GW01607505

WITHDRAWN

EMINENT PERSONS

WILFRED GREATOREX

WEIDENFELD AND NICOLSON
LONDON

First published in 1990 by
George Weidenfeld & Nicolson Ltd
91 Clapham High Street, London SW4 7TA

British Library Cataloguing in Publication Data
applied for

ISBN 0 297 84034 7

Typeset at the Spartan Press Ltd
Lymington, Hampshire
Printed and bound in Great Britain by
Butler & Tanner Ltd
Frome and London

For Beryl

Author's Note

The places and some institutions cited in *Eminent Persons* are real. The story, the banks and finance houses, and all the characters, are fictitious, particularly the Eminent Persons on Naisby's list and office-holders in the Cayman Islands. Any likeness to actual persons, living or dead, will be purely coincidental.

WG

ONE

'Naisby, Great Britain.'

He heard the tannoy call echo through the steep valley as he leaned over the lead-weighted skeleton, his eyes on the spectacular funnel of ice dropping to Stable Junction and Church Leap. His heart was bumping and he felt the race of adrenalin as he gripped the skeleton, keeping the sliding seat full forward, and ran past the start tape before throwing himself on.

It was essential to his ego to clock a good time. As the frozen mountain air stung his face below the visor he felt good about having put off his return call to Renwick in London. It could wait. He had a hunch it would mean bad news. Renwick himself was bad news.

The towering ice walls flashed by and he was soon doing around 50 mph, going into Stable and digging the steel rakes riveted to his army-style boots into the ice floor of the run. He raked with his left boot as he came into Curzon and his right boot as he banked to the right through Brabazon. He was making good time through Junction when he lost control for a moment, letting the heavy skeleton slide into the right wall, then the left. He heard the screech of his metal handguards scoring the ice, and felt the impact as the skeleton noisily rattled on. He had her going straight now on the 150 yards stretch to Rise, and cursed the disadvantage of his lean 154 lbs. The heavy boys' extra weight helped them clip seconds off their times.

Through Battledore now, and with the feared Shuttlecock looming, he took the ice-bank early, pushing back on the sliding seat so that the grooves at the rear of the runners bit the ice, grasping the back of the skeleton with his left hand, and raking hard with his left foot. He felt a stab of pain in the ankle and caught a split-second glimpse of the ambulance chasers, standing up there on the left bank like human vultures waiting with their Nikons for the sensational crash.

He would not be obliging this time. Going over the top at Shuttlecock was the prerogative of some of the spoiled Hooray Henries whose rich dads picked up their exotic tabs from the more ritzy St Moritz doss houses.

The world was a glacier. In a split second he was disorientated as he came down off the high wall, bumping through Stream into the straight, his body pummelled by the impacts. It felt like he was doing more than 75 mph but the twisty Battledore–Shuttlecock section had cost God knew how many seconds more than it should. He knew he was slower than yesterday, perhaps by six or seven seconds. He knew why. He was letting Renwick bug him. In that pre-breakfast call from Zürich, Elke had made it clear that Renwick had been at his autocratic worst, insisting that Naisby return his call 'instantly', even if it meant that Renwick took it in his Mercedes between Ascot and the City. 'If he comes on again, love,' Naisby had told Elke, 'just say you're still trying to locate me.' Ever since he'd taken over at Cromwell, Jaynes and Co. six weeks back, Renwick had been spoiling to get him.

He was going so fast now he thought the tough little skeleton might disintegrate. It was Scylla first and he banked to the left, very fast, then he was into Charybdis, banking right, the big rake on his right boot clawing at the ice-track. Into the final stretch, he knew he'd clocked a lousy time and tried to compensate by riding in such a streamlined posture his chin was almost being shaved by the ice.

He was made even more aware of his bad run by the looks on the faces of the riders before him who were waiting at the finishing hump for the truck to take them and their skeletons back to the club pavilion. Keller, the big modest Genevois, his scarlet helmet tucked under his arm, shrugged and winked. Ercole, the dark playboy son of a Milan tycoon and one of the most promising – and practised – young Cresta riders, screwed up his nose and grinned. It was a pity the ineffable Brit, Wetherby, had to be there. The latest in a short line of fringe aristocrats, he was pole-thin with buck teeth and had a habit of sniffing, which made him appear to disapprove of most people and things.

He sniffed now, and smirked. 'You missed the announcement, old chap,' he said as Naisby tugged his helmet off. 'Sixty-eight point two secs. Least that's what I think they said.'

Naisby nodded, sliding his skeleton clear of the track.

Keller confirmed the timing. 'Happens to the best, Rollo,' he said.

Yes, but it never happened to Keller, tipped as a future champion and record-breaker and said by the experts to have more talent than the legendary Bibbia.

Ercole pulled a face. 'You should have been a rich man's son, Rollo,' he quipped, his English perfect. They all knew what Naisby thought of the playboys and Hooray Henries whose silver spoons enabled them to practise every day through the Swiss winter, from the day the Cresta opened to the day it closed.

'Just wait till your old man goes bust,' Naisby said, without malice. He liked Ercole.

They were on the way up the hill to Top when Wetherby waxed sniffy about the arrival of a group of RAF Tornado and Harrier pilots from NATO duties in West Germany. 'These heroic proles don't trust our helmets. Bring their own hats, all pale blue and shitehawk crests. Then have the neck to eat into our practice time.'

'Tell you what, Sniffy,' Naisby said with an earnest look. 'You get your old man to use his pull with the Almighty to give us three days of hot sun. That'll mean Clancy will close the run.'

Wetherby was stumped. 'Then *we* couldn't ride either.'

'*They're* only here three days. You're here for ever.'

'*Very* funny,' Wetherby sniffed. And he dressed Naisby down with a superior glance, the grey eyes cold and insensitive.

Keller and Ercole couldn't make sense of the animosity and made a point of checking the runners of their skeletons.

In the clubhouse at Top, Naisby ran his eyes over the riders' running order.

'Yeah, you're in with the chance of another run, Rollo.' It was Clancy. 'As long as the sun doesn't get up too much.' He was protective of that ice face. It could have been made of platinum, not ice. Legend had it that Clancy had never seen natural snow or ice, having grown up in California, until he was posted to Germany with the USAF. But that didn't fit the fact that he'd first put on skis in Colorado and had served with a transport unit in Alaska. He was vague about his curriculum vitae. 'Best try get you another run this morning. You cocked that one up for sure.'

Others were listening, but it was no more than a mini-humiliation. All that really mattered to Naisby was that he was stretching himself, dicing. He went over to the public phone kiosk and put in a collect call to London. Waiting, he could see the riders fretfully weighing up their chances of another run, of beating the rising temperature and Clancy's ban on further riding till tomorrow. Keller was swigging down vitamins, Ercole was reading a telex, and Wetherby was still whingeing about those Tornado and Harrier crews. They could drop him in the North Sea any time they liked, Naisby thought.

'We have a slight delay on calls to UK,' the operator said, impatient for lunch.

'I'll hold.' Naisby saw three riders having quiet words in Clancy's ears. Queue jumpers all, and Wetherby was among them – no doubt implying some class privilege. His first name was a bit special and he was entitled to be addressed as 'The Honourable Gervaise'. Naisby had tried it on him once, but Wetherby had not been amused by the heavy irony in Naisby's North-country voice.

It was another minute before Renwick followed his personal assistant on the line. 'Rollo,' he snapped. 'Where in hell are you? Skiing?'

'If I were so lucky.' It wasn't quite a lie.

'If you're sunning yourself up some mountain, you better come down, eh?'

'I was with a potential client interested in currency funds.' Naisby was amazed by his laid-back line. He knew Renwick was coming up with something nasty.

And Renwick's tone was harsh. 'Well, you just give him my most sincere regards and get back here right away, right?'

'Tomorrow?' Naisby was still watching Clancy, who was like some queen bee in a fur hat and khaki British Warm, being fussed by eager riders trying to beat the rising sun. Its beams were creating light and shade patterns in the clubroom.

Renwick's voice took over. 'What's wrong with right now?' The tone was spiky. 'You could be on that next Swissair out of Zürich. Unless you *are* up in the mountains.'

Naisby wanted to tell him to go to hell. He could see the bastard, ten floors up in that new City block, imperious and hair-gelled, *enjoying* the moment. Just outside the kiosk, Clancy was doing his best to cope with the pressures from the eager riders – Wetherby, stars like Keller and Ercole, five playboy sons of America and the UK, a couple of committed Germans, and two of the RAF contingent. It was time

Naisby got in there. The yuppie had his place, too. 'I'll make that flight,' he told Renwick.

'Good,' Renwick said. 'See you around four thirty then.'

Naisby left the booth to buttonhole Clancy and tell him of the sudden recall to London. 'Any chance of jumping the queue?'

Clancy weighed him up through hooded eyes. 'Only if the other guys consent.'

Wetherby was listening. 'I know,' he said, the cynical mouth curling in what passed for a smile. 'Your old auntie's been taken with something terminal?'

'Just work,' Naisby said, weighing up the others' reactions.

'We should blackball all proles and tradesmen,' Wetherby sniffed, and won an uneasy laugh.

Naisby threw the superior brat no more than a passing glance.

'I'm next in the run, Rollo.' It was a fresh-faced youngster from Ohio. 'You can have my slot.'

'Thanks,' Naisby beamed. He started to gear up – knee pads, elbow pads, metal handguards.

Clancy went to the door to check the state of the ice under that bright sun. 'Okay, Rollo. You first, then three more.'

Nobody was sure if Clancy had figured it deliberately, but Wetherby was fifth in the queue. His pale eyes were alive with suspicion. 'Where the hell does that leave me?'

'First down tomorrow,' Clancy murmured.

'Oh no. To hell with that for a lark!'

Clancy adjusted that fur hat. 'You know the rules. We don't bend 'em for anyone.'

'The Committee wouldn't like this one bit.' The threat to Clancy was clear.

Naisby's dark brown eyes came alight with anger as he glared at the titled brat before turning to Clancy. 'Don't deprive the under-privileged, Clancy. Give the lad his dummy.' And he was already peeling off the pads and handguards. There were murmurs of protest from the other riders, and Wetherby was suddenly public enemy number one. Some urged him not to ruin the arrangement. It was too late. With a nod of thanks to the tax lawyer's son from Ohio, Naisby was already on his way, discarding his raked boots and pulling on his black moccasins.

He took a helicopter taxi from St Moritz and caught a glimpse of the ritzy Badrutt's Palace Hotel where the trendy rich mingled with the royals, the sheikhs and the top brass of multinational corporations. Wetherby had a room there. The snow-covered Engadine Valley glittered below and Naisby caught a brief glimpse of the Cresta Run as the pilot set course for Geneva.

Just over four hours later Naisby faced Renwick in the discreetly-labelled chief executive's tenth-floor office with its view of Lloyd's and St Paul's Cathedral. The décor was different. Two large oil paintings by Munnings dominated the rosewood panelled wall behind Renwick. A further reminder of Renwick's horsey interests was a two-foot-high bronze of a black stallion, and a solid gold horseshoe was in use as a paperweight on the only documents in sight. The vast rosewood desk was bare but for a desk lamp converted from an antique Chinese porcelain vase. In Goodall's time the office had been more traditional, full of English watercolours and old Persian rugs. Now the wood block floor had vanished under a Royal blue wall-to-wall carpet, its pile so deep it was like treading in snow. Whereas Goodall had given it the feel of an office belonging to a finance house and merchant bank founded around 1790, though it was only born after World War Two when the founders Cromwell and Jaynes were demobbed from the Army and Navy, Renwick had put the money-tycoon's mark on it.

He shook hands limply, leaving Naisby to stretch over the acres of desk. 'Do sit down, Rollo.' Immaculate in a pin-striped dark blue suit, he shot his gold studded cuffs and checked his Piaget as if to make it clear the interview had to be brief. He was nearly a perfect stereotype of the pushful middle-class businessman who had latterly come through in the City of London – overly laid-back, and with a phoney accent meant to suggest an upper-crust family tree. Ice-cold as the Cresta, Naisby thought. And a bit of a ham actor with that creaseless wardrobe – the only creases were on his sun-tanned forehead – and that careful voice projection. Even the tan now looked as if it could be makeup.

Renwick didn't sit down himself. He let his six-foot-two frame loom over Naisby for a second, then crossed to the window as if to seek succour from St Paul's. 'I'll not beat around, Rollo.' He paused, watching a passing helicopter. 'How would you feel about a stint back here?' His manner wasn't kind.

Naisby knew it wouldn't matter a damn if he were to come clean and say he would hate the prospect. 'There's still plenty to do in Zürich.'

'And more here.' Renwick peered at him over the half-lenses of his black-framed glasses. 'I want you to help Antony rebuild the UK operation.'

It was even worse than Naisby had feared. Tony Friell and he had been rivals ever since they joined the old Western Bank on the same day twelve years back. 'So it's demotion.' His eyes met Renwick's and it was Renwick who looked away, aware of Naisby's sense of injustice. 'Demotion? After what I've done over there?'

'I'd choose to call it a sideways move, Rollo.' The voice was laden with fake tolerance. 'I'm fully aware of all you've managed to do in Switzerland, though it hasn't gone unnoticed that you've been a touch harder to get of late.'

'I've taken no holiday in eighteen months.'

'And that's not a good sign.' He was sucking the end of the right arm of his glasses. 'It's in the interest of this house that we strengthen our UK accounts. You're just the chap to help Antony.' He put his glasses back on and began to show interest in the papers under the golden horseshoe. The gesture was symbolic. The interview was over.

'Salary?' Naisby made no move to rise.

'Unchanged.' He sat in the high-backed navy-blue hide chair which could have been made for a judge. The intent pale blue eyes were unyielding. 'We can't, of course, be quite so liberal over expenses. Zürich does call for somewhat special arrangements.'

They weren't all that special, Naisby thought. 'Do we know yet who'll be replacing me there?'

'Yes.' Renwick knew it would cause pain, but that wouldn't deter him. He managed a frosty smile as he said, 'Rodney Howard.' Naisby might have known. The upstart nephew of the bank's deputy chairman had clearly been put on the fast track from the moment he came over from Bradstreet's. It wasn't Naisby's first encounter with nepotism and nephews. 'I trust you'll do all in your power to ease him into the chair, Rollo.' The voice held menace now.

Naisby said nothing. His mind was pinwheeling ideas. He had rehearsed his options many a time for this professional crisis. He saw Renwick spread the fingers of his left hand over the edge of the desk, with the thumb underneath, and knew the hidden 'EI' button was being pressed. End of Interview. All senior staff knew of it. Renwick's secretary would be in any moment with an urgent call.

'I had hoped we might engineer this essential change without difficulties being raised.' Renwick was clearly waiting for the call.

'I'm raising none.' Naisby surprised himself. He could hardly wait to get the first flight back to Switzerland. He had settled on his chosen option.

'Excellent.'

Naisby got up just as the red phone buzzed.

'Yes?'

It was the secretary, right on cue. 'Lord Hadley for you, Mr Renwick.'

'John!' The voice was transformed, warm and welcoming. 'Let's make the club, eh? Settle it. Six fifteen, say. Just so that you can do your homework, I'll be arguing that a thirty million valuation on that outfit's a bit steep. Twenty-six should do the trick with the underwriters. Anyhow, think it over.' He hung up, came to his feet, and held out his right hand. 'I'd like to give you a drink, Rollo. But it's a touch early.'

'And I've a lot to settle in Zürich.'

'Get things shipshape for Rodney, eh?'

Naisby nodded, though that was the last thing on his mind.

Even with an hour added on for Swiss time, Naisby made the Kulm Hotel bar on St Moritz's main street in time for a drink with the Cresta riders he'd left around midday. Little more than four and a half hours since his encounter with Renwick, he ran straight into a black look from Clancy, who drained his Glenlivet and said, 'Recalled to London, eh?'

'There and back, Clan,' Naisby smiled. 'Believe me.'

'So you can buy me a Glenlivet to prove it.'

As he sought the barman's eye, Naisby saw the RAF pilots were being made to feel at home by Keller and Ercole and some of the American and British playboys. Wetherby was at the centre of a knot of non-members of the Tobogganing Club – skiers, bobsleigh loons, and elderly tourists there for the fresh air and the *Glühwein*. He caught sight of Naisby and pointedly held his nose in a gesture of contempt. His court broke up enough to enable Naisby to see that some were signing their names on a plaster cast propping up Wetherby's neck.

Naisby threw a look at Clancy. 'I see the brat copped it.'

'The usual collarbone, though his real problem's the brain.' He ran a wrinkled hand through his sandy moustache. 'Never learns.'

'Shuttlecock?'

Clancy nodded. 'Silly bugger shoots over the top three times out of four there.'

The drinks came up automatically. The barman knew Clancy well, and Naisby fairly well.

Naisby raised his glass. 'I need an early run in the morning, Clan – and need is the word.'

Clancy savoured the Glenlivet. 'Bad time in London?'

'Hell, no. I got promoted.'

'I'd have asked for a triple if I'd known.' Clancy's grin was knowing. 'I can get you in early. Fifth, right?'

Naisby's eyes sparkled. 'Not in place of Crestabrat?' He indicated Wetherby, who was still attracting autographs.

Clancy scratched his head and tried to look naive.

'Bloody hell!' Naisby enthused. 'That's poetry!'

Half an hour later he made his way down the street to the modestly-priced hotel in the town, enjoying the sound of his fleece-lined boots crunching the ice. He felt oddly light-hearted, knowing exactly the option he had chosen. Down the valley, from the grounds of the lush Badrutt's Palace Hotel, fireworks exploded in vivid reds, blues and golds in the clear night sky. Probably some rich man's party for his daughter's celebration of eighteen years and five months, four days on this earth. Real birthdays in that set would merit a salute by a regiment of nuclear artillery. The world was an unjust place. For a reason he couldn't fathom he kept seeing Tara's face. In his brief stay in London he'd not even called her – and he thought he knew why. There would have been questions about the purpose of his visit – and he could no more have told her the truth than he could have lied to her. He was a survivor. Demotion was no part of his scene. And she might have asked why he couldn't make time to see her in London. It would have been no answer to say he *had* to get back to St Moritz to make one final run – or two – on the Cresta, and then see Oscar Leiden in Zürich. Neither engagement would have been understood.

He was tempted to call Oscar right away. His mind was churning over his chosen option. He could invite Oscar to join him in St Moritz, but that could prove a liability: Oscar could never forget the time he flew over the top at Shuttlecock and needed an ambulance and surgery. Ever since, he'd been a ski marathon nut, hauling himself punishingly over miles of cross-country snow, urged on often by Reza, an ample woman of stern Zürich puritan stock. She saw it as part of Oscar's treatment.

The day's events had left Naisby both tired and wound-up, and he slept only fitfully. He was wide awake long before the pocket alarm clock sounded at six thirty. He called Oscar right away. Another half hour and the workaholic would be driving to his office at Seifert et Cie.

Reza took the call.

'Morning, Reza.' He tried to seem more laid-back than he felt. 'Rollo Naisby.'

She wasn't best pleased to hear him. Oscar would be into muesli and sausages. 'I'll get Oscar for you.'

'You're all well, I hope.'

'Yes.' The voice was brusque and contralto.

'Good morning, Rollo.' Oscar could not hide his apprehension.

'I'll not keep you now, but it's essential we meet.'

'It's rather difficult.' Oscar was hedging. 'We're into our annual audit just now.'

'Tonight won't be too late,' Naisby insisted.

'Tonight I have tickets for the Schauspielhaus.'

'A good play?'

'Brecht.'

'Give him a miss, Oscar.'

A long moment of silence.

'Remember where we last met?' Naisby had a mental image of Oscar going pale in the hall of the compact villa up on Leonhardstrasse, to which he and Reza and their troupe of kids had moved from their mini-mansion at Winterthur. Oscar had explained this downwardly-mobile change by saying he would be no slave to a property. And besides, the new place was near the campus of the University of Zürich, where two of his kids were about to begin courses. 'How about meeting there, say around eight?'

'Very well.' His voice shook even over the two words. He was anxious to get off the line.

'Look forward to it, Oscar.' Naisby was trembling himself. He went down to the restaurant for muesli and bacon and eggs. Just over half an hour later he was riding the Cresta, the cold air stinging his face, the sheer speed exciting him. He clipped nearly four seconds off his run of the day before, and stayed for a second ride. This time he took another second off. The price was torn ligaments in his ankle as he raked hard at Cresta Leap just before the finish.

'Getting back into your stride,' Clancy said in the clubhouse. 'Pity about that ankle, buddy. I could have you on again and you'd likely have clocked better than sixty-three five.'

It would do to be going on with. Besides, he had a lot to see to in Zürich. Oscar might be a problem. He was too jumpy by half.

TWO

Oscar was late.

Waiting in his black Porsche, Naisby had the heating on full and the front screen wipers doing a spasmodic sweep of the melting snow. Up here on the heights above the city he had a big view of the lights of Zürich behind the veil of falling snow, but his gaze was fixed on the approach to the restaurant car park. He was in the shadows, clear of the welcoming glare of the dining room with its picture windows. The place was quiet, as he and Oscar knew it would be at this time of year when Zürichers were the regular patrons. They dined around nine, and it was still only just after seven thirty.

It was Oscar who had named the time, and it crossed Naisby's mind that Reza had put her foot down and insisted on their visit to the Schauspielhaus. He could see the headlights of two cars on the road beyond. As those of the first car briefly took in the car park he froze behind the tinted glass. The car went on past the restaurant. The following car slowed and turned into the car park, its headlights briefly sweeping the Porsche. Naisby stayed absolutely still.

It wasn't Oscar.

As a couple left the red Audi, so muffled against the cold they could have been two males or two females or one of each, Naisby was suddenly haunted by the fear that Oscar had yielded to desperation and done something drastic – like killing himself or calling the police.

Another twenty minutes went by. He was so jumpy he had an urge to drive off, suspecting each car that turned into the lot was an unmarked vehicle of the Zürich Police Fraud and Corruption Squad.

It was another quarter of an hour – after eight – when Oscar Leiden's BMW drew into the lot. Naisby was surprised. He'd followed its approach passively, as it came from the wrong direction – assuming Oscar had driven from his house in Leonhardstrasse, or even straight from the bank in the Bahnhofstrasse.

The BMW did a semicircle, very slowly, its beams raking the parked cars and finding Naisby's Porsche. It reversed alongside. And Naisby marvelled at the precision of this repeat of their manoeuvre barely three months back. He could see Oscar's ample figure in the BMW's driving seat. He didn't move right away, and let a minute and more elapse – long after Oscar had turned off his lights – before crossing to the BMW. And he saw it had snow chains on its tyres.

'I thought you'd had a nasty skid, Oscar,' he said, offering his hand.

'I did say we're in the middle of the annual audit.' Oscar shook hands formally. 'It's a most inconvenient time.' His hand was damp with sweat and in the dim amber light coming from the dashboard his plump face was gaunt and his eyes desperate behind those vast owlish lenses. He waited for Naisby to fasten his seat belt. They were out on the road, with the chains rumbling over the thin snow cover, before Naisby was really aware of the whiff of heavy Italian perfume – Reza's, he remembered. It had a sickly odour.

'We could have settled things in the car park, Oscar,' Naisby said. 'For all I have to say.'

Oscar's reply was to raise the volume of the compact disc player. The sound of the Zürich Philharmonic playing Mahler filled the BMW. It had been the same at that earlier rendezvous. Oscar had an obsession about confined spaces and the bugging factor.

Neither said a word over the next eight kilometres. Naisby was finding the combination of Mahler and Reza's sickly scent depressing. He was still troubled that Oscar had come from the wrong direction, though he could see the reason for using chains now. The snow was thickening. A layby loomed.

'We could talk here, Oscar,' Naisby said against the loud music. 'Why go all the way?'

Oscar threw him a quick look. And shook his head.

The sticking snow was deeper now as they climbed the high ground away from the city. Up in the blackness ahead lay one of the high passes where Naisby had once been stranded in a snowstorm and reprimanded by the breakdown team for having tried to get through without chains. 'I still think we could get out . . . the next layby . . . it's not as if you don't know what I want to talk about.'

Oscar ignored him, his eyes set on the climb before them.

The snow seemed to be heavier by the minute. White light from the car's headlamps came back at them from the wind-driven fall. Naisby studied Oscar's intent profile. Oscar was nervous at the best of times, though these had been few and far between since his problems with the gaming-club owner Mallef had threatened to destroy him. He was more than just nervous now. His grim mood was getting to Naisby, who took in the perfume atomizer on the dashboard shelf and the skiing gloves protruding from the right pocket of Oscar's heavy-duty grey anorak. The air conditioning was having no effect on that sickly scent pervading the car.

It must have been another quarter of an hour, though it seemed to Naisby four times as long, before Oscar took the BMW left down a farm track almost innocent of snow in the lee of tightly-planted young firs. Naisby recognized the rendezvous. Their last meeting had been at dusk after a warm autumn day, but even the snow and low cloud could not hide the medieval cowshed-barn with its steep sagging roof.

'You still own this dump, Oscar?' His surprise was genuine. His flip tone was fake – meant to cover his misgivings.

Still set on silence while in the confines of the car, which was irrational unless he intended to search Naisby for bugs once they were outside, Oscar drew the BMW to within a few feet of the iron-hinged barn door. He buttoned off the disc player, cut the engine, leaned into the back seats to retrieve a breakdown lamp, and indicated that Naisby should get out.

Leaning out of the car, Naisby was puzzled. He came alert as he saw another set of car tracks almost, but not quite, obscured by those just made by the BMW. The wheels hadn't been chained. And now, nearer the farm track, he made out other tracks, like their own, pressed by chained wheels.

'Rollo!'

Oscar was at the barn door, trying to ease a heavy key into the lock. Last time they had just strolled round the outside of the barn. 'This could have been bugged, Oscar.'

Oscar wagged a dismissive finger.

Inside the place reeked of old dung and hay. The only light, apart from that of Oscar's breakdown lamp, came from log-barred spaces set high in the walls. Oscar indicated that they should sit on bales of fodder. He kept the lamp in his right hand, with the beam off himself but taking in Naisby. Odd. Oscar was left-handed at everything except golf.

'Go on!' The voice was abrupt, impatient.

'I want to revive that idea we talked about, Oscar.' He spoke slowly and simply. Oscar was on a knife edge.

'I assumed as much. But we dismissed it, Rollo. For ever more.'

'I didn't.' There was a rustling in the timbers.

'Only bats,' Oscar muttered. He leaned close to Naisby, his right elbow propped against a sack of fertilizer, his left hand deep in the anorak pocket. 'It would mean the end of a lot of problems.'

'For you or me?'

'Both.' He felt Oscar's eyes searching him. 'You *are* still paying Mallef?'

Oscar nodded gravely. 'In cash. Every month.' He made it sound as if he firmly intended to keep it that way.

'And Reza?'

'We've learned to live with it.'

Naisby raised his eyebrows.

'It would never have worked, Rollo.'

Naisby knew he had to tread carefully. 'It would get Mallef off your back for good.'

'Maybe.' The voice was weary yet on a high. 'And others even more dangerous would take his place.'

Naisby blew his nose. The dung and the hay were getting to his sinuses. 'Anyway, you managed to keep this place.'

'Yes.' Bitterness clouded his pale plump face. 'We lost the chalet, of course.'

'Chalet?' Naisby smiled. That place at Winterthur was more like a grandee's château. The downmarket move had been painful. 'And you're still paying the bastard?'

'The balance on the house move barely paid half the debt.' His nostrils dilated. 'I raised a bit more by selling securities.'

'And he's still bleeding you?'

Oscar's small mouth set firm.

'What was it? Thirty per cent interest?'

A long moment went by. Oscar said, 'Sometimes I think the bank should put me in charge of Third World accounts. But then I'd be no good. I understand the problems of people who can't get out of that noose of debt because the interest payments take most of what they earn.'

'Now thrive the usurers,' Naisby said, and sneezed. The sooner he was out of this dank stenchy hole the better – and not just because of the air. He was uneasy about Oscar's state of mind.

'How much do you still owe, Oscar?'

A rat scuttered over the muck-laden straw. Oscar followed it with deadpan eyes. 'I still worship every day. Well, most days I go into the Grossmunster and say a prayer.'

'Lead me not into temptation,' Naisby said with a smile that didn't go down well. 'I told you at the time, Oscar. You're the archetypal banker. You're not the sort to go gambling with your own money. Only other people's.' He paused. 'You *have* stopped gambling? You're not getting into anyone else's clutches?'

'I'm cured. I'll not go into another casino anywhere in the world.' He paused, staying behind the lamp's beam. 'And this idea of yours. It's a gamble. With odds much greater than those I faced at Mallef's place. And I've suffered disgrace enough with Reza knowing, let alone the bank, my children, my friends.'

'You don't want to tell me what you still owe Mallef?'

'Irrelevant.' He was assessing Naisby with the look of a hanging judge. 'Coming back like this . . . trying to revive this mad scheme . . . you could bring the whole world down on us.' The face was full of cunning. 'How can you be sure nobody knows we're here?'

'Neither of us mentioned the rendezvous on the phone.'

'And you told nobody?'

'No.' Naisby's heart had begun to race. He fought down panic as Oscar, eyes aglow in the half light, came to his feet and indicated that Naisby should move ahead of him to the barn's west wall. Naisby had an urge to run, to find some hiding place among the stacked bales.

'Over that way,' Oscar commanded.

Naisby took the line marked by the lamp's beam. It was an area where concrete slabs formed the base for a store of winter feed and fertilizers. Several slabs had been set aside. Earth had been gouged out and lay in two neat mounds by what looked like a crude grave, no more than three feet deep. The lamp beam went back. Naisby turned, very deliberately, on a hunch. The beam caught him full in the eyes. He raised an arm to shield them. Beyond the glare he could make out Oscar's bulky form and, briefly, the glint of metal. The lamp's aim was adjusted until Oscar was sure the Luger was in Naisby's eyeline.

'I wasn't praying to be forgiven my gambling,' Oscar said, 'though that was bad enough. Thou shalt not kill. That's what was behind it. The trouble is Mallef has bodyguards and that fortress on Sardinia.

And documents with his bent lawyer . . . and the Lord knows who else . . . to prove my debt.'

Naisby's mouth was so dry he could hardly speak. 'My way there need be no debt.'

'And I could rot in jail for the rest of my days.'

'Not if we do it right.'

'It's impossible.' Naisby caught the merest hint of doubt in Oscar's voice.

'Even you agreed it wasn't.'

'It is now. And I've had enough of guilt – and people on my back.'

'Oscar,' he said quietly. 'You're blinding me with that thing.'

For a long moment Oscar didn't adjust the lamp, but then the beam was lowered until Naisby's eyes were above its frame.

'Thanks,' Naisby said. 'Can *I* pray?'

Oscar grunted. 'The unbeliever praying?'

'Insurance.' Even in the freezing temperature of the barn he was sweating. His head throbbed behind the eyes. 'And others do know I'm meeting you.'

'Who?'

'Friends.'

'I didn't know you had any, Rollo.' Again that change of tone. He sounded sane all of a sudden. 'Except – for a time – me.'

'And if anything happens to me it'll not be long before they know where to start looking.'

'I don't believe you.'

'You never believed me when I warned you against gambling and Mallef.' Naisby heard the click of a safety catch. The only other sound was Oscar's laboured breathing, the result of an asthmatic tendency brought on by the Mallef predicament. Last time they met, Oscar had just come through his Army medical check, playing down his condition and proud of his rank of major and the refresher courses and military exercises he went on. It would be his Army issue pistol and bullets, which he kept at home with his gas mask, he was flaunting now.

Two rats came out and were mating in the straw. Naisby turned and saw the freshly-dug grave. Another rat was nosing about its rim.

'It's still a hell of a plan, Oscar.'

Silence – except for that laboured breathing and the rustle of mating rats.

'I'd get Mallef off your back.'

'You couldn't be sure.'

'An offer he couldn't refuse.'

'He'd still have my IOUs.'

'Which he'd have to return before seeing the money.'

'Photocopies!'

Naisby could see his face more clearly now. It was riddled with self-doubt. 'He would sign an affidavit that they were taken from a forgery.'

Oscar's only reply was to refocus the beam on Naisby's eyes. No more than a second, then the beam fell away.

'Don't forget, Oscar, I know the source of some of that fortune he's stashed away in the Caribbean.'

'You didn't have the details.'

'I do now.' Naisby prayed, *Please God – let this lie sound like the truth*. 'The Drug Enforcement Administration in the States, let alone the FBI, would make his life a bigger hell than he's managed to make of yours.'

The pause lasted a lifetime.

Then Oscar turned the lamp's beam back onto the bales. 'We'll talk,' he said. His voice was breaking. He put the lamp on a bale and, under its light, clicked the pistol's safety catch. Naisby now saw that he was putting it back on. He closed his eyes. When he reopened them Oscar was emptying bullets from the barrel into his right hand, his pale cheeks streaked with tears. His lower jaw was trembling.

Naisby let Oscar put the pistol back in his anorak pocket before he spoke. 'Eminent persons, Oscar. You remember. The Great and the Good. Yanks. Brits. Germans. French. Those Third World supreme idealists creaming off the dollars into their own accounts via the UN and other institutions bent on giving a hand to suffering mankind.' He put on a nervous grin. 'Bent being the word.'

Oscar bit his lip and checked that he had actually emptied the pistol's chamber, and for a split second Naisby thought he was going to reload and carry out what he had set out to do. That perfumed BMW made sense now. Oscar must have reeked of dung and hay after digging that grave. And those car tracks were clearly all made by the BMW – first without chains on the outward trip, then with chains to the rendezvous, and back with Naisby for the burial.

'How many?' Oscar asked grimly.

'Mmmmm?'

'Eminent Persons.'

'Oscar, you were the one who reckoned you could finger more than forty of Bank Seifert's clients in that category. Or were you boasting?'

'No, that was true.'

'*Is* true?'

Oscar shrugged as he wiped his eyes, then his steamed-up glasses, using the same handkerchief.

'Ten will do to be going on with,' Naisby said easily.

'To be going on with?' The scale of the proposal alarmed him.

'Oscar, I sincerely wish to be rich – and to see you out of Mallef's clutches. I really do. And with such nepotism in the way of my ever achieving this by hard work and inspiration I must fall back on just the inspiration.' He was feeling more himself now, though far from sure that Oscar's mood wouldn't suddenly change again, turning him into a homicidal nut. 'I want the names of the first ten of those EPs, the good and the great – and the better and greater the more I'll like it. I want their account numbers, the state of their accounts, and dates when the more interesting deposits reached the haven.'

'Not easy.' Oscar aimed the lamp's beam towards the grave and ran a shaky hand over his forehead.

'That's what you said before – and we sorted out the way we'd go about it.'

'Easier said than done.'

'Of course. What isn't?'

'Besides, the bank's whole security setup is more sophisticated now.' He was so scared the sweat from his face was steaming up his glasses again. 'Since Wasserman became security director it's been like living in Moscow, not Zürich. Hidden eyes all over the place.' He'd once spent three months in Moscow trying to negotiate a role for Seifert's various Soviet clients, including the Government diamond-mining arm. Nothing had come of it, and despite *glasnost* he could no longer pass the Soviet Embassy in Berne without a twinge of fear. Not that he felt any better when passing Wasserman's office up there on the second floor in the Bahnhofstrasse.

'I've never assumed that any accounts, never mind those belonging to the Eminent Persons, would be anything but hard to crack.'

'It's now a technological minefield.'

'Tread gingerly, Oscar. You've got privileged access to the computer. You know the codes.'

'Not everyone's.'

'Just take your time, that's all. But not all that much. And feed me the info as you get it. I'll have some digging to do once we have names and numbers.'

Oscar was tugging at the loose folds of flesh under his chin. 'And you mustn't try to reach me – either at Seifert's or at home.'

'You'll contact me?'

Oscar nodded.

'I'll need progress reports.'

'Yes,' Oscar said absently. He was preoccupied with that grave he'd dug. He went over now and began to spade the earth back into it.

'Let me help,' Naisby said, peering into what was to have been, if not his last resting place, one that would do to be going on with. It was deeper than he'd first reckoned and its base was white. 'Not a shroud, for God's sake?' He knew what it was.

Oscar couldn't face him and was demonically sweeping the earth over the quicklime.

'Bloody hell!' Naisby muttered, only half to himself. Oscar didn't seem to hear. Naisby found a shovel near the byre's water butt and helped Oscar fill in the grave and relay the three concrete slabs. He wondered how Oscar had managed to lift them unaided. Maybe Reza had helped. It was unlikely, though she had the muscle.

As they left the byre and Oscar locked the door, Naisby said, 'Best not try to get me at Cromwell Jaynes's office. My successor has big ears.'

Just for a moment Oscar's face lit up. 'I see,' he said, as if some mighty truth had dawned. 'I see now.'

'Good,' Naisby said, as if the snow before his eyes were quicklime. 'I'm glad, Oscar. No calls either way, okay? Same rendezvous, same time, then. Should we say Friday evening?'

'I promised to take Reza to Winterthur. Our Selie's in the skating finals.'

'Saturday?'

Again Oscar shook his head. 'We're all going to the Bernhard Theatre.'

'And you'll be in church on Sunday?'

Oscar nodded, a touch sheepishly.

'Monday, then?'

'Monday is good.'

All the way back to the restaurant car park, and long after Oscar had gone home, Naisby's mind pinwheeled with images of that awful quicklimed grave. He was cold and hungry, but avoided the restaurant as a precaution. He drove down to one of his favourite eating houses on the Limmatquai, and had *Glühwein* and steak fondu. As he dipped his first chunk of steak into the sizzling fat he spotted two girls in their early twenties in the compact, discreetly lit bar. One threw him a smile and he returned it.

But his mind was on that grave among the coupling rats in that byre in the hills.

Naisby let the crowded tram go by before crossing through the Bahnhofstrasse's slush to the gleaming new edifice of glass and marble owned by Seifert et Cie. He zipped up his anorak against the driving sleet and trod carefully in his calf-length boots.

It was mid-morning and the rich Zürichers weren't being put off their luxury shopping by the thaw. The main lobby of Seifert's was busy, too – with Zürichers playing money games. In the pubs and clubs of Britain it would be coming up to darts and shove ha'penny time and in New York they'd be getting over a night of pool. Here it was money games. The lobby had the look of some lush space centre with 3-D electronic maps showing the main financial centres of the world, its time zones, price movements in dollars, sterling and yen, and the rest, and in cocoa and soya beans. General Motors was up there in bright green, its share price winning a plus even as Naisby followed the gaze of Zürichers old and young as they worked out profits and losses. Some made for the public phones, a few others for the bank counters, but for most it was vicarious dealing. Never-never land. The atrium with its profusion of hot-house plants, all scarlet and green, climbed up five floors, each floor with its encircling balconies behind sea-green glass. Only on the second floor, where top management worked, was there a section more private than the rest. Oscar Leiden's room was on that level, with a view of the Bahnhofstrasse.

Naisby crossed to the inquiry desk. He weighed up the woman clerk's fleshy arms and elbows as she completed some notes before acknowledging he was there. Too many sugar buns and *bricelets*, he thought.

She finally took him in without a smile.

'Herr Leiden please.' He might have been asking to see the Swiss President.

'You have an appointment?'

'Yes,' he lied.

'And your name, sir?'

'Rollaston Naisby.'

'And how will you spell that?'

'Like I always do.'

She knew it was a joke but didn't react. Naisby spelled out his name and half turned away from her, his elbow on the counter, and took in the real-life Monopoly-money game going on all around. An old man nearer ninety than eighty lit a cheroot and ran a marker pen over the names of stocks on a business page of the *International Herald Tribune* as if he were picking winners for the day's race meetings. A young woman in a tartan suit with elegant laced black leather boots – and aware of the quality of her crossed legs above the boot-line – was using a mini-computer to transfer the big screens' information into her own data bank.

She was aware of Naisby's admiring look and took it as a routine – and merited – tribute.

Naisby turned to watch the three elevators climbing and descending inside their glass tubes. It was another seven minutes before he saw Oscar in the left-hand tube – and he was pulling on a heavy suede coat. His quick eyes behind the owl lenses found Naisby in the crowded lobby even before the elevator had reached the first level. Having made sure Naisby had seen him, and checked that the inquiry clerk was busy on the phone, he made straight for the main doors.

They were already on the steps down to the slushy sidewalk when Naisby caught up. 'What's the hurry, Oscar?' he asked quietly.

Oscar steered them left and some hundred yards clear of the Seifert building and the possible prying eyes of some of its occupants before he spoke. 'You must have a death wish!' he snapped. He walked head down, hands clasped behind his back. 'I told you it would take time!'

They crossed the tram tracks and headed for the Rathaus Brücke.

'We agreed there'd be a progress report last night, Oscar.'

Oscar quickened their pace, tramping through the slush in his rubber overshoes as if it weren't there. They were on the Limmatquai and into the winding streets of cafés and nightclubs before Oscar rated it safe to reply. 'Last night was impossible.'

'Why?' Naisby indicated an empty café.

Oscar shuffled on past it. 'Jean-Pascal summoned a late meeting.' He knew Naisby didn't believe him. 'Wall Street was going crazy and the bullion market all over the place.' He looked hard at Naisby. 'Believe it or not. I couldn't make it and there's no more to be said.'

There was a hell of a lot more to be said. It was now close on a week since that nightmare at the byre. And most of it had been taken up showing Rodney Howard around. The superior silver-spoon artiste, having fixed himself up in appropriate style at the deluxe Atlantis Sheraton, where he was the most prolific user of the indoor pool and sauna, had grown more demanding by the day. 'I think it might be a good idea, old son, if we have a short season of taking our prime clients to lunch and dinner over the next few weeks,' he had said on Sunday. 'Starting with dinner tomorrow night.' The upstart had a Monday lunch date with his maternal grandmother, who was over for the curling at Gstaad. Naisby had replied that he already had a dinner date, no matter that it was a non-dinner date up in that car park.

Naisby was bursting to look the foxy-faced upstart straight in those tiny eyes, black as opals, and tell him to fuck off. The sooner Oscar came up with the goods, the sooner that would be done.

Sleet was falling now, driven by the wind from over Lake Zürich. Naisby tried to tempt Oscar into an empty bar. But Oscar's obsession about bugs in confined spaces was too strong.

Naisby stopped on the sidewalk. The sheer wetness of the day was getting to him. 'Oscar,' he said tartly. 'Friday, right? Same place. Same time.'

'You do know the penalties for disclosure of bank information here?'

'Sure.'

'I've been rereading the actual legislation and looking up some of the cases.' Oscar's face was a picture of fear.

'African jails are a damn sight worse,' Naisby scoffed. 'Friday, Oscar. And I want something – somebody – to begin work on by then. The first of our Eminent Persons. Better still, the first two or three. Names, numbers, state of their accounts, and dates when the bigger lumps of loot were deposited.'

'I know what you want.' Oscar hunched his overweight frame against the sleet. 'I've already made the first reconnaissance.'

The military metaphor amused Naisby. 'You still in the Landwehr, Oscar?'

Oscar brightened. 'I can't wait for the spring manoeuvres in the Ticino.'

Naisby felt that if ever neutral Switzerland got into a war, the Ticino was the canton Oscar would be happiest to fight for – with its Mediterranean sunshine and palm trees. 'Friday, then.'

He watched Oscar heading for the Munster Brucke and back to the office before he went into the empty bar. He ordered a double cognac and his brain became a visual *Who's Who*, conjuring famous faces from the constellation of American and British top people, with a German or two and a French vice-president thrown in for good measure.

Life was looking up.

Anything would be better than a life sentence as a nobody with Cromwell Jaynes & Co.

Every step he took along the soft plastic floor of the lower basement corridor rang out as if he were wearing his army boots. Or so it seemed. What he had on were his rubber-soled brogues, hand-made in Italy before his gambling calamity. All was dull grey: grey floor, grey walls and ceiling, grey filing cabinets and grey safes with folders and data discs holding material with a lower security classification than those which lay beyond the heavy steel door some twenty metres ahead.

It was grey, too – with a notice painted in red at eye level:

STERILE AREA
AUTHORIZED
PERSONNEL
ONLY

The duty security man put down his *World Football* magazine and came to his feet. His open-air complexion belied the time he spent in this dungeon three floors below street level, far removed from natural light and air. He was a sergeant-major in the same Landwehr unit as Leiden.

'Morning, Major Leiden,' he beamed.

'Manfred,' Oscar nodded. He was pleased it was Geissler. Hagen was an over-suspicious pain in the ass and Schumann an ingratiating creep who had a habit of doing spot checks on the Sterile Area whenever anyone bar the bank's president, Jean-Pascal himself, was inside. It could be unnerving.

'So it's to be the Ticino in the spring?' Geissler enthused. Landwehr exercises were like a get-out-of-jail card – an escape from the grey dungeon.

'Our turn, Manfred.' Oscar's breathing wasn't so good and he hoped Geissler wouldn't notice.

Geissler dialled a combination on the massive door, then swung it open just enough for Oscar to go through. The lights beyond came on along a shorter corridor. Oscar was fighting panic and an urge to wipe his damp hands, a gesture that would not have been picked up by Geissler on the TV monitors but might have been spotted by Wasserman in his security director's office on the second floor. Or by Jean-Pascal himself, who was known to check the Sterile Area monitor in his office fairly often.

The bare greyness of it all focused the mind. It was like walking through some sterile zone in a chemical weapons factory rather than a bank. Even the nine-foot-radius door of the bullion vault to his right was grey, *and* the prying TV cameras which between them covered every cubic millimetre of the corridor.

Oscar was sensitive not only to his footfalls but his heavy breathing. He strove to pick up some other sound. Even the air-conditioning was devoid of hum. The TV cameras up there near the ceiling, guided by sonar, were clearly tracking him.

He had always found it eerie. Now it was terrifying. He was walking too fast. And now too slow. His chest was tight and he was desperate to suck in air. His routine was to visit the Sterile Area eight or nine times a week. It was par for the course for each of the six directors with top security status. Klutz ran a higher average, but then he was having to cope with the task of rooting out Mafia and other drugs-related holdings. Klutz was using the Sterile Area maybe fifteen times a week.

Another steel door swung open. Oscar went through to the inner area. Three grey monitors were set in triangular formation close to the west wall beyond the probe of the TV eye. It wouldn't do for surveillance cameras to catch the confidential images on those monitors, any more than it would for anyone watching one monitor to be able to see another. In this area, the cameras' job was to identify people, not detailed figures on the inspection screens.

But first Oscar went to the row of wall safes – one for each of the authorized bank chiefs. He went to Safe Five, buttoned out his personal entry code – 761X0279 – and heard the slight buzz before the tiny door clicked open. He took out a resin tag, grey with faint blue stripes. It was the size of a credit card but thicker. He left the wall safe door open. It came between the TV camera's eye and Safe Four. He drew a plastic glove from his inside pocket, under cover of that hand-sized door, and put it on his left hand. He buttoned his wristwatch memory bank which came up with the number 483J1922. He knocked it out on Safe Four's frame.

Pins and needles ran through his neck and shoulders. And he coughed. It sounded like a roar. All being well, Klutz would be in Lugano investigating the Italian launderers who'd been pushing hoards of lire through eighty-seven of the Seifert Bank's accounts. He'd spent half the morning in the Sterile Area, checking. Klutz was beyond suspicion, a pious Calvinist rich in his own right through inheritance. He had failed his medical for military service many years back, and Oscar found it hard to forgive such men when later they could play a hard game of squash without obvious risk of a heart attack. Klutz was a fine squash player, even today. He was also a marksman – with a shotgun. He took holidays in southern Italy and Malta every year for the spring and autumn bird migrations, bagging the exhausted migratory flocks of birds by the thousand.

Oscar adored wild birds.

Hence, partly, his choice of Klutz as fall guy. It had taken no less than seventeen shared visits to the Sterile Area, starting long before this revival of Naisby's *coup*, to piece together Klutz's entry code. A few numbers here, another there. And then an overheard conversation when Wasserman, of all people, had told Klutz he had brought in the letter J for I to prevent errors caused by the similarity of the letter I with the figure 1.

The lock buzzed for an age. Then the little door snapped open.

Oscar removed Klutz's resin tag.

He closed Klutz's safe and left his own wide open.

Up on the wall the TV camera was blind to what Oscar had done. The only other surveillance was a 'glass eye' built into the wall beyond which the security men could patrol a nuclear attack shelter. They rarely, if ever these days, went there. Oscar had thought of blinding the 'glass eye' with sticky tape only to dismiss the idea as unnecessary and risky.

He went over to the first of the monitors, switched it on, and slotted Klutz's tag. The next routine was the most tricky. He had only once seen Klutz key out his personal password and then only the first four letters – T-R-I-S. Klutz was an opera buff and a patron of the *Opernhaus* in Zürich, where Wagner composed *Tristan und Isolde* while on the run from creditors. Oscar keyed in the letters T-R-I-S-T-A-N and waited for the control light to turn from red to green. It stayed red. He tried again, keying in T-R-I-S-T-A-N-U-N-D-I-S. The grey phone set in the terminal frame buzzed gently and almost lifted him from the chair. The shock set his heart racing. He cancelled the keying-in and took the call.

It was Geissler. Every call to the Sterile Area had to go through the security man. 'Frau Kellberg, Major Leiden. She called to say you have a visitor.'

'Tell her I'll be there presently.' He hadn't subdued his alarm and knew it.

'Thank you sir.'

'Visitor'? Only Schneider from a Hamburg finance house was due – and not for another hour. He sensed a trap. And the shock had paralysed him. He kept an eye on the door for another three minutes before he began to key in the full T-R-I-S-T-A-N-U-N-D-I-S-O-L-D-E. The red light stayed on. He was close to panic and almost tore off the glove in error. The condensation on his glasses made it hard for him to see. He pushed the glasses onto his forehead, afraid that some hidden eye would see him wiping them.

The red light changed to green. He peered at it for a long moment, unable to believe he was now into the interrogator unit on Klutz's password. All he had to do now was key in the first of the account numbers he wished to know about – Sir Rupert Mallory's. He'd looked at the account perhaps half a dozen times since he'd been made a director, but he had to rely on his wristwatch's memory bank for the answer. He keyed it in now – Savoie/V7032955, then the suffix oX9 telling the descrambler to decode the account.

The words and figures began to come up clear and bright green:

Savoie/V7032955		**SFR**		**MALLORY R UK CITIZEN**
Date	*Details*	*Withdrawals*	*Deposits*	*Balance*
29.4.78	Banque J9		6,000,000	
26.5.78	Transfer S2	3,000,000		
	Interest		51,623	3,051,623
18.2.79	Bank MX		1,500,000	
	Interest		76,290	4,627,913
16.2.89	Banque J9		1,250,000	
	Interest		4,284,457	10,162,370
	Transfer S2	2,000,000		8,162,370
4.1.90	Bank MX . . .			

It was instinct, and not any sound, that brought him alert. Wasserman was in the area, the door closing silently behind his solid, stoop-shouldered frame. His mouth was set in its reef of beard, his large head half turned as he took in Oscar at the terminal. Oscar wiped the screen instantly. His mouth was dry as an oven, his tongue stuck to his lower gums. He was seized with a spasm of horror as he feared he had left Klutz's safe door open. For a second he couldn't tell. Wasserman was in the way, collecting his own tag from Safe Two. He moved off. Oscar's breathing eased. He had an urge to run – anywhere. But he would have to sit it out until Wasserman had gone. He couldn't return Klutz's tag yet. And he began to feel sure that Klutz would be back early from Lugano, with an urgent need to follow up his inquiries there with research here in the Sterile Area.

Wasserman was taking his place at Terminal Three, and Oscar muttered a brief prayer of thanks that the terminals were so placed that their users couldn't see other users' faces. Those probing grey eyes of Wasserman's would have been too much.

Oscar put on a show of being preoccupied with his notes. But Wasserman hadn't sat down yet. Because of his height, he was still able to catch Oscar's eye from beyond the partition. 'Good morning, Oscar.'

'Morning.' Oscar couldn't bring himself to look up.

'You had notice of Exercise Palm Tree yet?'

God, the army had its uses. 'I wish they started now.' He meant it.

'The Ticino in the spring,' Wasserman enthused. 'Can't be bad.'

Oscar was set on showing how busy he was. Wasserman disappeared into his chair beyond the partition. It was another two minutes before Oscar buttoned the screen to life, re-activated Klutz's password, and got back into the account of Sir Rupert Mallory, Bt. It showed some activity. Stocks and shares being bought in New York and Frankfurt, and some recent activity on the Tokyo stock market. Two further deposits of more than three million Swiss francs had found their resting place via havens in the Bahamas and the Cayman Islands. The balance now was just over fifteen million Swiss francs.

Oscar took a full note of the dates and details. He knew Wasserman was still on the other side of the partition, even though he couldn't see him. It was a pity the big man wasn't a heavy breather. Oscar found himself beginning to enjoy the challenge, as once he'd enjoyed the risks of the high-stakes blackjack and roulette tables. He stood up and walked a few paces as if to stretch his legs and straighten his back. He found Wasserman's eyeline, but now it was Wasserman who was busy.

Oscar marvelled at his own cheek. He'd even left Klutz's tag in its slot. He could push in another order without having to go through the rigmarole of restating that he was Klutz. Big Brain had accepted him for as long as he dared hang about. And he couldn't leave yet. Wasserman had to go first.

It seemed easier on this one. He keyed in the account number of General Edison Gibb – 784387/KY – and the suffix oX9 to order the decode. He knew of an original five million US dollar windfall which had marked the opening of the general's account just over three years back. But he was surprised by the later accruals. His current balance must make him the richest officer in the whole US Army. Even Sergeant Bilko would have been proud of him. Those brilliant electric green figures on the screen could be a strain on the eyes, but clearly not on the general's. Payments had flowed in by the million. Every six months, roughly – in almost equal amounts. And the Bank had done some slick trading on his account. Currency deals, three Hunt-style coups in commodities, and some shrewd in-and-out trading on the London, Zürich and New York exchanges.

General Edison Gibb, of the Pentagon, Washington, was now misnamed, Oscar thought. He should have been called General Rothschild. Or Getty.

Oscar was relishing the discovery because he found something evil about soldiers getting rich. He felt he could stay at the terminal all day – and all night, for that matter. He didn't fancy an evening as the meek-and-mild sidekick to Reza at the annual meeting of the Red Cross support group.

He made a note of the current state of the General's account. The balance was just over fourteen and a half million dollars.

He stood up now, placing his hands on his head and pressing his shoulders back as if to compensate for the research posture.

Wasserman caught him looking and was so clearly deep into some inquiry over drugs-related funds that he didn't even acknowledge Oscar.

And Oscar had to outstay him. He held on to the Klutz facility and conjured up the account of Lord Justice Kenright, UK citizen. It showed that a deposit of four million pounds made four years ago had grown – with interest and cunning investment by the Seifert managers – to £9,423,625.70.

Wasserman was still beavering away.

Oscar was worried that he might be overdoing it. Executives didn't normally spend so much time in the Sterile Area. But what was good for Wasserman must surely be right for others. Unless Wasserman was timing him. He called on his wristwatch memory bank. It flashed up the number BZ/5371/Celle.

He keyed in his demand for a decoded statement.

The electric green figures raised his eyebrows. The current balance was twenty-three million Swiss francs. Or five million dollars plus, as its owner, the latest US woman ambassador to the UN, would very likely prefer it. Sarne, the statement began. Mrs Edwina. US Citizen. Oscar was a regular reader of *Time* and *Newsweek* and *International Herald Tribune*. She was an ex-schoolteacher from Maine whose husband had a business in New York. It would be up to Naisby to find out more.

He was peering at the detail of the emerging account when he was suddenly aware of someone behind him. He swivelled in the chair.

Wasserman loomed, cool. 'I'm sorry, Oscar. I didn't mean to distract you.'

It was just what he was trying to do.

'I'll be taking you prisoner next month, Oscar.' The bearded face was all malicious humour.

'I'm sorry?'

'Exercise Palm Tree.'

'Oh yes.' Oscar's hands were trembling, but he kept them under cover, especially the left one with the glove on.

'I'm on the invading side.' Wasserman's tone was meant to be light. But he could make a joke about Donald Duck and it would sound sinister.

He went to his safe and put back the tag.

Oscar wanted to look more closely at Edwina Sarne's account. He was shaking and was about to vomit. He called up no more data. It was another ten minutes before he retrieved Klutz's tag, got up, and put it back in Safe Four. He removed the glove and put back his own tag in Safe Five.

And he went out of the Sterile Area past Geissler, feeling elated.

He couldn't make out why.

THREE

Naisby was still jet-lagged.

As he edged through the crowd of US veterans reunited at the Vietnam Memorial, his mind was reeling from all the flying and time-zone confusions. He hardly knew what time of day it was as he got his first sight of General Edison Gibb. The general's hair was steel-grey now, the beaming boy scout's face lined, but the eyes were clear and shrewd, and he was clearly having a good day as the vets, many of them grey or bald, treated him as if he were a baseball star, crowding in for a word or to shake his hand. They were shaking both his hands. Their ex-colonel had been popular and had done well since those days of hell and little glory.

Naisby was tempted to put off introducing himself for another day and get back to his hotel on 16th Street behind the White House for about twelve hours' sleep. But he was on a high. It was the first moment of truth. In six weeks Oscar had given him the names of ten Eminent Persons – five in America, not counting the West African diplomat at the UN in Manhattan, three in Britain, and a German. Using the Library of Congress, newspaper libraries in London and New York, *Who's Who* and, briefly, private detectives, he now had enough research on three of the Americans and two of the Brits to begin business. Oscar had got carried away and had thrown in a senior minister in the Italian Government and a Cardinal said to be so close to the Pope they could have been Siamese twins. 'Just leave the Italians out of it,' Naisby had countered. Things would be dodgy enough without asking for trouble from the Mob.

He had also set the German aside but didn't know why.

His last meeting with Oscar had been three days and some hours ago, at the latest rendezvous in the Fluntern Cemetery where James Joyce was buried. Back in London for one night he had found a hostile letter from Renwick demanding an explanation for his absences from Rodney's side in Zürich. He had faxed his reply: 'Dear Renwick, Your management style is not to my taste. Don't fret. I shan't be pressing for a golden handshake. J. R. Naisby.'

He had then tidied up some research on Sir Rupert Mallory and taken Tara to the National Theatre. The play was a dud and Tara was still in trauma from a broken marriage. He'd been in no mood even for that dinner in Soho, so absorbed was he by the game he was in. He had nursed his flight tickets and passport in his inside pocket all through the evening. Tara had teased him about taking her. 'It won't be a holiday, love,' he'd said.

That had proved all too true.

The flight to the Cayman Islands, with a tedious four-and-a-half-hour wait at Miami International, had doused his zest. The early morning meeting with Ed Maxell had restored him, as Ed got him to sign legal papers involving the Cayman company now registered in his name – Raleigh House Securities Inc. 'Daft to come all this way just to sign the damn things,' Ed had said. 'I'm in the States myself all next week.' He'd always been one for shortcuts. Taking a few too many had led to an abrupt departure from Cromwell Jaynes & Co. Naisby had missed him. Being five years older, Ed had taught Naisby much about the real-life Monopoly games of the City of London. And he had taken a few more shortcuts and was a company attorney on Grand Cayman within six months of 'resigning' from Cromwell Jaynes. 'Oh, and this is the bank on Cayman that'll be handling your account, Rollo,' he'd said, giving Naisby a bank card. 'Let's hope investments come rolling in. Maybe you'll tell me one day how you're so sure some high rollers will come in with their cash.'

What he was really saying was that he didn't wish to know.

With barely enough time to get his swim trunks wet – he'd taken a 6 am dip off Seven Mile Beach just before the taxi ordered by Ed took him to Owen Roberts Airport for the flight over Cuba to Miami – Naisby had left them in his room with a note for the chambermaid saying he'd probably be back to wear them again. Old economies died hard.

General Gibb was still pumping flesh. A gifted populist, with his big wide smile and strongman presence, he had put on his four-star general's uniform for the day. Back in his Procurement office in the

Pentagon his everyday outfit was a tweed jacket and navy-blue belted slacks.

The vets were mesmerized. Big vets, little vets, vets from Detroit and Maine and Colorado, some laughing, some in tears. Vets with able bodies and vacant or staring eyes. And vets so sharp and bright nothing escaped them, but they were short of legs and arms and hands. One had artificial ears. A black vet shook Naisby's hand vigorously, as if they were old buddies. Close to the Memorial's roll of honour, vets scanned the names, thousand upon thousand, searching for those of buddies long gone. Naisby felt like crying. Maybe he was *too* jet-lagged.

He was close to the ring of ex-soldiers surrounding Gibb now. And between the heaving heads he had a good view of the weather-tanned face. At this range the general's eyes weren't at one with his hail-fellow-well-met election-winner's style. They weren't so much bright as twitchy.

'Hi, General. Great to meet you again.' It was a man with a stick and thick silver hair. 'I was with the medics at Dien. It's sure fine to see you looking so good now, sir.'

The general laid on his folksy smile and took the vet's hand in a two-handed grip. 'Mighty fine to see you again, soldier. And ain't it just some day?'

The vet was awed into silence.

But it *was* some day. It was the second week in April and Washington was blooming. On his way to the Memorial Naisby had been beguiled out of his jet lag by the stupefying cherry blossom, all lush pink and white. It didn't seem to go with war – or war memorials.

'Have a good day, soldier.' The General was talking to a vet with an artificial right hand, and shaking left-handed.

'Thank you, sir.' The vet began to move off to make way for others, on impulse turned and said, 'You can't really remember *all* these guys, sir?' He really meant himself.

'Not their names, least not *all* their names.' The General would have made a super presidential candidate. No fluffs. No hesitations. A straight guy. He even had the nerve to laugh this one off. And Naisby admired the dental job. The general's top front teeth could have been his own, just slightly irregular and discoloured, replacing almost to perfection those he had lost to a shell splinter just before the final pullout to Saigon.

The vet persisted. 'Weller, sir. Corporal Weller.'

Just for a moment Gibb suspected he was being put to a test. He had it all sorted out in a trice. 'So how's the wound, Corporal?'

'No wound, sir.' He displayed his artificial hand. 'I copped this on the Michigan Freeway. Some crazy guy overtaking.'

It was a measure of Gibb's talent that he survived even that fluff. 'Have a good day, Corporal.'

'Yessir.'

Naisby was through the cordon. 'Just a couple of minutes, General?'

Gibb spotted the British accent in a flash. 'A couple of minutes is what I don't have right now.' He turned to pump more eager hands.

'One minute then.'

'If you're media . . .?'

'No,' Naisby said.

'Just you write me, eh? The Pentagon?' He was pumping more flesh.

'I called your secretary there this morning.'

'I didn't get the message.' He reached out to catch opened hands. 'Try me in writing.'

'Better I don't.'

Naisby's tone was such as to call for a change of line. 'Later, okay?' And the General smiled.

'Now's better.'

The naive vets hadn't a clue about what was going on.

'Write me,' the General said, signing an autograph on a vet's tourist guide to Washington DC.

'Rather not.' Naisby's face was lean and cold. 'All I want is a word about a number beginning with seven eight four.'

The General shook another two hands before the message hit him. Even then he kept his big smile in place, aware of the vets' Nikons and Pentaxes. A beanpole vet got to him. 'Sign this for me, sir?' He offered a beer-stained menu card. It had some twenty or thirty names scrawled over it.

'You were with me, soldier?'

'Some of the way, sir. That Agent Orange juice got me.'

'You look pretty good.'

The thin man nodded. 'Except at nights, sir. The lungs. They erupt kinda.'

General Gibb signed the menu, then pushed his way through the throng with Naisby at his heels, making it clear he would be back after a moment of privacy with Naisby.

They were twenty yards clear of the old soldiers and heading even further away. Gibb's face was a picture of alarm. 'What's the game?'

'Seven eight four three eight seven stroke K Y'.

Gibb's face went taut. 'What do you want?' The populist was suddenly cut to life size.

'An investment.'

'In what?' Vets were moving closer, as if drawn by a magnet.

Naisby eased Gibb further away. 'In world markets.' Naisby urged the general to walk on, keeping distance from the vets. 'I have an investment company in the Caymans.'

'Really, sir,' Gibb said. 'This is no place to be discussing business.'

'Right,' Naisby nodded. 'So let's just call it agreed?'

Gibb hadn't known a trap like this since he'd been cornered with his unit a mile from Dien. 'If I knew what you were on about I'd . . . '

'I'm on about seven eight four et cetera.'

Gibb threw out his wrist and checked the time.

Naisby fixed him with a look.

'I didn't catch your name, sir,' Gibb half whispered as they put another few yards between themselves and the soldiers.

'Kilroy,' Naisby said. 'Tom Kilroy.'

Gibb didn't look satisfied.

'No rank. Just Kilroy. Call me Tom.'

'I wish I knew what you're on about.' The general was trying to rebuild his morale. His firm tone didn't fool Naisby.

'Three years back you opened that account – I'll not bother you with that number again. Five million dollars for starters. Three months later you gave evidence to a Senate committee that was a bit keen on knowing how some batteries of ground-to-air missiles, and some heavy artillery stuff, came to get in the hands of two Middle East armies that would never be on Israel's side.'

'I spoke as an expert witness, not as a suspect,' Gibb snapped.

'You got away with it,' Naisby said matter-of-factly. 'Otherwise you'd not still be in Procurement at the Pentagon.'

The General's eyes flashed. 'That's slander.'

Naisby ignored the sophistry. 'You'd be in Sing Sing. If the place still exists.'

Small beads of sweat glistened on Gibb's upper lip and he was twirling the thick signet ring on the little finger of his left hand. 'You're making dangerous assumptions, sir.'

Naisby shrugged. 'I don't know how far the FBI or your Defense

Intelligence moles delved into your affairs, General. I dug away at the other end. I don't even know where that first five million sprang from. Or those half-million-dollar top-ups that have been going in every six months or so since. I do know the Pentagon doesn't dish out bonuses to serving officers. Maybe you have a rich uncle.'

Gibb kept his back to the ex-soldiers in case they saw his cornered look. His deep brown eyes glistened like chestnuts as he shot out the word. 'Blackmail!'

'All I'm asking is for an investment, General. Two million dollars. Hardly ruinous. You'll still have around eight million left.'

'Where can I contact you, Mr Kilroy?'

'You can't. And General. Don't kid yourself. Unless I stay in one piece – indeed, in a state that would get me through a medical for the US Rangers – others are in place who're numerate enough to talk intelligently about that account.'

'It *is* blackmail.' The general was in such turmoil he took the ring off his finger and almost dropped it down a storm drain.

'Greedy world, General. People on the make wherever you look. Just send your investment to Raleigh House Securities Inc. PO Box 2007. George Town, Grand Cayman. Can you remember it?'

It would be a miracle if he ever forgot it.

Elated, Naisby took a yellow cab to Capitol Hill. He had chicken pot pie at the Library of Congress cafeteria, which he'd used every day on his research trip two weeks ago. He strolled down to the Capitol Building, found the basement, and took the open-car subway through the tunnel to the New Senate Office Building and its cafeteria. It wasn't likely he'd see Senator Pryde lunching. The great Waldo was inclined to grab a quick steak sandwich in the Senators' private dining room when he wasn't gourmandizing at his favourite bistro out by the Dupont Circle.

Naisby settled in a corner of the vast marble and gilt eatery to study the gluttonous lobbyists en route to their first coronaries, and the diet-conscious Senate secretaries. He had time to kill before his date with Waldo Pryde. None of the girls was heading for anorexia. Many had big bottoms and legs of puppy fat. They gossiped and giggled. The lobbyists were guzzling their Senate bean soup, thick and creamy, and their generous steaks, in a race against the clock between importuning sessions with senators.

Five young secretaries came in now. They bubbled. One was freckled and nubile with the most intelligent legs in the place. Naisby couldn't take his eyes off her. She had a look of Tara and the young

Ali McGraw. If her voice was up to the rest of her he would shanghai her to England. Unless she insisted on marriage. Never again. Not after Maeve.

Two senators were downing bean soup. Naisby knew Royd and Mitchell from their pictures in the last issues of *Time* and *Newsweek*. They were nosing into the dubious tax returns of some prominent citizens who had been giving liberal dowries to the other great Party. Money, money. He found it more congenial just to study the Tara lookalike.

Just over an hour later he was up in the public gallery gazing down into the steep canyon where senators, but not many of them, were in listless debate about illegal immigrants. By leaning forward between two heads in the row below, Naisby could just make out Waldo Pryde. The senator lolled in his seat, his arms spread out, like one who'd enjoyed a good lunch. He put on a lopsided smile to greet the latest idiocy from a brash old Republican, and not once did he turn to look up at the gallery. It was as if he had forgotten all about his date with Naisby, and what Naisby had said during that phone call to Pryde's town house in Georgetown. And that was odd.

Naisby had made the call around half past seven, one hour before Pryde would be leaving for Capitol Hill. A woman he took to be Mrs Pryde had answered, and when he asked to speak to Pryde she said, 'Would you tell me what it's about?'

'Rather not over the phone,' Naisby had said, pleasantly.

'If it's about foreign aid . . .?'

'Yes,' Naisby had said. 'You could call it that.'

'In that case you'd do better to call the Senator's office at the Senate Office Buildings.'

'It's rather essential I talk to him personally.' There was a click on the line, then silence, and Naisby thought she had hung up. It could have been the hotel operator. Or – please, not yet – the FBI. Then the woman's voice came back on. 'Call the senator's office in about an hour, all right?'

'No,' Naisby insisted. 'Would you kindly tell Senator Pryde I wish to talk to him about a number starting with a five and ending with a P?'

'I'm sorry?'

'It's a kind of code, ma'am.'

'Hold the line.' She sounded cross.

Pryde came on in less than half a minute. 'Yessir?' The voice was deep – and intolerant.

'I'm sure you'd not want me to refer you to the whole number?'

'You're British?'

'A citizen of the world, Senator. And I have to leave Washington tomorrow.'

'Okay. Let me think now. Make it three thirty this afternoon, eh? How'll I know you?'

'Doesn't matter, Senator. I know you.' He made it sound quite menacing and felt pleased about his voice control.

In the Senate chamber now a paunchy Democrat from the west coast was droning on about immigration. Naisby could see Pryde talking in whispers to two colleagues, probably about the foreign aid debate which was to follow and in which he would have a big say. If he was shaken by Naisby's quoting of part of that account number he wasn't showing any signs of it. He hadn't looked up at the gallery once. The tension was getting to Naisby. He fought an urge to get out of the place and disappear into the spring crowds in the Mall. And then it happened.

Waldo Pryde turned his eyes to the gallery, running the rule over the packed seats.

Naisby froze. Did Pryde have some alibi to explain that twelve million dollars in Switzerland? Had he tipped off the police or the FBI?

As if bored by the debate rather than prompted by the need to meet anyone, Pryde rose from his place, tucking his stack of papers under his left arm, and made for the doors. Naisby left his aisle seat, turned briefly on the stairs to look down. Pryde was looking up and watching him.

When he reached the awesome Rotunda, Naisby found Pryde engulfed by US citizens, most of whom had never seen a senator in the flesh before. They had come in parties from Maine and Detroit and Kentucky, and Pryde was responding with all the panache of a presidential candidate, which he was tipped one day to become. He was much bigger than his press photographs, and that glimpse of him on the floor of the Senate, had led Naisby to believe. His barrel chest was accentuated by the loose cut of his feather-weight cotton suit, the single-breasted jacket held by one button. His face and hands were brown from the sun, and he had the brash cockiness of a prizefighter shaking hands with himself, the clasped hands held aloft and waving as if he had just won something. His head was big in the physical sense, his shock of hair groomed precisely.

He was clearly a Very Important Politician.

Even Naisby fell for the macho style. He congratulated himself on having put Waldo Pryde into the top league of those Eminent Persons who would be the first investors in Raleigh House Securities Inc.

It seemed that Pryde would never tire of signing autographs. He revelled in the hero worship. He rattled off anecdotes about the Capitol and its history. He even got a big laugh for the one about Will Rogers saying that if anyone ever put a statue of him in the Capitol it would face Congress so he could keep an eye on the lawmakers. 'And that's why Will's been put there – watching us.'

He hadn't even noticed Naisby – or so Naisby thought.

The way he went on he might have invented Congress – or bought it. Then, quite suddenly, he'd had enough. He winked at an aide – a slim six-foot blond – to indicate the party was over and called, 'That's it, folks. You sure got plenty to see and be proud of without wasting any more time on me.' That went down a treat. Such modesty! The aide magically turned into the Pied Piper. The mid-America voters followed him. Pryde pumped a dozen more hands, then turned and chose Naisby from the hundred or more visitors who were still in the Rotunda.

He pointed an index finger. 'You're the guy who called me.'

Naisby nodded.

'We got ten minutes, sir. At the outside. I gotta big foreign aid debate coming up.'

And he led Naisby through those bronze doors. They were out near the steps to the West front. It was less busy. Pryde leaned his bulk against the terrace balustrade. 'Okay. So what's it all about?' He sounded like a politician disgruntled as hell by whingeing poseurs from pressure groups who flocked to Capitol Hill with their begging bowls.

'I'm sure you know very well.' Naisby saw that Pryde had lured him into a position facing the bright sun.

'You didn't even give your name.'

'Kilroy,' Naisby said. 'Tom Kilroy.'

'So shoot, Mr Kilroy. You got eight minutes left.'

'I'll need a good deal less.' Naisby was finding Pryde's vanity too much.

Pryde's gaze was hard.

'You've a big reputation, Senator, for getting Congress to cough up foreign aid funds for the Third World?'

'Right, sir.' He squeezed his nose as if he were embarrassed.

'At that Senate hearing last year into the business interests of politicians you said you had no business interests?'

'Right.' He looked unbreakable.

'You said you'd find it unethical to run a business *and* sit in the Senate?'

'You sure have done your homework.'

'And you said something else. You said politicians who grew fat on business couldn't do their job in Congress?'

'You're a well-read guy.'

'And you've made a big play in your campaign stuff over the years about coming from a poor farming family in Iowa?'

'I tell you what, Mr Kilroy. I'll have you ghost my autobiography.'

'Too much like hard work, Senator.' Naisby shut up to let a group of teenagers who had come close move out of earshot. 'And besides, I know nothing about Iowa.'

'Take a holiday there, Mr Kilroy.'

It was Naisby's turn to be tough. 'Like me to give you the numbers and letters between five and P?'

Pryde shook his head, very slowly. And he was wary of a group of tourists who were too close.

Naisby let them move off. Then he said, 'How come you have nearly ten million dollars in Switzerland?'

It was like Custer's last stand, only this was Pryde. 'Disneyland, Mr Kilroy. That's where you are.' The tone was desperate, though he didn't even blink.

'This ten million, Senator?'

Pryde was wilting.

'It was paid in from an offshore island bank used by a West African diplomat working for the good of the world at the United Nations in New York?'

All trace of defiance had gone now. Pryde was like a stripper down to the G-string. 'Okay, Mr Kilroy. What's your price?'

'And I'm one of nature's survivors, Senator.'

'Okay. Others know what you know. Give it me straight.'

'Two million dollars.'

'Two million!'

'An investment, Senator. Less than ten per cent of your current account.'

'This place is a magnet for nuts!'

'So just prove you're sane.' Naisby was playing Pryde's game himself. Every root of every hair at the nape of his neck was tingling.

'We'll have to meet again, Mr Kilroy.'

Naisby shook his head. 'Two million, Senator. An investment. Payable to Raleigh House Securities Inc. Box 2007. George Town. Grand Cayman.'

'Like Georgetown here?'

'No. Two separate words.'

The Senator looked homicidal.

'And don't forget.' Naisby fixed him with a stare. 'If I don't get home safe and sound with all my faculties in good order my friends will be sending photocopies of your account to the Justice Department, the FBI and maybe the *Washington Post* besides.' He made his way to the west steps. When he turned Waldo Pryde was already besieged by admiring groups of rubber-necking ordinary folk. His grin was wide and white. Shaking hands, signing guidebooks, throwing bold salutes, he might not have had a care in the world.

The scene gave Naisby a lift. He'd been right to go for populists. The general conned soldiers, the senator civilians. Both had too much to lose from being discredited.

Naisby strolled jauntily along the Mall, feasting his eyes on the sublime blossom and inhaling the scent which even the traffic on Madison and Jefferson wasn't able to snuff out. He came on two young buskers near the Washington Monument playing the flute and violin, a violin case open at their sandalled feet. He tossed in a hundred-dollar bill and enjoyed their looks of surprise.

He felt like a millionaire already.

And this was only for starters.

He'd forgotten all about his jet lag.

It was no place to be on a wet Sunday night.

The Bahnhofstrasse was deserted except for the odd masochists window-shopping under umbrellas. In the main the only lights in the banks were of the low-intensity security kind, giving off an amber glare. But even as he took the corner, Oscar Leiden saw the lights were on beyond the blinds in Jean-Pascal's office and the next-door boardroom of Seifert et Cie. As he glanced up the marble and glass frontage he saw the lights go on in Wasserman's office.

That made sense.

In all his years at Seifert's he could not remember a Sunday meeting of the board. The summons from Jean-Pascal had upset Reza, who had his favourite Zürchertopf nicely baking in the oven.

She had given him a bad day and was trying to make up for it. 'It's so unreasonable,' she'd complained. 'Surely it can't be so urgent it can't wait till morning?'

She would never understand the money game if she lived to be a hundred. And it wasn't as if there'd been anything on the TV news about the Russians invading Germany, or the dollar going through the floor, or even all of South America reneging on its debts.

Parking the BMW in the brightly lit street close to Seifert's side door, Oscar Leiden knew that none of those things had induced Jean-Pascal to round up the board. He hadn't even used his secretary to make the calls. Oscar climbed the steps and pressed the bell. It was Hagen who replied.

'Oscar Leiden,' he said into the brass speaker set into the wall, knowing that Hagen or one of the other night guards would have seen him already via the security camera with its night-sight.

Another few seconds and the reinforced door swung open.

Hagen stood at the steel gate four yards beyond the door. He was a sergeant in the Landwehr with short-cropped fair hair and a disciplined bearing. In his black roll-collar sweater and black leather jacket he looked more like the classic stereotype of a secret policeman. In time of war he would be a candidate for transfer from the infantry to an interrogation unit. He had a way of being ingratiating and disturbingly suspicious at the same time. 'Fine night for ducks, Herr Leiden.' The ten-yard run from the BMW had left Oscar damp, the rain was pelting so hard.

'I'm the last to get here, I'll bet,' Oscar said, knowing he wasn't. It would be politic neither to be the first nor last to reach Jean-Pascal's office.

'One to come,' Hagen said, following Oscar to the elevator.

'Good,' Oscar smiled, set on looking at ease.

He went to the washroom first. The night was oddly humid and he was sweating. He took off his jacket, opened his shirt and sprayed Aramis antiperspirant under his arms. He then dipped his face in cold water and took a long look at himself in the mirror. He knew it wouldn't be his eyes that might give him away but his chest. His breathing was tight and he felt an ache half-way between his heart and his throat. He brought out an atomizer, wrapped his mouth round it, and sucked the inhalant into his lungs.

He could hear Wasserman's voice even as he tapped on the half-open door of Jean-Pascal's suite.

'Do come in.'

Dread took over. It would be tricky enough to face Wasserman, but Jean-Pascal was a deeply intuitive man of the world it was hard to keep the truth from. And he wasn't at all confident he could look Klutz in the eye ever again. It was a relief to see Klutz was the missing director.

'Sorry about this, Oscar.' Jean-Pascal wasn't just being polite. 'No one enjoys breaking into the Sabbath.'

'If it has to be,' Oscar murmured. The suite smelled of roses, which Jean-Pascal was watering from the jug he'd taken from the refreshments tray. Deep reds and pinks and whites, they stood in three antique Oriental jars. Forty-eight of them. One for each year of Jean-Pascal's life. His wife Caroline had them sent Monday through Friday every week. These were Friday's roses. They had stood up well to the central heating. Gabi Seifert had her pert nose close to the red ones. 'Delightful,' she pronounced, with a quiet smile for Oscar. It was fatally easy to underrate Gabi. Elegant and still sexy at forty, she was more than just the great-granddaughter-in-law of the bank's founder, and not at all the rich suburban housewife from one of those prim havens with an eagle's eye view of Zürich some people took her for. One word from Gabi and Jean-Pascal had been known to fire grown men. Not those with access to those accounts in the Sterile Area, of course. They died in harness. Or lived long lives on the most generous pensions in Switzerland.

Wasserman hadn't said a word. He was dipping into a couple of folders as if they were imperative homework.

'Shouldn't be long now, Oscar.' It was Jean-Pascal. He was re-arranging roses. 'Klutz is having to drive in from Rapperswil. Awful nuisance. He was about to start dinner with his parents.' Laid-back as ever, he had the lofty grace of an aristocrat, the lean face intelligent and patient. Even in the middle of this crisis, Oscar thought, he was all dignity.

'And Willi's not the world's fastest driver,' Gabi said. She was trying to read Jean-Pascal's mind. Why the SOS?

Oscar reckoned Wasserman already knew. 'And Ulrich?' Surely Engel would have to be present – if the meeting *was* about those penetrated accounts.

'Ulrich's on his way to Washington.' Jean-Pascal's tone was calm.

That also made sense. As the bank's legal director, Engel was an authority on bank secrecy. He knew more about America's Internal Revenue Service than most of its senior officials did themselves, and much about the Inland Revenue in Britain and equivalent tax-raising institutions in France, Italy, Germany and even the Soviet Union. He knew how to see them off. But he'd also been at the heart of negotiations with Washington's Drug Enforcement Administration, the FBI, Scotland Yard and other forces eager to trap drug racketeers and organized crime bosses. It seemed Naisby had begun in America, after all. He had planned to make his first hunting ground Britain.

Jean-Pascal put the jug back on the tray. 'Do sit down,' he urged, heading for the long oval boardroom table, made from the same rosewood as the room's wall panels.

It seemed he knew Klutz was on his way up, and they had hardly taken their places when Klutz came in, his fresh young man's face full of apology. 'Driving conditions round the lake are atrocious.' He walked with a stoop. Something to do with a hip condition. He was fifty and could be taken for a thirty-year-old.

'A pity I had to get you here, Willi.' Using a button on the table to his left under the telex monitor, Jean-Pascal locked the door, pressed a second button to start the anti-bugging system, and clasped his hands under his chin with his elbows on the table. His lean face was suddenly grave. 'We have to make a critical decision,' he said solemnly. 'Here and now. This evening.'

He weighed them up in turn. And Oscar caught Wasserman weighing him up. Oscar outgazed him, and Wasserman had good looks at the others except Jean-Pascal. It was plain that Wasserman was the only one who knew why Jean-Pascal had put out the summons. Gabi was probably thinking it had to do with one of her obsessions – the moles of the IRS. Klutz, because of his recent hard look at large deposits coming in from Italy and New York, would have his mind full of menacing godfathers.

Oscar had developed a thirst. His mouth was dry, and his tongue felt like an abrasive pad. He tried to stop looking at the fruit juices and Cokes on the tray. His aim was to be the least conspicuous person in the room. And he felt sure that Jean-Pascal's drawn-out lead-up was meant to give Wasserman the chance to check each of them out. Don't for God's sake reach for a drink.

'I have the most disturbing news to report.' Jean-Pascal had trouble going on. 'Just about the worst news any bank can have short of being told it is about to collapse.' He bit his bottom lip.

Gabi and Klutz braced themselves. Oscar pretended to. He made furrows of concern wrinkle his forehead.

'Two of our private clients' accounts have been penetrated.'

The silence was such that the mild hum from the ionizer Jean-Pascal insisted on having to keep the room's air pure began to sound like a power plant. Gabi and Klutz were in shock. And so was Oscar – not so much from the disclosure as from the danger he now faced. Wasserman wasn't even feigning shock. He was busy watching Oscar, Gabi and Klutz.

'When I was told of the first incident I frankly didn't believe it. Then came this' – he indicated a message he brought from his inside pocket – 'second incident. I sent Ulrich to London right away. He's on Concorde at this very moment.'

Oscar was dying to know who were the first two clients Naisby had approached. He left it to others to ask the questions. Klutz was first. 'These reports, Jean-Pascal?'

'Incidents,' Jean-Pascal was adamant. 'Not just reports.'

'They're complaints direct from our clients?'

Jean-Pascal nodded. His mouth was taut.

'The two accounts? I suppose they're not to do with drugs-related offences or organized crime?'

Jean-Pascal looked to Wasserman for help. And Wasserman won his nodded consent to explain. 'Neither case according to our records has any such links.'

'Are they major clients?' It was Gabi.

Jean-Pascal nodded.

'Both American?'

Jean-Pascal nodded.

'Would it help us to know who they are?' Klutz was being very diplomatic, but Oscar was glad he'd spoken up.

'You're entitled to know.' Jean-Pascal scratched the back of his left hand, not at all keen on giving names.

'We understand,' Klutz said.

Gabi could take no more of the cat-and-mouse stuff. She fixed Jean-Pascal with those iceberg eyes. If only she had her knitting, Oscar thought, she'd have looked like one of the tricoteuses needling away at the guillotine in Paris. Somebody's head was going to roll – even if it had to be Jean-Pascal's. Her face made that much clear. 'Tell me this, Jean-Pascal. Why have you brought us here tonight?'

'You must surely see this is a crisis?'

'My great-grandfather-in-law will be turning in his grave! But why have you got us here? You could have told us all this at the routine meeting on Tuesday.'

'I told you. We have a critical decision to make.'

She didn't even blink.

Jean-Pascal reached for an orange juice. It was the chance Oscar had waited for. He helped himself to a Coke. Jean-Pascal took an elegant sip and said, 'You will see this is such a grave matter it will have to be reported to the Federal Banking Commission.' He paused, letting the silence get to them. 'Whether we do that immediately or – for the present – try to handle it ourselves is for us to decide tonight. All I can add is that if this incident becomes public knowledge – I mean if it becomes known outside this room to others except for Ulrich and the two clients – well, you can imagine!'

'The bank's doomed?' Klutz was shaking his head in disbelief.

All the rest were looking at Jean-Pascal now.

Oscar thought the Last Supper must have been something like this. The thought gave him courage. 'I think what Gabi's saying is that if we're to make such a decision, which some might see as criminal, we have a right to know the names.'

'Absolutely,' Gabi nodded.

'Very well,' Jean-Pascal conceded. 'The first was General Gibb of the US Army. The second is Senator Waldo Pryde.'

Gabi blew out her cheeks in surprise. Oscar helped himself to another Coke.

'Do we agree to handle this internally, then?' Jean-Pascal was putting it to the vote. He covered himself by adding, 'For the time being?'

They all knew it wasn't for the time being.

Their murmured vote was, of course, unanimous.

The delegate from Holland was still droning on.

In his aisle seat high in the tiered public gallery Naisby beckoned an attendant and asked if he could move to one of three empty seats at the far side of the gallery.

'Okay,' the attendant nodded. 'But quiet, right?'

With the world in another of its shoot-first moods, the Security Council of the United Nations was extra busy. Neighbours in South America were squabbling. North and South Korea were letting the sabre-rattling get out of hand, and there was more gunfire than usual in the Middle East. 'It is up to us, the peoples of the world, to ensure that the trigger-happy warriors lay down their weapons before we are all engulfed.' The Dutchman was talking about Syria and Israel in particular, and making old points and diplomatic clichés sound fresh. Only the hum of the air-conditioning and the occasional rustle of paper broke into the pious monologue.

Yet the public up in the gallery were gripped. Naisby crept over the thick carpeting to his new seat. He was right. It gave him a better view of Edwina Sarne. Sifting papers and sharing whispers with grey-suited swells from the State Department, she should have been speaking by now. It was 11.45 and Naisby was to meet her at midday. It hadn't been easy to fix.

His first call had been too early. The US delegation's office in the Secretariat building was unmanned. He tried again only to run into a brick wall by the name of Mary Ann, who insisted that if he wanted to meet America's latest woman ambassador to the UN he would have to put it in writing. He hung up, thinking it might be better just to buttonhole Edwina in the public lobby. But there was no telling when she would be there, and security was tighter than he'd thought. Understandable in a bomb-happy world, but it meant obstacles. He called again, telling Mary Ann it was crucial that he should see the ambassador.

'I did say to put it in writing, sir.' The tone was that of a tolerant social worker speaking to a nut.

It dawned on him that lots of nuts must be trying every day to get to ambassadors at the UN, so he said, 'Look, Mary Ann, just do her a favour, eh? Tell Mrs Sarne I'm on about that property she's interested in by Central Park. The one in the brochure she has. Number 5371.'

'She's busy right now anyway. She has a speech to make this morning.'

'Just remind her about that number, eh?'

'Five three seven one.'

'Right.'

He had given them ten minutes and called again. This time Edwina Sarne had come on, cool as the morning.

'I wasn't given your name,' she said, and he had a suspicion she was taping the call. That was up to her.

'Kilroy,' Naisby said. 'Tom Kilroy.'

'Make it midday, Mr Kilroy.' She sounded firm and unshaken.

'Outside the building's better.' He'd been looking at the statuary in the grounds, and the one from the Soviet Union was still in his mind's eye – a big sculpture of some Russian equivalent of Mr Universe, all body-built biceps as he wielded a hammer to turn a sword into a ploughshare or sickle. 'How about that Russian sculpture?'

'Not there, if you don't mind, Mr Kilroy. Make it the Barbara Hepworth one at the pool.'

Watching her now, he was struck by her self-control *and* her looks. *Who's Who* put her at fifty-two but she could have passed for forty. Her nose was neater than her photographs made out and her buck teeth were less horsey. He trained his binoculars on her – UN security had been difficult about them even after a double-check – and was taken by her good complexion and her taste in makeup.

The Dutchman ran out of clichés and gave way to her. She had the Soviet delegation in her sights as she warned of the folly of inflaming the Middle East. And she was briefly scathing about a resolution that seemed to blame Israel for everything except the natural decay of the Pyramids. 'The United States would for sure use the veto.'

She won Naisby over.

He saw her leave, a brisk woman looking more like an air hostess with her knotted silk scarf above a tailored suit in navy.

Outside he made for the Hepworth abstract and paced around the pool. He was gazing up at the thirty-nine-storey Secretariat when he was aware of someone behind him.

'Sir?'

It was one of a pair of svelte six-footers.

'Are you the guy who's looking for Mrs Sarne?'

His heart seemed to stop. Agents, he thought. Oscar had given him a dud – a legitimate account. He strove to get himself together. He'd done his homework on that account. If the evidence was circumstantial it was also damning. And he'd thought the FBI wasn't allowed in the UN buildings or their precincts.

'She'd prefer to change the venue, sir.' It was the paler of the two.

They led him across the plaza to the public lobby of the General Assembly building. At the security checkpoint the paler man drew off to talk into his walkie-talkie while the other saw Naisby to the head of the queue for screening. The two UN cops on duty weren't the ones who'd hassled Naisby over his binoculars. The check was repeated until they were all sure the glasses weren't guns.

The paler man took over. He led Naisby across the lobby to the meditation room with its huge block of iron ore under a dim spotlight. It was intermittently busy with tourists, but they weren't staying long.

Edwina Sarne came in, so cool it might have been the most routine meeting ever. 'Not in here after all,' she said, shaking hands with Naisby. There were too many people about. She led Naisby through the lobby, motioning to her two minders to keep their distance.

'It seems you're a very numerate man, Mr Kilroy,' she said as they went past the Brotherhood painting given by Mexico.

'You don't want me to go over the number again?'

'No. Just you tell me the next two and the last letter.'

'Four. Seven. And K.' He waited for a group of Chinese to move out of earshot. 'I can let you have a photocopy if you wish. Later. Clearly I don't carry such things in my wallet.'

'That won't be necessary.' She acknowledged a school party from Vermont whose teacher had recognized her. Awestruck eyes got their fill and visitor's guides and ballpoints appeared. 'Later, you kids.' Her smile was warm and easy.

'You're looking for a payoff, that it?'

Naisby shook his head. 'An investment.'

They covered another twenty yards before it was safe to say any more. 'How much?'

'Two million.'

She didn't even blink.

He gave her the name and address of his Cayman company. And she paused near the model of Sputnik One, took a gold-encased notebook from her bag, and wrote it down.

She shook hands and laid on her big politician's smile. But those hard brown eyes told another story. She walked past Naisby.

When he turned she was busy being a potential President to those kids from Vermont.

Jean-Pascal looked ill and trapped. 'Three now.' He had to struggle to get even those words out. 'And I fear it's not the end of them.'

'Another populist?' It was Gabi who was taking her mirror from her handbag.

'Edwina Sarne.'

'Isn't she being tipped as a presidential candidate?' Klutz asked.

'Vice-presidential,' Gabi said.

'*Herald Trib* speculation,' Jean-Pascal said.

'A most able woman,' Gabi said, as if checking her lipstick in that mirror.

It was the first time Oscar had ever seen her do such a feminine thing at a meeting. But then he realized she was using the mirror to check on Wasserman, Klutz and himself. And Wasserman was paying him attention, too. He had to make a move. 'I'd say we're near the point where this must be reported to the FBC.' They were all terrified of the Fedcom.

'I disagree.' It was Gabi in her iron lady role. She indicated Wasserman with a flash of the eyes. 'It's still up to us. I think Charles should get over there right away. Ulrich's a sophisticated tax lawyer.' She meant he was also too much of a gentleman – and by inference that Wasserman was anything but one.

'Charles?' Jean-Pascal was desperate.

'It's possible I could put an end to it,' Wasserman said. The cold eyes had lost their colour.

And it went through Oscar's mind that Wasserman meant murder. 'Is Ulrich getting anywhere in Washington?'

'No.' Jean-Pascal's gaze roved the table, dwelling with some uncertainty for a long moment on Gabi who was taking in Klutz's agonized face in the mirror.

Hitler's final meetings with his generals must have been like this, with mutual suspicion poisoning the air. Jean-Pascal fixed Wasserman with a look. 'I think you should get over there fast, Charles.'

'I'll check on flights,' Wasserman said.

He was hardly gone when Klutz said, 'If this is a real penetration of our security . . .?'

'Willi, for God's sake, of course it is!' Jean-Pascal's patience had snapped. The cross-suspicions had his nerves jangling.

'And our entire security system was devised by Charles.'

'I could never believe this could be Charles's doing,' Jean-Pascal said.

'He did say the system was foolproof.' Oscar surprised himself with his own boldness. He was being a bit reckless.

'I don't think we can take things any further just now.'

The meeting was over. Jean-Pascal went through to his office, leaving the others to go out through the boardroom door. 'Oscar!'

Oscar Leiden turned. Jean-Pascal, at the inter-connecting door, bade him to take a chair in the private office. It was the end of a dreadful day and Jean-Pascal was at his limit. He went to the antique Chinese cabinet, opened the fawn and blue doors, and brought out a bottle of Napoleon brandy. It was a sign of the way he felt. Abstemious and with a sense of moral rectitude, he would never have taken anything stronger than an orange juice before leaving the bank. 'Having one with me, Oscar?'

'I think we need them,' Oscar said, puzzled that he should be asked in.

Jean-Pascal poured two stiff ones. 'Tell me, Oscar, why did you make that comment about Charles's system being foolproof.'

Oscar twirled the ice around the glass. 'Oh' – he tried to be casual – 'he was very sniffy when I pointed out one day that no system is foolproof.'

'You suspect Charles?'

'Good Lord, no.' It would have been too obvious a ploy. And he was full of guilt. One of the good things about having Wasserman in the States for a bit was that any further checks and counter-checks on the use of the Sterile Area would have to be postponed.

'It must be one of the six of us.'

'That's just my point, Jean-Pascal. It wouldn't be the first time some outsider has hacked a way into a major computer. I seem to recall the US Department of Defense had the problem.'

Anything was better than to have a finger pointed at any of them, including Klutz. It all depended on whether Wasserman had built into the system a record of who had consulted which accounts over the past two months. It was beginning to look as if he hadn't.

'Thank you, Oscar.' Jean-Pascal went to the window to look down on the busy street. The Bahnhofstrasse's classy boutiques and jewellers' shops had their lights on.

'Good night, Jean-Pascal.' Oscar felt sorry for him.

In the corridor Wasserman was pacing, an airline timetable in his hand. He was clearly waiting for Oscar to leave. He stroked his beard and frowned, his eyes opaque with hostility.

Conrad Warri was elusive.

Even harder to pin down than his role at the United Nations, where he was no longer a West African delegate yet behaved like one. Neither was he a bureaucrat on the Secretariat's payroll. Since his year as a member of the Economic and Social Council, he had continued to push its interest not only in New York and Geneva but in the world outside.

Naisby stood near the reception desk in the lobby of the Secretariat building and heard the American girl at the desk tell two newsmen, 'Mr Warri has been delayed, but it's fine to go up.' She was piqued at having to relay the directions so often and pointed them to the noticeboard near the elevators.

Another half dozen hacks came in through the security checkpoint to be given the same message. Naisby joined them at the noticeboard. It listed meetings and their times. One of the hacks ran a long manicured fingernail down the list, showing her white gold wristwatch. Naisby caught the word 'Brazil' on her lapel badge, which also gave her name and that of her paper. Her figure-hugging costume and what he could see of her long legs implied she would cut a dash on those Rio beaches. Her finger settled on a line of white plastic letters – 1200 DP PHOTO EXHIBITION: MEDIA PREVIEW.

Naisby made to join the hacks in the elevator.

'Sir!'

He swivelled. A stocky UN security cop in shirtsleeves came over. He'd been watching Naisby on and off for some minutes.

'You media, sir?'

Naisby nodded.

'You ain't wearin' your lapel badge.' The way he said it, the offence was a capital one.

'I was invited by Mr Warri at the last minute.' It wasn't a total lie. One of Warri's aides – who *was* on the UN payroll – had said rashly after Naisby's third call in an hour, 'I reckon the only way you'll get him today is at the media preview. Or in the lobby just before. Say about ten to twelve.'

The security cop wasn't placated yet. 'Which paper you from, sir?'

'Freelance,' Naisby beamed.

It was Miss Brazil who saw him through. She leaned in the elevator doorway with her finger hard on the Stop button and a look on her dark face which said the press was inviolate. 'Aw, come on!' She sounded more like a New Yorker now as she ticked off the cop with a glare. 'He'll give the show a bad notice if you don't come on!'

The cop plucked at an earlobe, then nodded Naisby through.

'Thanks,' Naisby said.

She winked and her smile wasn't spoiled even by a gold tooth.

The reception room on the fourth floor was lined with the exhibits – photographs in colour and black-and-white meant to show the Development Programme through ordinary people. Some showing hungry children were clichés but heartrending all the same. Others with Third World workers coming to terms with factory machines were no more than imitations of old Soviet propaganda. Down the middle of the room ran a modest buffet. The freeloading hacks were helping themselves with only a few troubling even to look as if they were aware of the photographs.

It occurred to Naisby that it wasn't only food for the starving kids of Africa the UN was keen on. Yesterday it had been the delegates' restaurant in the Assembly block. Warri's aide – the same one – had said it was the place Naisby was most likely to find the elusive action man. There had been no sign of Warri. But Naisby had got a good look at the menu – ginger poached Norwegian salmon, fusilli with crayfish and shitake mushrooms, linguine with sun-dried tomatoes. The delegates also had a choice of five champagnes.

He helped himself now to a cheese fritter.

A UN official, a young American in a conservative blue suit and moccasins, suddenly raised his hands in the middle of the room. 'Ladies and gen'l'men. We just had a message from Conrad. He sends his apologies to you all. He's on his way by helicopter from JFK right now and should get here like soon.'

A few who knew Warri well threw in spiked comments. The rest were too busy eating.

It was another half hour before Warri came in like a black cyclone. His moon face glistened. He was smaller than Naisby had imagined but had the drive of three men. He was standing on a chair, squeezing his tiny moustache between thumb and forefinger, and calling for attention. 'I can see you folk have been helping yourselves to what's going. I hope the nibbles aren't too primitive.' He got a laugh and wagged a finger in reproof. 'And don't any of you go saying we're on a spree round here. The nibbles are a gift from a private friend of the Development Programme. As are the prizes for the best photos.'

'We know, Conrad,' a hack teased. 'We know *you* gave the eats and the prizes.'

Hand on heart, Warri put on the look of an innocent man.

'If we'd known it was your call, Connie, we'd have expected truffles and caviar.'

The hacks laughed. They were the same the world over, Naisby thought. Fill their bellies they'll go easy on you. Give 'em rides on the gravy train there's nothing they won't do for you.

'Anyway, just bear in mind who this exhibition's meant to help. The world's most needy peoples. Some of the best photos weren't even taken by professionals. I've even got a couple of my own prints in.'

'Fix,' came a cynical shout. But it was only a joke.

Warri wore a big grin. 'I wasn't on the selection panel,' he said, and stepped down.

He was in demand. Naisby pressed through the throng. 'Mr Warri?' He held out his hand.

'Yessir.' For all his bluster, Warri was guarded.

'Kilroy,' Naisby said. 'Tom Kilroy.'

Warri shook hands just as an ageing British hack came up. 'Did I hear Kilroy?'

'You did,' Warri said.

'In the last war he was all over the place. Funny little guy poking his face over walls. Soldiers' graffiti. "Kilroy was here".' He looked at Naisby. 'You could've got your name from him.'

'I did,' Naisby said, deadpan.

It was true but they all thought he was joking.

'Just a word to the wise, old son.' The old hack pushed his face confidentially close to Warri's. 'If you're going to make this a buzz round the world you should get the President to give you a print or two, and one or two of the Royals are dab hands. And the big boy in the Kremlin's no slouch with a Pentax.'

'I'll think about it,' Warri laughed.

'I need a minute, that's all,' Naisby said.

'Can't be any more, I'm afraid.'

Naisby pointed to a corner away from the crowd.

'What's wrong with here?' Warri's antennae sensed trouble.

'As you like.' Naisby probed his inside pocket and fished out a small brown envelope from which he took a postcard-size photograph. 'My entry for the exhibition, Mr Warri.'

Warri thought he was serious and took him for a nut – but not for long. One glance at the photograph was enough. He shielded it briskly from others' eyes. It was a close-up of a computer screen with a scarlet frame, showing an up-to-date summary of an account numbered 268/T/4749 belonging to one WARRI C – US RESIDENT. The current balance was 16,844,278.65 Swiss francs.

Warri hustled Naisby out of the room. 'So what are you saying to me?' he asked in the corridor.

'You're clearly a wise investor.'

'I'm no longer a politician. Or an international civil servant. I'm free to run businesses.'

Naisby shook his head. 'The main deposits coincided with multi-million-dollar tranches of aid to certain African countries.'

Warri tugged at his tie, with its UN logo, as if it were a noose.

'Those deposits weren't paid in from nowhere. We know the sources. If you'd like one or two more photos for your show?' In fact, he had no more photographs of Warri's account. Midway through his searches in the Sterile Area, Oscar had become alarmed at the time it was taking to note all the details. He had turned to his 35mm mini-camera. His first attempt was a fiasco. The snaps were underlit and murky. But then he'd come up with a good one. In London Naisby had keyed the information from the photograph into another computer – the biggest seller on the market – and it was the image from this computer's screen that was on the photograph which Warri could not bear to look at any more. Naisby had even disguised his own computer screen for the photograph, giving it a false frame of scarlet plastic. Oscar, for all he knew, was taking more pictures in Zürich.

'What's your price?'

'I want an investment of two million dollars in a company with great prospects.' He smiled. 'You never know. It might make you really rich.'

Warri's shoulders sagged and his bloodshot eyes filled with tears.

'Just as a matter of interest, what's your cut from this aid for the poor strugglers?' Naisby asked blandly. 'Tying up some of the deposits with the amounts of aid you got out of America and one or two other donors I worked out that you – '

'No United Nations money,' Warri insisted.

Naisby shrugged. 'I put your commission at two per cent.'

Warri was lost for words but his face told Naisby that he wasn't far out.

And it had been a try-on, a blind guess.

Naisby told him now where to send the two million. He didn't go back into the media party with Warri. He thought he'd see what it felt like to be a delegate up in that UN restaurant. He couldn't get that fusilli with crayfish and shitake mushrooms out of his mind. He thought he'd give it a try, whatever it was.

Jean-Pascal was restored to his statesmanlike best. He had prayed and for three nights had taken sleeping-pills, which had pleased his friend Dr Neumann. Normally Jean-Pascal would have declined pills even with a death rattle in his throat. 'I give you my solemn word that our security is the best on earth. Layer upon layer of it. We call it the onion-skin approach.'

'Then the onion's rotten at the core.' Warri was unforgiving, and frightened.

'That's unfair, Mr Warri,' Jean-Pascal soothed. 'A remark I'm sure you'll wish to withdraw soon.'

'How does this man, this total stranger called Kilroy, how does he come to hold a copy of my account?'

'I'm sure he doesn't.' He kept his finger near the panic button on the underside of his desk. Warri had the look of one about to take leave of his marbles. He was clenching both hands as if he were about to strangle someone. Less than five minutes after the two million dollar demand he'd made his excuses and found a pressing reason to visit Geneva on UN business. He had then taken an off-the-record flight to Zürich.

He stared at each of the four walls of Jean-Pascal's office in turn as he reached for his crocodile-skin briefcase.

'You needn't worry about devices, Mr Warri.' Jean-Pascal kept his voice low key. 'My office is proofed against them.'

'Like your computer?' The tone was sour.

He zipped the briefcase open. It offended Jean-Pascal. He was a committed supporter of the World Wildlife Fund, and crocodile skins were definitely out. That briefcase had cost Warri more friends at the UN than his brash salesman's style. He brought out a wallet, then the brown envelope, which he laid on the rosewood desk as if it were radioactive.

On a nod from Warri, Jean-Pascal took it.

The photograph of Warri's statement of account shook him so much he nearly lost his statesman's mask. Then he frowned.

'The best security on earth?' The rhetoric was dagger-sharp.

Jean-Pascal needed Wasserman, but he was in New York to question Edwina Sarne. His report in coded telex was due any minute. And it might have unhinged Warri to call in *anyone*. But something didn't fit. Then he knew what it was. The scarlet frame around the screen in the photograph was wrong. Every screen in the Sterile Area – indeed in the entire bank – was battleship grey.

'Explain that.' In his fury, Warri looked demented.

'Do please restrain yourself, Mr Warri,' Jean-Pascal snapped. 'This is a bank of repute, Mr Warri. So we assume our clients' repute is of equal quality.'

'What the hell are you suggesting?'

'*Our* assets are clean, Mr Warri. We never knowingly accept deposits that could be the proceeds of crime.'

Conrad Warri felt he had lost his last ally in a cruel world. 'You're telling me – now! – you're saying I must pay this ransom?'

'I'm saying, Mr Warri, that if your assets were properly acquired you have nothing to fear.'

Warri felt naked. Disgrace loomed. His Mr Clean image made it all the worse. All those leaders of integrity who were emerging in

Africa would treat him as a political leper. And the fact that he was black like them would only make it worse.

Jean-Pascal affected not to spot his sense of guilt. He was puzzling over something else in that photograph. On impulse he buttoned up a random unclassified image on his computer screen. It showed a statement from the Fed in Washington. And the media not the message mattered. The typeface was different from that on the screen photographed by Kilroy. And the typeface on all computer screens in Seifert et Cie. was uniform.

He couldn't explain that to Warri, of course. It would only make things worse. For it seemed that an outsider had somehow hacked into a foolproof system. He felt exposed now. The telex on the small table to his left had begun to stutter a coded message. He saw it was from Wasserman. He rose and offered his hand and showed Warri to the door. 'We'll be in touch, Mr Warri.' The soothing tone was back.

Warri, beaten, said, 'The photograph?'

'Leave it with me, Mr Warri. We need to look at it very closely.'

'And the ransom? Do I pay it?'

'Not if the deposits were clean, Mr Warri.' And with a smile he transferred Warri to his secretary in the outer office. 'Goodbye, Mr Warri. I do hope you'll be able to make the most of your stay in Switzerland. It's quite beautiful, you know. Especially at this time of year.'

Back at the telex he was mentally decoding as it stuttered Wasserman's message. General Gibb, Senator Waldo Pryde and now Edwina Sarne had all been approached by the same man, Tom Kilroy, an Englishman of slight build with grey eyes, dark curly hair and an outdoors complexion. Like Gibb and Pryde, Mrs Sarne had been invited to invest in a Cayman-registered company, Raleigh House Securities Inc.

And now there was Conrad Warri.

Where would it end? He looked at that photograph. It seemed to spell the collapse of Seifert et Cie. He called his wife and said it was high time they had a night out.

And then he sat with his head in his hands.

FOUR

The judge in the Court of Appeal was clearly out of sorts.

It was the ninth day of a complex case of insurance fraud in which the suave City gent in the dock wore his Old Etonian tie with pride. He was accused of embezzling £27 million of a syndicate's money, which had gone walkabout to wind up in some place still unknown.

The afternoon was unseasonably muggy, and the air-conditioning wasn't up to much. What made it worse was the droning performance of the tanned and overfed Queen's Counsel who was leading for the defence. The Rt Hon. Sir Corin Timothy Kenright MBE wriggled in that throne of a chair, adjusted the ample sleeves of his ermine robe, pushed up his wig to scratch his left ear, and gazed upwards as if seeking solace from the gods. All he could see was a representative selection of the British public up in the gallery, and a sick-making lot they were – unkempt voyeurs, young City gents there to learn how the accused had pulled off the coup, and the *schadenfreude*-driven lefties there to see a capitalist squirm.

He was about to turn his ire on the dreary QC when his gaze fell on a young man in an aisle seat three rows up. He looked neither a lefty nor a City money-grubber. And he was undoubtedly giving a thumbs-up sign, albeit discreetly close to his left cheek.

It had taken Naisby hours to make contact.

'You can't just go seeing Her Majesty's judges like that, sir,' the bulky old cop on the door of Court Four had told him when he asked for a quick word with Kenright before the day's hearing.

'It won't take more than a couple of minutes.'

'If you think you're a material witness, sir . . . '

'Forget it,' Naisby had said, going out to find a typing agency in Fleet Street, where he dictated a letter to Kenright:

Dear Lord Justice Kenright:
Please telephone me this evening on 237-1894 unless we can meet earlier. I will endeavour to be in the public gallery of your court, and will identify myself with a discreet thumb signal. It is a shade lèse majesté, I know. I had thought of holding a copy of the *Financial Times* rather prominently, but it appeared just now that most of those going into the public gallery were doing precisely that. Perhaps when you close the day's hearing we could talk briefly in your chambers?
Yours sincerely,
Tom Kilroy

Naisby was aware that Kenright had seen the signal. Kenright's eyesight was a bit of a legend. He didn't need glasses and was a crack shot at Bisley. And Naisby felt the power of his gaze now. Then Kenright took it out of the overweight QC. 'Are you saying, Mr Hyland, that your client was not at the relevant time effectively in control of this re-insurance company in the Bahamas?' The tone was acrid.

'With respect, milord, I thought I had made it clear this morning . . . '

Kenright cut him dead. 'You made very little clear this morning, Mr Hyland.'

Hyland bowed.

'Carry on.'

Hyland grovelled. 'I'll do my best.'

'As long as we don't confuse the jury. This whole case is maze enough to those familiar with the machinations of the financial world, let alone these good men and women.'

If the bench had permitted it, Hyland's forehead would have stroked Kenright's boots, the bow was so exaggerated. He resumed his cross-examination of a witness who knew more than he was letting on.

Again Naisby found Kenright fixing him with that laser stare. It told him what he wanted to know. Kenright had recognized that telephone number as the first seven digits of his Swiss account.

Another ten minutes, and Kenright ended the day's show. The QC was calling another witness when Kenright straightened his back and planted his palms on the dais. 'I think that will do, Mr Hyland. The jury has taken as much as it can assimilate of evidence of such complexity.' And he rose, tossing a quick look at Naisby.

Meeting the judge was easier this time. The police and court ushers had clearly been warned of his coming, and Naisby was in the judge's room before Kenright had finished disrobing. A grey-haired lackey was settling Kenright's wig on its frame as Kenright placed his robe over a chair and reached for the gin and tonic the lackey had poured.

Kenright indicated the gin bottle and another glass.

'I thought you'd prefer to meet in the open air,' Naisby said with an eye on the lackey.

'You're probably right,' Kenright said. He was even more judicially severe now than in court, and no longer the old man under that wig. Naisby knew how old he was – fifty-two – with lots of time to fulfil the predictions Naisby had read in the press clip, that he was a Lord Chief Justice in the making. He had a lot to lose. 'I telephoned that number, Mr Kilroy. It was unobtainable.'

Unless he was a fool the judge was lying. And he was no fool.

Naisby brought out a buff envelope and handed it over.

Kenright opened it, took one look at the postcard-size photograph, put the photograph back and the envelope into his inside pocket. 'We'll get some fresh air. You know Lincoln's Inn Fields?'

Naisby nodded. He had spent many a lunchtime in this lawyers' quadrangle up behind the Old Bailey watching the young secretaries playing netball.

'Give me twenty minutes. I'll see you near the north-east corner.'

He's setting a trap, Naisby thought. But even before he was outside he dismissed the idea. Even the most successful barristers, and especially the self-made ones – the cuttings said Kenright was the son of a Durham railway driver – didn't have seventeen million Swiss francs tucked away in Zürich. It was a simple account. One deposit of eight million francs put in seven years ago. Jean-Pascal's investment aces had created the rest. One withdrawal became a luxury chalet up in the Engadine mountains. The deposit was dated one week precisely after the end of one of Kenright's major victories in a £46 million shipping case. A hot commercial lawyer at the time, he'd ridiculed rumours of sky-high fees. 'Nonsense,' the cuttings showed him saying at the time. 'I'll be lucky to clear £100,000.'

It was half an hour before Kenright showed up. Naisby saw him coming from nearly two hundred yards away, a brisk and upright six-footer with the bearing and style of a retired Guards officer. Only the salutes were missing as young and not so young lawyers spotted him and showed their respect with bows and careful smiles.

Naisby rose from a bench, dropping his *Standard* into a trash bin.

'Keep walking, eh?'

'I don't mind,' Naisby said.

They let two groups of lawyers pass before Kenright said, 'I assume it *is* blackmail?'

'No. I'm asking for an investment, that's all.'

'In some offshore company?' He was so matter-of-fact he could have been on about a hundred pounds' worth of National Savings bonds.

'My own.'

'Ah! An entrepreneur?' He was used to tight spots. 'A substantial investment, I take it?'

'Two million.'

'Pounds, dollars or Swiss francs?'

Naisby let two gowned barristers pass out of earshot, after they had bowed in unison to the judge like grovelling Siamese twins. Kenright beamed his appreciation of Naisby's sense of danger.

'I'm not greedy. Make it dollars.'

A discarded plastic lunch pack blew across their path. Kenright trapped it with the élan of a football player. He stooped to pick it up. 'Can't stand litter, you know. They inherit this civilized place and can't be bothered to keep it tidy.' He dropped it in the next bin. 'You do know the penalties for blackmail, Mr Kilroy?'

'Funny, you must admit.'

'What was that?'

'I see you're to be the judge in what's likely to be the biggest tax evasion trial ever brought by the Inland Revenue.'

'That's funny?'

'Very.'

Four young barristers, wigless but still wearing their white cravats, were about to cross their path. They spotted Kenright almost as one, and two of them collided in their awed surprise. They bowed.

'Good afternoon,' Kenright said.

When they were clear Naisby asked, 'Should I give you the name and address of the company?'

'I think you'd better.'

They paused at a bench. Naisby put up a foot to use his knee as a writing table. 'I *have* taken precautions in case I should – er – be pushed under a bus. Others will have access to prints of the photograph and the research.'

'One would have been surprised if it had been otherwise.'

Naisby saw the judge frown. So he wiped his footmarks off the seat before handing over the slip of paper.

They parted without a handshake. Kenright headed back to the Old Bailey and Naisby cut through to Kingsway, where he hailed a cab.

'Buckingham Palace, please,' he said nonchalantly.

The driver smirked. 'You don't live there, I suppose?'

'Not yet.' Naisby was feeling it was fun to be alive.

The driver set him down at the right-hand corner of the railings. Naisby went up to the duty policeman. 'I'm here to see Sir Rupert Mallory.'

'You have an appointment, sir?'

Naisby shook his head. 'I believe he's been trying to call me on 703-2955.'

The policeman ran the rule over him, then put in a walkie-talkie call. A plainclothes man came out, took in Naisby's sober grey suit and Royal Air Force tie, which Naisby had bought for the occasion, though the nearest he'd been to serving in the RAF was a series of visits to several fighter-bomber stations for Cromwell Jaynes & Co. when they were advising airmen about investments. Both the policeman and the plainclothes man were strip-searching him without use of hands.

Presently the plainclothes man said, 'Hold on a tick, sir,' and turned to re-enter the Palace. 'Your name, sir?'

'Kilroy,' Naisby said. 'Tom Kilroy. Just say I'm the chap I believe he was trying to call on 703-2955.'

The plainclothes man made a ballpoint note.

It was another six minutes before the plainclothes man beckoned him to advance to the Privy Purse door. A brisk body search and he was on his way, to be met near the first staircase by one of Sir Rupert's aides.

The equerry's office was spacious and austere. An electric fan swivelled in a ninety-degree arc on a mahogany stand facing the baroque escritoire at which Sir Rupert sat behind two stacks of files and reference books. He stood up, a lean man with wavy silvering hair and a stoop. High cheekbones gave him a gaunt look. He tugged his half-lensed glasses off and scrutinized Naisby from head to toe, his nostrils quivering in the distinguished Roman face. There was no false bonhomie, no self-deception. He was so numbed he had the look of a man who has seen his end.

Naisby felt sorry for him. He had an urge to back out. Instead he brought out a buff envelope, leaving Mallory to open it and see the photograph of his Swiss bank statement. Naisby couldn't look into that stupefied face again.

He would raise the matter of the investment another day, in some other place, when Mallory might be better able to stand up to it.

He closed the door quietly behind him, and was glad to get back into the Mall's bright sunshine.

Jean-Pascal had hardly slept.

As he watched from the back seat of the Mercedes he could see that Wasserman was in a foul temper. Wasserman didn't travel well. Having left JFK International early on a balmy New York evening, he found the British dawn no less dispiriting than usual. He was mouthing some disgruntled comment to Duhrer who was carrying his two matching cases out of Terminal Four. He switched his tamper-proof briefcase from one hand to the other as they came through the automatic doors. It was heavier than it looked with its bugging and debugging devices, its radio-phone and telex decoding gear.

Jean-Pascal lowered the nearside tinted window. 'Good morning, Charles.'

'Morning, Jean-Pascal.' The tone was formal rather than friendly.

'You've taken breakfast, I assume?'

'Couldn't face it,' Wasserman murmured. He smelled of eau de cologne.

'Excellent. You can look forward to sharing some Loch Fyne kippers with me. The best thing about coming over here.'

They were on the Heathrow spur heading for the M4 before Jean-Pascal raised the glass privacy screen between them and Duhrer. Even the loyal Duhrer, Swiss-born and with thirty years' service to the bank in London, could not be privy to what Jean-Pascal was burning to say. A reading light came on as Jean-Pascal handed Wasserman a buff-coloured envelope, leaving him to take out the photographs of Warri's, Mallory's and Kenright's accounts.

They were an attack on Wasserman's professional self-esteem. He peered at each photograph with an intensity bordering on paranoia, adjusting the reading light this way and that. 'You've had fingerprints taken?'

'No,' Jean-Pascal said. 'No fingerprint man would have a high enough security status to look at those.'

Wasserman murmured his doubts.

'You know about Conrad Warri, of course. The other two are fresh.'

'Kilroy again?'

'He seems to have moved his base to London. Hence our need to have you here. I hope it wasn't too messy.'

It was messy as hell. Having met General Gibb, Senator Pryde, Edwina Sarne and Warri, Wasserman had built up an image of Kilroy in spite of some of their descriptions being at odds. Finding an Englishman called Kilroy without help from the police or other US agencies was a bit like seeking a white marble in the Arctic. But he had three private eyes helping to comb New York hotel registers. They had come up with a few Kilroys, but none the bellhops could recall, and mostly they were Irish-Americans with addresses in Boston, Philadelphia and even Texas.

He was still squinting at those photographs when Duhrer took the Mercedes on to the M4. 'Sir Rupert Mallory?'

'A Royal equerry,' Jean-Pascal sniffed. 'Works at Buckingham Palace.'

'Still the eminent persons, then? The good and the great.'

Wasserman fought his jet-lagged brain. It was part of his job to check on clients holding bigger sums than might be expected from their roles in life.

'One of Britain's top judges,' Jean-Pascal said of Kenright. 'In line for the very top.'

Wasserman took another close look at Kenright's account.

'This Kilroy has to be stopped soon.' Jean-Pascal's voice was desperate. 'He's the greatest threat to the bank in its one hundred and fifty years. Not even the Gestapo were more dangerous when old Seifert frustrated their efforts to pry into our German Jewish accounts.'

To Wasserman it sounded as if Jean-Pascal was blaming him for the security failure. 'Has anything struck you about these pictures?'

Jean-Pascal nodded. 'But you tell me what you've seen.'

'These screens aren't like any of ours.'

'Those scarlet frames?'

'And the print face.'

'Trace the computer, you have Kilroy.'

It sounded like another marble in the Arctic job. 'I'm only guessing,' Wasserman said. 'But I reckon this is one of the top three best-selling PCs in the world.'

The red light on the radiophone was glowing.

'You take it,' Jean-Pascal said. 'I've heard as much bad news as I can take for a while.'

'Jean-Pascal,' the voice crackled. It was Werner.

'No. Charles Wasserman. Jean-Pascal's busy.'

Werner was the upwardly-mobile young head of the dealing department who worked all hours and knew more about time zones than Wasserman would ever want to. And this was no time to be asking Jean-Pascal about switching dollars and yen. 'Won't it keep?'

'It's not a money-market problem, Charles. One of our London clients is trying to contact Jean-Pascal urgently. He's been through twice. I didn't say Jean-Pascal was in the UK, naturally.'

Jean-Pascal overheard the message and took the phone. 'Don't give his name over this thing, Werner. Get a coded telex to my hotel room, okay?'

Werner acknowledged and hung up.

Jean-Pascal and Wasserman read each other's thoughts. Not another eminent person, please.

In Jean-Pascal's room they decoded the message. It ran: LORD PLACKETT REQUIRES IMMEDIATE MEETING. SAYS YOU HAVE HIS NUMBER.

Every important client had the idea that Jean-Pascal kept his number in his head. It was no problem. Plackett was listed in the phone book. A Chelsea number. But Jean-Pascal wasn't ready to face the day. He took a cold shower while Wasserman ordered their breakfasts – Loch Fyne kippers.

Only after the kippers, which put him in better sorts, did Jean-Pascal call Plackett. He recalled him well. Plackett was no run-of-the-mill millionaire. He was a socialist life peer whose fortune had landed at Seifert et Cie. during the last Labour government. Even Wasserman knew of him, having run a defensive check on his curriculum vitae when the first deposit of nearly seven million Swiss francs had shown up via Bermuda.

'Jean-Pascal?' Plackett sounded as breezy as the morning. 'Where the devil are you?' He was known for this talent of treating people he hardly knew as intimates.

'The Connaught,' Jean-Pascal said easily. 'How can I help you at this time of day?' It was just after six-thirty.

'I'll tell you when I get there. Give me twenty minutes. Don't move.'

It would have been tiresome had not Jean-Pascal told himself that Plackett was victim number seven.

From his windows with their view of Berkeley Square, Jean-Pascal saw Plackett drive up in his Daimler and hand it over to the commissionaire for parking.

Plackett was in the room before they expected him. 'Didn't bother to wait for the lift,' he said. A diminutive power-pack of sixty-plus, he wasn't even breathing hard as he shook hands with Jean-Pascal and examined him with a head-to-toe look.

'Charles Wasserman,' Jean-Pascal said. 'One of my directors.' And his expression said Wasserman would be staying.

'Ah, kippers!' Plackett enthused, sniffing the air.

'You should have come for breakfast,' Jean-Pascal said.

'I would if I'd known.' The hyperactive little man unzipped his slim envelope-style briefcase like one who had to get through more appointments than there were minutes in the day.

And Jean-Pascal knew what was coming even before Plackett brought out a miniature tape recorder and set it on Play with his small, dainty hands. His rumbustious charm was gone – just like that – as he said, 'Just hear this, eh?' His northern accent made him sound hard and bossy.

'Lord Plackett?' a male voice asked.

'Speaking.'

'You're a difficult man to get hold of.'

'You know what time it is, young man?'

'Half past five.' The voice was unalarmed.

'In the morning.'

'I tried to contact you seven times yesterday.'

'Try again today then. Call me at the House of Lords.' Plackett sounded as if he were about to hang up.

'*You* could call *me*.'

'I don't even know who you are.'

'Kilroy,' came the reply. 'Tom Kilroy.'

Wasserman nearly spilt his coffee. Jean-Pascal leaned close to the machine.

'Goodbye then, Mr Kilroy.'

'Don't be like that, your lordship. Call me at 619-8023.'

In the silence Jean-Pascal could imagine the look on Plackett's ferret face.

'I don't think we should talk over the phone,' Plackett now offered, his voice no longer hostile.

'Name the time and place.'

'How about lunch with me at the House of Lords?' A pause. 'On second thoughts, maybe not.'

'Oh, I don't know. I just want to show you a photo and offer you a simple deal. But I'm off heavy lunches. So maybe we can just meet for a couple of minutes.'

'I'll be in the Lords' dining room between half past twelve and two o'clock.'

'Look forward to it.' And a click.

Plackett crossed and helped himself to a coffee. 'You know what all that's about? That number he gave me? It might sound like one from the London phone book. But that's what it isn't. It's my number . . . ' He stopped and took a long look at the room.

'The room's sanitized, Lord Plackett.' It was Wasserman.

'It's as secure as the bank,' Jean-Pascal said, and promptly regretted it.

'That's not saying much.' He was more blunt than ever.

'What you're saying is that it's your number with us?'

'Who is this little bugger? And how's he come by that number?'

Both Wasserman and Jean-Pascal put on a thespians' show of being numbed by the news as if this were some unique and incredible aberration. Yet Wasserman's hunter's eyes were alight. 'Why don't we have lunch with you, Lord Plackett?'

'That wise, is it?'

'I'd like to meet this chap.' He paused to imply he had forgotten the name. 'Er'm . . .?'

'Kilroy,' Plackett said. 'Tom Kilroy.' He was caught on the hop. But then he nodded, rose and began to put the tape recorder away.

'Mind if we have the tape?' Wasserman had voice prints in mind.

'Not yet,' Plackett said foxily. He zipped up the case. 'Let's see what this leak's going to cost, first.'

He was gone as swiftly as he had come.

'A cunning one,' Wasserman said.

Jean-Pascal nodded. 'That's as near as he could come to saying we'll be liable for whatever Kilroy demands.'

'Two million. It's always two million.'

'If his money's clean he's got nothing to fear.'

Wasserman's face said it all. If.

'The trouble is – we have. Whether it's clean or filthy. And he knows it. Pity about that tape, Charles.'

The Lords' dining room was no gourmet's haven. The prevailing smell was of boiled cabbage. Jean-Pascal played safe. Clear soup, then a steak and salad. Wasserman went for prawns and the chicken and ham pie. Wanting to impress a tableful of Tory peers close by, Plackett stayed defiantly loyal to his origins and made a show of choosing Lancashire hot-pot. 'You should try it,' he told his guests. 'Better than all your fondu things.'

There was no sign of Kilroy.

Three times Plackett went out to find him, in case some idiot in the central lobby had failed to show him up. They were on coffee and brandy when he made his last search. 'The blighter likely thought I'd called in the Yard.' It was a touch of bravura that didn't kid any of them.

No more than three yards away, within earshot, Naisby heard nothing to his advantage.

'You know that lot, Rollo?' said his host, Lord Darwen.

Naisby shrugged, feigning indifference.

'The midget's Plackett. One of our lefty life peers. One of those socialists turned company chairmen. Don't be taken in by the hot-pot. He's a caviar and venison chap really.'

Again Naisby implied that he couldn't care less. He knew more about Plackett than Darwen, who was no mere life peer but an hereditary blue-blooded lord with knobs on. They had been young learners together at Cromwell Jaynes & Co. Naisby had scrounged the invitation to lunch to keep an eye on Plackett and whoever he might bring at his ermine tails. Peregrine Darwen thought it was for a chat about the good old days. Naisby cut himself a piece of ripe Stilton and buttered his cream crackers, and all the time kept Jean-Pascal in his eyeline. Jean-Pascal being there personally was an eye-opener. It was good they'd never met. The big bearded polecat who'd had the chicken and ham pie had to be Wasserman. Oscar's description of him had been spot-on.

Lord Darwen raised his glass of Corton to Naisby. 'Anyway, Rollo, here's to your new venture. May it take off and stay airborne for years to come.'

'Oh I don't know about that, Perry. I'm not setting up a business for my children.' He smiled, his eyes on Plackett. 'I haven't got any actually.' He waited until Plackett had signed the bill and was on his way out with Jean-Pascal and Wasserman before he took a shocked glance at his watch. 'God! I'm late for an investment meeting.' He rose, knowing Lord Darwen had still to get his bill. 'No way to run a new venture, is it?'

'You'll survive,' Darwen said with a knowing grin.

'Thanks for the bite, old son. The next one's on me.'

'It had better be.'

They shook hands, and Naisby followed Plackett and his guests to the central lobby, keeping his distance in the long hall leading to St Stephen's door. He stayed at the top of the steps looking down at Plackett as he bade farewell to Jean-Pascal and Wasserman inside the security checkpoint. He let Plackett pass him on the way back along that endless hall, giving the two Swiss time to get well clear among the crowds ogling the Mother of Parliaments.

Half-way along he caught up with his man. 'Lord Plackett?'

Plackett knew the voice and swivelled in shock.

'Tom Kilroy.' He brought out a buff-coloured envelope. 'I promised you a look at this.'

Plackett held back.

'It's not a dirty postcard,' Kilroy grinned.

Plackett took the envelope and found the photograph.

'Good healthy picture, your lordship.'

'Hard-earned,' he said tartly.

'Hard-earned my backside!'

'What's the game, young man?'

'I read about your big speech in the Lords this week about the need to fund more hospitals.'

Plackett began to walk faster.

'You could have paid for one yourself.'

Plackett built up the pace. Ahead were three uniformed cops.

'I mean eighteen million francs plus.'

'What do you want?'

'Two million, that's all.'

'You must be mad.'

'Dollars. Just to keep the books tidy.'

'I should clear off before somebody takes you off to the cells.' It was a puny bluff.

'Two million dollars. An investment, that's all. You're chairman of enough firms these days. You know what it's about. Investment makes the world go round.' And he offered a card which he'd had instantly printed the day before. It was simple: 'Raleigh House

Securities Inc. Grand Cayman'. The printers had stipulated a minimum order of five hundred. He couldn't see he would need that many, but he took the lot. 'Just see the investment reaches us in forty-eight hours.' And Naisby turned back along the hall.

The place was crawling with cops, uniformed and in plain clothes. Plackett called none of them.

FIVE

Naisby felt vulnerable.

As far as he was aware, the only person on Grand Cayman who knew him was Ed Maxell. He had checked in at the same hotel on Seven Mile Beach he'd used on his first one-day trip, and maybe some of the staff would recall him. But only Ed really knew him as an individual and, more to the point, as owner of Raleigh House Securities Inc. And it was Ed who'd set the alarm bells off.

Landing from Miami at Owen Roberts around 2 pm, Naisby had barely finished his shower when there was a knock on his beach-room door.

It was Ed, blowing hard and soaked after running through a flash storm from the car park.

For a second Naisby had thought the game was up. He opened the bottle of brandy from the Miami duty-free shop and poured two trebles.

'I knew you were on the flight, Rollo,' Maxell had said, wiping his glasses. 'I didn't pick you up for the damn good reason that we've had a couple of nosey-parkers around asking about Raleigh House.'

Naisby had come alert.

'Don't let it fret you too much – we get this kind of moling quite often – but I reckoned I'd best play safe and not give anyone the idea you were some new big client.' He'd then taken a swig of brandy and asked, 'This investment money, Rollo? It *is* clean?'

'Sure it's clean.' He sounded resentful.

'Sure, sure. I knew it would be.' He seemed to be clearing himself for the record.

'But is this room?'

With a knowing look, Maxell had dipped into a pocket of his linen jacket hanging near the air-conditioner to dry, and brought out an anti-bugging device which he laid on the bed. 'I'm sure this place is okay.' He seemed to wind down a bit, propping himself on the bed with a muscled brown forearm with a scar running from wrist to elbow, the souvenir of a big-game fishing mishap. He wore a thick gold ring, a gold bracelet on his wrist, and a gold chain with a St Christopher charm round his neck. 'Anyway, you needn't have come here at all. Except for the sun and some diving on the reef.'

'I told you. I want to see these transfers go through. I want to see these dollars come in. And go out.' His mouth was drawn tight.

Maxell had shrugged. 'What can go wrong? Unless you don't trust me?'

'Rubbish.' Naisby had smiled. 'Put it down to the maternal instinct. It's like having a baby, I suppose.'

Maxell had then given him instructions and two keys.

It was nearly midday now. Naisby parked his hired Honda near the Post Office and made his way between the glossy new BMWs and the bangers of another age, many with bald tyres. He went past the old colonial shops and two new blocks, all sandstone and glass, that were totems of money and greed. The Drake Building loomed with its facade of marble and tinted glass. It was impossible to see inside. He crossed the street, dodging clapped-out taxis that were more rust than metal, and watched the main doors. The people moving in and out were a microcosm of George Town as a whole – blacks, browns and whites, in finely-tailored mohair suits and carrying briefcases. Many of the cases were so fat they could better be called hand-held offices. There were numerous banks in the Drake Building. And Maxell had made it clear that tales of these cases being packed with dollar bills were closer to the truth than myth.

Looking back over his shoulder, Naisby made his way into the foyer. The air-conditioning was a boon. He was eager to cool off and take a shower. An ageing security man in a short-sleeved grey-blue shirt and blue trousers with a walkie-talkie at his belt ran a lazy eye over him, but the young black receptionist hardly gave him a second glance as he made straight for the elevators. He walked alongside a wall of black marble, with most of its surface covered with the names of Cayman-registered companies inscribed on gun-metal grey plates. Hundreds, maybe thousands, of companies. Trusts. Investment corporations. Realty firms. List upon list of names. It reminded him of the Vietnam Memorial.

He called an elevator. The security man was studying him through narrowed eyes. He looked as if he had jaundice. Naisby wanted to risk a glance at the nearest names on that wall, in case Ed Maxell had added Raleigh House Securities Inc. to the roll. But that would only have made it clear he was a stranger and not one of the army of attorneys who worked there.

He pressed the fourth floor button and got out at the third, noting the security camera high on the wall. He turned left through swing doors, out of shot, and kept going to the end of the forty-yard corridor, through a door marked EMERGENCY EXIT in red, then down the stairwell to the second floor. He went through this emergency exit, and found Room 219. The discreet lettering on the door read 'Lammack Park Realty Inc.'. There were two locks. He used both keys. He passed through a secretary's den to an inner office with its blinds drawn. Not much of the bright day's sunlight was getting in, but he didn't need it. A heavy mahogany door set in the far wall opened.

'Sorry about the long way round. Keeps you a bit safer from those TV cameras this way. I sometimes wonder whether they're to protect us or put us in jeopardy.' Maxell laughed. He had a big cigar on.

'Anything in yet?'

Maxell's plump face broke into a grin. He was wearing an open-necked silk shirt with his initials embroidered on the pocket. 'I thought you'd be different, Rollo. Why's everybody so impatient these days?' He checked his watch. 'Let's see. Zürich time. They've another two hours. If that deadline you gave me was right?' He pressed a button on the glass-topped desk with its cane frame and legs.

Carrie came in – a slender Jamaican in a cool summer dress. It was meant to show off a model's figure, and it did its job.

'You met my Girl Friday last time?'

Naisby threw her a small smile and she threw him a big one.

'Will you ask my friend if he'd like a coffee or something stronger?'

'I'd prefer a fruit juice.' Naisby's throat was parched.

As she went out he took in the set-up. Just Ed and Carrie, two telephones, a telex, a word-processor, and a shredder. This was all they needed to represent one hundred and forty seven Cayman-registered companies. The handling fees were one per cent of turnover, and Maxell had grossed four hundred thousand dollars in the past year. At least that was the figure he'd given Naisby on that last visit. Knowing Ed, it was maybe twice as much.

The telex began to stutter a message.

Maxell leaned over for a quick look. He shook his head at the expectant Naisby, and gave out a deep-throated laugh of derision. 'Some guy in Houston who thinks he can keep his dollars *and* invest 'em! I tell you, Rollo, it makes you want to get the hell out of it.'

'But you won't.'

'Too bloody right, old son!'

Carrie brought in the coffee. Naisby sat drinking it as Maxell drafted letters for Carrie to type, received and sent out twenty or more telex messages, knocked out several queries to the word-processor's memory, and used the shredder twice. He patted it with affection. 'That,' he said, 'is God's gift to blokes in this game. Too many nosey-parkers.'

'You don't run to a shower up here?' Naisby was feeling like an intruder himself.

'In the basement, old son. Pool and sauna besides.'

'Sauna?'

Maxell nodded.

'I've no sweat left.'

'Go down the way you came up, old son.' He indicated a cane cupboard. 'Help yourself to a clean shirt.'

'Yours'll swamp me.'

'You mean around the middle, of course.' He'd always been able to laugh at himself. 'I keep 'em in different sizes for my nervous clients.'

Naisby thought it was a joke. But Maxell opened the cupboard to disclose a dozen shirts. Two couldn't have been better for Naisby if he'd had them made in Jermyn Street, which was one of the indulgencies he fancied once the money came through.

The telex stuttered again. 'No,' Maxell said after taking a look.

Naisby also borrowed a pair of swim trunks, which just about stayed up as he took a dip.

Forty minutes later he went back to Maxell's office by the circuitous route. He couldn't quite make out why it was so necessary.

Maxell slapped an arm over his shoulder and led him to the telex. He recovered a fold of the paper run and held it in front of Naisby. It confirmed the receipt by Peak National Bank of the Caymans of six million dollars transferred to the account of Raleigh House from an unnamed source in Zürich.

Naisby trembled and his heart was racing.

'Congratulations, old son,' Maxell said.

'There must be some mistake,' Naisby said, peering at the telex message. 'It should be fourteen million.'

It was just after four o'clock in Zürich, but more like high noon in the boardroom of Seifert et Cie.

Jean-Pascal sat squarely facing the rest, his hands steepled in front of his nose as if in prayer. 'We're in a corner,' he said irritably. 'A trap.' They waited on his next words, the entire board except for Klutz. It was the second summons meeting in succession that he'd missed. 'Only three of the seven clients under this threat have agreed to the payments being made. We have accordingly transferred six million dollars to Grand Cayman against their accounts. The other four flatly refuse to meet Kilroy's demands.'

'Three with something to hide and four with clear consciences.' It was Ulrich Engel, who always saw the world in black and white.

'I'm not sure it's quite so simple.' He spoke so quietly they found it hard to hear him. 'Three with something to hide, perhaps. It's the four refuseniks who pose the main threat to the bank.' He gave them a moment to work it out. 'If Kilroy discloses *their* secrets he discloses ours. So I must ask again – do we now go to the Federal Banking Commission?' He made sure they didn't see it as an ultimatum. 'Or do we hold out for a bit longer?'

No one dared advise the first option.

'Are we any closer to stopping this nightmare?' It was Engel again, looking at Wasserman.

'Charles is pursuing several lines of inquiry,' Jean-Pascal soothed.

Wasserman glanced at Jean-Pascal for permission to explain, won the go-ahead, and said, 'We now have a detailed picture of what this Kilroy looks like. And the office of this company of his – Raleigh House Securities Incorporated – and the Cayman attorney who runs it, I have under surveillance.'

'What does that mean?' Gabi didn't have much confidence in Wasserman.

'I'd rather say no more just now.' His hawk's eyes took in Gabi as if he didn't trust her – or anyone else present bar Jean-Pascal.

'We're having to take an awful lot on trust,' Gabi snapped. 'I mean we know little more about your inquiry into the security of the Sterile Area. Who might have been keying in to these seven accounts.'

Wasserman stayed tight-lipped.

'Charles is still checking the records.' Jean-Pascal said.

'*Still?*' Gabi was furious.

Again Wasserman sought Jean-Pascal's nodded consent before saying, 'I now know for sure when and for how long each of us, including myself, visited the Sterile Area over the six months prior to this – er – setback.'

'Can you tell us why Willi Klutz has missed the last two meetings?' Engel sniffed a set-up.

'Leave this to me, Charles,' Jean-Pascal said to Wasserman, then turned. 'It was my decision to send Willi to Milan on the Losone inquiry.'

Engel wouldn't be put off. He glared at Wasserman. 'Did you tell Willi he'd used the Sterile Area twice as often as anyone else?'

Wasserman stroked the edge of his blond beard. 'Yes.'

'Did you also demand from him a list of every account he'd keyed into in the last six months?'

'I asked each of you for such information, not excluding Jean-Pascal himself.'

'Asked, yes. *Demanded.* That's another word. You put the fear of God into him?'

Wasserman stared at the ceiling in contempt.

'And then challenged him about accounts he'd omitted?'

'He omitted more than anyone else.'

'He was dealing with twice as many as any of us. You've just admitted that. I omitted some. Because I simply couldn't remember whose account I was examining at twenty-three minutes past ten on the morning of January 11th, or some other arbitrary date. Gabi omitted some. Oscar did.'

It was clear a rebellion was brewing. Jean-Pascal frowned.

'Willi Klutz is a deeply sensitive man. Excessively so, perhaps. You needn't read into his absence that I or anyone else suspects him.'

But Engel hadn't done with Wasserman. 'You're not putting poor Klutz on the spot to divert us from a critical failure of security?'

'That's unfair, Ulrich,' Jean-Pascal said sharply. 'There's no evidence to imply such a failure.'

'Charles has more than once told us the system was foolproof.' It was Gabi, playing with an emerald and diamond eternity ring on the third finger of her left hand.

'Internally,' Wasserman said. 'No system in the world is one hundred per cent tamper-proof.'

'I see.' She was suddenly Portia. 'So will you now tell us – in layman's terms, of course, rather than computer jargon – why you *needed* to ask each of us *which* accounts we keyed into? Shouldn't the computer know?'

Oscar came near to a lightning attack of asthma. It was just the question he wanted the answer to. He'd planted it discreetly in Gabi's mind half an hour before. If the computer knew who'd looked into which accounts, Klutz would be able to deny having had any interest in at least some of the seven accounts whereas now his only queries were about timings. And Oscar had been careful to do most of his research only on days when Klutz had been in the building.

'I'd prefer not to answer that right now, Jean-Pascal,' Wasserman said with a furtive smile.

Oscar studied him closely. If the system had no record of who looked at what, Wasserman wasn't ready to admit it. And it wasn't professional vanity, Oscar reckoned. He wanted them all to sweat until he could finger the culprit.

The red light came on to Jean-Pascal's right. He took the phone. 'Yes?'

'General Gibb to see you, Jean-Pascal.' It was his confidential secretary, Francine, a mature Genevois who had just taken a law degree in her spare time.

He glanced at his watch.

'He's early,' came Francine's voice as if she could see him checking his watch.

'Thank you,' he said. He had been making notes, and now put the gold ballpoint back in his inside pocket. 'We must adjourn a while. This could well have some bearing on the way we proceed. Give me half an hour.'

He went through to his suite and told Francine to meet Gibb personally and bring him up.

As Gibb came in, Jean-Pascal's welcome was warm. 'You're early, General.'

'Sure,' Gibb said impatiently, waving away Jean-Pascal's offer of a chair. It was no business of a banker to know how he'd made such a quick trip. Having hitched a trans-Atlantic flight in a USAF jet to NATO HQ in Brussels, he'd found a flight commander to fix him up with a helicopter to the Swiss border. If the damn Swiss hadn't been neutral he could have made it all the way to Zürich. He strode to the windows, looking more like a show-jumping competitor in his heavy tweed jacket and cavalry twill slacks.

He turned. 'So where are we with this son of a bitch?'

'Kilroy?' Jean-Pascal wasn't sold on generals.

'Sure. Right. Kilroy.'

'We're after him, you can be sure.'

'You know how the hell he got into my account?'

'Not yet.'

'Shit! Not yet?'

Jean-Pascal was so laid-back he could have been a Brit.

'I tell you this. Straight. Not a dime, you understand? Not a dime will this son of a bitch extort from me!'

'I'm well aware of your feelings, General. You made them clear to Wasserman in Washington.'

'So I'm making 'em a bit clearer. To you. Here.'

'You're absolutely right to refuse to yield.'

'You think so?' He was blazing. Pale red veins stood out in the granite face. 'I refuse, okay? And this bum will spread shit about me on Capitol Hill. The *Washington Post*. Oh, *they'd* like that. Things have been thin on the ground since Watergate and Oliver North.'

'You've nothing to fear, General.'

'Oh no?'

'I'm sure your account is perfectly clean.' He was far from sure, really, after looking at the file Wasserman had built on Gibb.

'Listen, it could be clean as a cadet's rifle at West Point. Generals aren't expected to have Swiss accounts. I'd be flayed.' He came over and leaned across the desk, pointing an index finger at Jean-Pascal. 'The cock-up doesn't lie with me. Even my wife doesn't know the number of my account here. Or my lawyer. My will just mentions an account. The proof and the number I keep in my safe deposit deep under Washington. Nobody's seen that stuff except you and me. So the cock-up's here, sir!'

'We'll see who's to blame.' Jean-Pascal was tired of the Rambo stuff, but he had to go easy. Gibb looked distinctly trigger-happy. 'This bank has a long history, General. Our integrity is respected all over the world.'

'Likewise mine.'

'Indeed.'

'Just let me shoot one question, sir.'

Jean-Pascal leaned back.

'Give it to me straight. Am I the only client with this son of a bitch on my back?'

'Good Lord, yes,' Jean-Pascal said.

The smile of a smart strategist lit up Gibb's face. 'So it wouldn't be too much to expect the bank to keep this bum happy till you nail him?'

'You mean pay the two million dollars?'

'I mean exactly that, sir.'

It was Jean-Pascal's turn to go walkabout now. He went to the window to give Gibb time to cool down, then crossed slowly to the door to Francine's office. 'If your deposits were clean you've nothing to fear.'

'You'll not cover this bum's demand?'

Jean-Pascal was about to open the door.

'This guy starts spreading shit, you know where it'll stick. Right here. This bank.'

Jean-Pascal held out his hand. 'Nice of you to come all this way, General.' He'd had a bellyful.

'I can ride a lying attack on my character.'

'But do pause for thought, General Gibb. I doubt if a Washington inquiry would be easily sidetracked. The last one got nowhere investigating those US missiles and things showing up in Iran's armoury. In spite of all your help as a witness. And in spite of the investigators knowing when the missiles arrived in Iran. In the November of that year, wasn't it? And your first deposit of three million dollars arrived here less than a week later. I think you're right. A new Washington inquiry would flay you alive.'

Gibb's mouth fell open. He was like a landed fish gasping for air. But not for long. He straightened his tie, shot his cuffs and said, 'Pay the bastard!'

'You're authorizing that?'

Gibb nodded. 'Pay him!'

Jean-Pascal needed a moment to get over it. He poured an iced Perrier and went into the boardroom to look up at the portrait in oils of old Seifert, who started the firm all those hundred and fifty years back. 'Did you have funny-money generals in those days, Reine?'

Reine Seifert looked down benignly, but with a firm glint in his eyes.

By the time the others were back to restart the meeting, Jean-Pascal had drawn strength from old Reine. The others were still taking their chairs when he said with a grim smile, 'Well, that's another to the good. The general's gone over to the other side.' Only Wasserman of the rest knew about the Iran episode, but they didn't seek to know why Gibb was paying up. 'Four up and three to go.'

'The payers before General Gibb?' It was Engel.

'Senator Waldo Pryde, Lord Plackett and Conrad Warri,' Jean-Pascal said. 'I intend to meet Mrs Sarne, Lord Justice Kenright and Sir Rupert Mallory in the next forty-eight hours.'

The others had no doubt that Jean-Pascal had been tough with General Gibb, but none chose to ask how Gibb had come by his funny-money.

'It's possible, just possible, that these three are holding out because their accounts are pure.' His tone told another story.

'And if they continue to hold out?' Gabi asked.

'Let's hope we will have run this Kilroy to ground by then.'

'And if we haven't?' Oscar felt his silence was being noticed. Hence the question.

'If we haven't we may have to consider paying the outstanding six million from the bank's own reserves.'

Oscar gasped and Gabi, in that way of hers, blew out her cheeks. Engel said, 'When will we know something about the Cayman surveillance?'

Jean-Pascal directed an open hand towards Wasserman. 'Charles is going over there himself.'

'I leave tonight,' he said, making an impatient play of checking his watch.

'And I'll be off to Washington to see Mrs Sarne,' Jean-Pascal said.

It was enough to cut short the meeting. As it broke up, Oscar Leiden caught Jean-Pascal's eye.

Jean-Pascal got the message. 'Oh, Oscar. One moment, eh?'

Oscar closed the door on the rest. 'I've known Klutz for twenty-five years,' he said, holding his glasses across his chest as if affirming some oath of loyalty. 'I really do find it disturbing to see this cloud hanging over him. No more honest man ever lived.'

'What are you trying to tell me, Oscar?'

'Well, Jean-Pascal, this Sterile Area system?'

'Go on.'

'Only one man seems to know if its memory bank knows who consulted which accounts.' He was suddenly filled with horror. He was making a mess of it.

'Go on,' Jean-Pascal said. 'I have to be at the airport soon.'

'Charles Wasserman's pointing a finger at Willi Klutz. It makes one wonder.'

'Wonder what, Oscar?'

'Well, Wasserman *is* the only one who knows what that computer knows.'

'No, he's not, Oscar.' Jean-Pascal was on his way to his own suite. 'I know.'

And he was gone, closing the door in Oscar's face.

Oscar feared he should have let things be.

SIX

Steering one-handed, he pushed the visor up over his yellow crash helmet for a better look at the reef some fifty feet below. The microlight plane was on a course parallel to Seven Mile Beach, and he could make out the underwater edge of the coral cliff where the steep 6000 feet drop began.

It was Naisby's fourth day on Grand Cayman and the wait for the remaining eight million dollars from Zürich had begun to rattle him. He would give the defaulters a few more days' grace, but no more. Ed Maxell had counselled patience and some island activities that might take his mind off things. Having tried parasailing and windsurfing, and then a deep dive down the North Wall at Rum Point, Naisby had gone back to the office to find that no further investments had been made. Most of the six million dollars so far received had now been duly laundered in half-million dollar lots into a series of accounts in the Bahamas, Liechtenstein and the Isle of Man.

'I'd not be hanging about in here if I could help it,' Maxell had said pointedly during the morning. Rollo Naisby was only one of hundreds of clients, and Maxell was busy coping with a number of new ones, American citizens all, with assets beyond the ken of the Internal Revenue Service. Four were doctors, and two of them were on the island. Privacy was all-important, and Naisby's hanging about didn't help. What was worse was Naisby's vigilance over the money transfers. It left Maxell with too little scope to improve on his one per cent bite.

He had fixed the microlight trip. 'Go right round the island,' he'd enthused. It appealed to Naisby's love of dicing – 'your Cresta syndrome' – as Maxell knew it would.

Naisby had almost forgotten the missing eight million dollars as the warm breeze caught his sunburnt face and pierced his open sea island cotton shirt. Below, divers were leaping from a dive boat in their gaudy red and blue skin-clinging outfits and goggles. Catamarans tacked far from the long white beach. He put the midget plane into an easy turn to starboard and headed for a tycoon's ivory-coloured yacht anchored five hundred yards out. Two girls in bikinis lay sun-bathing on the upper deck as their sugar daddy mixed rum-and-Cokes, his Bermuda shorts so baggy he could have been a circus clown.

Naisby buzzed the yacht, making a pass so low he could make out the sticks skewering the slivers of lemon in the drinks.

The girls waved. Even that far out from the beach they didn't go topless. He hadn't seen a topless girl on the island. It wasn't the first time he'd been struck by the odd mix on Grand Cayman of the chaste, strait-laced and religious with the immoral big-money game.

He made another pass over *Gladehopper*, so low he could smell prawns cooking. Baggy Shorts down there had it made. And the thought went through Naisby's mind that he could go back by surfboard and make him an offer for *Gladehopper*, cash on the nail.

He got back on course now, flying low and some thirty yards out from the waterline. As George Town came up ahead he flew between the harbour and a cruise yacht from Miami anchored offshore, then hugged the shoreline round the point and into South Sound. Down to his left and set in wide flat gardens were the houses of Ed Maxell and his like, with their spacious garages, green gardens and TV dish aerials leaning to the sky. Scattered between them were old colonial homes, little more than shacks of wood and wattle with tin roofs and thatched roofs and patches of overgrown land hugging their garishly painted sides.

The whitish strip of Seven Mile Beach had given way to a tight necklace of darker hue, pebbled and rocky. He was close to Red Bay and about twenty yards out from the shoreline when it happened. Here the sea came right up to the tree line. Coconut palms and sea-grape trees leaned over the water, and for a stretch the tree line was unbroken by property, the vegetation so deep and thick he could see no light in it. He felt suddenly isolated. No one moved. An old rowing boat, its metal parts rusted, bobbed on the end of a frayed rope attached to a boulder. There was no beach. Only rock-strewn shallow water. Gone was the glare and the movement of Seven Mile Beach. Here were shadows and stillness. He found the motor scooter sound of the mini-engine a comfort.

He felt a blow on his left upper arm, then a stinging sensation. The microlight lurched to starboard, then to port as he overcompensated. He heard what sounded like a shot and took it to be a fuel explosion. And then another blow, on his helmet. He clamped his left hand against it and felt a ridge. Then he saw a hole in the wing fabric, and another in the foot platform. They couldn't have been due to a birdstrike and he'd not seen a single gull since he was over Seven Mile Beach. Another bang, like a backfire, and the little plane slewed to starboard. He righted it and found he was heading for a cluster of Australian pines and sea-grape trees that brought the bush down to the water's edge. He came out of a near-stall. The engine began to cough. He tried to put on more power, but there was no response. His head was reeling and his upper arm stinging. And then the engine died and he tried to glide the microlight into slightly deeper water away from the protruding rocks.

He hit the water sideways on, the microlight out of control, and the jolt sent a pain up his right leg. He unlocked his safety harness and struggled clear as the microlight, caught by the slight current, moved laterally and began to tip over on its nose. He caught a glimpse of two holes drilled through the wing and knew the fuel tank had been punctured. He was in no more than five feet of water. He would have found it difficult to swim, his left arm felt so numbed yet painful. He began to wade the twenty yards through the rocks, stumbling over some he couldn't see. There was no one to help. The thick bush looked sinister. He thought he heard some movement, but put it down to the ching-chings, the long-tailed birds he'd seen squabbling in the Australian pines near his hotel. Then he felt the stickiness on his right hand as he drew it clear of his left shoulder. The graze was deep, running up from just over the elbow almost to the shoulder. He was suddenly out of shock and frightened. He was still in three feet of water. He ducked behind a rock and waited. He stayed, hardly daring to breathe, for the best part of half an hour.

Nobody had appeared. The only movement was hundreds of yards out in the bay, where a miniature submarine which took tourists on deep dives among the coral was moving on the surface with its mother-ship tug near.

He clambered out of the water, taking care not to make a splash, found a soggy foothold in the swamp beyond the sea, and then crawled on all fours through the bush towards the coast road which lay somewhere beyond. Still jumpy and lying low in the thick foliage from time to time, he found the road. He let several cars go past, aware that hitch-hiking in his state, soaked and bleeding, would alarm the drivers, especially women. Better to wait for a truck with two big Caymanians in the cab. But when one came along, loaded with gravel, he stayed in the cover of the trees. He headed in the direction of George Town, keeping away from the road.

The first place he reached was a two-man garage. Two petrol pumps, a tin-roofed shack where a thin black Caymanian hammered at a veteran Chrysler with no wheels, and a concrete bunker where a bigger Caymanian, pale brown and wearing only an old pair of athlete's shorts, was sifting through a pile of clapped-out engines. Parked nearby was an ancient Ford with bald tyres, its front bumper secured with wire. On its roof was a sign – AIR CONDITIONED TAXI. One of its side windows was missing.

'May I use your phone?' Naisby asked the black man.

'You ask my brother,' the man said, eyeing him with mistrust.

The pale brown man turned. His hair and beard were fair, almost ginger. 'What happened to *you*, man?' The accent was Caribbean with a hint of Welsh.

Naisby was on his guard. On this small island, where rich men could have their millions laundered at the expense of the world's tax collectors with not so much as the blink of an eye, the crash of a tiny plane would have the bush telegraph humming. And it would have made the story of the century if he said he'd been shot down. He might as well jog round the island with a placard proclaiming, 'I'm the owner of Raleigh House Securities Inc.' He knew the brown man was suspicious. 'I just had a bit of an accident with my boat.'

The brown man pointed to his shoulder. 'You hurt, man.'

'It's nothing,' Naisby said.

The brown man showed him the phone. It stood on a stack of empty petrol cans, oil-grimed and sticky. Naisby dialled Maxell's office.

Carrie came on, brisk and concerned when Naisby said he needed an immediate word with Ed. 'He's out right now. Should I get him to call you?'

'Tell him to make for my hotel, it's that important.'

She knew better than to ask for explanations from any client.

As Naisby hung up, the brown man came up with a bucket of water and a sponge. He insisted on bathing Naisby's wound. 'Where's the boat, man?' He seemed to have salvage on his mind.

'Sunk,' Naisby said.

'Near-in? Or out deep?'

'Out deep.' He wanted no one finding bullet holes just yet. 'This working?' He tapped the Ford's rusted bonnet.

'Sure, man.'

'You've got a fare,' Naisby said, holding the wet sponge against his left arm. 'Drop me near the Holiday Inn.' It wasn't his hotel, but it wasn't all that far away.

Heavy black clouds were brooding over the island now, and as he got into the Ford Naisby felt the first heavy spots of rain. By the time they were skirting George Town the flash storm broke. The wipers wouldn't work. 'We just give her a few minutes, okay?'

'Fine,' Naisby said.

The brown man pulled into the side of the road. Naisby was seized with the fear that the Ford's lights wouldn't come on, and some passing police car would stop to ask what they were doing without them in this bad light.

'You here long?' the brown man said, lighting an American cigarette.

'Oh, a few days.'

'Holiday?'

'Holiday,' Naisby said.

'Our dad came for a few days,' he said, blowing smoke rings and admiring them. 'Sailor with de Royal Navy.' He turned to look straight at Naisby. 'You wondering, I see, man. You wonderin' why I'm brown-black with red hair and my brother's black with black?'

'No, I wasn't,' Naisby said. He was in a hurry to get back to his room with no hassle on the way.

'He's just my half-brother, you see?' And he laughed out loud.

The brown man said his name was Elwyn. As they waited for the flash storm to die, he sang a folk ditty all about rich doctors and lawyers. Naisby wondered why there wasn't a verse about bankers.

It was still raining when they came near the Holiday Inn. 'Here's fine,' Naisby said.

'Not right to the door?'

'Here,' Naisby said firmly. 'And thanks.' He gave the brown man a fifty-dollar bill.

'I don't have that kind of change, man.'

'Never mind,' Naisby said.

The brown man still looked as if he thought it was Christmas as he drove off. Fifty dollars. Not just American dollars. Caymanian dollars. Those fancy guys in George Town had their uses. They kept the Caymanian dollar ahead of its big uncle.

Naisby was glad of the downpour. He cut through a clearing near the Holiday Inn and went back along the beach to his own hotel. He had his shirt slung over his left shoulder to hide the bandage the pale man had put over the wound. His soaked state wasn't unusual for a beachcomber on such an afternoon.

Maxell, watching from the verandah bar, saw Naisby come in from the wet.

'I need a quack we can rely on,' Naisby said, stripping for a warm shower.

Maxell saw the wound. 'Christ, what's that?'

'Some loony shot me down.' He made it sound routine.

'Jesus!' Maxell said, crossing to the phone.

Naisby gasped in pain as the warm water gushed over his wound. He could hear Maxell calling a doctor friend. He rinsed off the caked blood and the wound started to bleed again.

'Shot down!' Maxell scoffed. 'You mean you cocked up the piloting, Rollo!' He was hooked by that wound.

'It's a bullet wound, I tell you. But I got it water-skiing, right? It's a rope burn.'

Maxell looked baffled.

'I don't want this all over the front pages of the *Caymanian Compass*, not to mention papers in Zürich, London and the States. You got any nearer to finding out who those moles were?'

'Not yet.' Maxell was twitchy. 'If you *were* shot down it's a matter for the police.'

'They're next to the last of those who should know. The last being those moles.'

'Maybe one of *them* did it. I don't wish to be nosey, Rollo, but there's nothing a bit dodgy about these rich investors of yours?'

'No,' Naisby said, soaking a clean handkerchief in diluted Dettol in the washbowl.

'So where's the plane? Down among the coral?'

'It's only partly under. Out past South Sound. The Red Bay area or thereabouts.'

'Problem,' Maxell mused. 'Any bullet holes? Not that there's much in that flying pram to have bullet holes in.'

'Two in the wing for sure. And almost certainly at least one more in the fuel tank. That's what ditched me.'

'Anyone saw you come down?'

'If they did they didn't come to the rescue,' he said bitterly.

'You're right about keeping it under wraps, Rollo.'

Maxell put in a call to the hirer of the microlight. 'Geoff. Our friend's had a slight problem with that flying pram of yours. Like to drop in at my office?' He paused. 'In about an hour, okay?' He hung up, looking even more uneasy. 'Geoff will have it insured. Lloyd's of London most likely. But suppose they want to assess the machine? They'd do some tut-tutting if they were to find bulletholes.'

'Right. That would put the fox among the chickens.'

'Can I tell him you'll pay him in full?'

Naisby nodded. He knew Maxell would take a slice for himself, but he was in no state to negotiate. 'And he can lose the damn thing in deeper water.'

There was a knock at the land-side door of the room. Maxell answered it, and let in Dr Clyde Haley, lithe and nutmeg-brown and so thin on top the freckles stood out under the strand of oiled hair. He dumped his case on the bed and swapped a look of concern with Maxell before checking the wound. He frowned. 'How did you get this?'

'Water-skiing,' Naisby said. 'I got caught up in the tow rope.'

Haley peered at the gash, dressed it with gauze and a bandage, then had a look at Naisby's eyes and checked his blood pressure. 'You'll survive.' His smile was mischievous. 'But you're in shock.' He sank his hypodermic lance into first one, then another phial, and jabbed the cocktail shot into Naisby's backside near the thigh. It made Naisby feel woozy. He could hear Maxell and Haley talking.

'That's no rope burn,' Haley was saying.

'Ed,' Naisby called. He was glassy-eyed. 'Ask the doctor if he was called Clyde because his father was a Scot in the Royal Navy.'

'Quite right, my friend,' Haley's voice came from a long way off. 'How did you guess?'

Naisby heard the door close. His head was spinning. He sensed Maxell was very close. 'Any idea, Rollo, why three of these investors of yours might have reneged?'

'Four, not three.'

'Three, Rollo.' The voice was calculating. 'I should have told you. Just before I came over, we got confirmation of the transfer of another two million dollars.'

'Great,' Naisby murmured. 'So which of those three tried to shoot me like a sitting duck up there?'

'Get some sleep, Rollo,' came the whisper in his ear. 'None of 'em, I reckon. Some nut, most likely. They've been giving out gun licences like this was little America. Some nut for sure.'

'Right,' Naisby muttered.

But he didn't believe it.

Maxell's face pinwheeled dizzily. Then there was the sound of a shot. Or perhaps it was the door closing. 'Ed,' he called. 'Make sure the other one's locked, eh?' There was no reply. He slid off the bed and crawled drunkenly to the sliding window-door leading to the beach. He tried to reach the locking slot, but it was too much.

He rolled over, unconscious, his right cheek against the grains of sand trodden in after his morning swim.

'Hold!'

It was Klutz, back in the fold but weighed down with the burden of having been taken for the Judas who had broken into the accounts.

Francine set up the video. On the big wall screen the picture froze on a thick-set man in his early forties looking up into camera. He held a wafer-thin document case in front of his chest and waited for something to happen.

'I'm sorry,' Klutz said. 'He does look a little like someone I've met, but he's not the same.'

Francine set the video rolling again. It was the fourth time someone had asked for a longer look at a face in shot. The edited tape was repetitious and dull. Every single visitor who had crossed to the elevators or stairs of the Drake Building in George Town over a period of four days was on show. And every face came into medium close-up for several seconds – a video procession of moving mug shots. Wasserman and his Grand Cayman collaborator had edited out some of the known regulars who worked in the building, but had kept in every shot of Ed Maxell. He'd come up five times on the first ninety-minute tape.

It was the second tape Francine was running now, and Jean-Pascal was testy. It was typical of Wasserman's thoroughness to set up this marathon identity parade, but hours of it seemed like madness with every director bar Wasserman ogling a screen in the boardroom when there was a bank to run. 'No more *holds*, please, unless you're in little doubt. Otherwise, make a note of the time, and we'll arrange for a further viewing to enable you to check.'

More faces came to the elevators. Most were of young well-dressed men in their late twenties and early thirties, but there were plenty of middle-aged American men and women. Most of the Caymanian secretaries, including those who were said to be the best-looking girls in the Caribbean, had been edited out to save time at the screening.

Klutz almost called for a hold as a businesswoman with a crocodile-skin briefcase came into close-up, but he made a note of the time instead.

'Hold!' It was Gabi's call.

Francine froze the image of two brisk men in their forties who had come in together. One had his left hand outstretched and out of shot as he called the elevator, but it was the other man, prematurely white-haired and with a leathery lined face, who had caught her eye. 'The one on the right,' she said. 'His name's Daniels. He works in Zürich and London. Gold and copper trading chiefly.'

'Hardly a prime suspect.' Jean-Pascal spoke tartly.

'You did ask us to name anyone we recognized, Jean-Pascal.'

Jean-Pascal had almost had enough. 'And Charles has another two tapes on the way over!'

The tape restarted. Each face had been given six seconds of screen time, Oscar had worked out. So they'd been looking at ten a minute for the best part of two hours. It had crossed his mind to call 'Hold!' on a face he'd never seen in his life just to give a hint of his keenness to spot the culprit. Jean-Pascal's impatient mood had put an end to that. But now Oscar came close to a call – and it would have been a disaster had he not held his tongue in sheer fright.

The man coming into close-up was Rollo Naisby.

Oscar's mouth dried out. He felt he was going to be sick. He stayed rooted as Naisby seemed to stay on-screen for ages. By the time Naisby moved out of shot into the elevator, Oscar was a wreck.

Jean-Pascal took another ten minutes of it, then left for his own suite, murmuring, 'We must have better things to do than watch escapers from the Internal Revenue Service of America and funny-money smoothies from everywhere just pressing lift buttons.'

'I agree entirely.' Engel followed his master out.

But Gabi Seifert stayed in her chair, having spotted Oscar's discomfort. Klutz stayed, too, being the one with most at stake until they nailed Kilroy. Oscar was riveted. It would be better to leave with a bored expression. But he couldn't. Faces came and went. Black faces, white faces, brown ones. Men's faces and women's, too. Ugly ones and some so beautiful they could have made it in Hollywood. He knew in his bones he was to see Naisby again. The second tape was half over, with the editing having deteriorated into rough cutting, when Naisby crossed the glazed marble floor of the foyer. He was in different clothes. A blue safari suit in place of the grey jacket and tie and fawn slacks. And his left arm was in a sling.

Oscar could stand no more. He let another half-dozen faces pass, then took his leave.

And Gabi never let him out of her sight until he was through the door. She glanced at Klutz, who had seen nothing amiss either on-screen or among the viewers.

'So much wasted time,' Oscar said, doing a fair imitation of Jean-Pascal as he went through Anna's outer office into his own. 'You did get those Tokyo Stock Market files out?'

'They're on your desk,' Anna said. 'But there's this.' She handed him a memo, immaculate from the word-processor. Everything Anna put through that machine was fine-tuned. *1107. Mr Naisby called to remind you of your meeting at midday.*

Oscar could have been put on hold himself.

The message was no reminder. It was an order. Five minutes ago Naisby was in the foyer of that marbled laundry nearly four thousand miles away. Oscar had to remind himself that the next rendezvous was at Uetliberg high above the city. It was 11.35 and he would be late even if he set out right now.

He lost no time on the drive up.

'I was about to call you again.' Naisby was checking his watch.

'I'm glad you didn't.' Oscar wiped his palms on his handkerchief.

Naisby led the way to a terrace table with a big view over Lake Zürich. 'You can stay for lunch, Oscar?'

Oscar shook his head. He was jumpy even though it was plain that the people at the other tables were tourists. They could all have been moles from the Federal Banking Commission, the way he reacted. 'I'd rather walk.'

'Not even a drink?'

What Oscar would have liked was a glass of iced water in some place beyond the snow-topped peaks across the lake, preferably a million miles beyond.

Naisby got them a lager apiece and they found a spot on the grass away from people. 'You're not looking all that well, mate.' Naisby's concern sounded genuine.

'Don't leave messages at the bank!' The voice was desperate.

'Reza mightn't pass them on if I left them with her.'

'Why come here at all? I gave you all the information you asked for.'

'Not all, Oscar.'

'I couldn't get into any more accounts, anyway. They've blocked the one loophole I was lucky enough to find.'

'Oscar! What do you take me for?'

'And you'd be well advised to keep away from Zürich.'

'I'd not even try to press you for more names,' Naisby said with feeling. 'Though we *could* go down in history if we got a lot more of the world's eminent persons shitting themselves for fear of being shown up for what they really are.'

'I'm not interested in crusades,' Oscar snapped. It wasn't really true. At some points he'd enjoyed the moling.

Naisby took a deep intake of bracing mountain air. 'What I want now's a bit of tidying up. I – er – approached seven of our big names.'

Oscar nodded.

'Four have coughed up.'

Oscar shrugged as if he wanted to be rid of the whole scam.

'Even a banker can work out that this leaves three.' Naisby grinned, trying to settle his glass on the grassy slope. It wasn't easy. 'All I need to know is – who's invested and who's holding out?'

'And then you'll leave me out of it?'

'No,' Naisby said. 'I might have to help you out yet, mate.'

Oscar sipped his lager. 'Leave it, Rollo. You've done well enough.'

'Names, Oscar. Please.'

It took him another three minutes to make up his mind, then Oscar said, 'Senator Pryde, Lord Plackett and Conrad Warri authorized right off. General Gibb was then persuaded.'

'Persuaded?'

'Jean-Pascal, our bank's president.'

'I know that.'

'He showed the general the yellow card.'

'Eh?'

'If the general's deposits were clean he had nothing to fear.'

Naisby fell back on the grass in delight.

'You find that funny?'

'Very.' Naisby forced himself up and leaned on his right elbow. 'So now I know who I'm chasing.'

'Careful, Rollo.' Oscar was in danger of being carried away himself. 'I shouldn't go hounding them.' He paused. 'Jean-Pascal saw Mrs Sarne in Washington, and Sir Rupert Mallory and Lord Justice Kenright in London. They're still prepared to defy you. If they do, the bank will probably put the six million dollars through.'

'Rather than risk the scandal of the world knowing its accounts have been leaked?'

'Don't get ideas, Rollo.'

'How can I help it?' Naisby hadn't been so thrilled since his last descent of the Cresta.

'You ever heard of Charles Wasserman?'

'Another eminent person? One of the good and the great?'

'No,' Oscar said quietly. 'Our bank's candidate for the Ivan the Terrible Award.'

Naisby laughed out loud.

'He's been on Grand Cayman for the past week.'

'Let's hope he doesn't get sunburn,' Naisby flashed, only to be hit by the memory of that shooting-down and the bullet-graze.

'What he does get is a good video service.'

Naisby was hooked.

'You must be crazy. Going in and out of the Drake Building in George Town like that.'

'Like what?'

'Like some healthy visitor one minute, and an accident statistic the next.'

'You've been dreaming, Oscar.'

'You seem all right now. What was wrong with your arm?'

It was Naisby's turn to freeze.

Mallory raised the twin-barrelled Purdy and took aim at a flock of wood pigeons heading for the copse to their left. His rheumy right eye unblinking against the sight, he pressed the trigger, and Gilliam saw two pigeons explode in a flurry of feathers in midair. Two more were coming down on one wing apiece, and another was flying in tight circles, all sense of direction gone.

'You really should try it, Gilliam,' Mallory said, reloading as his servant and three black gundogs made through the drizzle some fifty yards away to pick up the carcasses. 'Once you've got over the sentimental block you'll come to enjoy it.'

'Never,' Gilliam said, hands deep in his raincoat pockets. He peered down at the fragile-looking blood sports buff whose kind he had detested since his childhood in the hunt country of Leicestershire. 'I'd rather get down to some talking, if you don't mind.'

'Oh, come along.' The bossy aristocrat, all skin and bone with parched hands and face, and the air of one used to life in an austerely underheated country mansion, was insistent. Swamped inside a green windcheater reaching to the tightly-secured tops of his gumboots near the knees, he suddenly looked like a mischievous gnome.

Gilliam knew he had to handle him with care. For one thing, the Commissioner was in awe of Mallory's social status. And Gilliam was close to a promotion he had set his heart on. Last time round he had been so sure of making Chief Superintendent that he had taken it for granted and told Margaret and the three girls it was clinched – only to be denied by the Commissioner. 'Next time, Geordie,' the Commissioner had consoled. 'You're still only forty-one.' Gilliam couldn't lose face with his family again.

'As I was explaining, Sir Rupert, the Commissioner said you had something to tell me.' It was close on an hour since his arrival at Spiggett's Corner, Mallory's seventeenth-century house in a tree-crested private estate about the size of the town Gilliam had grown up in.

'What do you already know?' Mallory was no longer gazing up at the sky. A movement in the long grass and nettles fringing the copse had caught his eye. He took aim with the speed of a sniper. Even as the gunshot sounded, the leveret somersaulted in midair.

'I know you're being blackmailed, sir.'

Mallory nudged the inert brown corpse with the tip of his gumboot. 'You don't approve one bit, do you, Superintendent?'

'It's your right, Sir Rupert.'

'Rights! My God! Can't do as you like on your own land these days.' A cock pheasant's squawk came from the copse. 'Can't touch that chap between the start of February and the end of September, you know.'

It seemed to Gilliam that Sir Rupert had changed his mind about talking. If it took all day and he had to watch a thousand creatures die he'd stick at it.

They walked on another hundred yards away from the copse towards a line of lime trees. Mallory was complaining all the way about the Wildlife and Countryside Act, which laid down the closed season for shooting some birds. They came on a broken fence. Mallory studied it balefully, his swift small eyes about to burst from eyelids that seemed too tight. 'Lampers again.'

'Lampers?'

'Young hooligans from the town. Come out with powerful lamps. Blind anything that moves. Owls, squirrels, anything. Then down 'em with catapults and things. Nasty.'

Gilliam couldn't see the difference between them and blue-blooded killers like Mallory.

Mallory led them back beyond the copse, trailing the gun in the crook of his arm. The gaunt face was a mask. His puce lips trembled from time to time. Maybe it won't take as long as I reckoned, Gilliam told himself.

'You know,' Mallory said mischievously, turning to size up the copse again, 'I could raise squadrons of birds for you right now. Pigeon, collared doves, rooks, the lot. No closed season for them, dear boy.' He reloaded the gun and offered it.

Gilliam took it reluctantly.

Mallory smiled. It was the first time he'd really shown his teeth. They were as tight as the rest of his face. 'Aim right there,' he pointed. 'The west side of the copse.' It seemed essential to him that Gilliam killed something. Gilliam took aim.

'You're left-handed?'

Gilliam nodded, squinting through the sights.

Mallory clapped his hands. Birds came out in droves – collared doves and wood pigeons, crows and starlings. Gilliam couldn't bring himself to pull the trigger. When he did the flock had found sanctuary.

'You're a determined young man,' Mallory said, taking the gun.

There weren't all that many years between them. *Who's Who* gave Mallory's age as forty-eight. But he had the shrewdness of an old man.

They were almost back at the house, castellated and more like a château, before Mallory showed any sign of opening up. Gilliam hadn't pressed. He recalled the Commissioner's own caution at the briefing. 'It's a banana-skin job, Geordie. You'll have to tread carefully. But you're used to that in the Serious Crimes Squad. I'd not want the CID lads kicking up a din on this. We're not dealing with just some Labour politician up to his neck in graft or even some Tory swindler from Lloyd's.' The Commissioner was very class-conscious and was still changing his accent from North-country to one that would make him acceptable in the best St James's clubs. He hadn't quite got it right, either.

'I did make it clear to the Commissioner,' Mallory was saying. 'At this stage nothing will be taken down and used.'

'You have my word.'

'My chief concern is to protect the Palace. And by that I mean, of course, the Monarchy.'

Gilliam coughed his understanding.

'We've had enough scandals, the Lord knows. All the way from that equerry and the Princess to that appalling traitor Blunt.' He was distracted just briefly by a flight of starlings, which led Gilliam to think he'd not draw the line at shooting butterflies.

'Blackmail,' Gilliam prompted.

'Chap should be shot.' He shifted his arm against the trailing gun.

'He's said what he wants?'

'Very precisely. Two million dollars.'

'He's American?'

'British, I'm sorry to say.' He sniffed and wiped the edge of his nose with the back of his pink hand. 'Of a kind.'

'You're not going to pay, of course?'

'I'd like not to.' He said no more and even ignored two young hares playing in the hedgerow.

'If you've nothing to hide . . .?'

'That's one problem. I know blackmailers come again. But it's just too frightful to contemplate what would happen if this gets out. It would bring disgrace not only on the Palace but on the country.'

They were close to the house now. Mallory slowed their pace to say what he had to say before family or servants could overhear. 'I had hoped to see this Kilroy again.' He tapped the gun barrel.

'You've actually met him?'

'At the Palace, would you believe.'

It was another half minute before Gilliam brought himself to ask, 'What does he have on you, Sir Rupert?'

Mallory brought out a pigskin wallet, dipped into it and handed Gilliam a buff envelope. Inside was a colour photograph of Mallory's Zürich account, showing a balance of 14,347,814 Swiss francs.

'Most of that money's due to investment and some years' interest.'

'May I keep this?'

'No.' And Mallory let him take a second look before he took it back. 'I don't know where you stand on the matter of governments and people's liberty, Superintendent.'

Gilliam played a safe card. 'I'm not exactly sold on politicians and bureaucrats.'

'I'm glad to hear it.' He was tucking the wallet securely away in an inside pocket of the jacket under his windcheater. 'Are you aware, Superintendent, of one of our laws which forbids the export of certain valuable works of art without a government licence?'

Gilliam nodded.

'And that such a licence may only be given if some purchaser can't be found here, which in effect means museums?'

'Yes sir.'

'Let me cut a long story short. I detest controls. I helped a number of friends to escape the net. A service much appreciated, I can tell you. It meant the paintings and other bits and pieces went to market abroad without landing my friends with punitive bills for Capital Gains Tax and horrendous death duties.'

Gilliam was on a high, while fearing the worst. 'You can say who these friends are?'

'Good Lord, I hardly recall them all.' He hesitated. 'I helped Hugh Revidge to dispose of a Constable. He's the Duke of Leuchars, of course. And we moved a Gainsborough and one or two other works for Giles Arnott, the Marquess of Preston. And when Perry Forster was dying I saw to it that a Turner and a few other works found their way to Geneva to benefit his dear widow Lady Probert.'

'You're an art expert like Blunt?'

'Good Lord, no! My talents lie in other things.'

He reeled off more names now, and Gilliam was beginning to feel that half of Britain's privately-owned art heritage must have gone walkabout. He was vainly trying to memorize the names of the earls, viscounts and barons – some of them life peers – listed by Mallory. He gave up on the works of art.

'And that wasn't all,' Mallory said as they reached the gravel drive ringing the house. 'You may recall how the last Labour Government brought in exchange controls?'

Gilliam put on a disarming smile. 'They copped me taking out twenty-five quid more than was legal – to the Costa Brava.' It was a lie. He'd gone out on duty as aide to a senior officer on the trail of some expatriate villains who in those days were allowed by the

Spaniards to live in style on the proceeds of coups in Britain. And the expenses had been generous and free from control. But the lie would please Mallory.

Mallory responded with what could pass for a laugh. 'I was able to assist some other respected friends to transfer considerable sums.' And he gave more names until he ran out of patience rather than names. 'And that's that,' he announced flatly. 'I intend to resign. And if the Monarch strips me of my knighthood I will understand. I shall pray that all this never gets out to damage my country.' The grey face was sad. 'Pity about the shoot, Gilliam. I'm sure you'd have taken to it.' He stood absolutely still, chest-high to Gilliam. 'You missed deliberately, didn't you?'

'I'm left-handed,' Gilliam said.

'Some of the best shots are left-handers.'

'Ah, but I'm half-blind in the left eye,' Gilliam said. 'Don't tell the Commissioner, though. I don't want to be ploughed at my next medical.'

They shook hands.

All the way back to London Gilliam was making a list of all those titled tax-dodgers and exchange control evaders. Back at his desk at the Yard he ran the names for accuracy against the lists in *Whittaker's Almanac* and the biogs in *Who's Who*.

The Commissioner had been right about this being a tricky one. This list would have him shitting bricks.

SEVEN

'Edwina Sarne?'

Olsen nodded as he gazed down at Lower Manhattan sweltering in the May heatwave. 'You seen much of her lately?'

'I've been a bit tied up with Comrade Koslov and the rumba set,' Carrodus said edgily. He was wary of Olsen since the little man's recent rise in the Bureau, and this one-day visit from Washington could mean anything from some weird assignment to a shake-out of the New York-based agents.

'I know, Matt. I'm well aware of your good work.' He waved his short arms emphatically. 'I know the UN beat's no picnic when you can't even put your nose inside the joint.' The United Nations was one of his *bêtes noires*, and at one agents' spree he'd called it 'this festering sore on the ass of America'. He also had a grudge against the Army's top brass, seeing them as 'fancy-pants poseurs'. And his aversions were shared by the President. Only a change of President could now get in the way of Trigvye Olsen being the next Director. 'Anyhow, you can come back to foreign counter-intelligence here after this.'

'This being Edwina Sarne?' He watched Olsen through narrowed eyes.

'Right.' He sat down uncomfortably. They were using the office of Dan Lemont, one of the Special Agents in Charge in the Big Apple, a six-foot-four beanpole with long legs. His chair was set so high that Olsen's feet were off the floor.

'I'll let it down a notch,' Carrodus offered.

'No, no,' Olsen said dismissively. 'Guys that high should be kept out of the service.'

Carrodus put on a strained smile and squeezed his beak nose. He wondered if now was a good time to raise the matter of his transfer back to Washington, which Olsen had twice turned down flat. Liz had made up her mind not to leave Capitol Hill. She was too busy being patriotic at the Voice of America. All they had now was a marriage of inconvenience courtesy of the Bell Telephone Company. He kept telling himself they were losing marital prime time – and the chance of raising a family. At thirty-eight Liz was leaving it late. Four years older, he was becoming obsessive about fatherhood. Every other agent in the Bureau seemed to be making it these days.

'Seems like low-profile time for the lady?' Olsen wasn't talking about Liz. He had Sarne's FBI card up on the monitor to his right.

'The Security Council's having a quiet patch.'

'Maybe that's the best thing that could happen for world peace.' Olsen was swinging to and fro, swivelling the chair with his right hand, his feet six inches clear of the carpet. 'You got so near to nailing her, Matt.'

It was three years ago, but as clear in Carrodus's memory as if it were last week. First the tip-off from the State Department about the leak of hi-tech microchip and laser developments to the Soviet Union. The suspicion that the leak was through Britain, which had a share in the research programme. Then the proof that the route had been via Israel, then Turkey. A further leak of forbidden hi-tech. And the finger on Edwina Sarne, then an aide working with the US delegation, because of the time she spent in amicable diplomacy with the Soviet delegate Viktor Bakhirev, a known hi-tech poacher for the Kremlin. Yet her entire record – as lawyer, official and politician – showed no ideological taint. In the end Carrodus had gone through her bank accounts, and those of her husband Larry's import-export company, only to find no monies they could not account for.

The order to pull off had come from the White House.

'I always did reckon she did it for gain,' Olsen said, pushing an official memo over the desk. RE EDWINA SARNE, it read. FLIGHT RESERVATION TOMORROW CAYMAN AIRWAYS OUT OF MIAMI. TRAVELLING AS MRS SYLVIE DELMER. OPEN RETURN. KALDOR.

'Holiday?' Carrodus didn't fancy another run-around. He'd rather have talked about a Washington transfer. 'It's got the world's best coral reef for divers.'

'And around five hundred banks for 18,000 people, most of 'em Caymanians who don't run to having bank accounts.'

'Offshore tax haven, sure.'

'Tax and other things.' Olsen's square jaw was set in the lardy face. 'It's one of those little hideaways that makes the IRS twitch. If the lady who's always telling the world how to behave better in those Security Council speeches is just tax-dodging that's *their* ball game. Me, I don't think it's tax. I've watched for a move like this for three damn years, Matt.' He got up now, pressing his squat frame upright with his knuckled fist on the desk. 'You just about got time to make JFK. I want to know what the lady's up to when she's not scuba diving, okay?'

'I never did get to meet her, you know.' It was Carrodus's last try to opt out. He tried to catch Olsen's evasive eyes.

'I know.' Olsen murmured, looking down from 26 Federal Plaza. 'Otherwise I'd have sent some other lucky guy.' He was cutting a cigar and trying to look like the son of J. Edgar Hoover.

'That's it then?' There was a flash of defiance.

'That's it, Matt.' He wasn't known for his social charm but he added, 'Oh, how's Liz?'

'Living in Washington DC.'

He boarded the flight with ten minutes in hand. There was no sign of Edwina Sarne. It wasn't until he was in his seat in the first-class section of a Cayman Airways 727 at Miami International that he saw her. Dark and elegant, her makeup just so, she wore sunglasses and had a Pentax slung from a shoulder and a Cayman Islands tourist brochure in her hand. Two young men came in her wake. The first was a boy of eighteen or nineteen with a springheel gait, the other was all beefcake with a Rambo swagger and could have been three or four years older. Carrodus knew them from the mugshots in the Sarne file. Hal and Marlon, the bodybuilder, were Edwina's sons. Both wore T-shirts with slogans printed front and rear, and they had identical moustaches.

Soon after takeoff, Carrodus ordered a large unadulterated Scotch, then went forward to the magazine rack to collect a discarded copy of the *Wall Street Journal*. All the other first-class passengers were grey-suited men in their thirties with swanky tamper-proof briefcases. Did they really fly to Grand Cayman with those cases stuffed with dollars for the laundry? Going back to his seat he spared a shy stranger's smile for Edwina. She may have taken him for one who had seen her UN performances, but her face gave nothing away. She was Mrs Sylvie Delmer.

Marlon spotted Carrodus's look – and scowled before burying himself in *The Bodybuilder*.

*

'Raleigh House Securities Inc,' Gilliam said. 'And its Cayman bank.'

Hobart folded his arms and took a couple of steps back to let tourists board the pocket submarine. 'Geordie, for Christ's sake! Thousands of companies like that are registered here. They're common as lizards.'

'All I'm asking, Hobe, as a Met man of an ex-Met man, is for a bit of info.'

'*All* you're asking!' Chief Superintendent Hobart put on a lopsided grin. 'You're asking about the ownership of a company registered here. You're asking for access to a bank account. That's like asking for the keys to the kingdom. Didn't they tell you back in London what it's like here?'

Gilliam shrugged. The Commissioner had warned him about Grand Cayman. 'They're tough as hell at enforcing their secrecy laws. Even the FBI walked into a brick wall there, let alone the tax-collecting agencies.' There'd been some easing up over dirty money from the drugs racket, but then some US agents had gone hunting tax-dodgers while claiming they were drugs barons. 'Such fishing trips had to be blocked – and blocked they were.' Gilliam had gone to the Yard's library and read up the US-UK-CI treaty covering the proceeds of crime.

'I'm looking into a crime that's recognized here.'

'Sure,' Hobart said, folding his brawny forearms and stroking his grey moustache. 'Blackmail.' He watched the last of the US tourists – old couples and honeymooners mainly – go down into the submarine. 'And you'll say nowt about it.' His keen eyes twinkled and he chewed the tip of his sunglasses' frame. 'Who did you say the victim was?'

'You bastard!'

They laughed. Up in his fourth-floor office by the harbour, the Commissioner of the Royal Cayman Islands Police, Fenwick, had asked the same question when Gilliam paid his courtesy call. Gilliam had told him the name was strictly under wraps. Then the Deputy Commissioner, Peters, had asked. And Hobart knew of those meetings. At fifty-two he had seen it all.

Back in the UK there'd have been nods and winks between cops. Here secrecy was pervasive. 'I tell you this,' Hobart said as the submarine set out below the harbour wall. 'You might rate the Old Bailey tough. Here you'll need a case as hard as a nuclear bomb shelter to get anywhere. The Grand Court will hear your evidence.

In camera. The Governor and the Executive Council will meet. In camera. And you'll be advised to take a dive down among the coral.'

They headed for the Cayman Arms. The weather was in the nineties. Gilliam's shirt was sticking to him. Not a globule of sweat was showing on the stocky Hobart, and his short-sleeved white cotton shirt was crisp and dry. He read Gilliam's mind. 'Takes a bit of getting used to, Geordie. Like a lot of things round here.'

In the pub the Brits, out of habit, were on light ales, as were the Americans, out of respect for the Crown. Gilliam asked for a rum and coke, and Hobart talked of Liverpool FC and his daughter's progress at Cambridge.

Not until they were back on the hot sidewalk did Hobart get back to business. He indicated the Post Office with its wall of PO boxes being visited by well-tailored young men with keys. 'Turn right there. Cross over. You'll find the Drake Building straight ahead. You can't miss it. Your Raleigh House set-up's in there somewhere. Its name will be on the inside wall. It's represented by an attorney name of Maxell. Ed Maxell.'

'Is he . . .?'

Hobart put on a naive look. 'He's not popular at the nick as we reckon he's been taking black coral and conch from the reef, not to mention the odd turtle.' He shook hands. 'And that's all I *can* say, mate. Wish I could help. Christ, if I were to go nosing into bank accounts they'd have me in the local equivalent of the Tower in no time. Under the confidentiality laws.'

And Hobart was head of the CID.

Naisby studied his hand. The king of diamonds stood out in a fistful of trash. His eyes were smarting and he needed to take out his contact lenses. The gaming room was thick with cigar smoke. His bow tie was too tight and the starched white collar of his shirt had seared his neck.

The florid, bald-headed punter opposite raised the stake by a thousand pounds. Naisby covered it. The two other players threw in their hands.

He was aware they were interpreting his neck-fingering as some poker player's trick. The other punter raised the stake again. Naisby doubled it only to be topped. They were near the table limit. It had long been Naisby's ambition to play the no-limit tables at Beresford's, but it was much too soon to indulge. Newcomers who took on the sheikhs and sharks at that sky-high level were asking for trouble from men in dinner suits whose London nights out were covered by their expense sheets at New Scotland Yard.

He made a play of showing respect to Baldhead and tapping his wallet pocket in a way that hinted he might be at his own limit.

He threw down his cards, and there was a genteel murmuring of sympathy for a loser. On the way out he lingered near the no-limit table where an aristocrat and an Indian company promoter gazed at each other like polecats as the two other players tossed in their cards. The aristocrat was known for his loud complaints in the media about the way penal taxation had brought his family near to ruin.

In the washroom Naisby loosened his shirt collar and gently dabbed his sore neck with a wet handkerchief. It was the first time he'd worn a dinner suit since that stuffed shirt reception in Zürich for expatriate Brits – and it would be the last. He took out his contact lenses and put on glasses and took a long look at his face in the big gilt-framed mirror.

He winked at himself.

It had been quite a day. Not quite the one he'd planned to share with Tara, but she was at some show-jumping meet in Holland. Calling himself Kilroy he'd been given a test drive round Hyde Park in a Rolls Royce before being measured for a dozen silk shirts at a Royal maker's in Jermyn Street. He'd lunched at the Connaught, checked out some exquisite jade pieces in Belgravia, then called in at British Airways' West End office to ask about round-the-world flights by Concorde. But the best moments were those when a Mr E. J. M. Blackmore-Smythe had shown him over three London apartments priced between £700,000 and £1 million in Regent's Park, Mayfair and Westminster near the Abbey. Mr Blackmore-Smythe was a lithe Eton-and-Guards type in a blue pinstripe suit with a pale blue carnation. He had clearly made up his mind that Kilroy was no gentleman and didn't have the booty to purchase the palatial nests he'd asked to see. But Blackmore-Smythe's boss, of equal pedigree but with more experience of today's world, had given the order. Kilroy had to be shown around, even if he turned up wearing green linen slacks and a distressed leather bomber jacket.

They were in the sumptuous drawing-room of the Westminster pad, which more than lived up to the agent's brochure, when Mr Blackmore-Smythe could resist no more. He pushed open a window with a panoramic view of the Houses of Parliament, Buckingham Palace and the Thames, breathed in deeply as if he needed clean air in such company and asked, 'One's not being personal, sir. But are you a pop star?'

'But you *are* being personal, Mr – er – ?'

'Blackmore-Smythe.'

Naisby was tempted to say he would have the place, cash on the button.

He'd moved on to Bond Street to look at jewellery in Cartier's. He wasn't sure of the date but he knew Tara's birthday was in May.

He left Beresford's now, took a taxi to the King's Road, where he bought fish and chips in a wrapper, and walked back to the embankment.

It was close on 11 pm when he came to the line of public call boxes. He buttoned 100 and asked for a transfer charge call to Sir Rupert Mallory.

'And your name, sir?'

'Kilroy. Tom Kilroy.'

A man answered and the operator asked if he would take the call.

'I'm afraid Sir Rupert's not here at the moment,' the man's voice came back. 'Would you try again in about an hour?'

Naisby could have sworn the voice was Sir Rupert's, he might be stupid enough to have the later call traced.

'I'll do that,' Naisby said. He checked his pocket book and found Lord Justice Kenright's number. He was asking for the transfer call when three skinheads began to kick and thump the call-box windows. They wore bovver boots and studded belts. The smallest – a lightly built thug with earrings – snatched the door open.

'How long you takin', eh?'

Naisby abandoned the call and came out. They jostled him, but no more, and were clearly high on something.

There was no great hurry. He would call Mallory and Kenright in the morning, and Edwina Sarne later, when New York had come awake. He had a nagging realization that he might soon get bored with being rich, and that even the $6,600,000 Maxell had transferred from Cayman – $1,400,000 had gone walkabout in fees and the compensation for that microlight – was a lot more than he would ever need.

Even so, it had become imperative that Mallory, Kenright and Sarne should cough up.

It was past midnight when he used his key to let himself into the block. The night porter would be in his room at this time unless there was an incident. As the elevators had a way of breaking down, Naisby took the stairs to the second floor. On the last flight he was aware of movement in the half-light on the second-floor landing. He stopped, aware of a bulky presence above. The low-intensity lighting, brought in to cut fuel bills, was not enough to enable him to see the face, but it was certainly a man. And he stood four square at the stairhead now. Naisby, his heart racing, turned back.

'Rollo!'

Naisby turned and looked up. The dark figure was Oscar Leiden. In shock Naisby said in a hushed voice, 'What in hell are you doing here? At this time?'

'The porter said you were coming back tonight.'

'How long have you been here?'

'Three hours.' Oscar was agitated.

'Jesus!' Naisby muttered as he let them into the flat. He put the second lock on, and fastened the security chain. 'You shouldn't do that, Oscar.'

'I telephoned twice.' Oscar's hand trembled on the brandy glass Naisby gave him.

'Sit down, for God's sake!'

Oscar preferred to explain his trip standing up. He tugged a curtain an inch to cover a gap open to the sky. 'How reliable is this man Maxell?'

'Who's he?'

'Don't be stupid, Rollo. Your man on Grand Cayman.'

Again Naisby put on a baffled air.

'Wasserman's been talking to him.'

The news shook Naisby. It was in Wasserman's picture show that Oscar had noted that bullet-grazed arm. Wasserman had to be reckoned with. 'He'll get nowhere.'

'I asked, how reliable a man is this Maxell?'

'Totally,' Naisby lied. Maxell had ripped him off, deducting enough for the loss of that flying pram to buy a bloody jet. And then some.

'And his nerve?'

'He's got a lot of bottle.' He was desperate to sound unworried.

'He'd better have.' He held out his glass for a refill. 'Wasserman's given him an ultimatum. He comes up with your identity or . . . '

'Or what?'

'Or Wasserman reports him to the Governor. Our lawyers have been busy. The Governor in Council can authorize disclosure where there's evidence of crime.'

'Can but won't.'

'And he can stop Maxell in his tracks by revoking his licence.'

'Here, get that down,' Naisby said, handing him the glass. 'Make you feel less strung up.' He sipped his own brandy. He was reeling from Oscar's news but put on a front. 'Wasserman would be potty to go within a mile of the Governor. If it gets out your bank's leaking like a shower-head, Seifert et Cie's done for. Kaput.'

Oscar was shaking his head. 'And Klutz is the scapegoat again for all this.' He was close to tears.

'That was *your* doing, Oscar.'

'I fear for his sanity.'

'Not much you can do about it now.'

Oscar's eyes flashed behind those big lenses. 'I'm already doing it.' His plan was to use Wasserman's absence on Grand Cayman to acquire his entry code into the wallsafe in the Sterile Area, then his personal password to get into the computer.

'Where does that get you?' Naisby diagnosed Oscar as being half-demented.

'Don't you see?' Oscar said, as if talking to a simpleton. 'Wasserman has now built in a new safeguard. The system now records the identity of the inquirer keying into *any* account.'

Naisby felt close to the abyss where he said goodbye to computer buffs.

'If I use *his* password to key into an account it'll be on the record.'

'So?'

'So he'll be discredited. And nobody will believe him about Klutz any more.'

'There seems to be a piece missing.'

Oscar bloomed suddenly. 'That's you, Rollo. You go to just one more eminent person whose account I will penetrate in the name of Charles Wasserman.'

It was Naisby's turn to be on guard. 'Who is he?'

'Johnny Kirkham.'

The name rang only a faint bell.

'I saw his account about a year ago. The bottom line showed twenty-six million Swiss francs. More, much more, than any of those you've been working on.'

Naisby yawned. 'Maybe he's in the kind of business that lets you make that honestly?'

'He's an evangelist, Rollo.'

Naisby poured more brandies. 'And what good would that do?'

'I told you. Discredit Wasserman and help Klutz.'

'I thought you disliked Klutz?'

'He's being destroyed by this,' Oscar said through his teeth. 'Because of me.' He took another gulp of brandy. 'And Wasserman I hate!'

'Forget it!'

'You don't want another investor? Your greed is satisfied?'

'It's a loony notion!'

'You've got your fourteen million dollars, so forget it.'

Naisby put it down to the alcohol. 'Less than half that, as you know. I'm still chasing those three refuseniks.'

Startled, Oscar downed his drink and helped himself to another. 'Their payments were transferred days ago.'

It didn't quite register with Naisby. 'I tell you – Mallory, Kenright and Sarne haven't coughed up.'

'The bank settled *for* them, Rollo.'

'Days ago, you say?'

'Nearly a week ago.' Oscar made for the almost empty bottle of Napoleon, tripped over a stool, and collided with the TV set. He would have to stay the night. He was in no state to be roaming around Chelsea knowing what he knew. Naisby let him have the sole bedroom. He settled on the sofa with a blanket.

His head was spinning.

He knew that even with Wasserman swanning around the island, he would have to confront Maxell there.

He could hear Big Ben chiming one o'clock.

Up in the top-floor security room of the Drake Building, Gladstone Hooley fine-tuned the monitor covering the ground-floor lobby. Greyish pictures flickered on the other four screens showing office workers and early visitors entering and leaving the elevators on each floor.

He rose from his left knee and adjusted his metal-framed glasses. He was brown and lean with the look of an Indian. Running a hand through thinning hair held with gel that made his skull glisten, he said, 'That's as good as we can expect, I think.'

'That's just fine, Mr Hooley,' Carrodus said with a faint sidelong smile for Coke Rogers. Coke had pulled a nice one in Gladstone. Nobody knew who paid Coke's salary, though it had to be the US taxpayer in the end. He'd been on Grand Cayman three years now, and knew his way round the island like it was his own Chicago backyard. Whether he did *any* work for the US multinational whose plush office he occupied in the Elizabethan Centre was anybody's guess.

Gladstone Hooley was a bundle of nerves. 'It might be advisable if you wish to continue the surveillance over a long period that we make a different arrangement.' He nodded towards the VTR machines beneath each monitor. 'I can let you see the tapes in Coke's office, perhaps? As long as they're returned. Discreetly, of course.'

'Fix that with Coke.' Carrodus spread himself in the battered plastic couch, and Hooley had to step over his long legs to get out. Carrodus was hooked by that lobby screen. It was 8.50 am and all being well Edwina Sarne would come through those tinted glass doors on her way to see he knew not who. It had been worth all the angst of enduring the tired floor show and the din of the dreary nightspot to eavesdrop for a while on America's UN ambassador and her two sons. Hal and Marlon had kept their eyes on her even when they were girl-spotting from the bar seats nearest their table. Each had taken to the mini dance floor once – with her. The rest of the time they'd mooched at the bar, sticking to beer, with Marlon flexing those biceps till the fabric of his T-shirt was about to rip.

Beyond a formal nod to imply he recalled her vaguely from the flight out, Carrodus had shown no interest in her, and little more in the boys. In the quieter moments when the pop group was refuelling at the bar he'd been able to pick up the odd snatch of chat between them, but it was mainly about Hal's impatience to go diving among the coral on the North Wall, and Marlon's urge to find a gym where he could keep up his weight-lifting. Marlon was scared of the sea. It had got to midnight before the angst turned to relish, when Edwina sent Hal to the hotel lobby to order a taxi for 8.45 am to take her to the Drake Building in George Town.

Carrodus had left then through the beach door, taken off his socks and shoes, turned up his slacks, and walked at the water's edge for a mile or more under the clearest night sky he'd ever seen. The moon had been big and he thought he saw a man-made satellite among the stars. Maybe it was American, taking a look at Cuba. But it wasn't politics he had on his mind. It was Liz. This could be just the place to patch up a marriage.

It was 9.10 am now and he must have seen all of a hundred people enter the building – bankers, attorneys, computer operators and the like, mainly, but among them a sprinkling of spruce US executives with fat briefcases. Olsen had been right in speaking of the place as a paradise for agents of the IRS.

'I bet you're dying for a peek inside that lot,' Coke smirked as three obviously American citizens carrying fat cases waited for the elevators.

'We'd get our wrists slapped if we tried.'

'Worse besides,' Coke said, and the words were heartfelt. He'd seen grown FBI agents kicked off the island, and one or two from Justice, after embarking on what the Caymanians called 'fishing expeditions'.

Suddenly Carrodus was gripped by the lobby picture. He sat up and leaned forward for a better view. It wasn't Edwina Sarne. There was no woman in shot. He was studying a bulky Englishman with a furrowed brow and a vigilant manner whose nose and eyes gave him the look of an eagle.

'Who's he?' Coke asked.

'Dunno,' Carrodus said. 'Do they kick Brits off the island?'

'It's a British island, Matt.'

Carrodus nodded, keeping the Brit in sight as he went to the receptionist in the lobby. 'I'll lay odds he's a cop. If he were up to his nostrils in the Caribbean Sea I'd say he was a cop.'

But he lost interest now.

A woman was coming off the street. No fat briefcase. Just a small black handbag.

Edwina Sarne went over to the receptionist as the beak-nosed Englishman idly scanned that vast wall display of company names.

Two minutes later Edwina came into close-up from the camera set above the elevators, then went out of shot. Carrodus and Coke studied the other monitors. Hal and Marlon were in the lobby picture now. Marlon came into close-up, then out of shot. He was with Edwina as she left the elevator at the second floor. They turned left and into a corridor and were lost to the camera.

'Wander down there, Coke.'

Coke was already on his way.

The Englishman and Hal were still in the lobby. It was another ten minutes before Edwina came up on the second floor screen, with Hal in her wake. They took the elevator. Then Coke appeared from the left-hand corridor. In the lobby the receptionist gave the Englishman a signal and he went to the elevator.

'She was in office two-twenty,' Coke said, back in the security room. 'The Maxell Group Inc.'

Edwina was on her way out through the lobby. A thick-set man with a blond beard stepped aside on his way to let her pass. Carrodus thought he'd seen him somewhere, and recalled it was in the nightspot, but didn't give it another thought.

Charles Wasserman didn't call at the desk. He went straight to the lift.

Carrodus went down for a peek at the office of The Maxell Group.

Beyond the door and Carrie's room Gilliam faced Maxell, who wasn't pleased to see him. 'You told my secretary you wished to discuss the formation of a company here,' Maxell snapped.

'Right,' Gilliam nodded. 'Raleigh House Securities.'

'A new company, you said.'

'It *is* a new company. Well, newish.' Having sussed out the scene, Gilliam reckoned the bull-in-the-china-shop approach was best for starters.

'So perhaps you'll come clean and say who you are and whom you represent?'

'Superintendent Gilliam. Serious Crimes Squad, Scotland Yard. Sir.'

'In which case you should know better than to come here seeking information that's strictly confidential. Under our laws.'

'It needn't be confidential where there's evidence of crime.'

'If you have such evidence, Superintendent, you should be at the Grand Court or the Attorney-General's office. Not here. And I *am* extremely busy.' The telex was chattering, a monitor was flashing Wall Street prices, and a red light had appeared on one of the phones. It was no lie. He *was* busy. And he was up to his elbows in paper, much of it wrapped in red tape.

'I'm inquiring into crime, Mr Maxell.'

'So you're at the wrong address.' He stood up, indicating the door.

'In which you appear to be implicated.'

'What crime?' he snapped, coming round the desk to show Gilliam out.

'Blackmail.'

'Go tell it to the Grand Court, Superintendent.'

'I'm here to find out who is the beneficial owner of Raleigh House Securities.'

'Mickey Mouse,' Maxell said.

Carrie was at the internal door wearing her big white smile and ready to lead Gilliam out through her room to the corridor. As she opened the door she came face to face with Wasserman, who was about to knock. And passing behind Wasserman was a tall American.

Carrodus wore the uninterested look of a passer-by but he glimpsed the Englishman who was being shown out, and noted his frustration.

Taking advantage, Wasserman thrust past Carrie and went right through to Maxell's office. Maxell was still not over the trauma of Gilliam's call. His mouth set and he glared at Wasserman. 'I told you not to come here again!' His hand went to the button that would call Carrie.

'Think before you do anything stupid.' Wasserman's voice was measured. 'I now have the authority of my board to report you to the Inspector of Banks and Trust Companies.'

It made Maxell feel sick, but he said, 'Go ahead. Just do that!' Last time they'd met, Wasserman had served an ultimatum on the pretext that the millions of dollars being transferred by Seifert et Cie to the Cayman account of Raleigh House Securities might be drugs-related. It was an old trick of the FBI's, that one, to trap tax-dodgers. And Maxell had figured that Wasserman's bank had the wind up about its own involvement. What Gilliam had just told him put another slant on Naisby's new-found success as an investment manager.

'I'm giving you a chance to think it over,' Wasserman said. 'You give me the name of the beneficial owner of Raleigh House Securities now. Or I go down the road to see the Inspector.'

'Go, then,' Maxell said, near to breaking-point. 'Or I call the police and have you removed. Our immigration people will do the rest. You'll be off this island faster than a rocket.'

It was stand-off.

Wasserman left.

Gilliam was half way down the emergency stairs to the basement when he was aware of footfalls above.

'Sir?' The voice was far from respectful.

Gilliam saw a lithe brown man with thinning hair leaning inquisitively over the rail above. 'I'm trying to find my way out,' Gilliam said.

Gladstone Hooley wagged a finger to call him back. 'You're going the wrong way, man.'

'I was looking for the lift.'

'The elevator goes up and down,' Gladstone remonstrated. 'You want it to go sideways?' The voice was Caribbean mixed with British

West-country. He showed Gilliam through the corridor door leading to the lobby.

Gilliam had reckoned the basement might be interesting. Now he wasn't so sure, having noted the shredder in Carrie's room at the offices of The Maxell Group. Nothing would wind up in the basement rubbish bar shredded evidence.

And Maxell's office looked tamper-proof.

EIGHT

Spinning and stalling like some red-and-white top two thousand feet above the English Channel, the little Pitts Special came out of a dive close to the sullen sea, then went into an almost vertical climb. On the promenades and shingle beaches below, crowds watching the aerobatics speculated on whether the pilot was just exuberant or plain crazy.

Naisby knew it was an escape from Grand Cayman. Call after call to Ed Maxell had brought the same reply from Carrie. He was away in the US. And none of the outstanding six million dollars had found its way into Naisby's accounts. That shooting-down and Oscar's warnings about Wasserman's continuing surveillance and ultimatum to Maxell had scared him off going back to sort things out.

He took the Pitts straight and level across the bay on full boost, then into a vertical climb that ended with the Pitts almost motionless, standing on her tail. Into a stall now, and a spin, and he had her falling like a leaf. Then the power dive with the engine screaming on full boost. His heart was beating only slightly faster than it did normally. His brain had cleared of the fuzziness of the past few days. He gained height, put the Pitts into a straight-and-level run parallel with the shore line, and into a loop. The world was a kaleidoscope of rainbow colours, of dinghies and spring lambs, and land, sea and sky. Maeve loomed, frowning. It wasn't only his passion for stunt flying that had wrecked their marriage, but it had been a factor.

One more loop, another roll and spin, and a dive so steep it seemed the Pitts would hit the sea, and he was satisfied. His dicing, and the showing-off that had hundreds of people open-mouthed, had done the trick. As he landed he could see Nick Syler and his next death-defying client near the mini-hangar Nick had built from bits and pieces that had fallen off the backs of RAF trucks. Nick was looking at his watch.

'Sorry,' Naisby said, getting down from the Pitts and patting its lower starboard wing as if it were a horse. 'Charge me for the extra time.'

'Forget it,' Syler said, helping his assistant to refuel the Pitts. 'I thought you'd done no flying since you were last here?'

'Only in a microlight.' He'd have loved to shoot a line about being shot down. He bottled up the urge.

Syler introduced his next client, a young farmer with the complexion of a red apple. 'He's worse than you were, Rollo. Can't leave it alone.'

'You married?'

Syler knew why Naisby had asked.

'Good Lord, no,' the farmer pilot said.

'Substitute for sex, this,' Syler muttered, leaving the refuelling to his assistant.

'Substitute for nearly everything,' Naisby smiled. Nearly being the word. He felt almost ready now to face up to a visit to Grand Cayman.

They watched the farmer take off. 'Nice little job, that Pitts,' Naisby said, as they went into the ancient Portacabin that served as Syler's flying clubhouse. 'I thought you'd have had a squadron of 'em by now.'

'That and the Piper's as much as I can handle.' He indicated the two-seater trainer outside, and opened a small refrigerator. 'Alcohol-free lager, lemonade or dry ginger?'

Naisby chose the dry ginger. He looked around. The place was in need of a coat of paint, and the chairs could have been relics from some crew room in the Battle of Britain. An antique hardwood propeller was suspended on one bare wall from chicken wire. Initials and names had been carved into it. Graffiti and Page Three pin-up girls fought for the rest of the wall space.

'You doing all right, Nick?' It was clear that Syler wasn't making a pile.

'Pays for the bread and dripping,' Syler grinned, handing over the drink.

An open-topped Golf drew up outside. Through the open door Naisby saw the driver, all blond locks and leggy assurance in clinging jeans, turn to tweak the ear of her only passenger, a hound big enough to have led the Baskervilles pack. She came towards the cabin with a wave of greeting.

'I see now why you're on the breadline, mate,' Naisby said.

'Pupil.'

'Free lessons?'

'Cash on the nail. No bouncing cheques with this one.'

'Which boss's daughter is *she* then?'

'Self-made. She's a trade union official.'

As she got closer, Naisby had her thighs in focus. They were sensational. 'She'll probably rate me a right male pig if she can read my mind.'

Syler laughed. 'Says she'll not come here any more unless we take those pin-ups down. But she's been saying that for weeks.'

'You're early,' Nick said to her. 'No strikes?'

'Not even a go slow.' Her nose twitched and laughter lines crinkled around her mouth.

Syler mischievously thwarted Naisby for a long moment by not introducing her. 'Kerry Dorland,' he then said, pulling on his flying overalls. 'Rollo Naisby.'

She smiled and shook hands, then crossed to the line of wooden lockers with graffiti carved into them. Without a trace of shyness she unzipped her jeans and stepped out of them, while keeping up a running commentary on Syler's flying circus and ribbing him about the low wages he was probably paying his assistant.

'You haven't a clue what I pay him,' Syler said.

Naisby couldn't care less. He had an eyeful of leg that prompted him to think he'd never seen such limbs since he'd watched Shirley Maclaine two nights running at the Palladium.

She pulled on her flying overalls.

'The first genuine flying picket,' Syler chuckled.

In the half-light Naisby caught the flash of those green eyes. Her hair now looked more russet than blond.

'Right.' Syler weighed her up. 'Last time before you go solo.'

They started out.

'Keep clear of that lunatic up there.' Naisby's eyes took in the airspace over the sea where the young farmer was into a loop and roll. And he felt the macho urge. He wanted Kerry to know he'd just been up there with the Pitts. 'How much would you take for her?'

Syler did a double-take. 'Eh?'

'The Pitts Special.'

'Don't be daft, Rollo.'

'I'm dead serious.'

Kerry knew he was trying to impress.

'She's my living.' He gently steered Kerry to the door.

'What's she worth?'

'Around forty thousand.' His knowing face broke into a laugh. 'Kerry knows you flew her just now, don't worry.'

'I saw you while I was having lunch down the road, Mr Naisby.' She paused, tongue in cheek. 'I was *very* impressed.'

He knew it was a tease. Two could play. 'I've fallen in love,' he said, bringing out his chequebook.

She put a hand to her mouth, holding back a laugh.

'Fifty thousand,' Naisby said, picking up a biro from the logbook.

'Can't you see I'm busy?' Syler was now in two minds about Naisby's seriousness, but didn't want to admit it. 'Besides, how do I make a living without Esther?'

'Buy another,' Naisby said, the pen poised over the cheque. 'Deal?'

Syler still feared it was some practical joke.

'You can service her when I'm not here. We'll have a maintenance contract. But nobody but me flies Esther.' Naisby's eyes caught Kerry's as he spoke. The code was easy to break. She was tucking that russet hair under her flying helmet. And smiling at him.

'Deal,' Syler said. 'I'll really believe it when the cheque's cleared.' He felt it for bounce.

'All this depends on the brat bringing it back in one piece.' He looked skywards at the Pitts standing up there on its tail.

'He knows his stuff,' Syler said, pocketing the cheque.

All the way back to London Naisby felt exhilarated. The risks of the scam were justified in those moments at the airfield. He couldn't get the trainee pilot out of his mind. He reckoned she was about thirty-two. But he would have to rein back on such spending. At least he'd not bought the Rolls Royce or the Westminster duplex.

He buttoned out Maxell's office number. It would be around 9 am in Grand Cayman. He heard the call ringing out. It was a little time before Carrie came on.

'Morning, Carrie,' he said. 'Ed back yet?'

'Morning, Mr Naisby. No. He's been held up in New York. I'll get him to call you the moment he shows up, right?'

'Fine. Bye.' He hung up, sure that Maxell was there in that office. The Banque Giscard Frères' London branch was next.

The toady Waring came on. 'Yes, Mr Naisby? How can we be of help?'

'Any further payment from Raleigh House?'

It took Waring an eternity to confirm there was none. 'I'm sorry. Would you like us to make an inquiry?'

'No thanks.' Naisby tried the Banco Palomar Rubio's City office, where Mr Singleton-Starkie oozed integrity in confirming that no further transfer had been made from Grand Cayman. He tried four of the other banks – in London, Luxembourg and the Bahamas – where $500,000 deposits should have been transferred. None had been recorded. If Oscar had been right about Seifert's paying up, six million dollars had gone walkabout via Maxell, not counting the sums he'd stripped from the first eight million.

On impulse he put in a call to Thomas Cook's to book him on the first available flight to Miami–Grand Cayman. Then he had second thoughts and said he'd call back. He called Syler.

'I knew it,' Syler said. 'It was a gag. You're not buying the Pitts.'

'It's bought,' Naisby said. 'Is our one-woman answer to the Teamsters there?'

'Kerry? She left ages ago.' He chuckled. 'I thought you'd gone celibate.'

'Don't have her number, do you?'

'You move fast these days, Rollo. Must be all that Swiss goat's cheese.' He came up with her number. 'I think that's it.' Naisby knew what the doubt was about. All Nick Syler's paperwork was in a mess, much of it lost among stacks of *Flight* magazines or so grimed with oil it was indecipherable. 'Anyway, the best of British, mate.'

Naisby poured a large Glenfiddick and lit a cigar, then called the number and asked for Kerry Dorland.

'Yes, Mr Naisby?' The voice was more guarded than amused.

'I – er – don't know how you'll take this, but how do you fancy a few days of sunshine?'

'The forecast for here's pretty good for May.'

'I mean down among the palm trees.'

'Nick told me you fly fast.'

'He's exaggerating.'

'You meet someone for five minutes, then suggest a holiday in the Med.'

'Not the Med, love. The Caribbean.'

'Impossible.'

'No catches. No conditions. Separate rooms, I mean.'

'I should think so!' But she laughed.

'I know,' Naisby teased. 'You have a strike to picket?'

'No, but I do have a dispute. Some of my members working on an all-woman production line. Management's put in an inspection pit right under where they work. My members can hardly go on working in skirts and dresses with all those males looking up.'

'So you're saying no inspections?'

'No I'm saying the firm buys them slacks.'

'So tell 'em to agree now, and come with me tomorrow.'

'Call me when you get back, Mr Naisby. And do have a good time.'

Five minutes later he was talking to Tara. 'How about a few days in the Caribbean, love?'

'Sounds super,' she said. 'But I'm looking over some stables I'd like to buy.'

He wanted to tell her to buy them sight unseen and he'd meet the bill, but thought it unwise. 'Are they likely to be snapped up?'

'I'd not want to lose them.'

'How long have they been on the market?'

'A few weeks, I think.' Her voice was tired. 'Can I call you back, Rollo?'

'I'm talking about flying out tomorrow.'

'I'll call you back.'

Less than seven minutes later she was on the line. 'It should be super.'

He got back on to Cook's and asked for first-class open returns to Grand Cayman and two rooms at the best hotel on Seven Mile Beach. When they were confirmed he called Tara about the time they had to be at Heathrow in the morning.

It was around 3 am when he awoke from a dream in which he and Kerry Dorland were the only passengers in the first-class section of a Jumbo commandeered over mid-Atlantic by terrorists bent on martyrdom. His chest was damp with sweat and his eyes ached. Why the hell Kerry Dorland? Why not Tara? The nightmare brought it home that things might turn nasty in real life on Grand Cayman. He spent the rest of the night sitting in the window watching barges ply the Thames.

Dawn was up by the time he had the heart to call Tara.

'I know,' she said drowsily. 'The trip's off?'

'Problems,' he said lamely.

'I had a funny feeling this was going to happen.'

He knew she would have packed before turning in for the night. She was thorough and precise – and a planner.

'We'll make the trip another time.' He couldn't bring himself to say he would be going alone.

'Yes, Rollo.' And she hung up.

He made an early breakfast – omelette and strong coffee. Could he really have planned to take her as cover? Those who were after him and others who wanted him dead, would not have taken long to find he was no mere honeymooning tourist. But the deception had been in his mind when he first asked Kerry Dorland, certainly. He felt guilt-stricken about Tara now, not only for seeing her as cover, but for inviting her as substitute in that loony role.

He didn't cancel Tara's reservations. He switched on LBC Radio to keep him awake until it was time to leave for Heathrow.

'It's Klutz,' Reza said huffily, passing the phone to Oscar Leiden. 'Make it clear we're in the middle of dinner!' It was Klutz's second call during the evening, and there had been others in the previous two days.

'Yes, Willi?' He sounded testy.

'We really must meet, Oscar.'

'Let's make it tomorrow then.' Klutz had been at the end of his tether for days now. He was again being kept out of board meetings at Seifert's, Wasserman having persuaded Jean-Pascal that he was still the likely source of the leaks. It was most unfair, of course, as Oscar had told Klutz at their secret meeting in the little fifteenth-century church at Meilen on the lakeside. Having put in the extra security checks in the Sterile Area, Wasserman had noted that Klutz had significantly cut down on his visits and the number of clients' accounts consulted.

'That's just it!' Klutz had stammered. 'All this suspicion – it's made me think twice about going down there, I can tell you!'

'You must be patient,' Oscar had counselled. 'Things will sort themselves out.'

'Did Jean-Pascal tell the board straight why I wasn't present?'

'Of course not,' Oscar had lied.

'I can't take much more, Oscar. It's destroying my home life as well – everything!'

'Be patient.'

The last Oscar had seen of him, Klutz had been on his knees in the back pew of the church, deep in prayer.

He sounded worse now, his hushed voice giving Oscar the image of someone cringing in fear. 'Have a good night's sleep, eh? And we'll meet tomorrow. Usual place.'

In the silence Reza called, 'Oscar! It's spoiling!' It was another of her special offerings to compensate for the way Oscar's life was being made a misery by her mid-life crisis. She'd made a *Bernerplatte* – sauerkraut under a pile of pork chops, ham and smoked sausages. The aroma was superb.

'I'll call you back,' Oscar told Klutz.

'Can't you come round? Just for a half hour? I'd like to know a little of what's going on.'

'Let me see about it.'

The phone went dead.

'I hope he's not wanting to start that boating nonsense over again.' The look was fierce as she set the *Bernerplatte* before him. It was three years since those Rhine cruises on Klutz's boat when the two middle-aged bankers sought a last fling. Oscar had been gone every other weekend. The exercise had proved in vain, but Reza had never accepted that.

'He's under a lot of pressure,' Oscar said quietly, and tucked into the meal.

Reza went through to the hall. He heard her take the phone off.

'He'd not have called again,' he said when she came back.

'He's never off the line these days.'

'Delicious!' he said, savouring the *Bernerplatte* and seeking to disarm her.

'And don't forget you're taking Selie and me to the festival tomorrow night.'

'If I meet Willi at all, it'll be at lunchtime.' He didn't look up from his plate at the shrewish face.

After the meal he put the hall phone back on, went into his study with a coffee, and settled in his favourite high-back chair by the window. The light was going. He switched on the table lamp at his elbow, took the bookmark from page 193 of *A Neutral at War*, and started to read. But he couldn't rid his mind of Klutz. He put the book down and called him.

The call rang out. He hung up, gave it five minutes, and called again. There was still no reply.

Oscar went into the hall, put on his anorak and collected his car keys. 'I'll not be too long,' he called.

Reza came from the kitchen. 'I knew it!' she rasped. 'You're off to Klutz's.'

He went out without even a glance at the scornful face.

Half-expecting to find Klutz in his Alpine garden, so rich in spring flowers that gardening magazines sent photographers to it, Oscar took the BMW very slowly up the winding drive. Through the fringe of trees he could see the west shore of Lake Zürich under the bright moon. He lowered his driver's window and heard Klutz's lurcher dogs barking. The breeze was blowing cold off the lake.

The long red-brick villa was ablaze with lights. For a moment Oscar thought he might be intruding on a house party. But there were no cars other than his BMW in the drive. The front door was open. He pressed the bell. No one came.

'Willi!' he called.

Only the lurchers replied. The place was suddenly eerie.

'Willi!' His shout was louder. 'Willi? It's Oscar!' He was puzzled that Katrina or one of the older children hadn't come to the door. Klutz would often be in his study at this time.

Oscar shivered, and put it down to that cold breeze off the water. He went back outside and saw what had eluded him first time – a deep score in the gravel drive. It pointed to a car having skidded in a U-turn. A border of Alpine flowers had been churned up. The U began and ended at the triple garage. Its door was closed, but the lights were on over the nearby concrete steps leading to the nuclear war bunker. With a glance at the wire-meshed compound where the lurchers were barking, he went down the steps. The door to the bunker was open and lights were on inside. On the simple pine table lay a writing pad, a ballpoint pen and some unused envelopes. Two doors leading to other sections of the bunker were closed.

'Willi?'

He opened the doors in turn. The cells were empty.

Back at ground level he saw a chink of light under the garage doors. He lifted the first door up. Two cars were there – Klutz's blue Mercedes and the family Range Rover. The space Katrina used for her Jaguar was empty. He was aware of vapour fumes, then heard the hum of the Mercedes' engine. He knew now what had happened. Seizing the inside handle of the second garage door he flung it wide open, ran to the Mercedes, and found Klutz slumped in the driver's seat. He tugged the door open and saw the rubber hose leading out from Klutz's chest through a tightly-shut rear window to the exhaust. He dragged Klutz's heavy body out on to the gravel and gave him the kiss of life, remembering what he'd been taught in the *Landwehr*.

But there was no pulse and Klutz's body was turning cold. Oscar went into the house, called the ambulance and police, then went back to the Mercedes to switch off the ignition. On the front passenger seat, wedged in the pages of a Bible, were four envelopes addressed to Katrina, Jean-Pascal, the President of the Federal Banking Commission, and himself. Oscar slit open the letter. 'Dear Oscar, You mustn't blame yourself for being unable to come over. As ever, Willi.' He stuffed the letter in his back pocket. He could hear the sirens and see blue lights flashing between the pines on the lakeside road. On impulse he pocketed the letters to Jean-Pascal and the Banking Commission.

The sirens grew louder. He slit open the letter for Katrina.

> Darling, I have prayed for your return. My apologies to you and the children for my inexcusable behaviour over these past few weeks. I can only say that my situation at the bank has worsened and become quite unbearable. You and the children have my word on oath that I have done nothing wrong and that the scurrilous innuendo which has led to my fall from grace is totally baseless. I have seen to it that you are all protected financially.
> All my love,
> Willi. xxxxxx

A police car was on the drive, crunching gravel, with an ambulance right behind. Headlights fingered Oscar and the Mercedes. He put the letter back in the Bible, keeping the torn envelope in his pocket with the letters to Jean-Pascal and the Banking Commission.

Outside the ambulance men and a cop knelt at Klutz's body. 'He's dead,' one of the ambulance men said.

'I tried to give him the kiss of life,' Oscar said.

Another cop was checking inside the Mercedes.

Those letters in Oscar's back pocket felt as bulky as a mailbag. The cop from the Mercedes came over, lasering him with a look. Oscar prayed there was to be no body search. He exhaled heavily, and planted his right hand on his heart.

'You all right sir?' the cop said anxiously.

'The kiss of life,' Oscar murmured. 'It didn't work.'

'You can't win them all,' the cop said. He was reading that letter to Katrina. Suicides usually left only one note.

Oscar closed his eyes.

'I tell you he's not here, Mr Naisby.'

Naisby was sure Carrie was lying. He thrust past her into her office and went straight through to Maxell's room.

'I told you,' Carrie complained. 'And if you don't leave this minute I'll get the police.'

'So where is he?'

She had her hand on the phone, unyielding.

'Where is he?'

She began to call a number. He reckoned it was no real number – and certainly not that of the Royal Cayman Islands Police station down near Hospital Road – but he had no time for games of bluff. He was still only half awake, having checked in at the hotel on Seven Mile Beach after a delayed flight. Heathrow–Miami–Owen Roberts was a brute.

His face was set as he took the usual long way round the corridors to evade the TV security eyes. He picked up his hastily hired Honda in the Elizabethan Centre car park and drove to South Sound. Maxell's ranch-style bungalow, with its three-car garage and swimming pool, had sprouted a satellite TV dish in a garden ablaze with scarlet hibiscus. The spread was coming on a treat.

He buttoned the bell.

'Yes?'

He spun round to see Hannah had come round the side of the bungalow with a muscular black Caymanian in beach shorts. A rope thong was at his left ankle.

'Hello, Hannah.'

'Rollo.' She was big enough not to need minders – an overweight go-getter from Houston who'd married Maxell for love and found money. In one unguarded moment Ed had said she rounded up clients in Texas like a cowgirl.

'I can see Ed's not around,' he said, aiming a finger at the garage with only her new Chevrolet there.

'No, Rollo. He's right busy.' The brusque manner was not that of the Hannah he knew, chatty and outgoing.

'Any idea where I might find him?'

'Doubt if you can right now, Rollo.'

He knew for sure that Carrie had been on to her. Once Hannah would have asked him in for a drink. Now her alert eyes found the Caymanian.

'I'll call, right?' Naisby was certain she was in the picture. Not fully, maybe, but she knew enough.

She didn't even offer a handshake. As he drove away she was showing the Caymanian where to put the lawn spray on the thick sparta grass.

He knew Maxell was on the island. On a hunch he drove back through George Town and along West Bay Road to the golf club. If Maxell wasn't there, he would be out fishing for blue marlin or scuba diving.

He found him on the fourth tee.

'Hi, Rollo,' Maxell said, so laid back he could have been expecting him. 'Since when did you take up this waste of time?'

Naisby felt like hitting him with his own wedge. 'Don't mess me about, Ed. Where the bloody hell's that last six million?'

'I don't know what you're on about, old son.' He set the ball and got ready to drive off.

'Six million.' Naisby kicked the ball aside.

'Don't get emotional, Rollo.'

'We can talk about the excess deductions from that first tranche later. Six million.'

Maxell shook his head and looked towards the clubhouse.

'Not a cent of that six million's shown up in my companies.'

'None of it's shown up here either.' Maxell's lower jaw quivered. 'Some computer cock-up somewhere, no doubt.'

'Just see that six million gets transferred today.' Naisby was full of menace.

'Or what?' He leaned on his driver, all arrogance. 'You better be careful, Rollo. I'm not saying there's anything bent about this investment game of yours, but I'm having to keep people off your back.'

'Six million,' Naisby said, jabbing a finger under Maxell's face. 'Today.'

'Ever heard of a chap called Wasserman?'

Naisby had turned to go. He wheeled.

'Or Gilliam? Special Crimes Squad, Scotland Yard?'

His heart in his mouth, Naisby put on a show of composure. 'Never heard of either.'

'You will, I reckon.' Maxell stooped to tee up his ball. 'Oh, and there's this American woman. Sarne? Edwina Sarne?'

'Six million dollars. Today.' It was an order. Naisby went back over a fairway, vivid green and giving off its own humid perfume after a thunderstorm. He skirted the green nearest the clubhouse where a thick-set golfer with a blond beard was practising his putting.

Wasserman straightened up and watched Naisby leap a puddle and get into the Honda. He had no way of seeing the Nikon held from a side window of a grey station wagon parked deep in the shadows of a giant casuarina.

Gilliam took another shot of Naisby, the twenty-third person Maxell had met away from his office in the last few days. For good measure he knocked off two shots of the man with the putter.

He was wondering if Hobart would be good enough to put names to the mugshots before he sent prints to the Yard for Sir Rupert Mallory to check. He had his doubts. Hobart would very likely plead the Confidentiality Act.

Even under the casuarina the station wagon was like a cooker. At least it was big enough to let him spread his bulk. It crossed his mind to break the surveillance and go for a swim.

Then he saw that Maxell was abandoning his round and wheeling his trolley back to the clubhouse.

He followed Maxell's Jaguar down West Bay Road into George Town. Maxell pulled into his slot in the private car park of the Drake Building, and went inside.

Surveillance without back-up was hell. Gilliam again toyed with the idea of calling on Hobart.

Carrodus was pleased with Coke Rogers.

As they came out of the elevator on the top floor of the Drake Building he said, 'This could be the break I need, Coke.' Edwina Sarne had been a mite incautious, having booked a trip in the mini-sub around the coral of the North Wall for herself and Hal. Marlon had chosen to go muscle-building in the gym in George Town. Coke, knowing this, had bugged Mrs Sarne's room. In her turn she'd done nothing about debugging, which surprised and delighted Carrodus. On her return from the deep dive she'd called Maxell to fix an appointment for her US attorney, Mr R. S. Bryant, Jr. And Carrodus knew her US attorney was Jimmy Simon. He couldn't wait to have a look at Mr R. S. Bryant, Jr.

They reached the security room. Carrodus knocked quietly. As there was no response he tried the door. It was locked. 'Go find Gladstone,' he told Coke. 'Another ten minutes, we could miss our guy.'

He paced the corridor, fretting over the time.

It was very near to the time of Mr R. S. Bryant's appointment with Maxell when Coke hustled Gladstone Hooley round from the stair well. Gladstone was jumpy as one of the ching-ching birds Carrodus had watched in the sea-grape trees. He wrung his brown hands. 'I did say not to come here again!' he whispered. 'We did agree!'

'Sure,' Carrodus said. 'We're sorry, Mr Hooley. But picking up a tape wouldn't work this time. We want to see this guy now. Maybe we'll want to follow him out when he leaves.'

Gladstone Hooley ran thin fingers over his polished brown skull. 'One moment,' he said, unlocking the door and opening it only just far enough to let himself through. Carrodus caught a split-second glimpse of a bearded man he'd seen before – on the security monitor and in the nightspot. He was clearly watching a tape playback. He came out a few moments later with a brief nod for Carrodus and Coke. In his left hand was an unusually bulky copy of the *Wall Street Journal*. Carrodus had a hunch it was wrapped around security tapes.

Gladstone Hooley came to the door now and beckoned them in, frowning. 'One of my security staff,' he shrugged without conviction and with a nod towards the departing Wasserman.

All five screens were alive, covering the lobby and the floors above, but it was plain that the visitor had been running a playback on one of the channels.

There was still another five minutes before Bryant's appointment.

Carrodus hardly blinked as he scanned the lobby and the second-floor screens. Only one arrival fitted his mental image of Bryant. The man got out at the third and turned right to be met by a vibrant black woman who kissed him on both cheeks. Another three minutes went by.

'My dough's on this guy,' Carrodus said, watching a lean, grey-suited man enter to the desk. 'Get down there, Coke.'

As Coke sprinted down to the second floor, Carrodus peered at the lobby screen in case the face was familiar. The man was directed to the elevators, and then Carrodus saw something that *did* make him blink. Coming through those automatic glass doors was another man whose face he knew *very* well. He'd have recognized that lined yet boyish face and leathery complexion anywhere. The Bureau had once been much concerned about his links with the mysterious appearance in unfriendly Middle East hands of US ground-to-air missiles and artillery shells. General Edison Gibb had played it smart, coming out of the inquiry smelling like Mr Pure.

The files on him were still 'active'.

To Carrodus, up there watching Gibb in close-up on the lobby screen, it was like winning at the high-stakes tables in Vegas. Gibb was clearly being told to wait. He was soon scanning that wall of company names as if it were a war memorial. Whatever his business in the Cayman Islands, it couldn't have had much to do with the Pentagon. Unless Cuba had designs on its British colonial neighbour.

The second-floor screen showed the man who could be Bryant leave the elevator and turn left. Coke emerged from the right and followed him through the door.

Gibb wandered along that roll of names, hands clasped behind his straight back, looking stern.

Coke knocked four times and Carrodus let him in. 'The guy did go into Maxell's office. He's Bryant okay. I heard Maxell's secretary ask him through.' It disappointed him that Carrodus was more interested in the lobby screen.

'Can you work out what a Pentagon general's doing here?' Carrodus's pale face was animated.

'Diving?' Coke said blandly.

'My ass!' Carrodus said.

Exactly twelve seconds after Bryant came back onto the second floor landing, Gibb was called by the lobby receptionist to take the elevator. He got out at the second floor, by which time Coke was there to check it was Maxell he was visiting. And when he left the Drake Building, Carrodus followed his taxi to one of the biggest hotels on Seven Mile Beach, saw him collect his room key and enter a beach-facing ground floor room.

Using a pay phone in the hotel lobby not a dozen yards from the desk, Carrodus asked if General Edison Gibb was a guest. 'No sir,' came the crisp reply. 'We have no one of that name staying here.'

It came as no shock that the general was plainly not there on US Army business.

The photographs were burning a hole in his inside pocket as Gilliam held up his glass and toasted Mary yet again.

It was a perfect Caribbean night. Three sides of the restaurant were open to the sea and sky under the thatched roof. The conch soup and lobster had gone down well. And even before they had started on the wine Gilliam had warmed up with three scotches.

'And thanks for a lovely dinner.' Mary Hobart raised her glass, her eyes dancing with amusement. She knew from Hobe about Gilliam's problem, though he hadn't gone into detail. And she'd seen a few Yard and FBI men come and go, usually none the wiser except about coral and turtles. Poor Geordie, she thought. But what she said was, 'Enjoy your trip while it lasts.' Versed in the ways of the Yard she knew there would be envy of Geordie Gilliam back in London.

Gilliam winked at her and asked Hobart, 'Does anything *ever* happen here, Hobe? If there's no crime why the sinecures? Why all the cops?'

'Let me tell you,' Hobart smiled. 'We had one murder here last year. And a hundred per cent clear-up rate for murder.'

'You've won me over, Hobe.' He was swirling wine round his glass, wondering whether he could take any more. 'I'll apply for a job here.'

'Mind you, we're pretty hot on misuse of drugs.' Hobart gazed out at the becalmed Caribbean. 'Out there are boats carrying the filth from Colombia to Florida. We manage to knock a few off, not to mention the odd villain in this paradise who nips out to re-fuel the bastards.'

'I'd not mind doing a job like that,' Gilliam said haltingly.

'And here on the island we trample on the ganja and cocaine market. Hundred per cent clear-up rate.'

Mary smiled. Hobe did like to boast to visiting cops.

'How about commercial crime?' Gilliam pulled a face.

'The banks and trust companies have to behave.'

Gilliam leaned back with his hands behind his head. 'Hundred per cent clear-up rate, Hobe? Or nil per cent?'

They were in a corner of the thatched area. The nearest table was crowded with raucous young Americans there for the reef diving. 'I know how you feel, Geordie.' Hobe's face was intent in the candlelight. 'I tell you this, though. You can walk the whole length of Seven Mile Beach out there tonight – or go by West Bay Road – and you'll be safe. You'll not get mugged.'

'Anyone who tried to mug him would be asking for it!' Mary said, taking in Gilliam's six-foot-four frame. She felt for Geordie, chasing a commerce-based crime on Cayman. May as well seek a specific branch of elkhorn coral down the North Wall. And she sensed that Geordie's dinner treat wasn't just social. Excusing herself, she started towards the ladies' room.

Hobart and Gilliam stood up until she'd gone.

'There's no way I can help you, Geordie,' Hobart said. 'Much as I'd like to.' He took a small sip of white wine.

Gilliam felt in his pocket. The sea and sky out there were wobbling a bit, like the storm lamps with their candle flames. He brought out the paper wallet from the photo shop near the harbour with the pictures of Ed Maxell's encounters outside the office. In turning to get at the wallet, he saw a late diner taking his place at a table near the door to the kitchen. He screwed up his eyes. The image was fuzzy. He wished to God he'd not drunk so much. 'Who's that, Hobe?'

Hobart followed his glance, and shrugged.

His vision blurred, Gilliam leaned out of his chair to gain a yard in the sight test. The chair almost toppled. And the newcomer was still a blur. 'I'm afraid I'm slightly pissed, Hobe. Must be the climate.'

'I'd noticed.' Hobart's rock face was tolerant.

'You see the bloke I mean?'

Hobart nodded.

'You've not been out of the UK all that long, mate.'

Hobart moved his chair for a better look. 'I see what you mean'.

The newcomer was Lord Justice Kenright, scourge of City cheats in the courts.

Gilliam took a long drink of Perrier water, hoping it would dilute his vision problem. Hobart was wondering why he'd not been tipped off by Special Branch about the presence on the island of one of HMG's front-line judges.

The wallet of photographs lay on the table, forgotten by Gilliam in his excitement.

'This for me?' Hobart asked.

'Oh yes.' Gilliam screwed up his face, striving to regain clear vision. He saw Mary – greying and with a confident stride – coming through the tables. 'A few mugshots. I'd not mind knowing if you can put names to them.'

Gilliam hailed the waiter and mimed a writing sign.

'Let me settle this, Geordie,' Hobart offered.

'Not bloody likely!'

Mary laughed.

And Hobart no less than Gilliam was curious about Lord Justice Kenright's presence.

Maybe he was an ageing scuba diver.

Maxell's office was a shambles.

Hobart took in the strewn desk drawers, the toppled filing cabinets, the smashed word-processor and telex machine, and the mess of letters and documents littering the thick pile carpet. 'So where *is* Mr Maxell?'

'I told your policeman,' Carrie said, biting her lip. 'He's away.'

'Away where?' If he was out illegally fishing for conch or turtle, serve him right.

'He was at his other house on Cayman Brac. He's on his way now.'

Cayman Brac was some ninety miles away. It would take Maxell an hour or so to get back, and Carrie would be tight as a conch shell about his affairs. Hobart watched Chief Inspector Flack stepping carefully among the exhibits as Jepson took fingerprints from the violated wallsafe, and two young black detectives collected exhibits in the wake of Flack. He turned to the troubled Hooley. 'What went wrong with your TV security, Gladstone?'

Hooley led him back into the corridor and out to the landing. He pointed up at the camera point. The camera was shrouded with a diver's hood. 'Neil,' Hobart called, and Flack came out. 'Don't let 'em forget this.' He drew Flack's attention to the hood, then turned to Hooley. 'They had to put the damn thing on, didn't they? So you should have recorded a bit of 'em?'

'I might.' Hooley was so agitated he pressed the elevator's down button in error.

'And you might have something on the lobby tape?'

Hooley shook his head. 'There's no sign they came in through the lobby.'

'They had to get out.'

'They forced the side door to the car park. I've been down there.'

'I know,' Hobart said wearily, as the elevator came. 'You don't have a camera on that door?'

Hooley shook his head, disconsolate.

'Jesus!' Hobart's eye was caught by an incident outside Maxell's office. A young uniformed cop was telling a slightly-built man in a windcheater that he couldn't enter.

'What's going on, constable?' Naisby asked.

'I can't talk about it, sir.'

Full marks to the young cop, Hobart thought. They were learning. One day they'd be able to run their own police force. He saw the caller go back along the corridor, and wondered why he'd not come up in the elevator or by the stairs wrapped around it.

Up on the top floor Hooley let Hobart into the security room. Only the second-floor monitor had a blank screen. Hooley moved two empty glasses from the top of the lobby monitor. Both had traces of orange on their insides.

Hobart watched the live images for a minute. It was 8.30 am and office workers were arriving in numbers. 'How long do your tapes run, Gladstone?'

'Three hours.'

'So who changes 'em?'

'They're on automatic, Chief Superintendent.'

'How long's this one been on?' He indicated the second-floor VTR.

Hooley bent down to check. 'Two hours five minutes.'

'So if these villains show anywhere it'll be on the tape before this? Forty-five minutes before it runs out?'

Hooley scratched his shiny head.

'The break-in was at twenty to six.' It was a hunch. This was the time on the shattered face of an office clock among the exhibits.

Hooley changed the tapes, wound the replacement back beyond the time Hobart had given, and set it on play. There was a brief sequence – no more than ten seconds of a heavily-built diver in clinging wetsuit and hood as he stood on a chair and planted the hood over the camera. In the background for no more than half the time another diver nipped through the door towards Maxell's office.

'Run it again.'

Only after Hooley had run it five times did Hobart get bored. 'You keep a library of these things, Gladstone?'

Hooley was still jumpy. He shook his head. 'I have two sets only. Each day's recording must be wiped the next morning.'

Hobart's eyebrows shot up.

'Confidentiality.' It was the first time he had come near to smiling.

Hobart glanced at the two glasses. 'Who shares your drinking sessions up here, then?'

Flustered, Hooley grabbed the glasses between his fingers and put them under Hobart's nose. 'No alcohol, Chief Superintendent. Fruit juice only.'

'Come on, Gladstone. I was only kidding.'

As he made for the stairwell, Hobart saw Hooley carrying the glasses into the lavatory. Jepson's fingerprinting seemed to have got to him. Hobart gave a quiet laugh.

Nobody in the building had seen or heard anything of the intruders, though it looked as if they'd gone in before the offices closed the night before.

Back in Maxell's office, Hobart found Maxell staring at the havoc, speechless, drained of colour. His hand shook so much he spilt the coffee brought from another office by Carrie.

'Any ideas, Mr Maxell?' Hobart asked.

It seemed Maxell hadn't heard, but his head was shaking. He took in the open wallsafe, the filing cabinets, then the array of exhibits in their plastic bags. Burglary on Grand Cayman was in the same league as murder when a bank or licensed trust was the victim. He began to sort through the bags. 'Any computer discs in here?'

'No,' Hobart said. 'We'll leave you to decide how important *they* are.'

'They've gone,' Maxell murmured.

'Your entire records, sir?'

Maxell shook his head. 'I've got copies lodged in the bank, thank God.'

Motioning that he wanted a private word, Hobart led the way out past the beavering detectives. 'When I asked if you have any ideas, Mr Maxell, I meant do you know who might have done this?'

'No.' He was tight-lipped.

'You *are* sure about this?'

Maxell nodded. His eyes were like jumping beans.

'Only I had a reference yesterday from the Attorney-General's office about a complaint from you.'

Maxell put a hand behind his head as if he had a stiff neck. He was on a tightrope with a long way to fall, having called the Attorney's office in a flash of anger over Wasserman's ultimatum. It was in Wasserman's interest, and his bank's, to say nothing about the whole affair, just as it was in his own. 'I'm sure it's quite unrelated, Chief Superintendent.'

'But this bloke Wasserman – Swiss, isn't he? – was nosing into business covered by the Confidentiality Act? Wasn't he? Didn't you report he was on a fishing trip? Some tax hunt?'

'I probably exaggerated.'

'You were saying he should be declared persona non grata and kicked off the island?'

'I can think of several in that category. Internal Revenue Service and Inland Revenue moles.'

Hobart knew he was covering up. He knew in his bones that Wasserman wasn't fishing for tax evaders at all.

And two could play the disinformation game.

'All clear, sir. He's just gone into the Drake Building.'

Hobart took the call in the hotel manager's office. Wasserman had been lured by a bogus call put in by a woman detective posing as Maxell's secretary. The manager collected the duplicate key to Wasserman's room and let Hobart enter.

Room 9a was spotless with the hallmark of a fastidious man. Hobart first checked the pockets of the three suits and cotton jacket, creaselessly hung in the wardrobe. He found the leather-banded lightweight travelling case unlocked, rummaged and found nothing of interest. The in-flight bag was empty. He took the black hide briefcase from the wardrobe, expecting to find the two combination locks in place. It was unsecured. Inside were copies of a bankers' magazine, two weighty reports from the *Economist* Intelligence Unit on Third World debt and US trade, a Cayman Islands handbook on which someone had used a vivid yellow textmarker, and a diary. Not a single entry had been written into it.

There was no sign of what Hobart was after – a passport and computer discs.

He put everything back and rejoined the manager outside. 'The hotel safe,' Hobart said. 'Has he anything there?'

Back in reception the manager unlocked a drawer, checked the safe deposit book, nodded, and invited Hobart back into his office. He tickled the combination lock of the big safe and brought out a man's leather handbag with a wrist strap. Hobart unzipped it. Inside was Wasserman's passport and two wads of dollars – US and Cayman – but no discs. Two other objects took up the space – videotapes. In pencil on the labels was written 'am 10/2' and 'pm 10/2'. It was now May 12. The tapes were VHS. Hobart held one up. 'Can you replay a bit of this for me?'

The manager wasn't sure how to work the VTR, but Hobart shook his head firmly when the manager wanted to bring in a hotel technician. The manager wasn't the only one who was jumpy. Hobart had reckoned it would take half an hour for Wasserman to get back, and he wasn't certain that the young cop looking after the

George Town end would have the gumption to have Wasserman stopped for some traffic violation should he start back early.

Presently the manager got the VTR working. And Hobart was glad he'd taken the risk of staying on. The playback showed the lobby and second-floor elevator area of the Drake Building with people coming and going. The tape had clearly been edited.

'That's fine,' Hobart said.

The manager was relieved. He ran back the tape as Hobart scrutinised the passport. Wasserman was a Swiss national of forty-six, close on six feet tall, and a banker, which covered a multitude of roles. He was well-travelled. There were date stamps both for the US and the Soviet Union.

'I'm grateful, Leonard,' Hobart said as he left for George Town. It was fairly likely he would pass Wasserman coming back on the other side of West Bay Road.

Half an hour later he was up in Gladstone Hooley's security room in the Drake Building. And Gladstone sensed he was on the griddle. All five monitors were showing good images now.

'Just remind me, Gladstone,' Hobart said, settling back in the only chair and feeling the loose spring cutting into his backside. 'You wipe these tapes every day?'

'Right.' He was looking away.

'But some get away?'

'I'm sorry, Mr Hobart?'

'Some get away?'

'I don't know what you're saying.'

'You been doing favours, Gladstone?'

Hooley went on one knee to adjust the third-floor monitor. His hand was over-busy on the controls.

'Where did you learn to edit this stuff?'

'Can I get you a drink, Mr Hobart?'

'If you need one, Gladstone, you go get one.'

'No, I don't need one.'

'Mr Wasserman. Staying up on Seven Mile Beach?'

'Yes?'

'He's been nipping up here and nicking your videos.' Hobart gazed at the monitors. He felt sorry for Hooley and didn't want it to show.

The silence lasted so long that more than ten people came into shot, entering the lobby singly.

'Okay, Mr Hobart. I've been helping him. He's looking into drugs-related money.'

'He's Swiss, for Christ's sake, Gladstone! They got enough clients in that game to keep 'em busy till Kingdom Come!' He waited, not looking at Hooley.

And Hooley began to tremble.

'I'll tell you this for free, Gladstone.' Hobart turned his cool eyes on Hooley now. 'If you don't come clean about this you'll be doing more time in a hot cell than you dreamed of in your wildest nightmares.'

'Okay.' He was still fine-tuning the sets, obsessively. 'I've been giving Wasserman edited tapes.'

'For money?'

Hooley nodded. He was preoccupied with the picture quality of the monitors.

'This the first time, Gladstone? The only one?'

'Yes.'

'You sure?' He held off a moment. 'How much do you pull in this job, Gladstone? I mean your official salary.'

Hooley told him.

Hobart tut-tutted. 'That's the trouble with these multimillion-dollar money-boys. They don't spread it around enough.' He caught Hooley's eye. 'What they're paying you won't buy conch stew for that growing family of yours.' It was an awful whopper, but it did the trick.

'I did it once before.' Hooley pressed his fingers into his eyes.

'Is that all?'

'No.'

Hobart leaned back, waiting.

'I've been supplying tapes to an American.'

'What, lately?'

Hooley nodded. 'Name of Grant.'

'Don't stop,' Hobart said. 'Not for the present.'

He didn't take the elevator. He went down the stairs, two at a time.

All was quiet on the second floor now. He knocked on the office door of the Maxell Group. Carrie opened it.

'I hope you're well over the shock,' Hobart smiled, scratching the nape of his neck.

'Thank you,' Carrie said.

Hobart could hear the telex back in business.

Carrodus watched General Edison Gibb and two lean young Americans as they got ready to take out a small dive boat with an outboard engine. The young men were pale, and the taller one had a bad sunburn on the shoulders. Each carried a wetsuit – one scarlet, the other pale blue. Their haircuts were close. Carrodus thought they might be soldiers.

'Mr Grant?'

The voice was close, but Carrodus didn't react instantly.

'Why, sure?' he said, turning to face a square-set Englishman in a khaki bush jacket.

'Chief Superintendent Hobart, Royal Cayman Islands Police.' Hobart held out an ID card from his left breast pocket. 'If you've a minute or two, sir?'

'Sure, sure.' Carrodus came to his feet. Twice in the past twenty-four hours he'd had the feeling of being watched. Coke Rogers had dismissed the notion.

'I'll get you another.' Hobart gestured towards Carrodus's glass.

'My call here,' Carrodus said.

Hobart waved away the offer. 'I'm looking into a break-in at a trust company's offices in town,' he said. 'The Maxell Group.'

Carrodus didn't even blink.

'If you've some evidence of identity, sir?'

'I don't have my passport,' Carrodus said, producing a small wallet from his back pocket. 'We Yanks don't need 'em here.'

'Right.'

'Strange, that,' Carrodus grinned. 'When the Brits who run the place have to show 'em.'

'Indeed.' Hobart's secret smile spoke volumes. He glanced at the US driving licence and American Express card. Both showed that Carrodus was Walter J. Grant, Jr.

'You here on business or pleasure, sir?'

'Business,' Carrodus said, and saw Hobart was studying the departure of General Gibb and his two friends. 'I'm with the Mezmar Corporation. We have an office on the island.'

And Coke Rogers was the local representative, Hobart thought. Coke had once been named in a confidential memo as a possible IRS 'fisherman'. Handing back the licence and Amex card, Hobart squeezed his moustache and said, 'You don't know about the Maxell Group?'

Carrodus shrugged. The plump cop knew more than he was letting on, and was probably taking him for an IRS agent. It was unlikely he would see any FBI link. The Bureau would normally make an overt approach and send an agent from Mexico, who would be known by Hobart.

'I wonder if you'd mind letting us have your fingerprints, sir?' In this climate kid gloves could hardly be worn, but they were needed when you were dealing with US agents. And he would lay a hundred to one that Grant was from the IRS.

'It's a pleasure, sir.'

'Whenever you're ready, Mr Grant.' Hobart pointed out a black Caymanian in a precisely-ironed safari suit seated in the shade of the beach bar eating cashew nuts. 'He'll drive you down. And back.' He shot a look at the dive boat. It was about a hundred yards out – and stationary. And the older American was talking earnestly to the others. It reminded him of that old classic painting *The Boyhood of Raleigh*.

Carrodus was taking it all in, too.

Hobart went to the hotel car park and the two unmarked police Toyotas. 'Cayman Kai,' he told the driver. It was on the other side of North Bay which meant a trip halfway round the island past Rum Point.

As they drove out past the kitchens the smell of conch chowder wafted in through the open roof. It made Hobart feel hungry.

Wasserman had lunched well with the realty maestro Laycock when Hobart spotted them in the spread of coiffured lawns around the new house fronting the unspoilt white sands. Or so it seemed, as Wasserman patted his ample paunch. In the twenty-four hours Hobart had allowed for surveillance before making any approach, Wasserman had twice met Laycock – first in his Georgetown office, then at the golf club, where a young detective had overheard them making this lunch date. The detective had also caught snatches of talk indicating that Wasserman was in the market for offices for his bank and two houses for the staff. This only built up Hobart's hunch that Wasserman was behind the break-in. The property hunt would make a good alibi for what was turning out to be a long stay on the island.

He let Wasserman drive out from the Laycock spread before overtaking and stopping him.

'Mr Wasserman?'

Wasserman's face was taut with mistrust, even after seeing Hobart's ID card.

'I'm looking into a burglary at the offices of The Maxell Group.'

'Why me?' Wasserman's Gallic shrug said.

'You know the company?'

'I'm aware of it.' Wasserman tugged at his beard. 'I thought you were as strict about confidentiality here as we are in Switzerland.'

'More so, I reckon.' There was some feeling in Hobart's voice. Villains got away with too much in every tax haven. He now asked if Wasserman would let them take his fingerprints.

And Wasserman bridled. 'Sounds highly illiberal,' he snapped.

'It's a polite request, sir, no more.' He didn't want the Governor and Executive Council on his back. He wasn't the Governor's favourite cop, as Henry Cecil Davies had made all too plain at the last Governor's Residence garden party. Davis had turned more scarlet than his prized hibiscus over Hobart's contempt for some of the filthy-rich young bankers and attorneys who were gracing the lawns. 'It's time you realized, Hobart, this island has to survive in a harsh world.'

And His Excellency hadn't even been wearing his white plumed hat at the time.

Hobart was too close to an honourable retirement to get in HE's hair again.

Wasserman thought better of tangling with Hobart. He followed the Toyota back to police HQ. Jepson took his prints.

In his office, Hobart tidied up the crime file – thefts, disorderly conduct, carrying an offensive weapon, possession of ganja and cocaine, the usual pattern, plus the tricky one involving an eminent citizen who'd been caught red-handed taking black coral and turtle's eggs from the environment zone.

He left at five o'clock to meet Gilliam, who had set one up for him at the open-air bar. They went down to a pair of beach loungers by the water's edge.

'Did you have to carry it that far, mate?' Hobart put on his avuncular tone.

'Eh?'

'Busting that office.'

Again Gilliam was genuinely nonplussed.

'Maxell's.'

'Don't be daft, Hobe.'

'It was done over. Early hours yesterday.'

Gilliam flushed. 'Any ideas?'

'Except you were in and out a couple of times. Up on that second floor besides. I've seen you on the tapes.'

It brought only a shrug from Gilliam. 'Those mugshots I let you have could be more useful to you than me, then?'

Hobart had noted Wasserman on one of the golf club pictures. 'They could be.' They certainly showed some of Maxell's contacts who never met him at the office. 'You had any feedback from the Yard about 'em?'

'Give 'em time, Hobe.'

It was another ten minutes, when they were on their second light ales, before Hobart came to the point.

'Blackmail, you said? Who was doing it to who?'

'There's no way I can discuss it. You know who sent me here, Hobe?'

'Don't tell me the Prime Minister?'

'The Commissioner himself.'

'It *must* be hot.'

'Not just hot. Bloody nuclear!'

'And Maxell's been doing the blackmailing?'

'I didn't say that.'

Hobart watched two lizards frolicking in the sand. 'Have you noticed, Geordie? The little buggers don't run away from you. They just sit bolt upright with their tails curled.'

'I'm feeding a pair,' Gilliam chuckled. 'Every morning at breakfast. Bet you never knew they're nuts on white of egg?'

'Really?' Hobart was being flattering. He knew they also fancied bacon. 'Tell you what, Geordie. We've got miles of videotape down at the nick. Showing everybody who enters the Drake Building and heads for Maxell's office.'

'Not everybody, Hobe.'

'Mmmmm?'

'You can get out on another floor, and continue up or down by the emergency stairs. I tried it and it works.'

Hobart agreed. 'Gladstone's not the world's number one security artiste.'

'Who?'

'He's the reason the Drake Building's not Fort Knox.' He put on a secret smile. 'And you missed a trick or two there, Geordie.'

'So where are you leading?'

'I'm offering you a private screening. Talk about Royal premieres, mate! I mean your blackmailer could be my Watergate artiste.' He hated to admit it, even to himself, but it meant a lot to get a clear-up on this burglary. It reeked of the armpit perfume of greedy young smoothies, and in the crime file just now he'd seen none of them. But he had noted a charge of shoplifting – goods to the value of $9 CI.

'Great!' Gilliam would have bought him champagne.

'Just the one proviso, Geordie. You find your man, and he's also mine, you cough up, right?' The face was as hard as the harbour wall now. 'And to hell with the heat!'

Gilliam offered to shake hands.

'Don't be stupid, Geordie. We know each other better than that Freemasons' stuff.'

Gilliam laughed.

A third lizard had joined the frolics in the sand. 'Now for trouble!' Hobart smiled.

Gilliam was driving with extra care.

It was already dark and West Bay Road was under the lash of a rainstorm. The wipers of his hired Chevrolet couldn't cope with the splash.

'More water here than I saw in my submersible experience down among the coral yesterday.' Lord Justice Kenright gave a throaty laugh. 'I should take your time, dear boy.'

Gilliam *was* taking his time. The last thing he wanted was to reach the fish restaurant early. He cut his speed until they were crawling. He was so near to a coup, he couldn't bear the idea of a skid. He had eyestrain from all those hours cooped up in the tiny viewing room at police HQ. All those faces in the lobby and on the second-floor landing of the Drake Building had taken their toll. What had really got his dander up was the appearance of Kenright. And on one of the reruns he'd spotted two of the men in his golf club shot – confirmed by Hobart as Wasserman, the putter, and a Brit called Naisby.

Hunch was telling him that Kenright and Sir Rupert Mallory might be in the same boat. The Yard had still not come back about his mugshots.

He saw to it that they reached the restaurant twenty minutes after the time for which Naisby had booked his table. The place was small, and he counted fourteen tables. He puffed his cheeks in relief. Naisby was finishing his conch soup. And there was a lucky break. The head waiter showed him and Kenright to a table which gave them a good view of Naisby. Gilliam saw to it that Kenright had the chair which gave him the better eyeline – almost head-on.

The first sighting was at their soup stage, the next when Naisby was wiping his mouth after the lobster, and the last when Kenright held up his wine glass as if checking for colour and set his judicial gaze on Naisby instead.

Gilliam could have sworn they knew each other.

But they disclosed nothing. Not even a blink between them.

Carrodus began to button out Liz's Washington number. It would be around 7 am there, an hour before her usual time for leaving for the Voice of America offices. Having told Olsen by coded telex of Hobart's interest and Bryant's arrival, he'd added, 'The game's up. Subject of surveillance.' His bags were half-packed, and he wanted to let Liz know he could be back in the States in less than twenty-four hours, with the chance of making DC by the weekend.

It was his third try to call her. The line had been busy twelve hours before, and he'd got no reply around midnight. She was in demand socially.

The call rang out several times, then he heard the knock and Coke Rogers's voice. He killed the call.

'Great morning!' Coke raved. 'You saw that daybreak come up?' He took in the closed curtains and blinds. 'Pity. You really missed something.' He handed Carrodus a coded telex. Olsen's reply dwelt on R. S. Bryant. 'A lawyer with underworld ties. Skilled dirty tricks specialist. Worth a close look.' And Olsen was clearly pleased by the bonus of having General Gibb turn up. 'Hang on in,' the message ran. 'Maybe we can put pressure on this end.'

'Shit!' He burned the message in the ashtray. He'd built up some expectation of being with Liz in Washington by the weekend.

'Anything I can do?' Coke asked.

Coke didn't have the status to know what was going on. 'They tailed you here just now?'

'Sure,' Coke said, opening the curtains. He was used to it. 'They get to yawning after a while.'

'Go do a bit of tailing yourself, eh?'

'Sarne, Gibb or Bryant?'

'Sarne's gone back,' Carrodus said. 'She was on last night's flight to Miami.'

Coke put on a wry look.

'Never mind. You know now.' Carrodus was picking up the phone. 'Make it Bryant. See you around midday. Same place as yesterday. The general and his straight-backed playmates. They've hired that dive boat again.' He began to ring Liz's number. He heard the door close as Coke left. The call was ringing out.

There was a knock on the door.

He unlocked it and tugged it open. 'Coke, for Jesus' sake!' And then he saw Coke in the background, looking apprehensive.

'I know it's a shade early, Mr Grant,' Hobart smiled. 'May I come in?'

Carrodus let him through.

'What I really wanted to say, Mr Grant, is that we found none of your prints in Maxell's office.'

'Okay – well, you wouldn't.'

'But we did find some that are yours all right.' He paused and put on an air of sadness, as if disappointed in an ally. 'In the security room. You know, the one on the top floor. Can you explain, sir?'

Carrodus went to the phone. The call was still ringing. He hung up, turned to Hobart and spread out his hands in bafflement. 'I wish I could help.'

'You must have had some reason to be in the security room of the Drake Building.'

Carrodus saw that Hobart hadn't mentioned Gladstone Hooley, but there was time yet. 'You sure your fingerprint guys are up to it?'

Hobart squeezed the end of his nose. Jepson was one of the world's best. 'You're not from the Internal Revenue Service?'

'Hell, no.' If only he could get rid of Hobart he might still catch Liz before she set off. But Hobart showed no sign of letting him off the hook.

And instinct told him there would still be no reply because Liz wasn't home.

Hurt, he met Hobart's gaze full on, set on bluffing it out. He poured a heavy rum-and-Coke, mostly rum, Hobart noticed.

'Gilliam speaking, sir.'

He'd expected a call from the Yard but not from the Commissioner himself.

'Your photographs.'

'Yes sir?'

'Our friend has picked out the chap. No doubts whatsoever. He's in shots seventeen and twenty. The golf course stuff. Not the golfers, you understand?'

'Excellent, sir.'

'Oh, and Gilliam. Do remember the sensitive nature of this one, won't you? I can only repeat my advice to you before you set out.'

'Understood, sir.' He hung up and thumped his right fist into his left palm. Out there it was in the nineties with the white sands glazed under the tropical sun, but it seemed like Christmas. He brought out his set of photographs, knowing from memory the face he would come up with. Shots seventeen and twenty starred the lithe Englishman – medium height, late thirties, dark curly hair and eyes, one who'd never stand out in a crowd. Peering at them now, he made out the firm jawline and the sharp, intelligent gaze. Naisby may have meant nothing to Lord Justice Kenright, but Sir Rupert Mallory had no doubts.

Gilliam thought long and hard about calling Hobart. His man was Naisby. He'd need a warrant, which he sensed wouldn't be readily supplied in London, and he'd need evidence – commercial evidence – from the Maxell Group and its bank on Cayman. And that was like getting into Pandora's box.

He drove over to the hotel down Seven Mile Beach where Naisby was staying. Five tourists were on early beers and cocktails at the palm-thatched bar. Beachboys were chatting up American girls and plying them with canned beer. Sun-oiled bodies baked on loungers. But there was no Naisby. Two small catamarans were out in full sail, and three windsurfers. Gilliam would need binoculars to see those faces. And then he saw the jet-skier, a speck taking shape as a man as the powered water-bike headed in from the calm sea. It was a hot-rod show. The jet-skier did a fast turn like some waterborne version of a speedway rider, engine soaring.

Gilliam would have laid odds on the jet-skier being Naisby. But even when he pulled off another sharp turn much closer to the beach, the skier was lost in speed and spray. Another fast run level with the water's edge, and the sharpest turn yet. The engine screamed. The jet bike hit three ridges of water, bounced, and went on. It was the fourth that told. The rider came off in a spumy cascade as the bike squirmed. He swam to the bike, and soon had it going again. One more celebration run, and he came in, running the jet-bike up the sand and stepping off.

Gilliam applauded.

It *was* Naisby.

He came up the white sand to the shower, then stepped into the sandals he'd left on the concrete walkway. He was almost dry when he reached the hotel reception area. He waited patiently for two Americans who were checking in, then asked if his bill was ready.

The brown receptionist was all apology. 'I do believe they're still working on it, Mr Naisby.'

Naisby nodded, trying to hide his disdain. He found her interesting. 'I did ask for it an hour ago.'

'We'll send it over to your room if you like,' she said.

'No, I'll be back.'

He hadn't spotted Gilliam, deep in brochures about scuba diving and big-game fishing. The moment Naisby went out, Gilliam was on one of the pay phones.

'Chief Superintendent Hobart is out right now.' The policewoman's voice was sexy.

'You can get him over the radio?'

'Yes.'

'Tell him I need to meet him. At the airport.'

'Your name, sir?'

'Gilliam.' He didn't want to lose Naisby. If he was London-bound, all right. But he would have to go via Miami. And he could go damn nearly anywhere on earth via Miami.

'What's the panic?' Hobart asked when they met in the concourse of the airy Owen Roberts International. He was put out, having been taken away from watching Charles Wasserman in George Town.

And Gilliam told him that Naisby was the man he was after.

'On whose say-so?'

It was like one of those nasty dreams Gilliam had from time to time where he was trapped, getting nowhere. Hobart had him on the rack for a minute, then checked with Cayman Airways, came back and said. 'He *was* on this afternoon's flight to Miami. But he's cancelled. He's leaving tomorrow, same time.'

Hobart went to leave a message with Immigration that if a passenger called Naisby should show up, having changed his mind again, he should be delayed. He then called police HQ with an order that Naisby was to be traced urgently, kept under surveillance, but not detained. There was a whiff of high-level hot potatoes.

Twenty minutes later he went into Maxell's office to ask Maxell what he knew of Naisby.

'Naisby?' Maxell pouted.

'John Rollaston Naisby.'

Maxell shook his head and threw a sharp glance at the monitor which was showing New York Stock Exchange prices. He was very busy.

Hobart brought out the best of the golf club photographs. 'This lad you're with here?'

Taking the photograph as if it were tainted, Maxell said, 'Oh yes, I vaguely recall him. Came over and asked about setting up a company.' He ran the back of his hand down the folds of his chin. 'Never talk business during a serious round of golf, Mr Hobart.'

'He'd not have reason to do over your office?'

'Heavens! Why should he? I hardly know him.'

Hobart knew Maxell was lying.

Down on the street, his driver said, 'This guy you want traced, sir. He's in the jeweller's near the duty-free.' It was barely a hundred yards away.

Naisby was looking over the black coral display when Hobart came up close and showed his ID card. 'I'd like a quiet word about a break-in, sir?'

And Naisby shivered. He knew the face from that moment when he had passed the burgled office. He had his own ideas about the burglary, sure that it was a fix by Maxell to evade some commitments like those to Raleigh House Securities Inc. He'd tried to call Maxell eight times, but had kept his distance from the Drake Building in case of a set-up. He'd even put off his return to the UK for fear of raising suspicions. He replaced the necklace on the red display cushion.

On the way out Hobart gave him a formal caution, aware that in Naisby's case it might all have to become official. He'd not warned Wasserman or Carrodus. A leading Swiss banker and an IRS agent wouldn't wind up in the Grand Court. They'd be kicked off the island with as little fuss as possible.

'How well do you know Ed Maxell, Mr Naisby?'

'We've met.' Naisby was gritting his teeth. It was easier to seem laid-back when jet-skiing.

Hobart was no less cagey. Questions about trust business could set off alarm bells in this paradise. 'Any objection to letting us take your fingerprints? We're trying to eliminate people.'

Naisby shrugged. On his visits to Maxell he'd not even put his hands on the desk.

Back at police HQ, Hobart ran excerpts from the Drake Building videotapes. Edited down to those visitors who had turned left out of the second floor elevators they had an attached list of names, where these were known, and times. Naisby showed up three times. Jepson came in, having taken Naisby's prints and run them against those collected at the scene of crime.

'Nothing?' Hobart asked.

'Not a sausage.'

Hobart strolled over to the Drake Building, and Maxell.

'Jesus, Mr Hobart, we've a business to run!' Maxell exploded. The cutting edge was blunted with a smile.

'This Naisby?'

Maxell took his eyes off the money-market monitor.

'Did you tell me he'd never been in here?'

And Maxell was struggling.

Hobart read his mind. Maxell wanted the break-in wiped off the record. He had God knows what rich men's fiddles to cover up. 'Only we've just been looking at his fingerprints.' The videotapes could stay out of it. Gladstone Hooley's moonlighting was not only criminal but political dynamite.

Maxell took what Hobart was saying to mean the prints had proved Naisby had been in the office, which was what Hobart intended. 'I seem to remember he did come here once.'

'Once?'

Maxell nodded, but he was twitching. He tried to make nothing of it. Then he said, 'Confidentiality, Mr Hobart. I don't need to remind you, of course.'

This confidentiality was a helluva thing, Hobart thought.

'Confidential?'

It was Gilliam, almost choking. If anything, Naisby was even cooler than he'd been on that aquatic hot rod.

'Sure,' Naisby said, scuffing the white sand with his foot. They were passing the dive shop, and it was going through his mind to hire a boat and a divemaster and go down deep off the North Wall before he set off for home tomorrow. 'Since when has a citizen's investments been a matter for the Serious Crimes Squad?'

'When they're made under threat, when they're extortion.'

'Dangerous talk, Superintendent. Don't you go saying things like that unless you want to wind up in the High Court with a libel writ.'

'I'll take my chance.' Gilliam was feeling the heat, though the evening was cooled by a fresh breeze from Cayman Brac. He could see what Hobart was up against. He'd asked to be present when Hobart quizzed Naisby, only to be turned down flat. Hobe was like a man juggling potatoes so hot they sizzled. 'If you want to have a dig, Geordie, you go ahead. But I don't know about it.' He'd paused.

'Though you will give me the results?' Hobart's interest was a break-in, Gilliam's blackmail. And Gilliam would never get near those trust and bank accounts without evidence that would convince the Caymans' Grand Court, not to mention the Governor and Executive Council. Hobart knew it, Gilliam knew it, and it was clear now that Naisby knew it.

Naisby still had his eye on the dive shop. 'I thought Scotland Yard was hard up. The Commissioner's always pleading poverty, and here you are living the life of Sherlock on a barmy hunt that'll lead nowhere.'

'Forget the Met!' Goaded, Gilliam choked back his fury. 'I'm talking about *your* budget.'

'None of your business.'

'You're on your way back to the UK tomorrow.' The threat was heavier than Gilliam wanted it to sound.

'If they let me out,' Naisby chuckled. 'Somebody's been shoplifting in Ed Maxell's office, and I'm one of the suspects.' His face lit up. 'I suppose it wasn't you, Superintendent? You certainly had the motive.'

Gilliam gave him an ironic handclap. 'Let's cut out the frolics, Rollo.'

Naisby smiled at the intimacy.

'You demanded two million dollars from Sir Rupert Mallory for keeping quiet about some skeleton you think you found in his cupboard.'

'You're rambling, Superintendent. Could be the sun.'

'I trust you're not going to destroy the old bloke?'

'Eh?'

'He'll never cough up.'

Just for an instant, Naisby was off-balance. Mallory had paid, unless Oscar had got it wrong. Or unless Seifert et Cie had settled for him.

Gilliam saw the weakness. 'You're not telling me you don't know Sir Rupert?'

'Even if I did it would be on a confidential basis. I'm an investment manager. And I'd not go nosing into the affairs of bank and trust clients too much.'

Naisby, bare-footed and wearing shorts, moved a couple of feet into water that reached half-way to his knees. Gilliam, in slacks and sandals, was a touch out of range.

'How about a quick one?' Gilliam indicated the verandah bar.

'Not thirsty, Superintendent.'

Gilliam offered his hand. 'I don't know why you don't treat us to another display on that jet-ski,' he said disarmingly.

They shook hands at arm's length.

'Oh, by the way.' Gilliam turned quickly. 'You don't happen to know Lord Justice Kenright, do you?'

The dart went home.

'No,' Naisby said.

And Gilliam knew he did.

He went back up the beach.

'This American chummy of yours, Hobe.' Fenwick was drained and frayed after his meeting over the road in the government offices. 'He's not an Internal Revenue agent. And he's not Walter J. Grant. His name's Carrodus and he's FBI.'

Fenwick laid his Police Commissioner's cap on Hobart's desk. He'd come straight from the meeting rather than drive over to his own office in the Tower. 'Pity we weren't able to pass this on to the Governor and the Attorney-General instead of having to be told.' He'd clearly been in the hot seat, and was set on warming up Hobart's chair.

'So where did this come from?' Hobart was in no mood for martyrdom, especially at the hands of bureaucrats and politicians. He had a number of crimes to clear up, and the Maxell hot-potato was taking up too much time.

'Washington,' Fenwick said grimly, pacing the room. 'The FBI have come clean, up to a point. They want him left to get on with his inquiries, and are pretty sniffy about the way we've been watching him.'

'Well, bad luck.' Hobart had FBI friends in Miami, but he didn't like the Bureau throwing its weight around on his patch. 'Besides, he could still be on a fishing trip for the IRS.'

'Apparently not. He's after two top Yanks – one for getting weapons to an unfriendly country, the other for illicit export of American hi-tech.'

Hobart snorted. 'Which means fishing into accounts here.'

'Right.' Fenwick had been on the griddle, for sure.

'I'm surprised they didn't come the old one and say he was on a drugs-abuse mission.'

'The next best thing nowadays,' Fenwick said. 'Other crimes. You can imagine the Attorney-General's line.'

'Oh sure. One of those fuzzy legal situations.' He put on the Attorney's languid and cagey style. 'But the Treaty says the crimes must be the sort that would be crimes here, old chap, old boy.'

Fenwick raised a smile. He had no more time for Robley-Ware than Hobart had. 'You must have had the Governor's office bugged, Hobe.'

'I'm pissed off with fuzzy legal edges.'

'Aren't we all?'

'So where do I stand with Walter J.? Carrodus, rather?'

'Tightrope time, Hobe.'

Hobart leaned back so far in his chair he almost fell over backwards. He closed his eyes. 'Jesus.'

'Nobody wants to upset the FBI.'

'After those other traumas I'm not surprised.'

'But there's a feeling that when some of the politicians hear of it, they'll want your chummy booted out.'

'*My* chummy?' He could see where the buck was stopping.

'Unfair world, Hobe. I know you'll cope.'

And Fenwick put his braided hat back on, and was gone.

Hobart sat running his thumb and forefinger against the grain of that mini-moustache. He wasn't so much on a tightrope as up a creek without a paddle.

He called Gilliam at his hotel. Half an hour later they were on ice-cold beer at the verandah bar. Hobart told him about Carrodus.

'I've seen him around.'

'That's just it,' Hobart said, fascinated by a US senior citizen in shorts that reached below her knees as she crept along Seven Mile Beach with a metal detector. 'I reckon he's been even busier than you over Ed Maxell.'

Gilliam couldn't understand why Hobe was being so helpful.

'If I were you, Geordie, I'd try having informal words with him.' He pulled a wry face as the old woman found some small object in the white sand.

'Anything more about him?'

'Only that he's said to be chasing two US citizens for flogging weapons and hi-tech to countries that aren't supposed to get them from America.'

Gilliam's face came alight.

'You've got it, Geordie. People like that are open to blackmail, too. Maybe it's a long shot.'

'Where do I find him?'

Hobart looked south. 'Two hotels further down the beach. I shouldn't hang about. There's a chance he might be invited to leave a bit sharpish.'

'Thanks,' Gilliam said, finishing his ale.

'And I know nothing about it, right? And you'll tip me off if any useful stuff comes out of it.'

Gilliam nodded, and studied the American old lady. 'What *is* she after, Hobe?'

Hobart smirked. 'Easy treasure? Like a lot of folk around here.'

It seemed to sum up his mood.

'Blackmail?' Carrodus was still wary.

'That's why I'm here to look at Ed Maxell's outfit,' Gilliam said. 'It struck me you just might have a similar aim.' He had intercepted the American as he came out of the sea.

Carrodus was still drying off, his foot up against a beached catamaran. 'Special Crimes Squad, Scotland Yard, you said, sir?'

Gilliam nodded.

'And why do you figure I'm an American agent?'

'If you're not, forget it.' Gilliam offered his hand, a touch irked by Carrodus's reserve, though it was half-expected. He could hardly produce a letter of introduction from Hobart. 'So long, Mr Grant.'

'Mr Gilliam, sir?' Gilliam was ten yards away, and Carrodus came to him. 'I've seen you around a bit.'

Probably on those videotapes, Gilliam thought, wondering if Carrodus was the supplier.

'You've been seeing Maxell?'

'Once,' Gilliam said.

The lean American was watchful. 'But how come you figure I'm an agent?' He reckoned he knew. Washington had been onto the Cayman government, else why that hint of support in Olsen's telex? And some local civil servant had given Gilliam the wink.

'I'm at the next but one hotel up the beach,' Gilliam said. 'Call me if you have any thoughts.'

Carrodus needed time to work it out. 'Okay.' He went back for another swim. The sea was getting up a bit, and there might not be many more chances to enjoy the Caribbean. He still rated his prospects high of being back in New York, if not Washington, by the weekend.

He took a header into a roller. When he surfaced he could see Gilliam strolling along the water line back to his hotel.

Blackmail.

Now *there* was a thought.

NINE

Ed Maxell was reported missing by Hannah at 10.55 pm.

Hobart was told instantly, and it had taken him no more than half an hour to reach the Maxell spread on South Sound. The night was sticky with heat, and the sea angry as he pulled in off the road. Flack was already there, spruce in a khaki bush jacket.

Hannah was shaken but not distressed. 'Ed called me at seven saying he'd be working late and asking me to delay dinner for an hour. Usually we eat at eight. Around then he called again to say he'd be through in ten minutes and that we'd eat at nine. The drive would never take more than twenty-five minutes and at night less than twenty. I called him twice and no reply. So I tried to get Gladstone Hooley and . . . '

'And there was no reply?' Hobart was taking preventive action. Gladstone's entrepreneurial effort to make easy money like some of his young employers had to be kept under wraps for the present. Another of those political hot spuds. It had been Hobart's duty under the confidentiality laws to keep him from behaving any more like a video shop owner.

'Yes, it was Gladstone's deputy. Gladstone's off sick.'

'I see.' Hobart watched her settle on the arm of the sofa. She had the build of a swimmer, all wide shoulders and lean bronzed arms. The designer dress in peach and green was outrageously feminine and quite short. It came near to cancelling out her power-lady style.

'This guy did a check. He found the office empty and securely locked. And Ed's Jag wasn't in the car park.'

'He couldn't have gone to one of his clubs?'

Hannah shook her head with its short-cropped blond hair. 'I called both. He'd shown up in neither.'

'His secretary?'

She hesitated, the eyes stony behind the Big-O glasses. 'I called Carrie. She left the office at six thirty.' Hannah crossed her legs, and Hobart got an eyeful of sturdy calves and thighs. 'And if you're thinking what I think you are, Mr Hobart, don't. I'd know if anything was going on.'

Hobart played with the bristles of his moustache. No such dirty thought had crossed his mind. He'd been thinking of all those visitors who had lately found a pressing need to see Maxell, and Carrie was the one who would know most about them. He was also opting for Maxell having done a bunk to get away from a Yard man who wished to talk to him about blackmail and an FBI agent who was just as keen to discuss weapons and hi-tech dodges. Launder dirty money, you stand a good chance of being blanched yourself. 'Has Ed had any – er – *professional* troubles of late? I mean apart from the break-in?' The cynical thought flashed across his brain that she might plead the privilege of confidentiality.

'No more than usual.' The Texan accent was harsh.

He knew she was lying.

'Are you any nearer finding out who did that break-in?'

'Not yet.' She was getting at him, and he was tempted to think she might know more about why Ed was missing than she was letting on.

Hobart cooled it by turning to Flack. 'Check with traffic, Neil, to see Ed's not gone off the road between town and here.'

Flack went into the hall.

'Don't be alarmed, Hannah,' Hobart said. They had met at scores of functions and he could still see her commanding figure at the Governor's recent garden party. It came to him now that Maxell could be on one of those illicit fishing trips, defying the ecology protection rules and diving in secret for conch and turtles' eggs – and even, it was said, for those near-tame groupers that were the tourists' sub-aqua friends. 'Neil,' he called. 'Have 'em check Ed's boat and the hirers in the harbour. Just to make sure he's not gone fishing.'

Hannah's face set and she pushed back the Cartier watch on her wrist as if she were about to hit him. 'That's wicked, Hobart.'

'Ed's wicked when it comes to knocking off our marine life.'

'He could call me like that, then go fishin'?' Her eyes flashed in anger. 'That what you're sayin'?' She took a sip of coconut milk.

There was no chance to answer. The phone was ringing. Flack

had called a wrong number, hung up, then been beaten by the incoming call.

'That's probably Ed,' Hobart said.

Hannah picked up the coffee table extension. 'Yes?' She listened for a moment, then offered the phone to Hobart. For a woman whose husband was missing she was very calm.

It was police HQ. A young policewoman in the radio room. 'Mr Maxell's Jaguar has been found, sir.'

'Crash?'

'No sir. It's intact. But there are signs of a fight.'

'Where is it, Janey?'

'In the bush by a construction site on West Bay Road, sir.'

'Thanks, Janey.' He hung up, and turned to Hannah. 'We've located Ed's car.' He was on his feet, ready to leave.

'I'll come with you.' She was suddenly in tears.

'I'd rather you didn't, Hannah.'

He was sure now that Ed Maxell hadn't just gone fishing. And West Bay Road was in the opposite direction from the route he would have taken to drive home.

The rain was lashing down by the time he was directed into a right turn by a uniformed cop with a torch. Two police cars were parked by the Jaguar a hundred and fifty yards along the crude track cut through the belt of casuarinas and sea-grape trees for the construction trucks. Yet another tourist hotel was due to go up there.

Avoiding the deep puddles, Hobart left Flack to make sure the young cops weren't destroying evidence through näiveté while he checked the Jaguar. Its nose was buried in the bush, its two rear doors and the driver's were wide open, and outside the nearside door footprints and mud marks suggested a scuffle and the dragging of a body to a point where the tyre tracks of another vehicle had not yet been completely lost in the puddles.

He peered into the Jag. On the front passenger seat was the grey jacket of a lightweight suit, with a black leather wallet half out of the inside pocket. It carried the letters 'E.M.' in gold. On the dashboard shelf was a rack of compact discs. The stereo was intact.

Hobart took a torch from the black inspector and put the beam over the rear seats. There were fresh bloodstains on the grey leather, a shirt button lay on the carpet with a gold chain and a St Christopher charm. He had noticed the chain at Maxell's neck at their last meeting. On the way from South Sound he had called for an immigration and air traffic control check at Owen Roberts, almost sure that Maxell had skipped the country. Now he beckoned Flack. 'Make sure the marine section are briefed.'

He still hadn't ruled out that it was a put-up job by Maxell to elude his tormentors, but his doubts were growing. He went to his car and told the radio room to get in state-of-the-art reports immediately on the surveillance of Rollo Naisby, Charles Wasserman, Walter J. Grant a.k.a. Carrodus, and Gilliam.

Gilliam? Perish the thought.

Jepson and his black fingerprint apprentices were going over the Jag now. Hobart prayed the surveillance lads were as professional and hadn't gone to sleep on the job. It wasn't a task the land-side cops had much experience of, unlike those in the marine section who kept such a sharp eye on the sea traffic between the drug-producers of South America and Florida.

It was 1.10 am when Hobart got back to his office. He found a memo about the surveillance round-up. He was keen to see where the four targets had been since Maxell's call to Hannah at around 8 pm, though he knew Maxell could have been under duress when he made it.

Walter J. Grant
7.16-8.42 – Dinner. Hotel restaurant.
8.45-9.38 – Bar. Hotel.
9.38-9.58 – Beach walk.
9.58-11.20 – Night club. Hotel.
11.20 – Bedroom. Hotel.

Charles Wasserman
7.21-8.44 – Dinner. Sammy's Palace.
8.58-9.06 – Bar. Hotel.
9.08-9.17 – Walk. Hotel gardens.
9.22 – Bedroom. Hotel.

Geordie Gilliam
7.17 – Left hotel in hired Toyota.
7.32 – Arrived Commissioner's house.
10.47 – Left Commissioner's house.
11.03 – Arrived hotel.
11.09 – Bedroom. Hotel.

Rollo Naisby
7.24-7.52 – Dinner. Hotel restaurant.

7.56-8.10 – Drive to cinema. West Bay Rd.
8.16-9.56 – No visual contact.
9.56 – Returned hotel.
10.02 – Bedroom. Hotel.

Hobart wished he'd had the resources to set his voyeurs on to many of those seen to visit Maxell's office over recent days. Since the break-in he'd thought of putting Mrs Sarne's boys, Hal and Marlon, on the list. Yet the two burglars in wetsuits hadn't the build, either of them, to match the Mr America muscularity of Marlon.

He ran through the memo again. Wasserman had gone to bed early, if the voyeur was to be trusted. The 'no visual contact' on Naisby for nearly two hours was infuriating. But what had really got to him was the idea of Gilliam having dinner at the Police Commissioner's house. What were they up to?

In the gun room which had once been a cell, Hobart looked closely at the telescopic rifle now tagged as an exhibit under Missing Persons 09/F. It had been found in the Jaguar boot masquerading as a club in Maxell's golf bag.

'Did he have a licence for it?'

Flack shook his head and, full of himself, led Hobart to the next cell, now used as the exhibits room. He could hardly curb his delight as he laid a hand on a rusted fuel tank perforated with three bullet holes. 'Remember this, sir?'

Hobart checked the tag and nodded. The finding of the tank had caused a brief stir. It had finally been assumed it was a gruesome memento of some drug-running fight on the cocaine route between Colombia and Florida. It was about a month ago when Hobart had other priorities. 'In Red Bay, wasn't it?'

Flack nodded. 'We sent it to Miami for a ballistics report. And there was this clue or two that it had come off a microlight plane.'

'I recall it now. One microlight owner couldn't produce his machine.'

'Aldo Turner, sir. Said he'd flogged it for cash to a visiting yacht owner.'

'Didn't we run a check against the gun licence register?'

'And found only three that matched the holes.'

'And none had been fired for years?'

'I've got the file out, sir.'

'Sure. Have a look, Flackie.'

'Done, sir.' He paused. 'The bullets that holed the microlight could have been fired from this rifle of Maxell's.'

Pleased, Hobart went up to his office. He ran through his messages. There had been no trace of Maxell, dead or alive. Hannah Maxell had been pulled in at half past two in the morning for drunk driving up on North Side. He figured she had been on her way to make sure Ed wasn't shacked up with Carrie in her bungalow on Cayman Kai. He had other things on his mind. He badly wished to interview Rollo Naisby about that hundred missing minutes the night before, and Charles Wasserman about why he'd gone to bed two hours earlier than was his habit.

But it was Gilliam, with his twenty-two-carat alibi, Hobart called first. That bloody dinner with the Commissioner needed explaining.

Gilliam's line was busy.

'Yes, Gilliam. I thought I'd made myself clear first time. I want you back here.'

It was lunchtime in London and the head of Scotland Yard was hungry.

Gilliam couldn't believe his ears. 'But I'm so close to wrapping it up, sir.'

'It's highly likely that will prove impossible. Leave it where it is.'

'A couple of days is all I need.'

The clipped voice was stern now. 'First available flight, Gilliam. Our distinguished friend here now sees that that money he's been asked for *is* an investment and has chosen to pay it. And the DPP's far from enraptured by the case.' His voice was lost for a split second and Gilliam had the impression he'd put a hand over the phone to speak to someone in his room. 'I appreciate that place has its lotus-eating attractions. But I'm told there's a Miami flight in seven hours, around 2 pm your time. I'll expect you to be on it.'

And he hung up.

Gilliam went and stood under the cold shower working out who could have got at the Director of Public Prosecutions and the Commissioner. Somebody up there had the wind up.

The phone buzzed again. He left a trail of water across the bedroom to take the call.

'You breakfasted yet?' It was Hobart.

'No,' Gilliam said.

'Give me twenty minutes, I'll join you. Eggs sunny side up and pancakes, right?'

Hobart could have been a Yank.

Naisby was spreading sun oil over his browning left leg. 'I told you. I went to see a film.'

'You went into the cinema, sure,' Hobart said. 'But for how long?' All this trimming of the truth was irksome. First it was Gilliam whose version of that dinner was that Fenwick was mainly interested in gossip about some of his old mates in the Met. 'He didn't ask about this blackmail inquiry?' 'Not much, no.' And then Wasserman, who looked like a man who'd never touched an aspirin in his life, had said he'd gone to bed early with a headache. 'Too much reading of close print,' he'd laughed. Yet Hobart knew he was lying, and had made a mental note to ask if two voyeurs had been assigned, as Wasserman's room had doors both to the corridor and the beach patio.

Naisby shrugged. 'Maybe an hour. The film was a stinker.'

'Maybe?'

'Could have been longer.' He grinned, oiling his right arm. 'I know I left the moment the star said, "Kiss me before I die." Get one of your bright lads to time the film, you'll know when I left.'

Impudent young bugger, Hobart thought. 'And where did you go from there?'

'May I know why you're asking?'

'In case you saw Ed Maxell.'

'Haven't seen him for days.'

'So where did you go from there?'

'Back to my hotel. My room.'

Hobart had worked it out that this should have been around 9.30 pm. 'You could have ducked out of that cinema a lot earlier than you say.'

'I don't like being followed, that's all.'

Hobart summed him up as a survivor. 'How do I know you were in the hotel when you say you were?'

He half-expected another evasion, but Naisby said, 'I made three international phone calls.'

'Direct dialling?'

'Through the operator. You can check.' He'd phoned his contacts in two banks in the Bahamas and another in Bermuda asking if the missing transfers had gone through. They hadn't. It didn't much matter that Hobart should know the identity of these contacts. No monies had reached those banks yet, and he had a feeling none was going to.

He was oiling the lower part of his back above the band of his scarlet swim trunks. 'Now may I make the most of the little time I've got left in paradise? I'm on this afternoon's flight, assuming you're not going to hold me here.'

Hobart knew of the flight booking. He began to move off.

'Oh, Mr Hobart?'

Hobart turned to see Naisby trying to oil the skin between his shoulderblades.

'Just a spot there, please?' He offered the can to Hobart, who obliged.

Up the beach, Hobart washed his hands under the foot splash tap.

'Here they come.' Matt Carrodus nodded towards General Edison Gibb and his two young friends as they strolled up from their catamaran dinghy to join the queue for the gourmet's buffet.

'But you can't tell me who they are?'

'The older guy, no I can't, Geordie. And his buddies I really don't know, though I could put names to 'em soon maybe.'

It was mid-day exactly. Gilliam was sweating on Hobart's showing up with Naisby. Carrodus had taken some time to respond to Gilliam's offer of mutual aid. Then he'd fixed a meeting on Seven Mile Beach. The blackmail seed had taken root in his brain. 'This blackmailer? You reckon it's Maxell?'

'No.'

'You got some guy in mind?'

'Yes.'

'He's on the island?'

Gilliam had hesitated before confirming.

'Would this guy's victims know him if they saw him?'

Gilliam had thought of Sir Rupert, and of Lord Justice Kenright, and nodded.

Hence the buffet trap. Hobart had taken some persuading. As head of CID he could hardly be seen fraternizing with an FBI agent who'd come on to the island under cover. 'Just don't involve me,' he'd warned Gilliam.

Gilliam didn't hold out much hope. Even if Hobart used his

status to bring Naisby over, Carrodus's target and Naisby might repeat the Kenright fiasco.

Gibb and the young Americans stacked their plates with marinated conch and fresh lobster and exotic tropical salads. They found a corner of a wooden bench at a long table under a palm-thatched awning. Carrodus spotted the small table to their right that would give the best view of Gibb. He led Gilliam over to take the two most likely places.

There was still no sign of Hobart and Naisby.

The two young Americans were already piling second helpings on their plates as Gibb helped himself to a giant melon stuffed with tropical fruit cuts.

It was nearly twelve thirty when Gilliam nudged Carrodus. Hobart was crossing the concrete patio by the pool. And he had Naisby with him.

Hobart hadn't found it that simple. Naisby *had* made those phone calls from the hotel, and the Cable and Wireless timings backed up his alibi. He was now off the list of those who might have abducted Maxell – at least as a principal. He'd made a point of wanting to be on that afternoon flight to Miami, and Hobart had shown some reserve about letting him leave.

Hobart now took in Gilliam and Carrodus, and got the message as they vacated the two vantage places. He took one of them and urged Naisby to raid the buffet while he guarded the chairs.

Gilliam and Carrodus didn't have to wait long. Naisby was turning away with his conch and lobster and salad when his eyes and Gibb's met. The encounter unnerved both. Naisby reacted like some hunted fox, looking for exits. Gibb's eyes were staring. He feared to blink, and tried to catch the attention of his young friends.

'They know each other all right,' Gilliam murmured as he and Carrodus watched from the shade of a palm tree.

'Jesus!' Carrodus squirmed with impatience. 'Who is this guy of yours, Geordie?'

'Who's your bloke?'

It was standoff.

Gilliam gave his promised discreet thumbs-up to Hobart, who then told Naisby he was free to leave the island. There was barely two hours to take-off. Naisby had two more mouthfuls of salad and stuck close to Hobart on the way out.

Carrodus and Gilliam followed.

As they came off the beach, they were approached by two men.

One was a cool and suntanned white man, the other a black heavyweight with the most enormous forearms Gilliam had ever seen.

'Mister Carrodus?' It was the big man.

Carrodus nodded.

'Come this way, please.' He led Carrodus away from Gilliam, and handed him a warrant. 'Immigration, Mr Carrodus. This is an expulsion order.'

'Expulsion?'

'I'm afraid you're persona non grata.'

'And what does that mean?' Carrodus was so close to a coup he couldn't contemplate expulsion now.

'You'll be leaving here on the first flight to Miami.'

Out there in the car park, Naisby was already on his way to Owen Roberts International to catch the same 727. It was the flight Gilliam had made up his mind to avoid in order to put off his recall to London. He sensed now that Hobart was letting Naisby out. Shaking hands with Carrodus he said, 'Perhaps we'll be on the same flight.'

He raced back along Seven Mile Beach to pack.

In his office at police HQ, Hobart was half way through a beefburger and beer as he ran through the crime file. Nothing new had been reported in the Maxell case, and he was still sore that no one had told him about the deportation of Carrodus.

There was a knock.

'Come in,' Hobart called irascibly.

Flack came in, his sharp face animated, his white shirt dark with sweat stains. 'I've been talking to Aldo Turner, sir.'

The name meant nothing, Hobart was so taken up with the crime file.

'It was just a hunch. I told him we'd found the gun that was probably used to puncture that fuel tank, and now had evidence the tank came from that microlight of his. The poor sod caved in. He didn't sell the plane to that yacht owner.'

Hobart wasn't amused, and took another mouthful of burger.

'He sold it to Ed Maxell.'

Hobart stopped munching.

'And there's more, sir.' Flack could hardly contain himself. 'It was a client of Maxell's who was actually flying the damn thing when it came down in Red Bay.'

'What does the accident report say?'

The crash wasn't reported, sir.'

'Eh?' Hobart sat bolt upright to clear a sudden bout of indigestion.

'And Maxell paid for the wreck. Turner recovered it, except for the fuel tank, which was useless.'

'I'll say it was.'

'And that client who was flying it was Rollo Naisby.'

Hobart grabbed the phone and checked his watch in one move. Then he was on his feet, handing the phone to Flack. 'Get the airport to hold the Miami flight. It's due out in twelve minutes.'

'Owen Roberts and quickish,' Hobart told his driver.

Flight KX046 was already boarding at Owen Roberts International.

Carrodus was escorted to the door of the aircraft by two immigration officers, who stayed at the steps as other passengers went through. He was shown to a first-class window seat port side, which also gave him a good view of the forward compartment and the door. Three young US executives in the grey-suited uniform of their money business took first-class seats, and a snake of tourists wriggled down the aisle to the proles' seating. Behind them came Naisby in a shirt open to the waist. He half-recognized Carrodus as the man he'd briefly seen with Gilliam at the buffet lunch, and found a window seat on the starboard side.

Another twenty-odd people from mid-America, in headgear ranging from baseball caps to kepis and sweatbands, filed past before Wasserman showed up. He took in every passenger in the first-class section before hoisting his briefcase into the overhead rack. He held on to a man's handbag with a security loop.

Carrodus's mind went back to the time when the bearded man had left Gladstone Hooley's security room as Carrodus had gone in. It was clear that the man remembered him, too.

The rest of the passengers were seated and belted and a steward was closing the door.

Looking out of the porthole Carrodus saw Gilliam dash from the terminal building, a massive graceless figure with his shirt clinging damply to his body, his jacket slung over his shoulder on the end of a finger, and his passport still in his hand.

The steward reopened the door.

Gilliam boarded and gazed around. There were some empty

seats and the stewardess indicated he could choose any of them. He took in Carrodus first. His eyes roved on, and he recognized Wasserman as the golf course man with a putter who had so excited Hobart's interest. Only when he saw Naisby, half hidden behind *Skin Diver* magazine, did he choose a seat – on the aisle next to Naisby. As he put away his passport and tossed his jacket into the locker he threw Carrodus a wink.

The aircraft taxied out, and the stewardesses were going through their ditching drill when the aircraft stopped.

Two cars headed out from the terminal area.

'Ladies and gentlemen, this is Captain Marlow speaking. We have been asked to hold for a few minutes and should be on our way very soon. Thank you.'

Five minutes went by. Mobile steps were placed against the door, and two immigration officers and a plainclothes man Gilliam knew as a Special Branch officer came aboard. They stood aside for Hobart. He took in the scene, and was surprised to see Gilliam. He'd run the rule over the passenger list as part of the day's routine, and Gilliam had not been on it. Indeed, Gilliam had derided the recall to London. 'Inept if not downright evil,' he'd called it, swearing he'd stay on a while. So much for defiance. Wasserman *had* been on the list. And it had given Hobart pause. The Swiss bank official had bribed Gladstone Hooley in a way that could be an offence under the Confidentiality Act, but Hobart knew he had a cat in hell's chance of persuading the authorities to go public on that. And Carrodus was being kicked out discreetly for similar activities. Where the two were different in Hobart's eyes owed much to his suspicion that Wasserman knew something about the break-in and of Maxell's disappearance. Hot potatoes were rolling all over the place.

Hobart set his sights on Naisby. Leaning across Gilliam with a 'Pardon me, sir,' he spoke quietly. 'I'm afraid I have to ask you to stay with us a little longer, Mr Naisby.' Naisby knew better than to question the demand. Hobart reached up and brought Naisby's blue canvas holdall from the locker, apologized to Gilliam for the inconvenience, and threw a sympathetic fellow-sufferer's nod towards Carrodus.

He led Naisby out to his car.

As they set off, he saw two men leaving the aircraft in haste – Gilliam and Wasserman.

*

'I'm sure I'm entitled to have an attorney present.' Naisby was on a simple wooden chair at the bare table in the interview room.

'Why not call Ed Maxell?' Irked by the stonewalling, Hobart was in no mood for legal niceties. 'I'll put it to you again, Rollo. When you ditched that flying pram why didn't you report it?'

Naisby pulled a face. 'I thought that was the owner's responsibility, not mine.'

'And you didn't want to draw attention to yourself?'

'I'd not mind a drink.' His tongue was like emery paper.

'When we get the taps mended,' Hobart said. 'Why this shyness?'

'If I'd been so set on a low profile, Chief Superintendent, I'd not have been flying that plane. Microlights make everyone look up.'

'And nobody can see behind the goggles.'

'Flying helmet,' Naisby corrected.

'You came down among the rocks in Red Bay.'

Naisby nodded and ran his tongue round his parched lips.

'And walked out unhurt?'

'A few cuts and bruises.'

'So where did you get those treated?'

'Self-help, Mr Hobart. I believe in looking after myself.'

'Like most folk who come here on business.' He went and opened the door and called, 'Bring our guest a glass of water. No, bring a jug and two glasses.' He shut the door and said, 'I'll order the sleeping bag and cocoa later on.'

Naisby noted the threat. Overnight in the nick. Hobart had to be bluffing.

Hobart paced the room lasering looks at him, until Naisby said, 'I'm here on legitimate and confidential business, and I want an attorney.'

'Shouldn't be any trouble, Rollo. The island's crawling with 'em. Mind you, they're hotter on commercial law than the criminal stuff.'

Naisby's face was a question mark.

'Like extortion.' Hobart knew he was into poker now, playing a card he didn't have.

A black policewoman brought in a jug of water and two glasses on a tray. Hobart filled two glasses, and handed one to Naisby. 'Or blackmail.'

'It must be the heat in these places that gets you all,' Naisby said, raising his glass. 'Papa Doc in Haiti. Castro in Cuba. You.' He paused. 'Islands in the sun.'

'You forgot Devil's Island,' Hobart chuckled. 'Blackmail I was on about. Oh, and abduction. Murder even.'

Naisby put a forefinger to his temple and twirled it.

Hobart was still nursing a theory that Maxell had abducted himself. 'When did you last see Ed Maxell?'

'Sounds like when did you last see your father.' Naisby was brazening it out. 'I don't remember. Some days back.'

'Not last night?'

'Not last night. Or yesterday. Or the day before.'

'When you met him on the golf course.'

Naisby alerted. 'Right. We talked business.'

'And wound up good friends?'

'I'd not say that, quite.'

'Enemies?'

'No.'

'I'm told the looks weren't loving.' Gilliam had used the phrase during that photo-inspection.

'We had a dispute about some investments, that's all. Nothing too serious.' He took a gulp of water. 'And what we talked about comes under the confidentiality rules, Hobart.'

He'd dropped the 'Mister' and Hobart found that a good sign. 'I'm still not persuaded by your alibi for last night.' It was actually watertight, but he still reckoned that Naisby knew more about Maxell's vanishing act than he was letting on.

It was Naisby's turn to probe. 'Are you telling me Ed's been abducted? Or murdered?'

'Ed Maxell's missing. In suspicious circumstances.'

Suddenly Naisby looked excited.

'And you're here to . . . '

'To help the police with their inquiries. I know the routine, Hobart.' His eyes flashed. 'I hope when you find him you'll let me know where he is. I have some business scores to settle. Confidential stuff, of course.'

Hobart hesitated, then said quietly, 'You can go back to your hotel now, Rollo.'

'I booked out,' Naisby said.

'*I* booked you back in.'

'I hope you'll be picking up the tab.' Naisby stood up and made for the door. 'And I intend to be on tomorrow morning's flight to Miami.'

'I'm sure there'll be no problem.' Hobart hated it. Naisby was a law-breaker, but there was no way he could be detained. And Hobart felt a sneaking regard for the audacious bastard. 'You'll find all your baggage back at the hotel.'

‘Thank you.’ The irony was strong as Naisby peered at the dregs in his glass. ‘I hope this was bottled water, Hobart, and you’ve not been poisoning me.’

‘The water on this island’s fine,’ Hobart found himself saying. ‘It’s specially treated.’

Naisby felt really good. ‘You’d not like to get me a taxi?’

‘Not necessary.’ Hobart smiled. He took Naisby down to the car park where a plainclothes policeman let Naisby into an unmarked police car. The blue canvas holdall was on the back seat.

And Naisby was driven in style back to his hotel.

It was 6.30 pm.

He checked in, went for a swim, and dined early after confirming a reservation on the 8 am flight to Miami. Only a few of the tables were occupied in the open-sided thatched restaurant. He took his favourite table near the giant icebox where guests filled their room buckets. It gave him a big view of the tables and curving bar. There were no familiar faces except for the waiters’ and some were lost in the shadows of the discreet candlelit area and its hibiscus and poinsettia plants.

He was into his conch chowder when he saw Wasserman enter to a table less than three yards away. A minute later he was aware of Gilliam, standing by the bar watching both him and Wasserman.

Presently Gilliam came over, tugged at the icebox lid, and fed two cubes of ice into his double Scotch. ‘Mind if I join you?’

‘Very much,’ Naisby said. ‘I’m into peace and quiet.’

‘Doubt if you’re going to find much of that, Rollo.’

‘Do me a favour, Superintendent,’ Naisby said under his breath. ‘Bugger off.’

The restaurant was filling up, and Gilliam took a chair at the next table – facing Naisby. But Naisby wouldn’t be rushed, taking his time over the meal. It was around 9 pm when he went for his usual stroll along the waterline, having left his socks inside his shoes at the beach door to his room. It was a night of low cloud and high humidity, and he took off his shirt and rolled up his slacks almost to the knees as he came to the cooling shallows.

Normally he would walk as far as the brightly-lit beach-side frontage of the next hotel – some two hundred yards north – before turning back. Now, passing the towering casuarinas and sea-grape trees separating the hotels, he sensed danger. The moon was fitful, throwing light now and then on two joggers three hundred yards ahead and, when he turned to look, on three boys playing among the beached catamarans outside the deserted dive hut.

The first moving shadow he put down to a casuarina branch swaying in the slight breeze. He had no doubts of the second. The figure came out from the cover of the tree-line on a track that would lead straight to the sea ahead. Naisby turned to see that the casuarina branch was a second man in a black wetsuit and hood darting to a point that would cut off his retreat. He confused them by turning off his own water-line track to head for the trees. They changed course to trap him. He picked up the remains of a fallen coconut and a stone the size of a lemon. He was halfway between the hotels, but the lights of his own picked out the beach better.

Changing course again, he cut back towards the hotel. He could hear the grunts of the man behind him, who was also in a wetsuit. The man ahead had a knife strapped to his left forearm and made to draw it. Naisby left it as late as he dared, and then hurled the stone against the hood above the eyes. The man yelled and reeled, and Naisby then hit his partner with the coconut, full in the face. The man shrieked and fell over. 'For Chrissake, get the bum! Get him!' The accent was a New Yorker's. Naisby was running for his life. He could hear them coming after him, and closing, uttering curses. He was within sixty or seventy yards of the blessed line of light hitting the beach from the hotel when he felt a blow on his right shoulder. He thought it was a hand.

His legs were giving out and his lungs at their limit, but he forced a few faster strides.

Then, from the junction of the bush and the lighted beach area, came reprieve. Three American couples from a tourist party strode noisily down to the sea for their first swim.

Naisby fell at their feet as his pursuers vanished in the dark part of the beach.

They took him for a drunk until one of them was aware of the two receding men. 'I reckon we made it right on time. You need a medic.'

'No, I'm fine.' The beach, the American swimmers, were reeling.

'Sure is a nasty slash.' It was an American woman's voice.

Recalling the blow, he put a hand over his shoulder and felt the stickiness of the blood – and the pain.

Back in his room, a doctor and Hobart came at the same time. Naisby told it as it was, feeling grateful for Hobart's presence. His hands were still shaking and he kept closing his eyes in relief.

Twenty minutes later a young black cop came up from the beach with a black matte diver's knife, its serrated edge coated in blood and sand. He held it out on an open handkerchief.

'Good lad,' Hobart sniffed. He liked the way his young cops were learning to treat exhibits at scene-of-crime trips. What pleased him even more was Naisby's certainty that the two men had American accents and wore wetsuits. The hunt was narrowing. The break-in had been the work of two men in black wetsuits. And among the exhibits from Maxell's Jaguar was a maker's tag from a wetsuit. Hobart was looking for a pair of youngish Americans. It was time he had another look at Mrs Sylvie Delmer's boys – and the other pair who'd caught his eye when he delivered Naisby to that buffet, General Gibb's young lions.

With the doctor gone, Naisby said, 'I hope you're not going to make this an excuse for keeping me here again.'

Hobart scratched his moustache. 'I don't think so. As long as we know where you are in the UK.'

It was crossing Naisby's tormented brain that the time had come when no one, absolutely no one, should know where to find him. 'Understood.' Naisby muttered the lie. He liked Hobart. 'And I hope those cops you've had on my tail will be around tonight.'

'I'll see to that.' Hobart had taken Naisby off the voyeurs' duty list.

Naisby shot him a wicked look. 'After all, it's because of you, Mr Hobart, I'm here tonight.'

'And it's because of me you might be with us no more, that what you're saying?'

'I'd not want my death on your conscience, would I?'

'That's a thought,' Hobart chuckled. 'You've no idea who might have done this?'

'No.' He was lying again. Any number of people now wanted him dead.

'Not even Ed Maxell?'

Naisby shook his head. A stab of pain ran through his shoulder and his head was bursting.

'Night, Mr Naisby.'

Hobart knew that Gilliam would be agog for news as he propped up the open-air bar, and would also know something from his FBI friend about General Edison Gibb and those two husky young Yanks who did so much diving.

Naisby feared the sturdy, bearded middle-aged man in the aisle seat port side more than he did Gilliam. Like Gilliam, he'd left the previous night's flight in Naisby's wake, and checked in at Naisby's hotel.

They were half an hour out from Owen Roberts to Miami when Naisby went to the lavatory, acknowledging Gilliam in a window seat starboard. He gave the bearded man the once-over, and on his way back had another good look. He had it now. The man's face fused with the time he'd confronted Maxell on the golf course.

Wasserman looked up from the *Tourist Weekly* and the granite face was blank.

Grateful for the buffer of an American matron in the aisle seat, Naisby retreated behind *Time*, working out escape routes.

At Miami International, Naisby found the British Airways desk and switched from the routine jumbo to a Concorde flight to Heathrow.

He boarded Concorde with some relish, until he saw the bearded man board. A moment later it was Gilliam, looking worn. Not only would he have to explain to the Commissioner why he'd walked off the earlier flight from Grand Cayman, but why he was claiming exorbitant expenses for the Concorde transfer. It would all come clear after Naisby had been picked up at Heathrow following the coded telex Gilliam had sent from Grand Cayman.

All the way across the Atlantic, Naisby permutated survival options.

He didn't know it, but the Establishment was on his side.

He was passed through Heathrow immigration on a glance. He saw that the bearded man was having questions to answer at the 'Foreign' gate.

Gilliam was already through. He couldn't believe his eyes as he saw Naisby re-enter Britain without so much as a tap on the arm. He was at the baggage carousel looking for Naisby when he felt a tap on the shoulder.

He wheeled.

'Nice holiday, Geordie?' The Commissioner wore a wintry smile. He was almost unrecognizable in a roll-neck pale blue sweater and linen jacket.

Out of the corner of his eye Gilliam saw Naisby lifting his bag from the carousel and making for the 'Nothing to Declare' exit. 'Sir,' he said. 'That's our laddie.'

'You've had too much sun, Geordie,' the Commissioner said soothingly. 'Find your bits and pieces, there's a good lad.'

Gilliam plucked out his case and holdall.

There was now no sign of Naisby.

'And I'd appreciate a few days' furlough,' Carrodus said, handing Special Agent Lemont his report on General Gibb and Mrs Sarne.

'Sorry, Matt. We got too much on right now.' He didn't look up.

Others in the squad room in the Federal Plaza had been just as evasive, even his buddy Ken Stacey. Carrodus had hardly expected a hero's welcome after that inglorious expulsion from Grand Cayman, but this cold-shoulder treatment was so unlike anything he'd known in all his years with the Bureau he was baffled. 'I was planning to go up to Washington for a spell with Liz. It'd give me a chance to put Olsen in the picture about General Gibb in particular and also ask him how I came to be kicked out.'

'I thought that was all in here?' Lemont flicked a fingernail against the report.

'Not all of it. Not what happened between Washington and the Cayman government.'

Lemont hoisted his lanky frame out of the chair and reached for a file on a table beyond his desk. 'I sure doubt whether you'll *ever* be told that. Take my advice, you'll not go chasing Olsen. He got near to throwing things when you got blown and then bust a fuse or two himself when you were kicked out. He's planning reprisals of some kind.'

Again, Carrodus had the feeling he'd lost status and was being unfairly blamed. 'I figured he'd have been tossing his hat in the air over General Gibb.'

'Sure,' Lemont said dourly. 'He likes top brass on the griddle.' He was still sifting papers and hadn't looked at Carrodus once for some minutes. 'But he made a point that he's assigned others to stay close to the general. On the grounds it's a Washington DC task and he wants you to stick to Mrs Sarne.' He paused. 'And one or two others around the international talk-shop.' He passed some of the papers to Carrodus. 'Like to go over these notes on some of your UN folks?'

'How about forty-eight hours?' He'd called Liz twice since his return to New York, first in the early hours from JFK when he could get no reply from her apartment, then an hour ago when her assistant at Voice of America had said she was out on assignment. It was high time they got together.

'Not yet, Matt.' Lemont settled in his chair and switched on his computer terminal.

Carrodus had never known him look so embarrassed.

He went back to the squad room. Passing Stacey's cubicle he leaned inside the partition and said, 'Stace? You ever get the feeling the world's gone off you?'

Stacey ran a hand through his thin crisp hair. 'Got time for a quick one?'

They found a bar off Foley Square.

'How long is it since you and Liz were together, Matt?'

Carrodus's cheeks tingled. 'Why?'

'Forget it.'

'Why, for Christ's sake?' It was like a bad dream.

'If I were you I'd be heading pronto for Washington DC, buddy.'

As they came off the slip road onto the M4, Naisby turned for the fifth time in as many minutes to look through the taxi's rear window.

The black Saab was still keeping a measured distance behind. It stayed in the slow lane. Naisby would have been surprised if he hadn't been followed. Enough people knew he was on that Concorde. And he was now sure that the thick-set middle-aged passenger with the Teutonic look and the German accent who'd shown so much interest in him on the flights was Seifert et Cie's security chief, Wasserman. He could hear Oscar's warning all over again now.

The taxi's radio came alive. 'Jacko one nine?'

The driver leaned into his microphone. 'One nine.'

'Where are you, one nine?'

'M4 London. Just out of Heathrow.'

'Destination, Jacko?'

'Chelsea.'

'I could have a nice pick-up for you. Where in Chelsea?'

'Dalston Mansions.'

'Thanks, Jacko.'

Naisby had an urge to give the driver another destination, sure that the call had nothing to do with the next fare. It went through his mind to go straight to Tara's place, which would mean losing the Saab and doing a U-turn via Junction Three, then making sure the driver said nothing about it over the radio.

He decided against it – in Tara's interest.

The Saab was being driven well inside its optimum speed, keeping its distance with such precision it was scary. It was still hanging on as the taxi turned right off the Cromwell Road. And it was still there along the Embankment. The taxi slowed to enter the Mansions' courtyard. Naisby saw the Saab carry on. He had a glimpse of three men beyond the tinted glass of the nearside windows. As he paid off the taxi he saw the Saab go left off the Embankment. He memorized its number without knowing what he could do about it.

'Goodness, you caught the sun, Mr Naisby.'

Herbie's affable Cockney voice bucked him up. Naisby felt he'd never needed a porter so much in his life. There wasn't much of Herbie, but he was all sinew and had once been a corporal in the Paras. 'Great to see you, Herbie.'

Herbie went ahead with the bags as Naisby cast a wary glance at the corner where the Saab had turned off.

Up on the fourth floor, Herbie used one of his security keys to let Naisby into his apartment. 'Home again, sir,' he said with a joyous grin.

Home, thought Naisby. Hardly that. He loathed the bachelor pad. Even its view of the river he found less than inspiring even on the best days. It was dark inside and musty. He switched on the lights from the hall. He was puzzled. He'd left the curtains open. 'Mrs Teviot been here to clean, Herbie?'

'Should she have been, Mr Naisby?'

'She's not due till tomorrow.'

And then he saw the mess.

'Gawd!' Herbie said, his mouth wide open.

The apartment had been taken apart. A mirror lay shattered on a crumpled Indian rug. Naisby's mahogany desk was upside down, its sides splintered, its drawers ransacked. Papers and files lay in unruly heaps on the floor with icons and watercolours which had been trampled under foot. The word-processor was intact, but the storage discs had gone. So had the videotapes, but not the music discs. Books lay strewn all over, swept from the now-bare shelves.

'Enough to break your heart, sir.' Herbie was near to tears. 'I'll get the police.'

'No, not yet,' Naisby said, picking up two vandalized photo frames from which the photographs had been stripped. One had shown him with his parents six months before they died within a few days of each other, the second was a recent one of Tara with two of her favourite ponies at the stables. There was no sign of the photos. One other frame was intact, the photograph showing Naisby with the sheepdog he'd adored.

'Should we get tidying up, sir? Or wait for the police?'

'Just leave me for a while, Herbie.' He felt he'd been hit in the throat.

'Get you a drink then?'

'Good idea.'

Then Herbie saw the drinks cabinet was a shambles. One decanter was smashed, its contents staining the rug, another was toppled on its side, almost empty. 'There's only Martini left, Mr Naisby.'

'Skip it, Herbie. I'll call if I need you here.'

Herbie went out quietly.

'Oh, Herbie. Leave the police to me, eh?'

Herbie had put the vandalism down to wifely revenge. He knew there had been matrimonial problems in Naisby's life.

Naisby heard the door close. He took the phone and began to call Tara's number. Then he had second thoughts. On impulse he went down on all fours, searching the debris around his desk. He widened the range, scavenging among the paper and other debris. His filofax had gone, and so had his diary. He tried to focus his mind on any papers he'd left behind that could be dangerous in others' hands. He went meticulously through the pockets of his clothes which had been wrenched from the wardrobe hangers. On the overturned bed were brochures and mail shots and a travel agency handout listing trans-Atlantic and Miami–Cayman flights. He still had one in the paper wallet that had held his air tickets. This copy had come with Tara's tickets, which he'd left in a pocket after changing his mind about taking her to Cayman.

He searched every square inch of floor.

But there was no trace of the wallet and tickets.

Naisby made up his mind. He showered briskly, changed, and went down to Herbie's lodge, where he got Herbie to call up a taxi.

'Victoria Station,' he told the driver.

Checking that he wasn't being followed he made for the payphones on the station concourse. He called her number and heard Tara's voice. He felt enormous relief. 'Too late to ask you out for dinner?'

'Rollo, you're mad. It's nine o'clock and I'm half way through.'

'Time for a drink,' Naisby pressed.

'It would take me an hour to get in.'

'So I'll come out there.'

She laughed. 'And then come on and say you've changed your mind.'

'I'm sorry about that, but it's just as well you didn't come. I'll explain one day.'

'Let's make it tomorrow. Today's been one of those days.' She sounded tired.

'Just a quick one at the Gardeners Arms?'

'Oh, Rollo. Come here then.'

He doubted if that would be wise, but he'd been contrary enough with her. 'Less than an hour, then.'

'Thames Valley this time of night, guv?' the taxi driver said. 'It'll cost you.'

'That's all right.' He'd have paid anything.

It meant only a three-mile run for Tara to the Gardeners Arms in the Buckinghamshire village, but Naisby was there first. He kissed her on the cheek, briskly formal, fetched a vodka and tonic, and followed her to a corner of the snug. In her jacket and skirt she was hardly the archetypal horsey lady, and had the looks and confident style of a young businesswoman. Slight and with a complexion so clear she could have modelled for a skin cream commercial, she studied Naisby with amused brown eyes. 'So it's as well I didn't go.' The brittle voice was laden with mischief.

Naisby was so solemn she laughed.

'All work and no play,' he said evasively.

'Ditto,' she said.

'Trouble is, I'm up against sharp businessmen.'

'And me, Rollo.'

She had sexy hands, he thought. 'I thought your problem was to keep little girls upright on ponies.'

'If only it were so simple.' She smiled. 'Anyway, I'd rather talk about the Cayman Islands.'

'So what *is* the problem?'

'The stables and cottage.' She rented them with an eight-acre paddock from a retired vicar who'd spent his life closer to Mammon than God. 'Old Geoffrey and his wife are selling up and going to live on Malta.'

'So you can buy the place?'

She shook her head. 'He's got two offers way beyond what I could afford. One's from someone who wants to run the stables and school. The other's the sort who'll put up the rent way beyond what Geoffrey's charging me.'

'What's the price?'
'The rent?'
He shook his head. 'The asking price for the spread?'
'A quarter of a million. Ridiculous, isn't it?'
He couldn't resist it. He brought out his cheque book and wrote out a cheque for £250,000.
'Rollo!' She laughed. 'How high would it bounce?'
'Buy the place, love. Get him out of your hair.' He looked quite normal.
She held the cheque in those fine fingers, folded it, and gave it back to him. He opened it out and tucked it in the side pocket of her handbag.
And she still thought it was a joke.

TEN

Hobart's eyes glistened in the reflected glare from the full moon and the boats' floods as he crossed to *Lima 3* from the dive boat which had ferried him out to the reef at Trinity Caves. The crew of the police boat were helping Vic Bray as he got ready with his assistant for another dive.

'Hi, Vic,' Hobart called, feeling a touch elated. 'My first reaction was it's a body.'

'My first reaction was keep-your-distance,' Bray replied. 'It could be radioactive.'

Everybody laughed – the cops as well as those voyeurs in the circle of boats. Vic Bray was a larger-than-life thirty-year-old with a healthy suspicion of authority.

'Touché,' Hobart smiled. The husky freelance was one of the most experienced divemasters on the island. Diving ran in his blood. The son of a diver, the grandson of another, he'd know as well as anyone that the odds on a perforated oil drum impaled on the coral were that it would contain something that would decompose without the perforations and bring it to the surface – lifted by gases released from a body. Hobart would have laid ten to one on a body being down there – and five to one on its being that of Ed Maxell.

Bray was lining up the liftbags to strap round the drum. Hobart took in the dive boats full of voyeurs like knitters at the guillotine. The first sighting of the drum had been by a honeymoon couple from Houston in the two passenger seats of a glass-eyed submersible diving around the spectacular coral of Trinity Caves.

The pilot, who knew the reef like his own garden, had made two further passes. He knew the oil drum hadn't been there the day before. And he knew that oil drums with vents could mean something nasty.

Hobart had been tipped off at home by the radio room. They hadn't mentioned the vents, and Hobart had suspected some cocaine offence. It was the later news about those vents that had set his pulse racing. 'How far down is it, Vic?'

'About a hundred feet,' Bray said, checking the liftbags and the block and tackle. 'It's stuck on staghorn. Smashed a lot of it and some giant sponge besides.' His tone was angry. The reef was his living and he couldn't stand attacks on it. 'Another ten feet and it would have gone down the Wall.'

Hobart wiped sea salt out of his moustache. Down the Wall meant six thousand feet, which would have meant goodbye for ever. He was thinking that if the oil drum contained what he was half sure it did, the dumpers weren't Caymanians. A Caymanian would have made sure the drum went down well clear of the Wall.

'It *is* a new dumping, Vic?'

Bray gave a thumbs-up sign. 'It's fresh. No slime on it. No growths.'

Bray jumped into the sea with his young assistant, and took the liftbags down.

Hobart turned to the photographer, a lithe black Caymanian who was towelling himself after his last dive. 'Good stuff, Bruce?'

'I got all we need, Mr Hobart.'

Hobart threw him a wink. Young Bruce was to undersea photography what Lord Snowdon had been to Royal portraits.

It took an hour for the float to begin. The drum broke surface some twenty yards from the port side of *Lima 3*, the inflated liftbags strapped on it by Bray looking like deformed octopi. It was lifted aboard *Lima 3*, seawater squirting from the vents. Using a torch, Hobart peered into one of the vents, but could see only what seemed to be oily rag.

'Hobe.' It was Bray, his wetsuit glistening. He was looking into another vent under the beam of his diver's headlight.

Hobart went round the drum and put his face close to the vent. Almost right up against the opening was a human elbow. Its position suggested the body had been bundled into the drum in a V-shape, backside first.

The *Lima 3* crew forced the drum's lid with metal cutters.

The corpse was even more grotesque than they had imagined. The head was lost between the knees, the plump lower legs were distorted round the inside of the drum, the arms followed the drum's contour behind the man's back, and the whole effect was of some yoga nightmare.

The body was too tightly wedged for removal, and was rigid. Hobart pondered whether to let the crew cut a panel from the drum only to rule out the move as it might destroy evidence. Immersion would wash off fingerprints, but not where they were on patches of oil. And the drum was still oiled up, inside and out, despite the wiping effect of those liftbags.

Hobart called for a mirror. As a marine section sergeant went off for one, he caught Bray staring at the drum in contempt. Hands on hips, his mask and flippers on the shelf of the hold, Bray said, 'It's made a right bloody mess down there. It crashed through staghorn nearly all the way. Broken branches all over the place. Crazy. Just think. Another ten feet it would have missed the big yellow sponges at the edge of the drop and gone right down the Wall. Six thousand feet and no damage.'

'And we'd have had no evidence.'

'Would that have mattered so much?' Bray was pulling the clinging wetsuit from his 225-pound bulk.

Hobart knew how he felt. Bray saw the reef as the most beautiful living garden on the planet.

The sergeant came back with a mirror. Hobart leaned into the drum, holding his nose with one hand and using the other to position the mirror under the drooping head of the corpse. 'Now give me some light.' The sergeant sent a beam into the drum.

Hobart could see a gash and some bruising around the nape of the neck, but had to adjust the mirror before it reflected the face. It was lardy and white, a gargoyle of fear.

The man had been given a hard time.

'Okay,' Hobart said. 'Let's get him to the pathologist.' Bray had made no sign of wanting to look into the mirror at what he'd fished up. He looked straight at Hobart. The look said, 'Do we know him?'

'Ed Maxell,' Hobart said coldly, reading Bray's mind. Maxell might have been better left to decompose into food for the fish. Bray had long suspected him not only of taking conch and turtle's eggs, but of speargunning some of the big fish half-tamed over the years by friendly divers around the reef.

Bray finally got out of his wetsuit, his nostrils twitching as if they were catching a bad smell.

*

'Yes, Mr Naisby?' Waring's spurious voice was more fawning than ever. 'If you're concerned about further payments from the Caymans, I'm afraid we've had none.'

'That's not what I'm on about,' Naisby said, lying against the pillows in the antique four-poster bed. 'I spoke to your assistant yesterday and asked him to transfer a quarter of a million pounds to the bank I named.'

'Ah yes, I did see a note to that effect, Mr Naisby.'

There were the sounds of shuffled papers. 'It *was* transferred?'

'Yes, Mr Naisby. It was transferred immediately.'

'Thank you.' Naisby hung up the ageing classic phone with some relief. It was more than twenty-four hours now since he'd said goodbye to Tara, having spent that first night in her cottage. He'd spoken to her last night when she still hadn't presented the cheque. Still in shock from the break-in he'd not gone back to the mansion flat, fearing he would be under surveillance if he did, and not only by Gilliam and the Yard. Too many people were after him. He shuddered at the memory of that beach escape, unsure whether the two frogmen were bent on murder or forcing him to talk. Both, probably. Even this remote and peaceful Cotswolds hotel hadn't induced him to sleep well. He'd tossed and turned, his mind a turmoil of questions about his future moves, his appetite for risk gone. He would write off that six million that had gone walkabout via Maxell, give himself a new identity and a new life – with Tara, maybe.

He called her.

A man's voice announced her number, and Naisby became alert.

'Tara there, please?'

'Who *is* that?' It wasn't the voice of some young stable groom, but that of a mature man.

Naisby slammed the phone down, and cursed himself for being so jumpy. It could have been her brother, who went over to see her now and then. Or her lawyer. Or the estate agent there about the property deal. He dialled again, but hung up as the call rang out.

An hour later he drove a run-of-the-mill hire car to Tara's place, only to come close to panic as he saw police cars on the approach road, a uniformed PC at the gate, and two cars with press stickers drawing into the verge.

On the front lawn close to Tara's rose arbor was a tarpaulin suspended high enough for people to enter at the crouch, and he saw two men go under, then a woman.

And then another man – tall and dark-haired with a tanned face.
Naisby would have known Gilliam at twice the distance.
He cruised past, terrified to touch the accelerator.
He wanted to be sick.

Under the tarpaulin tent, Gilliam stooped to shake hands with Superintendent Demain, of the Regional Crime Squad.

'Serious Crimes Squad?' Demain said testily. 'We must feel honoured.'

Gilliam let it pass. The regional lads were touchy about the SCS. He wanted to ask Demain what he knew so far about Tara Lynn's murder. Her semi-naked body was being examined by Dr Protheroe. White-smocked and clinical, she threw them a professional's warning that they could stay and keep their mouths shut – or leave.

Gilliam offered her a smile of apology, which Elly Protheroe coolly declined to acknowledge. A well-set woman with assured eyes and capable hands, she set about the scene-of-crime pathology yet again. She detested gossipy cops.

Gilliam and Demain crept out into the drizzle.

Demain ran a podgy hand through wisps of red hair which ran almost laterally across his dome, ear to ear. 'I don't know about you, but women like that put the wind up me.'

Gilliam laughed as he watched detectives marking footprints on the lawn and tyre marks on the gravel.

With a backward look towards the tarpaulin Demain said, 'I always think she'd get a special kick out of pickling my balls.' The black humour was meant partly to cover his aversion to Yard stars turning up to meddle. The days were over when the Met's big heads from the Murder Squad were rated as the only ones who wrapped up homicide cases. Now they showed up from fancy departments like the Serious Crimes Squad instead.

Back in the cottage Demain's scene-of-the-crime team were still collecting fingerprints and exhibits in the cosy living-room-cum-office which had been systematically turned over. Two filing cabinets had been ransacked. Letters, bills, contracts lay strewn across a rolltop desk which had been smashed. A small wall safe had been exposed and jemmied open.

'They were disturbed,' Gilliam said, noting that a wall cupboard with an arc front had not been touched.

'Right,' Demain said. 'And they left that oak chest next to it. Its lock would have been a doddle.'

On the Chinese carpet under the built-in shelves by the fireplace lay two silver trophies and a pair of gold stirrups inscribed, 'To Tara Lynn. Outright dressage winner.' Three twenty-pound notes lay on the mantelpiece under a small brass horseshoe.

'No ordinary burglary,' Demain said, leading Gilliam to a point at the foot of the stairs where a woman detective was marking bloodstains on the hessian wallpaper. 'I reckon she came downstairs while they were turning the place over, hit somebody with this' – he pointed to a walking stick – 'then ran out for help.'

Gilliam threw a look up the stairs.

'They never got up there.' Demain was set on showing Gilliam he was a bit ahead. 'Just *her* bed had been slept in. And it's a single.' He moved gingerly through the living-room-cum-office with Gilliam to a rear patio with rubber plants and cane furniture. 'They came in through here.' He pointed out the forced patio door. 'Beats me that nothing went off. She's got a burglar alarm system that must have cost a packet. With an attack alarm besides.'

'Sir?'

It was a young policeman. Gilliam turned but it was Demain who was wanted.

'The young lady's here, sir.'

'Tara's secretary,' Demain explained. 'Come and listen if you like.'

Gilliam nodded. He'd also be asking questions if he needed to.

Annabel was a wisp of a girl of about twenty-five. Short blond hair gave her a crisp look, but the pale face was crestfallen as she took in the havoc. She squeezed a handkerchief in her right hand and was set on not giving way to tears.

'I'll not keep you here longer than's needed,' Demain said, having shed his chauvinist cynicism. 'Any ideas about who might have been looking for something?'

Annabel blinked, still in shock.

'I mean, it's a pretty competitive business, isn't it?'

'In a way.' Annabel's grey-blue eyes roved the room.

'She was divorced, wasn't she? Unpleasantly?'

Annabel nodded.

'Any dispute over property?'

'Nothing special.'

Her gaze had settled on the jemmied filing cabinets. 'Have your men removed the files, Superintendent?' She was suddenly back in control of herself, very county and superior.

Demain looked for confirmation at his exhibits officer, who shook his head. 'No.'

'We kept the really important files in there.'

'What on, Miss?'

'Oh, everything. Contracts. Bank statements. VAT receipts. All sorts of information about horses, breeders, competitions.' She put a hand to her mouth as a thought shook her.

'Yes, Miss.'

'She was worried about having to leave here.'

'Leave?'

'The whole place is for sale – cottage, stables, paddock. Everything.'

Demain and Gilliam saw the tears surge.

'The most likely buyer wants his own horses and staff here. He told her there was no way he could let her stay on.'

'You have his name?'

She pressed her shaking hands against her forehead, striving to remember.

'Never mind,' Gilliam said. 'The present owner will know.'

Demain sniffed. Gilliam hadn't even said why he was here. The tears were rolling down Annabel's face now, and Gilliam had never seen such globules. Demain called over a policewoman. 'See this young lady home, Maggie.'

'May I see Tara?'

'Better you don't, love,' Demain said, putting an arm round her shoulder and steering her to the WPC. When they'd gone he led the way back to the front lawn and the awning.

WPC Maggie and Annabel stayed on.

'Sir,' the WPC said. 'Annabel would like to ask you something.'

'Sure.' Demain looked more like a social worker.

'They're saying in the village Tara was raped?'

'They'll say anything at times like this.'

'Was she?'

'I'm ninety-five per cent certain she wasn't.' He would soon know.

Annabel was led off by the WPC.

'You never told me why you're here,' Demain said as they went over to the awning.

'No, I didn't,' Gilliam said. It was more than his job was worth to tell the funny little Sherlock with the sagging shoulders. And, besides, he'd come unofficially, having seen the murder report on the routine computer summary. Tara Lynn was the woman for whom Rollo Naisby had bought air tickets to the Cayman Islands, only to show up without her. He could hardly tell Demain about that. Even the Commissioner himself didn't know yet.

They were some ten yards from the awning when Dr Protheroe came out, pulling off her surgical gloves. Gilliam took in the imposing presence. She must have been all of five feet eleven, not all that much shorter than himself. She towered over Demain. In her green gumboots and well-cut belted waterproof she might have been taken for the owner of the stables. Gilliam could see her assistant packing Protheroe's surgical pinny and mask in a bag inside the awning.

'That's all for the moment,' she told Demain. 'You can send it to the path lab now.'

'Thank you, Elly,' Demain fawned. 'Any findings yet?'

'She was strangled,' Elly said, pulling on a see-through plastic helmet against the drizzle. 'Her neck was broken by a blow, not a fall.'

'And – er'm . . . ' Poor Demain gazed upwards, not quite knowing how to put it.

'There are no signs of sexual assault, if that's what you were about to ask, Mr Demain.'

'None?'

'None.' And she turned away over the glutinous lawn and paddock entrance where Demain's men were still stooping in search of bootprints among the hoofmarks and horse shit.

'Oh Christ,' Demain muttered. He'd just seen that Elly's Mercedes might be blocked in by police cars. 'If they're in your way I'll get 'em to move,' he called.

'If they're in my way *I'll* tell them,' she called back.

Gilliam and Demain went back into the house, where the exhibits officer indicated a wallet among the labelled samples. 'We found this under her pillow, sir.' Demain hesitated. 'It's okay, sir. We have the prints.' Demain brought out a cheque, holding it by its tip. It was made out to Tara Lynn.

Demain stared at it. 'A quarter of a million quid.' It was signed 'John Rollaston Naisby'. 'Sugar daddy time?' He found the only other contents – a book of stamps and a postcard from the Cayman Islands showing the Governor's residence with its necklace of scarlet royal poincianas.

Gilliam remembered them well. He was trying to curb his excitement and would have liked to take the card and cheque back to London.

Twenty minutes later he shook hands with Demain and made his way to his car.

'Sir?' It was one of the young detectives. 'A call for you.'

Gilliam felt nervy. It could be the head of the Serious Crimes Squad or – more likely – the Commissioner in a fury. 'Gilliam here.' He spoke quietly.

'Rollo Naisby,' came the reply. 'Could we meet?'

'You're in London?'

'No, I'm quite close to where you . . . ' He went quiet. 'I just saw you at Tara's house.'

'Yes.' He tried to seem calm.

'I phoned and a man replied, so I drove over to see what was going on. I know now. I've heard it on the radio news.'

'I'm sorry, Rollo.'

'You know the Abbey House Hotel?'

'In Fulton?'

'I'll see you there.' The voice was jaded, resigned. 'In twenty minutes, right?'

'Right.'

Gilliam was tingling all the way there. The entrance hall of the converted medieval mansion was a coffee bar with a hatch for a reception desk. Middle-aged and elderly guests sipped their filter coffees. There was no sign of Naisby.

'May I help you, sir?' The porter was more like a butler – staid and stately.

'I'm meeting someone, thanks.'

'Mr Naisby, sir?'

Gilliam nodded, bewildered. The porter handed him an envelope. Inside was a brief note on the hotel's elegant stationery.

Dear Gilliam,
Sorry. Second thoughts.
We must avenge what has just happened to dear Tara.
It will help if I'm not hunted. I promise to meet you. Just give me forty-eight hours.
R.

Gilliam felt cornered. The Commissioner would have to be told now.

'Beautiful morning, sir.' An ancient guest with apple cheeks and silver hair leaned on a walking stick with a dog's head handle.

Gilliam nodded. 'Beautiful.'

As Jesse Blair manoeuvred the dive boat into the shallows, turning it until its stern raked the beach, Hobart could see eight young scuba divers aboard, all displeased to have their romp among the rainbow fish so rudely scuppered.

Jepson was shaking his head as the young divers came up the beach. If there'd been any fingerprints on *Reef Rider II* they would have been destroyed by a thousand touches, even though the young divers had been told by Jesse after the radio call to avoid touching the boat. He was shaking hands with the last of them and pointing to the dive shop. 'My wife will refund your money. Or you have the full trip free tomorrow, okay?'

Hobart went up to the dive shop with Jesse as Jepson, Flack and Jepson's young assistant went aboard *Reef Rider II*.

'I don't see they'll find a thing, Mr Hobart,' Jesse said, pained by the spoiled voyage. 'She's been swabbed down twice since that hiring, and kids have been swarming all over her.'

Hobart could believe it. Jesse Blair's boats were always as bright as a Cayman cop's boots and he treated the dive crowd of mainly young Yanks and Canadians as family. 'Pity you didn't tell us about those two guys right at the start.'

'I didn't hear what you'd fished up out over Trinity, did I?' The indignation was clear.

Hobart knew he'd been unfair. His detectives had done a trawl of the island's boathouses and dive shops trying to find a link between a boat and the estimated time of Ed Maxell's dumping, based itself on the pathologist's estimate of the time of death. Jesse had been out over the reef when they first phoned, and his wife had been unable to find the hiring book and guessed Jesse had it aboard *Rider*. He then confirmed this over the radio, and recalled having seen *Rider* over Trinity Caves or thereabouts two hours before the time given by the police.

Hobart had then asked him to come back.

'What led you to be around there at the time, Jesse?'

'Mr Hobart, you're in a no-lose situation in your job, right?'

'I'd not say that exactly.'

'Salary. Pension. You don't run risks.' Jesse was still boiling over the recall.

'Let's cut out the sermon, eh?' Hobart said tartly.

'You hire out your best boat, you fret over it, baby.'

'You checked them out before you hired?'

'Sure. Far as I could. They put down $10,000 CI as security.'

Hobart puffed out his cheeks. 'Cash?'

'Sure. Cash.'

'*I'd* have been a bit pushed to put that amount down. You knew they were competent to handle a twenty-five footer?'

'I gave 'em a test. They were used to a boat just like it, they said.' He screwed up his leathery face, finding it hard to be tolerant. 'I ask these guys where they're planning to go, right?'

Hobart nodded.

'They say up by Rum Point and No Name Wall. And I warn 'em about the Environment Zone and the regs. No fishing round there. Leave the turtles, the lobsters, the conch. The lot. No anchoring without permission from the Ministry. No diving. Zilch, right?'

'Zilch.' Hobart smothered a laugh.

'I even go aboard just before they start, okay? In case they've smuggled a speargun.'

'You didn't trust 'em much?'

'I did not, Mr Hobart.'

'So why hire them your best boat?'

'Business risk.' He ran his hairy forearm against his nose. 'Something you know nothin' about.' He greeted his wife who was busy with souvenir hunters in the dive shop. 'I hope the Lord forgives me.' He noticed a dismasted catamaran beached close by, went over to it, and set about its repair. 'Well, they didn't go near Rum Point. Some friend tips me off that *Rider*'s becalmed between Sand Shute and Slaughterhouse. I can't believe it. These Yanks said they'd be going round by East End. They shouldn't be anywhere near Sand Shute. So I take *Angelica* up there.' He nodded towards a smaller boat with an outboard motor. 'We find *Rider*, north of where I was told she was. Over Trinity Caves. I think these know-alls might be using an anchor in the coral, so I go in close to tell 'em it's illegal.'

'Were they?'

'No. They wave and say everything's okay.'

'You see anything aboard? In the hold?'

He shook his head. 'I was looking for an anchor line, not an oil drum, Mr Hobart.'

'I still don't get it. How can you know they didn't go round South Sound and the East End?'

'To wind up at Trinity when they did? They'd have needed a powerboat and then some.' His head was shaking in despair at the baseness of the human race. 'So why did they lie to me?' He had the catamaran's mast back in its socket now and hoisted the vivid scarlet and yellow sail. 'And I tell you this, Mr Hobart. They can't have gone much further up West Bay at any time.'

Hobart was interested.

'I check the fuel they used, don't I?'

Flack came up from *Rider*, empty-handed. 'Jeppo's collecting prints by the ton, but they're all very fresh. There's just one thing. Some black scores on the rim of the hold and the dive platform.'

'I saw those,' Jesse murmured crossly. He made towards the boat store evidently set on doing an instant paint job.

'Let's just cool it, Jesse, and go over and have a drink,' Hobart smiled. 'I want you to concentrate for a few minutes.'

They found stools at the corner of the next door hotel's verandah bar. Hobart brought out a notebook. 'Right, Jesse. I want to know just what these two looked like. You must have seen quite a lot of 'em.'

'I saw every bit of 'em. All they had on were swim trunks.'

'They were Americans?'

'Sure.'

'Not Canadians?'

'Well, maybe. But I still think they were Americans.'

'From their accents?'

'*And* their style. More hustle than Canadians have.'

'Height, shape, colouring?' Hobart said. 'And their ages?'

'They're both in good shape. You know – like water-skiers. All wiry and no paunch. One's around six foot, dark-haired, but none on his chest or arms to speak of. The other's medium build, mousey hair thick at the neck. The tall guy's was cut short close to the skull. He's around twenty-two. His buddy's maybe thirty or a bit younger and sure of himself. He did the negotiating for the hire.'

'He sign any contract?'

Jesse nodded.

'He give you any proof of identity?'

'His driving licence.' Jesse bit his lip.

'American or Canadian?'

'American.'

'You sure, Jesse?'

'I'm sure.'

'You don't sound it.'

Jesse's fists were clenched. His dark eyes flashed in the pale brown face. 'I should have checked better.'

'Did he say where they were staying?'

'Holiday Inn.' He screwed up his face.

'You didn't check that either?'

Hobart squeezed his moustache and peered at Jesse over his glasses.

'So I'm crazy.' He paused. 'But the guy did put down $10,000 CI cash.'

'Thanks, Jesse.' Hobart left half his ale. Jesse's Yanks seemed like the two wetsuited heroes who had tried to grab Naisby, and he wanted to look again at the blow-up photographs taken from the video of the two intruders who broke into Maxell's office at the start of it all. He wished now that he'd kept up surveillance on the two sporting Americans, and their older friend who had signed the hotel register as Elmer Stone, but who was now known to Hobart as General Gibb, US Army. Mrs Sylvie Delmer's boys, Hal and Marlon, didn't fit Jesse's descriptions.

Over at the dive hut, Hobart ran his eye over the signature on the crudely filed contract for the hire of *Reef Rider II*. It was no more than a squiggle, but it could be taken for John B. Plant. He left it for Jepson to check for prints. He needed to know how Immigration were doing with his call for a check on American males between the ages of eighteen and thirty-two who were on the island when Maxell was abducted.

'Hobe, you expect miracles, old son,' said Templar, head of Immigration, when Hobart phoned from police HQ. 'We've more than 4,250 Americans here just now. As of now, we've found 2,073 US males in your category. I'll give you a final figure as soon as we're through.'

Hobart called the Holiday Inn. They had no record of any guest named John B. Plant or with a name remotely like it. He leaned back, perusing the airlines' lists of confirmed departure reservations. John B. Plant was unlisted, which caused him no surprise at all. Maxell's killer or killers could also have left by sea. Three cruise ships and a few private yachts had been in and out since he had gone missing.

The sun was high and it was like a laundry out in the streets. Hobart sent out for a fish takeaway and a half-bottle of white wine. Then he phoned the hotel where Gibb was staying. 'Mister Stone left last night,' said the receptionist. She clearly didn't know he was a general.

'Any other guests went on the same flight?'

'Two, Mr Hobart.'

His spirits lifted, though not by much. 'Give me their names, will you?'

'Mr Franklyn Senior and Mr Franklyn Junior.'

Hobart leaned into the desk. 'Young men?'

'Heavens no. Mr Franklyn Senior had his eightieth birthday with us last week. His son is about mid-fifties. You can speak to Mrs Franklyn. She's staying on till they come back next week.'

'Don't bother.' Exasperated, he hung up.

He was enjoying his takeaway when Larry Howell came on from the Miami forensic labs where exhibits and certain parts of the late Ed Maxell had gone for sophisticated checks. The post-mortem at the Cayman hospital had established that Maxell died from cardiac arrest not directly due to that scar and bruising on the back of his head and neck. 'These specimens, Hobe,' Howell said, using vagueness as a code.

'Anything unusual?'

'You got a beaut on your hands.' Hobart heard him suck his teeth in delight. 'We found traces of scopolamine.'

Hobart gazed up at the ceiling. Scientists who talked in conundrums got him down, so he forced himself not to ask what the hell scopolamine was.

'You there, Hobe?'

'I'm here.'

'And some traces of phenothiazine besides.'

'Interesting,' Hobart said, lost. He could imagine the little forensic nut, with his piggy little eyes and pianist's pale hands, exulting.

'Scopolamine's a depressive drug, Hobe. Side effects of aggression so they add the phenothiazine and give it as a serum which makes the victim docile. Got it?'

'I think so.' He felt battered.

'Drug-induced hypnosis, okay?'

'Right.'

'The victim in that state will do anything you ask, give you his life savings.'

'Or answer questions?'

'Sure. And not recall a thing afterwards.'

It figured. Goodbye, confidentiality.

'Tell you what, Hobe. I reckon they were after information, then the guy goes and has a c.a. That's my theory. What you call a – what's it?'

'Cock-up?'

'That's it!' Howell enthused.

'Where the hell's this trash from?'

'Colombia, Hobe.' The voice was serious now.

Where else? Hobart thought. He could already see the need for more Marine Section boats like *Lima 3* – with mounted machine guns. Geography had put the Caymans in a right spot on the late twentieth-century drug routes.

The news had given him a touch of indigestion. He left the rest of the takeaway, pushed the tray aside, and leaned back, pondering Howell's news.

The phone buzzed.

It was Immigration. 'Final figures, Hobe,' Templar said cheerfully. 'Two thousand three hundred and forty-four US males in that age group of yours were here at the relevant time.'

'Thanks.' Hobe was jibbing at the task ahead.

'And since then 785 have gone back.'

'Hell!'

'All the best, Hobe.' Templar chuckled down the line.

Hobart scratched his moustache. You could hardly move for scuba divers these days, and they all seemed to be between eighteen and thirty-two.

The Commissioner of the Metropolitan Police was like a man behind bars.

He let the note from Naisby to Gilliam slip through his precise, manicured fingers on to the pristine rosewood desk, then paced slowly to the window, hands behind his ramrod back. 'You do realize, Gilliam, what a damn bind this could get us into?'

'I've tried most of the afternoon to get hold of you, sir.'

'I don't mean that!' Sir Alan snapped. He had spent most of the day lecturing at the Police College in the country, and had brushed off the messages from Gilliam as being no more than some heartcry from an officer who had been removed from a case he cared too much about.

The last reply Gilliam had got was an order to hang on at the Yard until the Commissioner got back.

It was now close to 7 pm.

'I'm aware of the sensitivity of the thing,' Gilliam said. The Mallory blackmail case wasn't the only pitfall now. Holding on to that letter without informing the Regional Murder Squad could be seen as an effort to pervert the course of justice. 'I *was* tempted to disclose, sir.'

'You're tempted to do things off your own bat too much.' The Commissioner was livid. 'You've been long enough in the force to know how essential discipline is.' He turned from the window, his whole body weighed down with gravity. 'Go on like this you're going to find yourself suspended. Or even worse, dismissed.'

'Yes sir.' Gilliam wouldn't cringe, especially to a Commissioner who was plainly terrified of someone up there. And he fancied he knew too much for the Commissioner to get really rough.

'And you've still to explain to me why the bloody hell you went nosing on someone else's patch!'

'This girl's been murdered, sir.' He let his own anger show. 'And I knew she was a friend of Naisby's, who nearly went to the Cayman Islands with him.'

'Did I, or did I not, order you off the case?'

'Yes sir.'

'Did I, or did I not, make it clear that the matter of Sir Rupert's investments was to go on the back burner for a while?' It was the voice of some prissy barrister being upwardly mobile with his accent. Indeed, Sir Alan had taken his bar exams and some unfortunate elocution lessons.

'Yes sir.'

The Commissioner drew himself up to his full five feet eight and a half inches – there were rumours he'd begun to shrink – and said, 'Get on with the work you've been assigned, Gilliam. Don't go near the Sir Rupert inquiry until I tell you to. Understand?'

'Yes sir.'

'That's all.'

Gilliam turned to go.

'Oh, and Gilliam.' He was holding Naisby's note very gingerly. 'Leave this with me, all right?'

'Yes sir.'

As he left through the Commissioner's outer office he noticed the shredder.

The wizened immigration officer at Zürich Airport weighed up Naisby as if he were a disease on legs intent on debasing the purity of Switzerland. A security officer by the man's side was also running the rule over him. Naisby was seized with fear: Wasserman had somehow tipped them off about his games with clients of Seifert et Cie. Yet it didn't make sense. Seifert's had too much to lose.

The IO suddenly relented. 'Thank you, sir,' he said, handing back the passport. 'Enjoy your stay.'

'Thank you.'

Naisby had half-expected to be picked up at Heathrow on his way out. He had deliberately not made for the airport immediately after standing up Gilliam. If Gilliam had intended to nab him he'd have alerted Immigration right away. Instead, Naisby had bought himself two off-the-peg suits in Savile Row and gone into Bond Street to set himself up with shirts, socks and underwear while the suits were being altered.

It was like starting a new life. He would never go back to that Chelsea apartment.

He checked now into a cheap hotel on the Limmatquai never used by the banking set, showered, then went out and took the escalator down to Shop-Ville, the shopping centre beneath the Bahnhofplatz. It was busy with home-bound office workers buying their delis and booze for the evening. He found the pay phones and called Oscar.

Reza answered.

Naisby feared the line might be bugged. He spoke in German, asking if Oscar could come on the line. He gave his name as Gottfried.

'I'm sorry, who is it?' Oscar asked.

'Gottfried,' Naisby said. 'Usual place, Oscar? In an hour?'

It took Oscar a few moments to catch on. 'Yes, fine,' he gulped. He'd almost forgotten which was the next 'usual place' for their rendezvous, it was so long since the last one.

Naisby was already in the unimposing café in one of the narrow streets near the Grossmunster cathedral. The nightlife of the district had hardly begun. The café was sheltered from the garish glare of the clubs and cinemas. It was the sort of place where you would never expect to find Wasserman.

'I've prayed you'd never come back,' Oscar whispered. The owlish look had gone. He had lost so much weight that his round face was now another shape, all sunken cheeks and sharp jawbone. In the buttonhole of his jacket was a minute strip of black fabric. He touched it. 'In memory of Klutz,' he said morosely. 'He killed himself because of all this.'

'I'm sorry,' Naisby said. 'They've put it down to him?'

Oscar's eyes blazed. 'So far.' The accusation was blatant. 'Wasserman knows who you are, for God's sake.'

Goose pimples tickled Naisby's face.

'You should never have come here.'

Naisby went over to the bar and brought two large brandies. 'I came to find out just how far Wasserman's got.'

'I just told you. He knows who you are. He knows you're the one behind Raleigh House Securities.'

The news shook him, and Naisby hid behind his raised glass. He knew that Wasserman *suspected* him, but the Raleigh House connection could only have come from Ed Maxell. 'He doesn't *know*. Not really. He suspects. He followed me back to London.'

Oscar was pressing his temples as if to keep sane. He gazed round the café, which was empty except for three teenagers at the bar and an old man reading a theatre programme. 'He could have followed you here.'

Naisby waved the notion aside, less dismissive than he pretended.

'Answer me this.' Oscar ran his tongue round his dry mouth, the brandy overlooked. 'Do you keep any documentation, any at all, about me?'

'Calm down, Oscar.' Naisby's eyes were on two heavyweights who glanced into the café, then went on their way. Anti-vice patrol, he thought. 'I don't keep a single bit of paper with your name on it.'

'*Nothing* that could lead to me?'

'Nix. Rien. Zero.' Naisby weighed-up the agonized face. 'What's going to give you away, chum, is your slimming campaign.'

'I'm sorry?'

'You've gone to skin and bone. You look like a bloke at his wits' end.'

Oscar's teeth came over his top lip. His eyes filled up. 'I've lost a little bit.'

'A little bit?' It was causing Naisby some alarm. Oscar was all but a broken man. 'Reza not feeding you that super Zürchertopf of hers any more?'

'She tries. She tries very hard.'

'Go on fading away like this, Oscar, you'll have 'em swooping on you. Then on me.'

'I've told you.' Oscar was near to a crack-up. 'Wasserman's on to you now.'

'So why wasn't I plucked out by the immigration people?'

It brought a spark of fire from Oscar. 'Why? You must know why. If this got out – what you've done – from our boardroom, Seifert et Cie would be doomed. And the whole confidentiality set-up here – our banking system – would be damaged.'

'Haven thirteen,' Naisby murmured.

'What was that?'

'Bad luck.' Naisby hadn't much time for usurers, and none at all for those working under the self-righteous Swiss flag.

'I shouldn't feel smug, Rollo.' He held out his empty glass, which came as a surprise to Naisby, who got him another brandy. 'Wasserman's a formidable and dangerous enemy to make.' His mouth was grim.

'So you've told me before. He's not the sort I'd like for a neighbour, I must admit.'

'He's working hand in glove with one of your investors.'

Again, Oscar had Naisby in a jumpy state. 'Go on.'

'General Edison Gibb.'

Images ran through Naisby's head. Gibb's laser eyes fixed on him. Gibb with those two athletic young Yanks. Those two wet-suited muggers on that dark stretch of Seven Mile Beach hurling Anglo-Saxon oaths in American accents.

He felt scared. Oscar sensed it.

'Oscar,' Naisby said, seeking to cover up. 'Klutz. The bank looking after his family?'

'There's some bitterness, but any meanness might suggest the bank had something to hide.'

'So they *are* going to see the family's okay?'

'It's still to be decided by the board.'

'When will they decide?'

Oscar shrugged. 'They're in no hurry.'

'They'd better be.' Naisby was back on beam, assured and provocative. 'If they won't see the widow and kids all right, we will.'

'We?'

'I will.' He studied the wrecked Oscar. 'And you can have what *you* want and get the hell out of it with Reza.'

Oscar shook his head. 'I'd not know what to do with it.'

'That makes two of us, Oscar.'

Oscar gazed across his brandy glass, hollow-eyed. 'Not you, Rollo? Not after all this?'

Naisby rolled his brandy glass around his palms. 'I'm fed up being a millionaire, Oscar. Bored to hell with the stuff, in fact.'

It seemed to Oscar, knowing him, that Naisby was playing another of his disinformation games.

Naisby knew otherwise.

But there was no going back.

Walking to his hotel on the Limmatquai, he kept glancing over his shoulder, half-expecting two masked muggers to pounce.

Naisby's self-imposed forty-eight-hour parole was long past, without a word from him.

Gilliam dropped another videotape into the recorder and checked the time on the TV screen. Coming home from the Yard to an empty house – Jenny was at a night school course on word-processing – he had put on the TV and caught a presenter doing a trailer for items in the second half of the magazine programme. ' . . . And then we meet Sir Rupert Mallory, who has given up his job at the Palace to turn his house into a stately home . . . '

It wasn't news. The announcement had appeared briefly in *The Times* yesterday.

Gilliam had to sit through two tedious items about hard-up teachers and deprived civil servants before Mallory came on. A long shot of a yellow tractor trundling across a meadow before it slewed into camera and came up close. The driver, in rough cords and gumboots, got down with a tight smile. Sir Rupert hadn't changed. The grovelling woman interviewer threw him a look of veneration. 'You drive it very well, Sir Rupert.'

'Had a lot of opportunity to learn, young lady.' He wiped a soil-grimed hand across the skull-like aristocrat's face. No makeup artist could have done better. He walked in step with the interviewer. 'One had to set one's hands to things. So much to be done.'

It was propaganda. Gilliam knew what was coming as they reached a broken five-barred gate. 'Don't you feel a tinge of regret, Sir Rupert, that you had to give up your important work as a Royal equerry to do this?'

'Of course I do.' He was bent double examining the hinge of the gate. The hack went down on her haunches beside him. 'I had to make a difficult decision. Unless I came down here to put things right, it was likely that my heirs would have no Spiggett's Corner to inherit. Quite appalling, really. Costs shooting up all the time. High taxes. High wages. That sort of thing. One had to choose. It's a heritage matter, you know. It's up to us to preserve the national heritage.'

Gilliam blew a raspberry. He could see those notes he'd made as if they were in front of him. The illegal export of works of art not only on his own behalf but of half the bloody hereditary peerage. And all that sterling spirited out of Britain for his blue-blooded comrades during the time of exchange controls.

Mallory was working on that hinge, and puffing a bit. 'We're having to turn our house into a stately home . . . visitors and all that . . . otherwise we'd go under. Lot to do, you see.'

'Your estate workers, Sir Rupert?'

'Wonderful chaps. Hard workers all of 'em. One would like to take on more. But the costs . . . ' The camera came off the gate. He was getting nowhere with the repair.

'You know,' Sir Rupert said, walking in step with the girl hack, 'if one could afford to pay a factor to look after all this, one wouldn't have problems. Factors are highly-paid individuals, you know.'

'So now you're your own factor?' the hack simpered.

'Factor, organizer, bookkeeper. And now, one sees, publicity manager.' He showed his small teeth in a stiff grin, climbed into the tractor seat, and roared off into what was meant to be a brave sunset. But the clouds hung low and dark, so the effect was that he was riding to his end.

All the same, Gilliam had to admire the brazen courtier. For sheer nerve the blue-bloods were in a class of their own. He was about to run the tape when he switched it off, and called the Yard to ask if there were any messages. The office of the Director of Public Prosecutions had been on about a property fiddle in one of the great departments of state, and three anonymous grasses who would call again.

Nothing from Naisby.

'The Commissioner wasn't trying to contact me?'

'No sir, he wasn't,' came the reply.

Somehow, Gilliam was not surprised.

He strolled down to the Crown and Anchor, telling himself he'd had enough of the peerage and would now meet the beerage. The thought gave him a laugh, but not much of one.

'Yes, Waring,' Naisby said. 'I want the entire initial deposit of one million dollars transferred. The accumulated interest can stay with you.'

'You will be giving us the agreed confirmation?'

'Right away,' Naisby said. 'You'll get the coded telex with the password.'

'Shall be done,' Waring said.

The bank which was to receive the transferred funds was the Banque Auroux in Luxembourg. Beyond the window of the first floor office Marcel Dufoix had let him use to sort things out, Naisby could see the horizontal bands of red, white and blue on the Grand Duchy's flag.

He called the number of the Banco Palomar Rubio's London office and was put through to the pompous Singleton-Starkie. 'Dear boy, what a pleasure to hear from you.'

'Hello, Nigel. Simple matter really. I'd like you to transfer one million dollars to a trust account in Luxembourg.'

'No sooner said than done. Usual confirmation, of course.'

'Coded telex on the way giving password and account number.'

'Must have you for a drink at my club when you've a minute to spare.'

'Look forward to it, Nigel.'

Naisby went on to instruct his contacts in other banks in Bermuda, the Bahamas, the Channel Islands and the Isle of Man to make similar transfers to the Banque Auroux. In less than an hour he had cleared the way for the transfer of most of that first eight million dollars from the Cayman Islands. This was the easy bit. Marcel Dufoix had not only set up the Auroux arrangement but had spent the best part of two days lining up a global web of accounts in other banks as far apart as Nassau and Hong Kong. The funds reaching Naisby's account at Auroux would be mesmerizingly recycled, in and out of far-flung places and back again. On the way, payments not exceeding $50,000 in each case would be made to charities named by Naisby. Larger sums going to charity could bring out the sniffers. Not that they'd get far after this latest recycling.

Naisby called Marcel's office on the intercom. 'Done.'

'Come through and celebrate.'

Marcel Dufoix worked in style. His office was princely, all mahogany and twentieth-century oils and rare Oriental ceramics. Naisby heard the pop of the champagne cork as he went through Marcel's secretary's office.

'I always knew you'd make it,' Marcel laughed. He wore a short-sleeved silk shirt with a monogram on the pocket. He was pencil-slim with the lean predatory look of a sparrowhawk. He came round the boomerang-shaped desk with Naisby's glass and the grace of a ballet dancer. 'My father often asked what became of you.'

Marcel had not made it on his own, but he did have a genius and appetite for hard work that set him apart from the British silver-spooners. 'I did think once or twice of coming to see you,' Naisby said.

'You should have done. Surprises me you stayed so long with Cromwell Jaynes.'

'It was a mistake.'

'Well, here's to recycling,' Marcell said in his high-pitched voice.

'It needed to be done.' No more explanation was required. 'I'd like to see the first million go out to the charities right away, Marcel.'

Marcel nodded. 'You'll let me have the names of the rest of them?'

Naisby nodded. 'Give me twenty-four hours.' He had listed fifteen charities so far, but wanted the money spread among many more.

'You want receipts, Rollo?'

Naisby shook his head. 'But we'll need to monitor their annual accounts. Fix that as part of the service?'

'No problem.' He studied Naisby over the rim of his glass. 'We'll need a pseudonym so they can acknowledge.'

'Yes.' He had toyed with the idea of 'Tara', but that would be asking for trouble. 'How about a simple number?'

'Fine.'

'Two three five.'

Marcel made a note, his not to reason why.

Tara was born on the twenty-third of May.

They finished off the champagne and Naisby left in a Mercedes with Marcel's chauffeur. All the way to the airport his brain was churning, without finding any loopholes in the recycling scheme. Whatever happened to him now, the funds had gone on the walkabout of all time. After the one-million-dollar immediate windfall to charity, the rest would be an everlasting trust, handing out its annual growth above inflation minus Marcel's fees.

On the flight to Heathrow, he was making a list of those he wished to benefit – charities involved in medical research, children's and old people's welfare, wildlife protection, human rights, animal rights, famine relief. Famine relief! He had never intended to emulate Bob Geldof, but it wasn't working out badly.

He was beginning to feel virtuous – and guilty, as his mind's eye tried to cope with a close-up of Tara.

*

Gilliam saw Naisby pay off a taxi near the Serpentine restaurant then stand checking a road map of London.

Nobody had followed, so Gilliam put his *Standard* in a wastebin and saw Naisby get the message. It was mid-morning – close on seventy-two hours since that non-meeting.

They shook hands.

'Sorry I'm a bit late,' Naisby said. 'It wasn't intentional.'

'No second thoughts then?'

'None.' Naisby's mood was grave. 'Are you any nearer on who killed Tara?'

'Not my case, Rollo.'

'You were there.'

'Because of you, that's all.' He motioned towards the *Standard* protruding from the bin. 'Latest seems they're looking for two males. One medium height, the other taller.'

'Any sexual thing?'

'It seems they've ruled that out.'

They were walking round the water's edge. Naisby took in a deep breath of cold air. 'You remember that bloke Wasserman?'

'The Swiss with a beard?'

Naisby nodded. 'And the American general, Gibb?'

Gilliam's nostrils twitched. He could see where Naisby was leading. The same thought had come to him when reading the *Standard* story.

'And the two young Americans with Gibb?'

'Vaguely.' He remembered them *very* well. But one more false move now, and the Commissioner might want his guts for jockstraps. He stooped to pick up a takeaway carton and tossed it into a bin labelled 'Keep London Tidy'.

'They're the murderers.'

'I know how you must be feeling, but . . . '

'I want the buggers caught, Gilliam. Caught and punished. And quick.' He paused. 'You went into the house, didn't you?'

'Briefly.'

'What was it like? I've seen one press story that says it was burglary, that Tara disturbed them.'

'I'd go along with that. They gave downstairs a real going-over. Three-quarters of it anyhow. Then she probably showed up.'

'You should be hunting those two Yanks. I reckon they're the same pair who tried to grab me on Seven Mile Beach the night before we came out.'

Gilliam put on a puzzled look, though he knew about the incident from Hobart.

'You should have been told about it by Hobart.' Naisby was suddenly bemused by Gilliam's apathy. 'Tara was murdered, for Christ's sake!' He paused. 'Probably the same people who turned *my* flat over.'

'Your flat?'

'They were looking. Like to come and see?'

'Sure.' Gilliam could hardly admit the break-in had been a Yard job which had yielded the evidence of those air tickets for Tara, but nothing about Naisby's connection with Maxell and Raleigh House Securities on the Caymans. It was shortly after this raid that Gilliam had been ordered home.

Herbie was at the entrance to the block when they got out of a taxi. He turned pale on seeing Naisby. What was more, Gilliam looked more like a Yard man than anything else except a staff sergeant in the Guards.

'Herbie,' Naisby said, shaking hands.

Herbie tugged his sleeve and drew him clear of Gilliam. 'I'm sorry, sir, but I had to call the police. I've got to rely on them most of the time.'

It was clear that he took Gilliam's presence to be tied up with his 999 call. 'That's all right, Herbie. Have they been?'

'Been, sir?' He threw a nonplussed glance at Gilliam.

'Don't worry, Herbie.'

'Oh, and there was this, Mr Naisby.' He brought out an old wallet and took from it a laboriously-written note in a sprawling hand. Handing it over he said, 'I just happened to be in your flat when this gentleman phoned. I – er – wasn't nosing. Just tidying up after the police went.'

Naisby hardly heard. The note read: '5.20 pm. Mr Faraday called. Says will you phone him at Maxell Group office. Caymer Islands. Herbie.'

'Cay*man* Islands, Herbie.' Naisby put an arm over his shoulder to show the little man all was forgiven, even the spelling.

He'd never heard of anyone called Faraday.

The flat had been spruced up by Herbie. Naisby wanted to call the Caymans but he told Gilliam, 'If you'd like to phone in about these two Yanks, it's all right.'

'I'll report your suspicions when I get back in.'

'And yours, surely?' Gilliam was confusing him.

'Mine as well.' Gilliam feared he was close to giving the game away. 'I thought you'd made up your mind to come clean about the blackmail, Rollo?'

'I have.' Naisby was pacing the room like a caged zoo animal. 'Catch those murdering bastards, I'll tell you more than you could dream of.'

'Give me an appetizer, eh?'

'Eh?' He was looking at the photograph of himself with his sheepdog. The frame that once held Tara's picture was back on the mantelpiece. 'They must have reckoned the dog couldn't talk, Gilliam.'

'I'll help you get them.' Gilliam was steeling himself for an all-out scrap with the Commissioner. 'Just an appetizer?'

Naisby wondered what he was on about.

'You didn't have the judge on the hook as well?'

'Who?'

'Kenright?'

'Yes,' Naisby replied, and Gilliam couldn't read him now. 'He was cut down to size on the beach, don't you think? Nothing like the giant up there at the Old Bailey.'

Gilliam saw what he meant. 'Did he pay the blackmail fee?'

'He *invested*, Gilliam.'

Lord Justice Kenright was in trouble, but Gilliam couldn't help feeling *he* was in even deeper. He ran his finger and thumb round his neck as though he felt a noose.

Naisby had sussed him out. 'I'm interested, Gilliam. How the hell could I have been let out and then back into the UK without real challenge? In view of what's gone on?'

'Maybe the Immigration lads and lassies were on strike about overtime.' Gilliam was at the end of his tether. 'Or maybe they were just tired.'

'Or they didn't know I was of any interest to the Yard?' Naisby threw off his jacket, took the Victorian chair by the telephone, and got set to make a call. 'Either you level with me, Gilliam, or you can leave this minute.'

Gilliam's head went into a 180-degree turn as he feared they were being bugged. He had to force out every word as he said, 'Rollo, you're a bright spark. Who can knock you off for taking investments?'

'The Fraud Squad could try.'

'And the DPP could see 'em off.'

'So I'm free to go about this business?'

'Don't get too cocky.'

'Who's cocky? I'm depressed as bloody hell. And I will be till you get those bastards.'

In the long silence Naisby put an impatient hand on the phone as Gilliam studied him. Presently Gilliam stood over him and asked, 'What do you have on Her Majesty's judge, then?'

'Seventeen million Swiss francs gathering interest in a Zürich bank account.' Naisby's face was icy. 'Will that do for starters?'

'It's adequate,' Gilliam said. His mouth was dry and his head was throbbing. Somehow roles had got reversed and he was under scrutiny.

'Think of that,' Naisby said. 'Then dig up his press clip. And match the two.'

'Jesus, you don't have anybody else on the hook?'

'Oh yes,' Naisby said tartly. 'I don't know why you talk about hooks, Superintendent. Nets is the better word. Or trawl. I could fulfil all your professional ambitions at a stroke.'

It made Gilliam shudder. 'You're going to need a minder, Rollo.'

'I've made more than a will. I have an all-will-be-told codicil in a safe haven. You'd need access to half the world's banks to get at it. Knock me off, it's trouble in high places, I assure you.'

'I wasn't making a threat.' Gilliam was rubbing his left temple, which was aching fiercely. 'I was advising.'

'As a friend?' The cynicism was laser-sharp.

'You might say that.' Certainly Gilliam was now more interested in the greed of Sir Rupert Mallory and Lord Justice Kenright than in Naisby's exercise in extortion.

'Let's meet when you've got these murderers charged, eh?' Naisby was making it plain he wanted to make a private call. Gilliam leaned over to shake hands. 'You can see yourself out, right?'

With Gilliam gone, Naisby called the Maxell office in Grand Cayman.

Carrie answered.

'Rollo,' Naisby said. 'How are you, love?'

Naisby heard the intake of breath. 'One moment, Mr Naisby.'

'John Faraday, Mr Naisby.' The accent was Caribbean-American. 'Glad you called.' The tone changed like some aural chameleon. 'We seem to have some unfinished business here.'

'We certainly have.' Naisby was on guard.

'There are certain assets of yours, Mr Naisby, that appear to have been improperly allocated, but are now available to you.'

Naisby held his breath.

'Mr Naisby?'

'I'm here.'

'Maybe we should meet, eh?'

'I have to be over there soon,' Naisby said, sharing Faraday's fear of giving anything away to international eavesdroppers. 'I'll call you, right?'

'That's fine.'

Naisby sat back in the chair and wondered why somebody named Faraday should be calling to say that six million dollars hadn't gone walkabout after all.

He was dying for a Scotch, but the flat was dry. He called Herbie, who came up with a half-bottle.

The Commissioner was dumbstruck.

He faced Gilliam for a full minute, rolling one thumb over the other, his hands resting on Gilliam's note. Then he said, 'I just don't believe it.'

'I do.' Gilliam was only just managing to control himself.

'But Kenright's shortly to try one of the biggest tax fraud cases in the country's history.'

'Exactly.'

Sir Alan put his glasses back on and reread the note. 'Seventeen million Swiss francs?'

Gilliam let him stew.

'I dimly remember that shipping case.' He checked the note. 'Nine years ago, you say. I thought it was longer.'

'I've just gone through the press clip, sir.'

'I see Kenright claimed at the time his fees were around £100,000?' He paused. 'There's no proof this seventeen million is related, even if it actually exists.'

'So why did Kenright pay Naisby to keep quiet?'

Again – bleak silence. Then the Commissioner leaned back in his high-backed chair, running the tip of his well-manicured forefinger against a bottom tooth. 'And I thought I ordered you to lay off Naisby until you heard further from me.'

'*He* called *me*, sir.'

'You agree to meet every caller?' The bafflement was giving way to anger.

'I thought this merited my seeing him.'

'Doing your own thing again?' He was like a prosecutor. 'I told you to leave the Mallory inquiry.'

'I didn't see Naisby about that. I thought he might help over the murder of that girl.'

'Not your case, Gilliam. Not your responsibility.'

Gilliam's face was stern. 'All murder is my responsibility. As, with respect, it should be yours.'

It was too much for the Commissioner. He stood to his full five-feet-eight-and-a-half, tugging down the edges of his immaculate tunic. Tilting his chin upwards he said, 'Consider yourself suspended as from this moment.'

Gilliam stood up now, looking down into the Commissioner's taut, pallid face. 'May I first pass on some information to the Regional Crime Squad about the possibility that two young Americans could be that girl's killers?'

'You can clear your desk and go home,' the Commissioner said huffily. 'Until you hear from me.'

Gilliam had an urge to clout him.

Outside hailstones were pelting the Commissioner's windows. For all Gilliam cared they could have been bullets.

Jepson invited Hobart to peer through the magnifier.

The image was black – an oval rim with the faintest impression of lettering. It was one of the prints Jepson had taken from the oil drum which was meant to have been Maxell's tomb. It had been ingrained in a patch of oil.

Hobart straightened up.

'Then this.' Jepson held out the oval wetsuit tag found in the back seats of Maxell's Jaguar. He took the photograph from under the magnifier and married it to the tag, which carried a brand name – ScubaSure. 'The guy must at some point have leaned against the drum, maybe it was pressing on his chest when the drum went over the side.'

It meant that one of those boat hirers had been in the Jaguar when Maxell was abducted. And Hobart was grateful for such minor advances. He was in limbo. Gibb's two young friends had not been identified, and young American males had been leaving the island in droves. Even now he would find it difficult, if not downright impossible, to get authority for Customs to rummage among young Americans' holiday baggage for a wetsuit missing a ScubaSure tag.

First it was the business confidentiality laws, then it was tourism. The Cayman Islands would disappear into the coral without them.

It was like trying to work with handcuffs on.

He was still feeling sore as he made his way back to his office. The FBI had not come back with any news of the palm and fingerprints Jepson had found on the boat hire contract, which were not those of Jesse Blair or his wife. Nor had the Bureau even acknowledged receipt of the list of 2344 American males between the ages of eighteen and thirty-two who were on Grand Cayman when Maxell went missing.

Hobart couldn't believe the great FBI would be uncooperative over the way Carrodus had been booted off the island – they had much to gain on drugs-related crime from the Royal Cayman Islands Police – but he still resented the incident.

The initials FBI caught his eye on a document the moment he got to his desk. But it was not about the Washington lab and computer checks. It was a memo from the Commissioner.

Nineteen Cayman Islands bankers and trust attorneys were being held at Miami International Airport after a pounce by US customs and the FBI. The elegant money men had been plucked from the Immigration queue 'like ripe apples'. Their bags and briefcases had been rummaged, and the fifteen men and four women had been taken behind closed doors for strip searches. One attorney they had let go – 'so that he would tell us, I imagine,' the Commissioner noted – had overheard an FBI man saying, 'You can't talk to us over there, but you're going to while you're here.'

They were still being held.

'Humiliating stuff,' the Commissioner had written. 'We've not heard the end of this.'

He could say that again.

As he came briskly through the terminal building at Washington National, Carrodus was met by a middle-aged agent who flashed his commission card. 'Matt Carrodus?'

Carrodus nodded.

'Ned Rennie. I have a message for you from Special Agent Lemont.'

The interception didn't catch him unprepared, so Carrodus put on a mildly interested look.

'You're needed back in New York right now. He suggests you get the first shuttle.'

'Thanks,' Carrodus said, heading for downtown Washington. He saw Rennie leave, then made for the cab rank. He'd put up with enough conjugal exile in New York, and far too much coolness over the phone from Liz, not to mention an excess of zeal by Lemont in keeping him doubtfully occupied in Manhattan. Although Stacey had dropped no more hints about his need to get to Washington, it had gone through his mind several times to defy Lemont and just go. It was last night's phone call that decided it. Twice he'd found her linc busy, and when he got her at the third try she had rebuked him for phoning too often. 'I'm coming over tomorrow,' he'd told her. 'I'll see you at the usual place at 12.30.'

'The usual place?'

In a way he wasn't shocked that she'd forgotten. 'The Cascade in the National.'

He had told nobody of the rendezvous, not even Stacey. He had made no call to report sick, no advance reservation for the flight. Only a tip-off from Liz could have brought the greying messenger boy Rennie to Washington National.

Down in the Cascade he strolled past the waterfall, checking the tables for signs of her. There were lots of women of her age from the offices on the Mall and Capitol Hill, but none with her stunning looks. It got to 12.50 and she still hadn't shown. He was about to find a payphone and call her at Voice of America when he saw her checking the buffet area. She was easy to spot in a crowd with that long russet hair, rounded figure and open face. And she had lost none of her dress sense. Her green costume was a sensation.

'Usual place I said, darling,' he said, coming up behind her. 'We never met in the buffet.'

'Same old Matt,' she said. 'Always table service or nothing.'

He made to kiss her, but she turned slightly to take it on the cheek.

He made a face and gazed into the wide hazel eyes, innocent of makeup. 'Let's eat,' he said.

They had hardly settled at the plastic table when she made a conspicuous gesture of checking her watch. 'I've got less than an hour, Matt.'

He had the menu open and was about to hand it to her. He laid it against the pepper pot. 'I was going to say I'd stay over tonight.'

She met his probing look. 'I'd be too shy, Matt.'

Carrodus had known all along, really – and especially since Stacey's warning on his return from the Caymans. 'There's another guy?'

She picked up the menu. 'Something light. Quiche with salad.' The menu was between them. He tugged it from her hands.

'There's another guy.' He dropped the question mark.

She was leaning down to her right to reach her handbag. He put out his arm, long and muscular, and drew her upright to face him. And she seemed to be light years away.

A frail-looking, hyperactive waitress came up. 'Hi. You decided yet?'

'Not yet,' Carrodus said, sending her away with a glance.

'I'm sorry, Matt.'

Her gaze was straight, and there was not even a hint of a tear.

Carrodus's head began to shake, very, very slowly. He set the menu precisely back on its stand.

And then he rose and walked out, past the pay desk and round by the waterfall. He didn't turn his head once. He made his way out to the Mall, past the chattering secretaries and the family groups of mid-America, his eyes smarting. It was one of those balmy Washington days when the blossom perfume obscures the gasoline fumes, but he didn't notice. His mind was pinwheeling with jigsaw pieces. The Bureau's bloody-minded denial of a Washington posting. His trip to the Caymans when normally it would be a case for the field office. The length of his stay there going unquestioned. Ditto, his expulsion. He'd expected to be summoned to the Alamo fortress in the Federal Triangle to elaborate on it. His report had not been mentioned since he submitted it.

On impulse he stopped, and looked back towards the National Gallery. He turned and broke into a run. He saw Liz getting into a yellow cab. As the cab moved off he ran in front of it. The driver braked and skidded. Wrenching the nearside rear door open, Carrodus took Liz by the lapels of her costume.

'Hey, buddy!' The driver was getting out.

'It's Olsen! It's Olsen!' He was shaking her.

The driver was looking for help from the growing crowd of lunchtime office workers. He was a diminutive Mexican who was reluctant to tangle with a giant.

'It's Olsen.' He pulled her out of the cab, passed over her handbag, and stood looking her up and down for a long moment, his mouth formed into a downward arc, his head shaking slowly in contempt.

'Hey, buddy,' the driver pleaded. Nobody had moved to help him or Liz.

Carrodus flashed his commission card. 'The J. Edgar Hoover Building,' he said, getting into the cab.

'Yes sir,' the driver said.

At the brownstone fortress, Carrodus flashed his card again, and made for Olsen's office on the top floor. He wanted to race up the stairs rather than take the elevator. But he moved sedately into the car, and walked in a measured way to Olsen's office. Ten to one the bastard wasn't in. He went into Olsen's outside office and headed past Olsen's secretaries to the internal door.

'Can I help you?' It was one of Olsen's secretaries.

'I doubt it.' He pushed the door open.

The secretaries expected Olsen to press the panic button. There was a whole pack of safeguards against crazies. But Olsen pressed no button. One of his secretaries went to the internal door and saw Carrodus facing Olsen across that acreage of desk. 'Okay, Mrs Quayle,' Olsen croaked, and she could only just see his square-jawed face beyond the towering intruder. 'Just leave us.'

'And close the door,' Carrodus said.

Olsen sat bravely in his swivel chair. 'There's a time and place, Matt.'

'Liz,' Carrodus said.

'We can talk about it some other place, okay?'

Carrodus's mouth went taut and he was round the desk so fast for a big man that Olsen was left blinking as he was hoisted out of his chair like a rag doll and planted on his own desk like some ridiculous Humpty Dumpty. Carrodus held him one-handed at arm's length as Olsen's wild despairing blows fell short. 'Let's talk.' Olsen was trying to convey urgency without raising his voice so loud that his secretaries could hear. 'Let's talk about it, Matt.'

'Talk, shit.' Carrodus said, pushing him across the desk with such force that Olsen skated on his backside, scattering files, papers, computer discs, paper clips and his ceramic pen-holder in the image of J. Edgar Hoover. He went over the far edge on his back and lay between two chairs said to have once belonged to mob bosses of the thirties.

He was whimpering, and holding the back of his head.

Hoping it was more than concussion, Carrodus stepped over him, and went out past the awed secretaries.

'It's okay, Mrs Quayle,' Carrodus heard him say. 'Don't call anybody.'

Nobody challenged Carrodus on the way out of the Hoover Building, and he made straight for Washington National, wondering all the way how Liz could leave *him* for such a cringing specimen.

Back in his compartment in the Federal Plaza, he caught Stacey's knowing look, and ran his eye over the messages on his desk, sure that none would be urgent enough to have merited Lemont's recall order. And none were. But one message did interest him.

'Superintendent Gilliam of Scotland Yard phoned from London. He'd like you to call him.' Carrodus noticed that the number was not that of the Yard.

He put the call in.

'Hello, Matt. How goes?'

'Just great,' Carrodus lied.

'I've advised somebody to get in touch with you, Matt. Naisby. He shared our blissful holiday on Cayman?'

'Sure.'

'You can help him, I think. And he can help both of us.'

'Great. I'll look forward to it.'

'He's on the island at the moment, but he'll break his return trip in New York just to see you.'

'I can't wait, Geordie.'

His mind was full of Liz.

All that was different about Maxell's office was the male perfume. Maxell had been an Aramis user. This was altogether more exotic. Carrie was still around and identical replacements for the equipment smashed during the break-in – the computer terminal, the telex, the shredder – were in the old places.

'So perhaps you'd give me instructions about the six million dollars and the interest it's acquired?' Faraday was a precise, thin Caymanian, brown-skinned and smooth, and Naisby had the impression he would never sweat, even in the clammy heat of George Town.

'It should have been transferred immediately to those overseas accounts I named.'

Faraday took a sip of filter coffee. 'That can be done, Mr Naisby.'

Naisby almost came out with it and said he had a new idea about the money. On second thoughts it was better to keep his new Luxembourg arrangements to himself. 'Send half of it. Keep the other three million here for the time being.'

‘As you wish.’ He made a note with a fine gold ballpoint. The handwriting was microscopic.

‘I’m still not clear about your role in the Maxell Group.’

The smile was shrewd. ‘If you have any doubts about my credentials, Mr Naisby, I suggest you find reassurance from the Inspector of Banks.’

He was in, quite clearly, to clean up the Maxell business.

As he came out of the elevator into the marbled lobby, Naisby saw Hobart raise a hand and move towards him. ‘Fancy seeing you here again.’ Hobart ran the back of his forefinger against the grain of that straw-coloured moustache.

‘Not for long,’ Naisby said.

They were out on the hot street before Hobart spoke again. ‘I’d have thought this would be the last place on earth to find you – after what happened.’

‘I wasn’t safe in London,’ Naisby replied brusquely. ‘You did hear from Gilliam, I’m sure?’

‘What about?’

‘The murder.’

Hobart shook his head slowly.

‘Tara Lynn.’ Naisby bit his lip. ‘A friend of mine. They got her. The same two bastards who set on me on the beach.’

‘Go on.’ Hobart became alert.

It was pure speculation. Naisby was matching the two beachcombers against the media stories of Tara’s murder. The descriptions of her killers were close enough to those he had given of his own assailants. ‘I told Gilliam you might now know who the bastards are. I want ’em caught and put away, though that’s too good for ’em.’

Hobart was still awaiting the FBI response to those palm- and fingerprints: a bitter inquest was still raging between the Bureau and the Cayman Government about the humiliation of that herd of bankers at Miami. It looked now as though he could expect more help from Scotland Yard. ‘Pity you’re not staying a bit longer.’ Hobart knew of Naisby’s arrival from Immigration. Naisby’s embarkation card showed it was a one-day in-and-out trip.

‘I’ll tell you who you should be looking for,’ Naisby said, hailing a cab. ‘Two youngish blokes who used to go sailing with General Gibb.’ He turned as the driver waited. ‘Maybe they’re the ones who rubbed out Ed Maxell.’

'I wondered if you knew about that,' Hobart said, lowering his voice.

'I've just been told. Five minutes ago.'

'That's why you're in deep shock.' It was irony. He'd never seen Naisby so keen and organized.

'I suppose so,' Naisby said. 'Give my regards to Gilliam.'

And he was gone.

Hobart felt some relief. He wanted to get back to see that those young Americans' prints were sent to London right away.

'You're telling me you *know* General Gibb had fourteen and a half million dollars in a Swiss numbered account?'

'Yes.'

'How come?' Carrodus had his doubts about Naisby's claim.

'It doesn't matter how come,' Naisby said, holding his hair down in the breeze as they leaned over the side of the ferry. 'I know.' He still had his doubts about Carrodus's integrity.

'You came a long way, sir, just to pitch me a rumour or hunch.' He had no trouble with the breeze. It was cooling his balding dome pleasantly. 'I sure sympathize with you wanting to hit these bums after what they did to your friend, but that's not my game, as they say. My only interest is the general.' He threw a quick glance around the tourist deck. Nobody was near enough to eavesdrop. It had been Naisby's idea to rendezvous on the ferry plying Manhattan–Staten Island. He'd felt insecure from the moment he landed at JFK. 'Maybe we can help Scotland Yard trace these guys.' His tone hinted that he was distancing himself from a routine UK homicide.

Naisby traded his ace, handing over a buff envelope. Leaning over the rail, Carrodus slit it open and found the postcard-sized colour print of a computer screen heavy with statistics. In the top left corner it read: *Gibb, Edison – 784387/KY*. It showed some debits for investments, credits for interest and realizations, and the bottom line was $14,526,000.88 in the black.

Carrodus felt his heart bumping. He turned away from the rail as if to make sure of not dropping the photograph into the ocean. 'It could be a fake?' Something told him it wasn't.

'It *could* be,' Naisby murmured. 'It's a hundred per cent authentic.'

'Which bank is this?'

'Seifert et Cie.' It meant nothing to Carrodus. 'You see there's a reference – top right hand – to the date the account was opened?'

'Sure.' He was making out he was unimpressed.

'When you get back, just have a look at the press clip around that time. Three years ago. There was a bit of a ding-dong in the Senate about some missiles and artillery stuff made here that got in the hands of some Middle East enemies of America.'

'I'll check that out, Mr Naisby.' Check it out! He actually knew every detail of that scandal so well he could recite the whole episode in his sleep. 'Can I hold on to it?'

Naisby nodded.

'If it's a fake, Mr Naisby, you could be in trouble like you've never known.'

'If it's a fake, why did the general invest two million dollars in a company of mine rather than have it put to the test?'

'Invest?' Naisby's role was emerging. 'Or cough up?'

Not a muscle moved in Naisby's face. 'Invest, I said. And I don't want you turning on me, Carrodus. It happens that I can help you pin the four-star tycoon, and you can help me nail those killers. But it needn't end there. I've got two more eminent Americans in the net, and others who could easily be hauled in. Not to mention some Brits, who wouldn't interest you.'

'Oh, they might.' Carrodus couldn't make Naisby out. Either he was a romancing con-man or the kind of talent the FBI was crying out for. Something else was bothering Carrodus. If Naisby was such a catch why had Gilliam handed him over on a plate?

A group of German rubber-neckers took up places at the rail on either side of Naisby and Carrodus, who moved to a more discreet place nearer the stern.

'Anyway, what makes you so certain these two guys killed your friend?'

'They were after information. The sort I've just given you. From their descriptions they were like the pair who tried to snatch me on Seven Mile Beach.'

'Nobody told me about that.'

'You'd already gone.' And for the first time Naisby laughed to show he knew that Carrodus had been kicked off the island.

Maybe Gilliam had told him. Or Hobart. It didn't matter. 'Hardly makes a case we could make stand up.' Carrodus blew his nose. The smell of the sea often got his sinuses.

'Remember Wasserman on the Caymans?'

'The big blond German with the beard?'

'Swiss,' Naisby said knowingly. 'Seifert et Cie's minder. He's got together with Gibb to stop me and repair the damage.'

'Damage?'

'I've penetrated their secret accounts, Mr Carrodus.' He said it with such grace he had to be taken seriously. He took in a lungful of brine. 'I want two things out of this. And neither's money. Not now. I'm sick of the bloody stuff. Somebody once wrote about the stench of money. Never knew what he meant till now. I want those two killers to pay the price for Tara – and I'm next to absolute certainty Gibb's young buddies did it – and then I want to feel free. I'll need a guarantee that after we've nailed Gibb for you and that pair for me, I'll leave the great US of A with a new identity.'

'And these other US eminent persons?'

Naisby nodded. 'I'll give you their accounts, too. Slightly less up to date, maybe, but enough to give you a professional field day.'

And Carrodus was bursting to ask if one of them might be Mrs Edwina Sarne, who had also shared those Cayman days and nights. He sneezed again. It could be his sinuses playing up. Or emotion.

Olsen was in no position to frustrate him on this one. He was in a funk lest the story of his Humpty Dumpty encounter with Carrodus should leak, especially upwards to the Director. If there was blackmail in the air, so be it.

He was starting to admire and understand the slight Englishman who was now taking snaps of the Manhattan skyline.

ELEVEN

Sprawled on the brocaded sofa, Carrodus averted his eyes as the needle went into Naisby.

He was squeamish about hypodermics.

He didn't even turn to the TV screen, which was raucous with baseball. It was Byrom Hayes he studied. And even Byrom wasn't looking at the box. He had his feet over the arm of a wide chintzy chair and was deep into the *New Yorker.*

It was nineteen days since that meeting on the ferry. Byrom was hardly Naisby's doppelganger but, wearing the same maker's slacks and short-sleeved shirt, he was more than a passable double. For days Carrodus had operated like a casting director seeing mugshots of Naisby lookalikes sifted by the Bureau's computer. One agent in Chicago and another in Nevada looked more like Naisby, but Byrom from the field office in San Juan not only had Naisby's spare dark looks but a talent for speaking like an Englishman – and even a northern Englishman.

Carrodus saw Byrom put down the magazine and watch Naisby giving blood. It was the best part of a week they'd been together, and Byrom was so close to Naisby now he felt it was his own blood that was flowing into that bottle.

'Bear up, Rollo,' he called to Naisby, in a flawless English accent hard on the vowels. 'She'll not take every drop, mate.'

Naisby threw him an up-you V-sign, and the FBI nurse smirked.

Carrodus went over to the picture window with its vista of meadows and sycamores. It was the kind of house he and Liz might have revelled in, and Manhattan wasn't all that far away. Impossible dream. He was a cuckold. And, besides, the FBI owned the property.

'Just lean back and relax,' the FBI nurse was telling Naisby. 'We'll get you a coffee.'

'I'd prefer tea,' Naisby said, mainly to annoy them.

'Well done, Rollo,' Byrom called, practising his English accent.

Carrodus was on a high without benefit of needles.

They were nearly there.

An hour later he was on his way from upstate New York to central Manhattan, with a drowsy blood-donor. In the FBI garage he helped Naisby transfer his baggage to a car marked as a yellow cab, switched to a waiting cerise-coloured Chevrolet with a driver who had lost half an ear in Vietnam, and watched Naisby leave in the cab.

As he went through the lobby of the midtown East Side family hotel, Carrodus saw Naisby checking in. Carrodus took the stairs two at a time to the second floor. He brought out a key and let himself into room 236. The room had endured much wear-and-tear over the years. Its grey carpet was ragged and the old oak furniture scarred. The bed had seen better days. Stains on the off-white wall were souvenirs of some zany marital spats, or worse. But there was a TV, and Carrodus found the commode on which it stood well-fixed with booze. He helped himself to a can of ale.

It was another ten minutes before there came the sound of movements in room 237 next door. Carrodus heard the ageing bellhop leave, then turned the key in the connecting door, drew the painted bolts which were meant to be permanently locked, and entered to find Naisby pouring a Scotch. The room was a touch more civilized than his own, but equally a relic of the 1920s and musty. The air-conditioning unit behind the heavy curtains rattled like an unlicensed cab.

'How the hell anybody can sleep in here I don't know,' Naisby said, kicking off his shoes.

'Suffer in the cause,' Carrodus quipped. He was feeling good. It was virtually *his* operation. Olsen had said so. He didn't have to report to his squad supervisor, or the assistant special agent in charge at the Federal Plaza, but only to Special Agent Lemont. And Lemont knew the score. 'Anyways, you'll not be here long,' Carrodus now told Naisby.

Naisby switched on the TV. A hearty newscaster was on about a swoop by the Drug Enforcement people in the Bronx.

'You don't want to see that,' Carrodus said, with a look at his watch. 'How about it, then?'

Naisby took a miniature notepad from his shirt pocket, and referred to it as he used the phone. The call rang out several times before the voice of a middle-aged woman came on. 'Hello, this is Washington 392 . . . '

'Mrs Gibb?'

'Yes?' The voice was guarded.

'General Gibb there right now?'

'I'm afraid he isn't. Who is that calling?'

'Oh, I know him from the Army, Mrs Gibb.'

'Then you call him at the Pentagon, right?'

'He's there now?'

'He'll be there. Goodbye.'

'Goodbye, Mrs Gibb. I'm sorry to have bothered you.'

'That's okay.'

Naisby hung up, consulted the notepad, and called the Pentagon.

Gibb's line was busy.

'You'll hold?' the operator asked.

Carrodus shook his head.

'I'll call back,' Naisby said, and hung up.

'The Pentagon security guys often trace even routine calls,' Carrodus said. 'We'll play it safe.' He gave it another five minutes, then asked Naisby to call again.

Gibb's secretary came on.

'I'd like a quick word with the general, please,' Naisby said. 'My name's Kilroy.'

'Does he know you, Mr Kilroy?'

'Very well,' Naisby said, and Carrodus gave him an approving thumbs-up sign. Carrodus was doing a precise time check on how long it took Gibb to come on.

It was twenty-two seconds before the line came alive, but it was the secretary once more. 'If you would like to leave your number, the general will call you. He's in a meeting right now.'

Carrodus, propped up against the stacked pillows and the bedhead, suffered a sudden hunch that Naisby was about to back down.

But Naisby said, 'I'm sure he could come out for a moment. It's essential we have a few words. Just tell him I'm due at the Senate Office Building quite soon.'

Carrodus blew out his cheeks in relief at this whopper. And waited for another eighteen seconds.

'Yes, Mr Kilroy?'

'A slight development, General . . . ' Naisby began.

'Leave your number, Mr Kilroy, I'll be back with you in ten minutes.'

It was about the time it would take him to get out from the Pentagon.

'Afraid not, General.' Naisby sounded sharp as a fox. 'It's a simple request. I'd like you to see your way to giving me further support. An investment like the last one would be fine.'

Carrodus leaned close to the phone, and Naisby held it out so that he could hear Gibb's heavy breathing.

'I don't see that will be possible, sir.' The general was keeping it all low-key. 'But I'd sure meet you to discuss it.'

'It doesn't call for a meeting, General,' Naisby rasped. 'Same amount. Same fund. And it's urgent. Twenty-four hours, all right?'

'I'll call you if you give me your number.'

'Just invest, sir.'

It was Gibb who hung up first.

'That's just great, Rollo.' Carrodus enthused. He was so carried away that he poured a stiff chaser of Naisby's Scotch before calling Stacey at the office. 'We got all that, Stace?'

'Loud and clear,' Stacey said.

Carrodus dialled 12 for the manager. 'The lady on yet, Jack?'

'Hold on, Matt.' A pause, then, 'Yeah, she's here.'

Carrodus hung up, took a swig of Scotch, and said, 'You can go down now, Rollo.'

Naisby was finding the ordering about a bit irksome and his look showed it. All the same, he went to his briefcase, drew out his passport and black leather wallet, and headed for the door.

'The more prints the better,' Carrodus said.

And Naisby fingered the two exhibits.

'And the cards.'

Naisby handled his American Express and Access cards and two of his London club cards. 'More of this, Carrodus, you'll have me a candidate for the hatch.'

But Carrodus wasn't listening. The phone buzzed and he took it.

Stacey said, 'Our guy's left early for home.'

'Thanks,' Carrodus said, and hung up. Given good traffic conditions and his usual Army driver, Gibb should get to his mansion beyond the Maryland line in less than an hour. Carrodus went through the connecting door and out via room 236. In the lobby Naisby was collecting a receipt for his wallet and passport from the woman cashier. It was her last stint for two weeks. She was going on vacation to California in the morning, and showed no interest at all in Naisby. Carrodus felt he'd been too fussy about Naisby handing in his stuff for safekeeping. It could have been done later by Byrom Hayes.

Carrodus was sussing out the lobby in relation to the stairs and elevators. Guests coming down to the lobby had to pass directly in front of the reception desk to make the doors to the street, but the layout was such that those manning the desk had to go a long way round to intercept anyone leaving in haste via the stairs or elevators.

Naisby knew what he was up to, but ignored Carrodus and headed for the stairs. Only now did he realize he'd left his room key on the bed. He gave a discreet gesture to Carrodus, and took the elevator.

Carrodus went up the stairs.

'I thought you were street-smart enough not to need a baby minder,' Carrodus joked back in room 237.

'Relax, Carrodus,' Naisby shot back. 'You could get the Purple Heart for this.'

'Touché,' Carrodus smiled.

The byplay eased the tension.

They watched TV, switching between newscasts, until the phone buzzed again. Carrodus took the call.

Stacey said, 'Our guy's home.'

It would have been clumsy to call Gibb right away, so they started to watch a quiz show until Naisby felt it was driving him crazy.

'Okay,' Carrodus said. 'You get busy giving the place a few daubs.'

Naisby's nose twitched, but he set about leaving his fingerprints on the bedhead, the wardrobe, the cheap dressing table and the brass weight on the curtain rope.

'Don't forget the bathroom,' Carrodus urged.

And Naisby obliged. When he came out of the bathroom Carrodus said, 'One or two on the walls, eh?'

'The bloody walls?'

And Carrodus put on a film director's performance, standing cross-legged by the bedside, the phone in his right hand while he used the left as a buttress against the flaked paint on the wall. Then he leaned a hand on the wall by the window as he pretended to look out. The blinds were drawn. Naisby delivered, though he felt they were overdoing it and that with less time on his hands Carrodus might have thought the same.

They watched a couple more newscasts before Carrodus dialled 9 for an outside line, then called Gibb's home number in Maryland.

Mrs Gibb answered.

'Mrs Gibb?' He was laying on the caution.

'Speaking.'

'Is the general about, ma'am?'

'Who is that?'

'I'm afraid I can't tell you that, ma'am.' Carrodus could have been taken for an eminent person himself. 'But I sure need to talk to your husband.'

'Can't you write to him?'

'I reckon he'd prefer I didn't.' He paused, giving her the idea he was about to abandon the call. 'Just do one thing for me, ma'am, okay? Tell him I'm in the same boat over a guy named Kilroy.'

'I'm sure it's better you write.'

'And that I know where Kilroy is.'

'One moment.' She made no effort to hide her annoyance.

Carrodus was biting his thumbnail as he hung on.

'General Gibb here.' He was wary.

'General, I'm having problems with a social nuisance.'

'Can you declare yourself, sir?'

'No,' Carrodus said, carefully. 'And you'll know why, sir.'

There was no comeback.

'We're not the only ones, General. I know that for sure. I don't know how to stop the guy.'

The line went so quiet Carrodus sensed Gibb had hung up. Then Gibb said, 'I understood that you know where Kilroy is?'

'Yes.' Again Carrodus was unhasty and deliberate.

Gibb took his time, too. 'Okay. Give me his address and I'll see what we can do.' He made it sound as if someone was transgressing against the US Army rather than himself.

'I know he checked in at the Craigmount on Lexington in New York,' Carrodus said. 'I don't know the room or how long he's there for. But he's at that hotel.' The lack of precision was an off-putter. The FBI would have such information.

'Thank you,' the General said. 'Goodbye.'

Carrodus hung up and blew out his cheeks in relief.

Naisby made a gesture of applause. 'I'll nominate you for an Oscar.'

Carrodus ran a hand through his thin hair, and the phone buzzed. He took it.

'Got it,' came Stacey's voice. 'Loud and clear.'

'Great,' Carrodus replied. He turned to Naisby. 'Be seeing you, Rollo.'

It was a busy time in the lobby, and unlikely that anyone saw Naisby go out on to Lexington. He crossed over, turned right for thirty yards, darted over the street, and saw the yellow cab door swing open. He carried no bags, nothing except a copy of the *New York Times*. The square-set driver with the wrestler's neck didn't even turn round, but was having a good look at him through the internal mirror.

In the hotel Carrodus lay back on the bed and let the TV run on. An hour went by, and nothing happened. Then he heard the key scratching in the lock. He moved back into room 236, closing the connecting door behind him.

A quick rap on the door and he re-opened it.

'Jesus, Matt,' Byrom Hayes said. 'You got this going like some infidelity snoop.'

And Byrom went and dug out his shaver from the toilet bag Naisby had left.

Carrodus stayed another hour hoping for a call from Stacey. None came. 'Don't get too bored, Byrom,' he said, going out through the connecting door to room 236. He was putting the locks on when he heard the phone buzz beyond the door. He went back in fast, and took the call. 'Yes?'

'It's happened,' came Stacey's voice. 'Our guy's called Zürich, Switzerland.'

His instinct was to celebrate with Byrom, but Carrodus had put back three Scotches already. And he wanted to hear the tape of Gibb's call to Zürich. He went back through room 236 and out down the stairs. He turned left off Lexington and saw his FBI 'cab' across the street.

Back in the Federal Plaza, Stacey played back the tape of Gibb's call to Wasserman. The dialogue was meant to suggest they were old buddies fixing a golf date.

It was to be at some course in New York.

Carrodus was half asleep.

'Matt!'

Stirred by the nudge from Stacey, he sat up on one elbow and squinted at the security monitor in room 236.

It was 5.15 am and the monitor showed two young men – one a six-footer, the other of medium height – enter the lobby from Lexington. They went to the desk where a night security man was dozing, and a white-haired bellhop had the weary air of one who should have been in bed. The smaller man pointed to the key rack and the bellhop gave him the key to 309.

'Find who booked 309, Stace.'

Stacey made a note.

Carrodus watched the second monitor. It showed the deserted second floor area around the elevators and stairwell. In the thirty-five hours since Gibb's call to Wasserman, the Swiss had been busy, flying in to JFK, checking in at the Grand Hyatt, phoning General Gibb from a payphone at Grand Central, and sussing out the Craigmount on the pretext that he might soon want to stay there. The phone tap on Gibb's home had yielded other calls – one to a man called Luke in Queen's, another to Wasserman to confirm a rendezvous in Mott Haven. The calls were thinly coded as if they were doing a business deal with an unnamed visitor from Europe. 'I must talk to him before he departs,' Gibb had said during the second talk with Wasserman. 'That's essential for me, too,' Wasserman had replied. Even so, Carrodus had covered Byrom in case somebody chose to take a short-cut and forego the dialogue. He briefly looked away from the monitor at the two agents with their holstered guns ready to break into room 237 through the connecting door. Others were posted near the stairwell and in the lobby.

The two men came from the stairs to the second floor.

In the half-light Carrodus could make out their almost identical gear – navy blue T-shirts and black bomber jackets. They moved with the brisk awareness of trained infantrymen.

Carrodus tapped on the connecting door. 'Wait for it, Byrom.'

'I'm ready,' Byrom replied.

'Rather him than me.' It was Stacey, checking his gun under the bedside lamp. The light caught the bottle of blood on the table.

They heard the gentle tap on Byrom's door, then another, a touch firmer.

'Yes?' Byrom put on a sleepy voice.

'Mr Naisby?'

'Yes, what is it?'

'House security, Mr Naisby.'

In the next room they heard the bedside lamp snap on and Byrom complaining loudly in an English accent about having been wakened up. He would be checking his visitors through the spy hole now. Carrodus, Stacey and the two agents drew their guns. They heard the chain being released, and the bolt being drawn, and the door swing against the wardrobe with a bang. Then it was closed.

'Get dressed!' The accent was Brooklyn.

Suddenly there was the noise of a fight, and the thud of a bedside lamp hitting the floor. The two agents and even Stacey glared at Carrodus, wanting him to order them in.

Carrodus shook his head. Byrom's shouts were muffled. His first one would have been louder if things were out of hand.

Then there was silence until the door of 237 was re-opened. They heard shuffling outside their own door and waited, still trigger-conscious.

The second monitor showed movement.

'Christ!' Stacey murmured.

The two men were dragging the inert Byrom down the stairs. They were no longer in black and navy. They wore long white smocks and looked like medics.

'No.' Carrodus snapped as the two young agents made to move. 'Not yet.'

The lobby camera picked up the abduction party. The security man was still dozing behind the desk and the bellhop immersed in an old copy of *Sports Illustrated*. The bellhop took in the departing party through rheumy eyes.

One of the men in white smocks called out some alibi. Only when they had gone out did the bellhop rouse the security man.

'Okay,' Carrodus said, turning on his walkie-talkie and following Stacey into the next room. There was little damage. One of the agents put on gloves and added to it, slewing the bed, emptying Byrom's case and scattering the contents. Then he wrenched the phone cable from its socket and kicked in a bedside cabinet.

Stacey was spattering blood from the bottle over the threadbare carpet. 'Time they had a new one, anyways,' he muttered.

Carrodus's radio crackled, murky with static. 'Hobo One,' came the call.

'Hobo One,' Carrodus said.

'We're with 'em, One. Route okay.'

'Thanks.' Carrodus snapped his thumb and forefinger in delight. 'Route okay' meant they were heading north, and that figured. He had chosen the call sign. It was short for Hobart, the Cayman cop who hadn't liked it a bit when they kicked Carrodus off the island.

Carrodus released one of the agents, who would rejoin the operation in Mott Haven.

The radio came on again. 'Hobo One.'

'Hobo One.'

'Right off Lexington at 116th.'

'Thanks.' Carrodus got up and paced the room as if it were a cage.

Two minutes later he was about to release another agent, but thought better of it as the radio crackled. 'Hobo One?'

'Hobo One.'

'Left off 116th on to First Avenue.' It could have been a yellow cab net. Carrodus released himself. 'Give it another ten minutes, Stace, before you leave.' He turned to the other agent. 'Twenty minutes after Stace, okay?'

The agent nodded.

His driver had the engine running as Carrodus jumped into the battered black sedan which at least gave him legroom. The only modern thing about it was the state-of-the-art two-way radio.

'Hobo One?'

'Go ahead.'

'Pick up Willis Avenue Bridge – now.'

'Thanks.' Taxis they might seem to be, but the less chat the better. The last thing he wanted was for the blues of the NYPD to prick up their ears. He saw the scene in his mind. The intercept, with the car carrying Byrom forced to stop between the two compacts that were less unkempt than they seemed, with supercharged new engines under the bonnets. The taking of Byrom. His agents in the role of mobsters letting the kidnappers go with a sinister warning. And then other agents taking over the tailing.

Coming up now to the Manhattan side of Willis Avenue Bridge Carrodus saw the Chevy compact with four of the agents who had been watching the transfer of Byrom and who would now join him in Mott Haven. One, Tarrant, threw him a thumbs-up sign.

Carrodus saw the Chevy coming up behind them in the wing mirror.

The turn-of-the-century house in Mott Haven was dilapidated. Carrodus had done one recce and wondered how a US Army general could have an interest in such a dump. The sedan fitted into the shabbiness of the scene. If he hadn't known of the other cars in the street he would have been unaware of the stakeout. As his driver slipped the sedan into a space by the sidewalk, the radio came on, clear as hi-fi but not so loud.

'Hobo One?'

'Hobo One.'

'They're still going round and round the blocks.'

Give 'em time.' He stretched his legs, until his feet were hard against the bulwark.

Half an hour later the abductors were still too jumpy to stop and approach the house.

'Hobo One?'

'Hobo One.'

'Switch completed.'

'Thanks.' He could have howled for joy.

'Matt.' His driver nudged him. The two abductors were leaving a convertible fifty yards up the street. Still jumpy and watchful and back in their bomber jackets, they walked another hundred yards up the street, then half-way back again. For a long minute they stopped to talk near a house three doors away from the target house.

Then they went to number 78.

'Not yet,' Carrodus whispered into the radio. The agents knew the score. If anyone came out of 78 they would pounce. If not, they would give it an hour.

The hour was like a year to Carrodus. He put up with all but four minutes before ordering the raid. Agents broke into the house from back and front, all armed.

They found a black housekeeper in the kitchen making breakfast pancakes, her husband in the pantry mending a fuse, one of the abductors in the lavatory, and the other with Wasserman and Gibb in the dining room finishing their corn flakes.

Gibb had begun to bluster about his civil rights when Carrodus came in to spoil the performance. 'General Edison Gibb, sir,' he said with a half bow. 'Herr Wasserman?'

Gibb sagged for a moment, the colour draining from his blotchy face. Wasserman held his head high in an arrogant way that reminded Carrodus of pictures of Mussolini. Then Gibb stood upright as one captured in combat who was ready to face the music.

'Haven't we met recently?' Carrodus could not bring himself to cut out the touch of *schadenfreude*.

'You have the suntan to prove it,' Gibb said bravely.

Head in the air, Wasserman might not have heard the question.

Carrodus turned an incurious look on the two abductors. 'I don't know where you two fit in,' he said loftily, as if unaware of their morning crime on Lexington.

Stacey, who had joined the party, marvelled at his talent for disinformation.

Carrodus was making it clear he had eyes only for Gibb and Wasserman – and especially Gibb.

The smell of freshly-ground coffee was coming from the kitchen, and Carrodus felt it was a pity they couldn't stay to enjoy some.

Homicide was in the air.

Carrodus went past the uniformed cop on the door, stretched a long leg over the crouching detective from the Crime Scene Unit who was collecting blood samples from the carpet and skirting board, and found Lieutenant Saul.

Room 237 of the hotel on Lexington was a shambles. The writing desk had been overturned, the TV set lay on its side on the bloodstained carpet, and bedside lamps and tables had been smashed.

Lieutenant Saul was sifting through the contents of a black leather wallet and holding a passport as the CSU photographer packed his camera case.

'Morning, Linc,' Carrodus said.

Saul barely spared him a glance. 'Matt,' he nodded. 'So what brings the superbrats here?' He was a bright, squarely-built detective with a chip on his shoulder about the FBI. It was beyond him that he should still be with the Major Case Unit of the New York City Police Department when others like Carrodus found it so easy to make the Feds.

'Just a hunch,' Carrodus said, watching a young detective taking fingerprints from the wall above the bedside table.

Lt Saul was used to tight-lipped agents who got carried away with notions of grandeur. He watched the fingerprints officer a moment. 'So many daubs this could be the fingerprints museum.' He moved to the connecting door to room 236 and said, 'You looked in here, Don?'

The fingerprints officer nodded. 'Barren,' he said. 'Like it was wiped.'

Saul squeezed his nostrils with a podgy hand. His brow was very wrinkled for one so relatively young. 'So two guys come in and less than two minutes later two guys go out in white coats dragging this Brit?' He was sort of talking to himself, but hoping Carrodus would offer a hunch without being asked. Carrodus would have to do the asking with so many young cops around.

Carrodus obliged. 'So there's a third guy in here' – he nodded towards room 236 – 'to open up for 'em?'

Saul looked worried.

'Well, they *were* let in?' Carrodus said. 'They didn't kick the door open.' He paused. 'And who'd open a room door at that time?'

'He was a crazy Brit,' Saul said. 'No American would be such a nut as to open up.'

A walkie-talkie crackled somewhere on the corridor and a detective came in to pass on the news. 'They found the first vehicle, Lieutenant, up by Pelham Bay Park.'

'Great.' Saul's tone didn't match the word. He was mesmerized by that trail of blood, and less interested in that old Lincoln convertible than in two other cars. He caught Carrodus looking at him. 'They used this Lincoln from here, and two witnesses have called in to report it stopped near Willis Avenue Bridge, and a body was switched, dead or alive, into a cherry-coloured compact. Some Big Ears called in to report a splash. We got the Harbour Unit diving.'

'Willis Avenue?'

'Yeah. They picked the right bridge, okay. They could go lots of places crossing there.' He laid the wallet and passport on the bed with other exhibits ready for the labs.

'Okay if I take a look?' Carrodus had to play it by the book with Linc.

'Sure. Help yourself. We got the daubs.'

The passport showed the holder to be John Rollaston Naisby, citizen of Great Britain, a finance house officer 1.82 metres tall. The face on the photograph was lean and alert under a high forehead and dark curly hair. Naisby was no great traveller. In the first three years after the passport was issued he had visited only Switzerland. He had been more mobile in recent weeks, with a number of entry and exit stamps for the Cayman Islands and the USA.

Carrodus knew all this. He heard the crackle of a walkie-talkie and the young detective telling Saul, 'Lieutenant. They got somethin' on that cherry-coloured compact.'

Saul swivelled.

'Some break-in's been reported at a funeral parlour in the Bronx, and this vehicle was seen there around six o'clock.'

Saul was already on his way. 'Coming, Matt?' he invited.

Carrodus was checking his watch. He hadn't aimed to stay long, having more pressing matters to deal with back at 26 Federal Plaza. He also wanted to compliment Agent Stacey on his precision. But he followed Saul out to the police car.

Saul told the driver to get the siren singing. It gave him a nice sense of importance as they raced through the mid-morning traffic northwards to the Bronx.

A precinct car stood outside Miller's Funeral Parlor when they arrived.

Inside, Eugene Miller and his son were in the Haven of Rest section, where three coffins stood on trestles, two covered with flowers, the other bare and sad. The son was rocking on his trainers as if about to start a run at a pole vault. Eugene was a more phlegmatic soul, pink-cheeked and welcoming. He had seen too many people on their way into the next world to let such hassles get him down in this. He threw an amused glance at Carrodus as though recognizing a fellow-member of some secret lodge.

'A break-in? Here?' Saul had begun to think spooky thoughts.

'Right, sir,' Eugene said brightly. He patted one of the raised coffins. 'This is new. But right here on Stand 1 this morning there was another box with this guy in it all set to go.'

Saul winced.

Eugene led them through to the stock room, thick with the smell of wood shavings and metal polish. Coffins stood in wall racks, some ready for occupation, others only half-made. Eugene's son stood in the doorway between the stockroom and the Haven. He was still rocking.

'Now look here,' Eugene said, removing the lid of an uncompleted coffin. They looked at the wizened white face of a very old man gone to skin and bone. 'He's the one who was in the coffin on Stand 1 when we locked up last night.'

'God Almighty!' Saul ran his handkerchief over his wrinkled forehead. The truth began to dawn. 'So where's *that* coffin?'

'The crematorium.' Eugene wore a look of apology as he checked his watch.

'Why the hell didn't you report this earlier?' Saul said tartly.

'We called the moment we found what had happened.'

Saul looked for his walkie-talkie, then remembered having left it in the car out of respect for the dead.

The crematorium was five blocks away, but they made it fast on full siren.

Two men and a woman in black were leaving the crematorium chapel, and another group of seven were moving in from the waiting room for the next service. Saul fought an urge to run past them through the door marked Staff Only. Carrodus restrained him with a gentle grip.

The cremator – a stooping veteran in a plastic apron – looked up as they came in.

'The one just finished?' Saul breathed, flashing his police card.

The man nodded and took in Carrodus at a glance. 'That's the last from Miller's today. We're on Welensky's now.'

Saul was asking himself if forensics could do anything with human ashes.

'God!' he whispered as he and Carrodus went out. 'RIP John Rollaston Naisby.'

'I sure go along with that,' Carrodus said.

They made their way south through Manhattan, Saul to the vast sandstone tomb of 1 Police Plaza, Carrodus to Foley Square. The delis were filling up with office girls taking early lunches. Carrodus had lost so much of the morning he would have to settle for a Chinese takeaway between interrogations.

'You never said what your interest is?' Saul queried as he got out, leaving Carrodus with the police car.

'No, I didn't,' Carrodus replied. 'It's a long story, Linc.'

Carrodus waited for the crucial call from the labs in Washington.

The prints of Gibb, Wasserman and the two young ex-soldiers, Martin Luke and Roly Furnival, had been transmitted instantly, and the phial of serum found with a syringe in Wasserman's toilet bag in the brownstone house in Mott Haven sent by special air delivery.

The detainees could sweat a bit. He whiled away a few moments by going through the little-used passports of Luke and Furnival found in their run-down apartment in Queen's.

The phone buzzed, but it was Stacey, who was having to put up with Gibb's imperious demands to have his lawyers called.

'Give the general a dummy to suck,' Carrodus said.

It was another ten minutes before Alder came on from the labs. 'The prints are negatives,' he said, and Carrodus's heart sank. 'These guys are not wanted.'

'Blast!'

'But there's one curious thing.'

'Yes?'

'We got a friends-in-need task from the Cayman Islands. They sent us a palm print and partial fingerprints to figure. Some homicide rap. Well, these prints are those of one of your guys.'

Bad times, good times. Carrodus sat bolt upright. 'Which one?'

'Set A – Furnival's.'

The boost was tremendous. Carrodus put in a call to Hobart on Grand Cayman, who could hardly believe it was Carrodus being so friendly after that unceremonious departure.

'You sent some prints to Washington, Mr Hobart?'

'And I'm still waiting for the result.' Hobart sounded aggrieved. 'Not surprising – as you'll be the first to agree.'

'Oh, I don't know.' He paused for effect. 'I got the guy here who owns the fingers.'

'One of those young friends of an eminent American we'd best not mention right now, okay?'

'Right.'

'Homicide?'

'Ed Maxell, Mr Carrodus.'

Carrodus whistled.

'The prints were on a hire contract for the boat they dumped him from. You don't have his wetsuit, I suppose?'

'His wetsuit?'

Hobart told him about the missing tag and the print Jepson had found of the oval mark and the word ScubaSure.

'I'll see what we can do, Mr Hobart.'

'Another thing. I don't know what you've got this bloke on. But we found traces of scopolamine in Maxell's remains.' He was clearly proud of the word.

'Sco-what?'

'Scopolamine,' Hobart repeated with no hesitation. He'd been saying it in his sleep for days. 'With phenothiazine.'

'I don't have time for funnies, Mr Hobart.'

'It's true. More trash from Colombia, I'm afraid. It causes a kind of hypnosis. The victim does everything he's told, including talk.'

'You'd best spell those two words.'

Carrodus took them down very slowly. He hardly needed forensics to tell him what was in that phial. He could tell *them* now. 'Thanks, Mr Hobart. I'll be in touch.'

He fixed another search of Luke's and Furnival's nest – for wetsuits.

The sooner he had these two off his hands the better. He wanted to dig into Gibb's private dealings in missiles.

He went to the interrogation rooms, where Stacey was becoming bolshie over the General's demands. He called Luke and Furnival to the first room, leaving the door open so that Gibb and Wasserman could overhear.

He opened both their passports. 'I see you two guys were in England recently?'

Neither spoke, standing very straight as if it were a court martial.

'And in the Cayman Islands?' His eyebrows rose. 'You must make lots of crackle to go there.' He let a half-minute go by. 'Well, you can leave here right now, okay?'

They couldn't believe their ears.

'Sure grateful, sir.' Furnival came near to saluting.

'Don't thank me. Thank the New York City Police. Some crazies up in 17th precinct want you more than I do. Homicide, they reckon. Some guy you had incinerated after whisking him from his hotel.'

It was Luke who cracked. 'Not true! Not true!'

'That's what the message says.' He was waving the bit of paper on which he'd written those hellzapoppin drugs' names.

'Not us, sir!' Luke was abruptly hoarse. 'Some mob took him away from us near Willis Avenue Bridge. He was alive then.'

'You go tell that to Lieutenant Saul, eh?'

As they were led off, Carrodus took Stacey aside and asked, 'Did the general and the big neutral hear all that?'

'You should have seen their faces.'

Carrodus called in Wasserman. 'Sit down.' He waited until Wasserman took the simple wooden chair. 'Now you tell me in plain English what those two bums were doing with you and General Gibb.'

'I'm saying not a word without my lawyer being here.'

Carrodus got up. 'Not like some lush chalet in the Swiss mountains, this place, Mr Wasserman. I'll drop in sometime tomorrow, okay?'

That finely trimmed beard was looking straggly, Carrodus thought. He went into Gibb's room.

'You're wasting your time,' Gibb said. 'I'm saying nothing until my lawyer's here.'

Carrodus shrugged and went out, closing the door on the General.

'Carrodus?'

The General was at the open door. 'Okay. I'll tell you all about it.' He spilled for an hour.

The newscast was showing the arrest in Manhattan of Martin Luke and Roly Furnival as suspects in what was being called the Cremation Homicide. It made Lieutenant Saul out to be a super crime-buster in the same league as Maigret and Sherlock Holmes.

Carrodus beamed with sheer joy.

'And you gave it him on a plate?' Naisby could see the funny side, but the shots of the funeral parlour and the crematorium were giving him the creeps.

'Okay, Rollo,' Carrodus said, sitting up and leaning across the coffee table to make notes. He had never felt better in his life, not even on his wedding day. The wetsuit had turned out to be Luke's and the serum in that phial of Wasserman's *was* the stuff Hobart had told him about. The knowledge had enabled him to bemuse the top scientist in forensics. Agents weren't expected to know things like that. 'Settlement time, right?'

They were in the cushy villa set in the meadows and among the Virginia creepers of upstate New York, but Naisby was bored by his pleasant jail. He leaned back, closed his eyes and conjured up images of those Swiss accounts. 'I gave you the Gibb stuff.'

'Right. Edwina Sarne.'

'Account number 537147K.'

'Bottom line?'

'Eleven million. The deposits went in nine years ago, three months before an inquiry into the way one of her husband's companies was rumoured to be into illicit hi-tech exports to the Soviets.'

'I remember,' Carrodus said. The rumour had been killed, only to revive. 'Any details?'

'I'll have to send you a photo.'

'You said there were others?'

Naisby said, 'Senator Waldo Pryde,' and Carrodus whistled.

'Nine million eight hundred thousand dollars. Account number starts with a five and ends with a P. Ditto. I'll send you a photo. There were hints that some foreign aid was sticking to the Senator's palms.' He helped himself to a filter coffee. 'Conrad Warri. A West African at the UN.'

Carrodus's face lit up. Warri had been one of his assigned targets.

'Nearly seventeen million. Deflecting some US aid to the Third World to himself. Can't recall the account number. Ditto. Photograph.'

Naisby then named Johnny Kirkham, the evangelist, a State Department official, and a human rights celebrity. He could remember neither account numbers nor bottom-line figures, but none of these people were the sort who should have amassed fortunes in a Swiss bank.

'Photographs?'

'Sure,' Naisby said easily. 'More for your album.'

'Homesick?' Carrodus asked.

'Very.'

'Let's get you on your way.'

Naisby packed his clothes, which had been returned to him. Two hours later he felt a heart flutter as he presented his passport at Immigration, but Carrodus was with him, and the grizzled black officer stamped him clear in a second. In the departure area the jumbo flight was called, and he shook hands with Carrodus.

'Beats me you're not flying Concorde,' Carrodus quipped.

'Can't afford.' Naisby kept a straight face and Carrodus thought it was a joke, not knowing that Naisby was sick of the stench of money.

'I like it,' Carrodus laughed.

'Just one thing, Matt,' Naisby said, turning back from the gangway.

'Sure.'

'That coffin.' It had been on his mind. 'What the hell was in it? Not another corpse?'

It was Carrodus's turn to keep a straight face. 'Bones and offal,' he said lightly. 'A hundred and thirty pounds of the stuff. A deal with the abattoirs.' And he chuckled.

Naisby would never begin to understand Americans.

He slept most of the way over the Atlantic, after watching an in-flight movie about a bank scam involving much underground labour with picks and shovels. The robbers were no more than Stakhanovites. He could have saved them all that digging.

As he came out into the Terminal Four concourse at Heathrow, emotional family reunions were going on all round him, and he felt lonely.

'Rollo?'

He looked up at the towering Gilliam. So it was a double sting, after all.

'You owe me some photographs,' Gilliam said, picking up Naisby's suitcase and leaving Naisby with only the in-flight bag to carry.

'My dad always told me never to trust a copper.'

Gilliam laughed it off and led them to the first taxi. 'Let's get to wherever you keep this dynamite,' he said.

'It's in a clearing bank in the King's Road.'

'King's Road,' Gilliam told the driver.

'About half-way,' Naisby said.

They were on the slip road leading to the M4 when Gilliam started to cast some keen looks through the rear window. A maroon Sierra and a black Toyota were some fifty yards back in the inside lane. Two miles on they were still there.

Gilliam's face hardened. He rapped on the glass partition, then brought out his police card and passed it to the driver. 'Forget the King's Road,' he said. 'Make for the West End and lose these two, right?'

'Easy,' the driver said, taking in the Sierra through his wing mirror and pulling out to the centre lane for a better view of the Toyota.

'Don't answer any radio calls,' Gilliam said.

In London they left the Cromwell Road and headed through Hyde Park and Mayfair. The two cars were still hanging on. On Regent Street the driver took the taxi into the buses-only lane, and still the followers kept close.

'Who are they, guv?'

'Villains,' Gilliam said.

The driver coughed, unable to work out why a cop should be avoiding villains instead of nabbing them.

'I thought you'd have shaken 'em off by now.' Gilliam had the disappointed air of some inspector of taxis.

'Hold on,' the driver called. He threw a thumbs-up signal to another cabbie, who let him cut in front into the outer lane to make the tightest of U-turns. It was all so quick they were riding past the following cars in the opposite direction before the enemy drivers caught on. The two cars were impossibly placed for U-turns.

'Where now, guv?'

'Savile Row police station.'

Naisby shivered. 'I knew it,' he muttered. 'No freedom, though, no evidence!'

'You should learn to believe in your fellow sufferers a bit more, Rollo.' Gilliam laughed. He was on a kind of high. 'You got anything in the suitcase you really need as baggage for the rest of your life?'

'I'm sorry?'

'Personal stuff you'd not wish to part with? Business stuff even?'

Naisby shrugged. He was growing used to losing sets of clothing these days.

'Fine,' Gilliam said. Getting out under the blue lamp at Savile Row, he collected Naisby's suitcase from the taxi's luggage platform and told the driver, 'Less than two minutes, right?'

He was back in less than twenty seconds, minus the suitcase. 'Cork Street,' he told the driver, then turned to Naisby. 'Leaving that anywhere in haste would have brought half the Met down on us, not to mention the anti-terrorist chummies.' He winked. 'Makes a difference when a senior Met officer leaves stuff in London nicks.'

Naisby studied him intently. Either Gilliam *was* on the level, or into some crafty double sting.

Nothing was on their tail when Gilliam paid off the driver. He gestured towards the Burlington Arcade. 'Imagine having to run through this Regency monument to the greedy rich with a bloody great suitcase.'

Naisby saw his point.

Out on Piccadilly they took another taxi.

'King's Road,' Gilliam said. He held out his long arms, linked his hands, and clicked his knuckles in satisfaction, all the time keeping a lookout for followers. There were none. An awful thought hit him. 'This bank, Rollo?'

'If you're asking if the security box is in my name, forget it.'

'Great.' Then his face clouded. 'Not Kilroy, for Jesus' sake.'

'I'm not that daft,' Naisby sniffed, beginning to think Gilliam *was* on the level.

In the bank Gilliam waited at a circular table with a five-year-old girl with ringlets who was scrawling doodles over the blotter with a tethered pen, which she offered to him. He drew a comical face, its nose hanging low over a wall. He fought back a temptation to caption it 'Kilroy was here'. The visual joke was good enough. The little girl was laughing.

'Ready?' It was Naisby.

They found a more discreet table, where Naisby handed over photographs of the Swiss accounts of Sir Rupert Mallory, Lord Justice Kenright and Lord Plackett.

'Plackett?' Gilliam was shaken.

'Our humble life peer and lifelong socialist,' Naisby said quietly. 'Eighteen million plus. Greedy comrade. It's not only the aristos and judges, Geordie.' He tucked an envelope with photographs of the American investors' accounts into his inside pocket. He had a feeling that Carrodus would get much further in the States with those than Gilliam would get in Britain with the others. Gilliam was having similar thoughts himself. He would lay odds that the two cars they had just lost were from the Yard, working at the behest of the Commissioner of Police.

'I'll get you a cab,' Gilliam said.

Suspicion came back in Naisby's face.

'No trick intended, Rollo. No stings.'

They shook hands.

Even so, Naisby went round two blocks half-expecting a heavy hand on his shoulder before he hailed a taxi. 'Paddington, please.' The West country would do for starters.

Nobody was on his tail.

He badly needed some peace and quiet.

THE END